PRAISE FOR
Gretel and the Dark

"As haunting, lyrical, and enchanting as the fairy tales Krysta is so taken with, Granville's bittersweet first novel will keep readers hooked, guessing and wondering how Lilie's and Krysta's stories relate, right up to the end."
—*Library Journal* (starred)

"In *Gretel and the Dark*, Eliza Granville masterfully entwines two richly layered and compelling stories of two seemingly different worlds. Filled with remarkable historical detail and stunning prose, both Krysta's and Lilie's stories captivated me, and Granville kept me quickly turning the pages to discover the connection between these two girls. By turns beautiful and frightening, magical and dark, this is a novel that will stay with me for a long time to come."
—Jillian Cantor, author of *Margot* and *The Hours Count*

"Dark and intriguing . . . a highly clever, original book."
—*The Daily Mail* (UK)

"A powerful story, sensitively told . . . a terrifying tale about the stories we hear and the stories we tell ourselves to understand our experiences . . . it's impossible not to find yourself racing through the pages, desperate to discover the connections . . . heartbreaking and heart-racing."
—*The Times* (UK)

"Atmospheric and beautifully written . . . a subtle and thoughtful novel. It seems soon to call it, but *Gretel and the Dark* will be one of the best books of 2014."
—*The List* (UK)

Gretel

and the

Dark

Eliza Granville

RIVERHEAD BOOKS
New York

RIVERHEAD BOOKS
An imprint of Penguin Random House LLC
375 Hudson Street
New York, New York 10014

The Library of Congress has catalogued the Riverhead hardcover edition as follows:

Granville, Eliza.
Gretel and the dark / Eliza Granville.—First American Edition.
p.   cm.
ISBN 978-1-59463-255-6
1. Girls—Fiction.   2. Imagination—Fiction.   3. Fairy tales—Fiction.
4. Psychoanalysts—Fiction.   5. Psychoanalysis and fairy tales—Fiction.
6. Psychological fiction.   I. Title.
PR6107.R378G74   2014   2013042686
823'.92—dc23

First edition: Penguin Group (UK) 2014
First American edition: Riverhead Books 2014
First Riverhead trade paperback edition: January 2016
Riverhead trade paperback ISBN: 978-1-59463-395-9

Printed in the United States of America
1   3   5   7   9   10   8   6   4   2

Book design by Meighan Cavanaugh

Gretel
and the
Dark

Prologue

t is many years before the Pied Piper comes back for the other children. Though his music has been silenced, still thousands are forced to follow him, young, old, large, small, everyone . . . even the ogres wearing ten-league boots and cracking whips, even their nine-headed dogs. We are the rats in exodus now and the Earth shrinks from the touch of our feet. Spring leaves a bitter taste. All day, rain and people fall; all night, nixies wail from the lakes. The blood-colored bear sniffs at our heels. I keep my eyes on the road, counting white pebbles, fearful of where this last gingerbread trail is leading us.

Has the spell worked? I think so: coils of mist lap at our ankles, rising to mute all sounds, swallowing everyone around us whole. When the moment comes, we run blind, dragging the Shadow behind us, stopping only when my outstretched hand meets the rough bark of pine trunks. One step, two, and we're inside the enchanted forest, the air threaded with icy witch breaths. The day collapses around us. Phantom sentries swoop from the trees, demanding names, but our teeth guard the answers so they turn away, flapping eastward in search of the cloud-shrouded moon. Roots coil, binding us to the forest floor. We crouch in a silence punctuated by the distant clatter of stags shedding their antlers.

We wake, uneaten. Every trace of mist has been sucked away by the sun. The landscape seems empty. We haven't come far: I can see where the road runs, but there's no sign of anything moving along it. It's quiet until a cuckoo calls from deep within the trees.

"Listen."

"*Kukułką,*" he says, shielding his eyes as he searches the topmost branches.

"*Kuckuck,*" I tell him. He still talks funny. "She's saying '*Kuckuck*'!"

He gives his usual jerky shrug. "At least we're free."

"Only if we keep moving. Come on."

The Shadow whimpers, but we force it upright and, supporting it between us, move slowly along the edge of the trees until we come to fields where ravens are busy gouging out the eyes of young wheat. Beyond, newly buried potatoes shiver beneath earth ridges. Cabbages swell like lines of green heads. When we kneel to gnaw at their skulls, the leaves stick in our throats.

We carry on walking, feet weighted by the sticky clay, until the Shadow crumples. I pull at its arm. "It's not safe here. We must go farther. If they notice we've gone—" Keep going. We have to keep going. Surely sooner or later kindly dwarves or a softhearted giant's wife must take pity on us. But fear has become too familiar a companion to act as a spur for long. Besides, we're carrying the Shadow now. Its head lolls, the wide eyes are empty, and its feet trail behind, making two furrows in the soft mud. It could be the death of us.

"We should go on alone."

"No," he pants. "I promised not to leave—"

"I didn't."

"Then you go. Save yourself."

He knows I won't go on without him. "No good standing here talking," I snap, hooking my arm under the Shadow's shoulder and wondering how something thin as a knife blade can be so heavy.

Another rest, this time perched on the mossy elbow of an oak tree, attempting to chew a handful of last year's acorns. Only the sprouted ones stay down. The Shadow lies where we dropped it, facing the sky, though I notice its eyes are completely white now. Without warning it gives a cry, the loudest noise it's ever made, followed by a gasp and a long, juddering out-breath. I finish spitting out the last of the acorns. The Shadow isn't doing its usual twitching and jumping; it doesn't even move when I push my foot into its chest. After a moment I gather handfuls of oak leaves and cover its face.

He tries to stop me. "Why are you doing that?"

"It's dead."

"No!" But I can see the relief as he pulls himself onto his knees to check. "After enduring so much, still we die like dogs . . . *pod płotem* . . . next to a fence, under a hedge." He closes the Shadow's eyes. "*Baruch dayan emet.*" It must be a prayer: his lips go on moving but no sound emerges.

"But we're not going to die." I tug at his clothes. "Shadows never last long. You always knew it was hopeless. Now we can travel faster, just you and me."

He shakes me off. "The ground here is soft. Help me dig a grave."

"Won't. There's no time. We have to keep going. It's already past midday." I watch him hesitate. "Nothing will eat a shadow. There's no meat on it." When he doesn't move, I trudge away, forcing myself not to look back. Eventually he catches up.

The path continues to weave between field and forest. Once, we catch sight of a village but decide it's still too near the black magician's stronghold to be safe. Finally, even the sun starts to abandon us, and our progress slows until I know we can drag ourselves no farther. By now the forest has thinned; before us stretches an enormous field with neat rows as far as the eye can see. We've pushed deep between the bushy plants before I realize it's a field of beans.

"What does it matter?" he asks wearily.

"Cecily said you go mad if you fall asleep under flowering beans."

"No flowers," he says curtly.

He's wrong, though. A few of the uppermost buds are already unfurling white petals, ghostly in the twilight, and in the morning it's obvious we should have pressed on, for hundreds of flowers have opened overnight, dancing like butterflies on the breeze, spreading their perfume on the warming air.

"Let me rest for a bit longer," he whispers, cheek pressed against the mud, refusing to move, not even noticing a black beetle ponderously climbing over his hand. "No one will find us here."

His bruises are changing color. Where they were purple-black, now they are tinged with green. When he asks for a story, I remember what Cecily told me about two children who came out of a magic wolf pit. They had green skin, too.

"It was in England," I tell him, "at harvesttime, a very long time ago. A boy and a girl appeared suddenly, as if by magic, on the edge of the cornfield. Their skin was bright green and they wore strange clothing." I look down at myself and laugh. "When they spoke, nobody could understand their fairy language. The harvesters took them to the Lord's house, where they were looked after, but they would eat nothing at all, not a thing, until one day they saw a servant carrying away a bundle of beanstalks. They ate those but never the actual beans."

"Why didn't they eat the beans like anyone else?"

"Cecily said the souls of the dead live in the beans. If you ate one you might be eating your mother or your father."

"That's plain silly."

"I'm only telling you what she said. It's a true story, but if you don't want me to—"

"No, go on," he says, and I notice in spite of his superior tone he's looking uneasily at the bean flowers. "What happened to the green children?"

"After they ate the beanstalks, they grew stronger and learned to speak English. They told the Lord about their beautiful homeland where poverty was unknown and everyone lived forever. The girl said that while playing one day they'd heard the sound of sweet music and followed it across pastureland and into a dark cave—"

"Like your story of the Pied Piper?"

"Yes." I hesitate, remembering that in Cecily's story the boy died and the little girl grew up to be an ordinary wife. "I don't remember the rest."

He's silent for a moment, then looks at me. "What are we going to do? Where can we go? Who can we turn to? Nobody has ever helped us before."

"They said help was coming. They said it was on its way."

"Do you believe it?"

"Yes. That's why we must keep walking towards them." Beneath the bruises, his face is chalk-white. His arm doesn't look right and he winces whenever he tries to move it. There's fresh blood at the corners of his mouth. And suddenly I'm so angry I might explode. "I wish I could kill him." My fists clench so hard my nails dig in. I want to scream and spit and kick things. He continues to look questioningly at me. "I mean the man who started it all. If it hadn't been for him—"

"Didn't you hear what everyone was whispering? He's already dead."

Again, the small shrug. "Anyway, my father said if it hadn't been him there'd have been someone else just like him."

"And maybe then it would have been someone else here, not us."

He smiles and squeezes my hand. "And we would never have met."

"Yes, we would," I say fiercely. "Somehow, somewhere—like in the old stories. Still I wish it could have been me that killed him."

"Too big," he says weakly. "And too powerful."

I knuckle my eyes. "Then I wish I'd been even bigger. I would have stepped on him or squashed him like a fly. Or I wish he'd been even smaller. Then I could have knocked him over and cut off his head or stabbed him in the heart." We sit in silence for a while. I think about all the ways you could kill someone shrunk to Tom Thumb size. "We ought to go now."

"Let me sleep."

"Walk now. Sleep later."

"All right. But first tell me a story—one of your really long ones— about a boy and a girl who kill an ogre."

I think for a moment. None of my old stories seem bad enough until I realize there are other circumstances in which an ogre really could be killed. Thanks to Hanna, I know where. And I even know when. All of a sudden, I'm excited. "Once upon a time," I begin, but see immediately I can't start that way. It isn't that sort of tale. He's still holding my hand. I give it a sharp pull. "Get up. From now on I shall only tell you my story while we're walking. The moment you stop, I shan't say another word."

One

he town of Gmunden, with its placid lake surrounded by high mountains, was a peaceful summer retreat until the morning Mathilde observed that a certain General Pappenheim had brutally suppressed a peasant rebellion there in 1626. The name stirred up a hornet's nest of resentments. Pappenheim was also the family name of that Bertha creature—the young patient Josef had been so preoccupied with. The one he had never stopped talking about, worrying over, at mealtimes, bedtimes, morning, noon, and night, even when his own wife was so heavily pregnant. Why was that? Actually, she had a very good idea why, thank you very much, *Doktor* Josef Breuer. And she wasn't the only one who thought along those lines. Ask Sigmund. He'd verify it.

Mathilde simply could not let the subject rest. The fact that almost two decades had passed made not a scrap of difference. Neither did Josef's protestations. On and on the argument went, growing more accusatory, weighted with increasing bitterness, until he could stand it no longer and returned to Vienna alone. With the exception of the children's old nurse, and the boy, of course, the house was empty.

At least it was quiet here. Or rather, after so many years, Josef was used to the muted noises from beyond the window. His mind no longer registered the distant rumble of trams or the grind and rattle of horse-drawn vehicles, the street cries, the high-pitched chatter of passing maid-servants. Even late-night revelers and their cacophonic renditions of melodies by the recently deceased Strauss were barely noticed.

Within his consulting room, only the somnolent pulse of the ancient clock usually broke the silence that filled the spaces between patients—and none of those would beat a path to his door until the rest of the family returned, marking the official end of his vacation. This morning, hunched over his desk, Josef became aware of another sound, a tremulous beat, a whisper-soft *allegrissimo* countermelody to the groan of the clock. It seemed so much a part of him that he clutched at his chest, suddenly alarmed. However, it was not, after all, the arrhythmic fluttering of his heart but merely the frantic escape bid of a rag-winged butterfly confused by the glass. That this realization took so long was a measure of how disturbing he'd found the earlier incident.

It had required enormous effort to unlock the girl's fingers. He'd never before encountered such prehensile determination. The cat was still hiding beneath the bureau. Perhaps it was dead, for during the struggle, Gudrun, shrieking with fury, had seized its head, forcibly yanking it free of the girl's hands. Clawing empty air as it fell, the animal added its own banshee howl to the din. Benjamin, lurking beyond the door, had immediately bounded into the room. Pandemonium. And yet the girl continued to stare straight ahead, wordless, blank.

What had the animal done to warrant her assault? Plenty of people disliked cats, and some were reputed to have found them terrifying—Napoleon, Meyerbeer, the dissolute Henry III of England— but there were few who, expressionless and without even glancing down, would seize one by the neck and proceed to crush its windpipe.

Josef rose from his desk with a sigh, keeping well back in the shadow of the curtain as he opened the window. After a moment's hesitation, the butterfly—a *Großer Kohlweißling*, summer ravager of cabbage patches, against whose progeny Benjamin waged constant war—exited to certain death. He watched it flutter upwards, keeping close to the building as it battled against the breeze. Not, after all, a Cabbage White: the sooty black spots on the forewings were too large, unusually pro-nounced, even for a female. It was a rare subspecies, perhaps, though it hardly mattered. The dying year had a voracious appetite for such deli-cate creatures. Today Josef could smell autumn on the air, a mixture of wood smoke and fungus, death and decay. He sensed worms wreaking their transformation in the dark loam beneath the leaf mold. The trees were changing color. A few leaves had fallen. Faced with the prospect of a bleak winter, his mood always veered towards the melancholic, never more so than this year, which marked not only the end of the present century but also the end of love. Mathilde had turned from him. Her moods, this difficult passage marking an end to her fertility, would pass; life would settle down again. But the harsh words, those vile accusations. He tugged angrily at his beard. Things could never be the same between them.

What remained? How could his declining years be faced, emotion-ally lacking, with affection rationed, touch denied? At least there was the steady acquisition of knowledge to sustain him—*suum esse conser-vare*. Thank God for work. And, as if to underline it, this intriguing case had simply fallen into his lap.

Josef returned to his chair and stared at the virgin page, as yet unsullied by whatever agonizing secrets were waiting to be unlocked. The facts would have to be recorded. He wrote a single word, *Fräulein*, and stopped. He scratched his head and looked about him at the familiar faces of his daily companions—the ancient clock, increasingly dragging its feet over the passing of time; the carved-wood deer's head mounted with hugely branching six-point antlers, its gaze fixed on each patient, its ears pricked as if eternally eavesdropping; the portrait of his father, Leopold, watching, waiting. For over thirty years Josef had sat at this desk, never once lost for words. He should simply choose a name, any name, and alter it as soon as the girl's identity was established. But still he hesitated. It was not an easy thing, for to name something established dominion over it. As with an infant, it shaped and molded the namer's expectations of that which was named. It set apart. It emphasized human aloneness. A pseudonym was different, a mere cloak.

Josef thought back to his first glimpse of the girl in Benjamin's arms, swaddled in a horse blanket, its coarse folds framing her pale and bloodied face, the gash on her throat a gaping second mouth, the shock of the naked skull, her eyes open but unseeing, as though fixed on a grim hereafter. In that moment, she had put him in mind of a broken flower. A flower name, then, for such was almost an endearment. Since she was so pale, so slender, and because it was his favorite flower, they would henceforth refer to her as Lilie.

> *Die Rose, die Lilie, die Taube, die Sonne,*
> *Die liebt' ich einst alle in Liebeswonne.*

The decision galvanized Josef into action. Squaring up his notebook, he began to write.

Fräulein Lilie X

Fräulein Lilie X appears to be in her early twenties and in good physical health. Nothing is known about her past life. Her well-kept hands and fine features suggest that she comes from the upper stratum of society. She was discovered unclothed on rough ground near the Narrenturm (27 August 1899). It is difficult to ascertain how long she lay there, but probably no more than twenty-four hours, as what has become known as the Tower of Fools is a favorite meeting place for schoolboys who congregate to throw stones at the lightning rod. Lilie's condition was such that the boys who stumbled across her thought she was dead.

My primary examination revealed an exceptionally slow heartbeat and hardly discernible breathing. She appeared to have no awareness of self or others, neither reacting to the external world nor to the passage of time. Her eyes remained open but were similarly unresponsive to stimuli. Skin and mucous membranes appeared normal. The teeth are all present and sound. The patient's head had been crudely shorn. There was severe bruising behind the ears and around the left eye. Two shallow incisions had been made in the throat, close together, probably with a small pocketknife. There was further bruising on the lower arms and wrists, partially obscuring a line of inked characters on the left, which appear to be permanent. I also found bruising on the inner thighs and buttocks but no indication of very recent sexual assault. There were abrasions on both left and right scapulae consistent with the patient having been dragged along the ground by the feet. The patient has remained comatose for three days, during which time she has not eaten or taken liquid apart from a few drops of water spooned between her lips.

Josef put down his pen, reluctant to revisit the moment of change. Instead he made his way to the kitchen, drawn by his nose to the prospect of freshly made *Shlishkes*.

The relaxed, almost *schlampig* way in which the house was run in Mathilde's absence was a holiday in itself. To perch on a stool amid the scrubbing and chopping, the beating and mixing, the basting and tasting, transported him back to childhood, when his grandmother had taken charge of his father's house, especially as Gudrun was familiar with so many old Hungarian recipes. He took advantage of Gudrun's turned back to palm surreptitiously one of the warm dumplings with its coating of sugar and caramelized bread crumbs.

"Leave them alone," said Gudrun, without turning, and in the fearsome voice formerly reserved for the nursery. "They're counted." Josef said nothing. The old nurse had strict rules about speaking with one's mouth full. She brought him coffee without being asked. "I've made some soup for the patient."

"I doubt she'll eat it."

"She will, if I feed her." Gudrun stood before him, arms akimbo, glaring.

"It's no good forcing food into her mouth if she can't swallow—"

Gudrun snorted. "Can't? *Won't*. I'm surprised you're still taken in after this morning's little episode. Vicious, that was. The girl deserves a good hiding. She needs locking up."

Josef ignored the venom. "She'll stay in her room for another few days. I've come to the conclusion that we brought her downstairs too soon."

"And I've come to the conclusion that she's playacting, pretending to be dead to the world. You mark my words: there's more to this than meets the eye. She'll probably wait until we're off guard and then let in her accomplices to ransack the silver and murder us all in our beds. Vienna's not what it was, with all these strangers pouring into the city. I told you, plain as plain, you were bringing trouble into the house. Would you listen? No. Am I right? I am. And what's the mistress going to say, tell me that? *Frau Doktor* Breuer won't want her nicely brought-up daughters associating with a wench who's probably no better than she should be—"

"The girl was brutally attacked," said Josef, in an attempt to stem the flow.

Gudrun moved the plate of *Shlishkes* out of reach. "There's no need to raise your voice."

Josef was on the verge of forbidding force-feeding and then beating a hasty retreat when Benjamin clumped in carrying a frail piled high with vegetables, distracting Gudrun, who turned her bad temper on his muddy boots. The young man grinned, ignoring the ensuing threats.

"How is she now, *Herr Doktor*?"

"And you'll scrub the floor until it's clean enough to eat off," Gudrun finished, adding: "Never mind her. It's the cat's health you should be asking after. If the poor creature's still alive."

Her eyes gleamed. Josef recalled that she'd never liked the animal. He set down his empty cup, nodding as Gudrun hovered with the coffeepot. "Thank you." It was not his practice to discuss patients, but Benjamin's quick action in bringing the girl . . . in bringing *Lilie* . . . here earned him the right to inquire. "Physically she's much improved. The bruising—"

"I told him already, the bruises are fading," Gudrun put in. "Almost gone, thanks to me. And those nasty cuts on her neck have more or less healed." She sniffed. "I can't shift those ink marks on her arm, though, no matter how hard I scrub."

"They're tattoos," Benjamin muttered, rolling his eyes. "Tell her, *Herr Doktor*. She takes no notice of me." He glanced defiantly at Gudrun. "They're tattoos. They won't come off."

"Sailors have tattoos," Gudrun said scornfully. "There's a reason for that, which I won't go into. No reason for one to be on a young woman's arm."

"Perhaps it's decorative," hazarded Josef. "People have decorated their bodies with tattoos since the beginning of time. They used to pierce the skin with thin sticks and sharpened bones. A painful process, I should imagine, but I understand a New York man's invented a tattooing machine."

"Must still hurt." Benjamin winced as he unlaced the offending boots.

"Leviticus 19, verse 28," declared Gudrun. "'You shall not make gashes in your flesh for the dead, or incise any marks on yourselves: I am the Lord.'"

The two men glanced at each other but said nothing. Josef had taken the presence of those marks to confirm Benjamin's suspicions that Lilie could not possibly be a Jew. It mattered now that Vienna had lapsed into one of its periodic bouts of anti-Semitism: taunts and slogans, occasional skirmishes—nothing new. This time he suspected it was being fueled by Mayor Lueger for his own political ends, and exacerbated, as always, by ill-educated Roman Catholic priests exercising their fervid imaginations to embellish age-old myths of ritual murder, including the sacrifice of Christian babies. The blood libel trial of Hilsner in Bohemia hadn't helped. The similarities between the discovery of Anežka Hrůzová's body—throat slashed, clothes half torn off—and that of Lilie had prompted the boy to act quickly for fear of reprisals against the Jewish community. Lucky for them it was Benjamin's younger brother and his friend who'd found her: within an hour the girl was safely concealed within the respectable Breuer house. Benjamin was to be commended for taking their late-night conversations so seriously.

"Anyway," Gudrun continued, plunging her knife into the heart of a cabbage, "what self-respecting woman wants a string of lines and numbers decorating her wrist when she could have a nice bracelet? Whatever she is, the girl doesn't look like a savage."

"Lilie," said Josef. "I've decided we should call her Lilie."

"Lilie," echoed Benjamin, savoring the word. "Lilie. And has Lilie recovered since this morning? How is her mental state?"

"Never mind that," said Gudrun. "What about this soup?"

Josef stood. "I'll take it up now."

"Let me go. I'll get her eating, see if I don't," Gudrun promised.

"No," insisted Josef. "Since she took water only from me, I should feed her." He was immediately oppressed by a sense of déjà vu, and a tiny frisson of something akin to fear ran the length of his spine. This was history repeating itself. He remembered long passages when Bertha had accepted food only when he extended the spoon. Perhaps it might be better . . . Then he remembered Mathilde's offensive accusations and turned his back on good sense. "I will feed her," he said, more firmly this time.

"Then I shall carry the tray," Gudrun said, just as firmly, fixing him with her eye. "You shouldn't go alone."

Josef's mouth tightened. For a moment the voices of his wife and Gudrun seemed to fuse into one. "The young woman needs no protection from me." He avoided looking at Benjamin.

"It's your reputation I'm thinking of, *Herr Doktor*. What with the mistress away."

They trudged upstairs, both breathing heavily, both oppressed by their age. On reaching the guest-room door, Josef knocked out of courtesy, but Gudrun shoved past him, balancing the tray on one generously padded hip. Lilie was exactly as they'd left her, sitting bolt upright in the chair and staring straight ahead. Her eyes were wide open. Dull. Blank. The only difference Josef could find was that her left hand lay loosely cupped in her lap.

"Some water first." He held the glass to Lilie's mouth. Meeting no response, he pushed a small spoonful of water between her lips. It spilled from the corners of her mouth, trickled down the sides of her neck, fingered under the plum-colored fabric, and continued stealthily downwards. Josef looked away. Gudrun had dressed the girl in outgrown family garments. Dark shades didn't suit the girl's pale complexion; some other arrangements would have to be made. After a moment he refilled the spoon.

"This time drink it," commanded Gudrun. "Hurry up, the soup's getting cold."

"Shouting won't achieve anything."

"How's it going to look if she starves to death, *Herr Doktor*? What then?" Gudrun leaned closer. "No good sitting there, mooning over whatever happened, my girl. Chances are you brought it on yourself anyway. What's done is done. Get up and get on with life, that's what I say."

"Enough," said Josef. "From now on, please remain silent at all times in Lilie's presence."

"Very well." The direct order didn't stop Gudrun from tapping Lilie sharply on the back of the neck as she passed. It couldn't have hurt, but Lilie responded immediately with an audible intake of breath, jerking her head vigorously to one side and wriggling her shoulders. A soft pink, the color of wild-rose petals, crept up her cheeks. Her eyes brightened.

She blinked and focused, not on Josef, who sat opposite her, but on an area somewhere above his left shoulder.

"*Vous êtes qui?*" Lilie's voice was low, melodic, totally pleasing to Josef. He stared back, transfixed by her irises, which were a curiously intense blue-green, almost turquoise, with a ring of amber flecks around the pupil. Now that her face was animated, he realized Lilie was possessed of a rare beauty, her features perfectly symmetrical and in proportion. A hazy recollection of some painting hovered on the edge of his memory. He struggled to remember the artist. "*Vous êtes qui?*" she repeated, and still receiving no answer: "*És ön? Cine esti tu? Kim?*" Her voice rose a fraction. "*Który jesteście ty? Kdo ar tebe? Wer sind Sie?* Who are you?" Her lips continued to move, but Josef was unable to pick out any words.

"Forgive me, *Fräulein*. My name is Josef Breuer. I am a physician—"

"Josef Robert Breuer," said Lilie, looking directly at him for the first time. "Born Vienna, January 15, 1842, graduated from the Akademisches Gymnasium in 1858—"

"That is correct," said Josef, a little startled. "And what is your name?"

"I have no name." Lilie turned her left arm so the wrist faced him. "Just my number."

"Number?" snorted Gudrun. "How much more of this nonsense—?"

Josef shot her a warning look before turning his attention back to the girl.

"Everyone has a name, *Fräulein*. It is what distinguishes one human being from another."

"Why do you assume I'm human?" Lilie inspected her cupped hand and slowly opened her fingers, revealing a white butterfly, its blotched wings ragged but otherwise undamaged, for it immediately fluttered away, joining several others dancing aimless figure eights against the ceiling. "So many," she murmured. "Thousands, millions, one for every stolen soul. Already there are too many to count."

"Ah, yes," agreed Josef, "the butterfly has long been associated with the human soul. In Greek myth—"

Lilie closed her hand. "Not butterflies. They're flowers."

Josef glanced at Gudrun. Tight-mouthed and resentful, she sat pleating the hem of her apron between her fingers. He cleared his throat and steered the conversation back to the girl's feeling of exclusion from the human race. He smiled. "I see no reason not to assume you're human."

"I am not part of the human race. First I was an idea. Then I came into being charged with a very important task."

Josef nodded but made no comment. "And were you born here in Vienna? No? Then can you remember where you spent your childhood?"

"I wasn't born. I was created just like this."

"As were we all," agreed Josef. "The creator of the universe—"

"Do you think I'm an angel?" asked Lilie, staring straight in front of her. "No. I'm not that, either. I'm sure you've heard of Olimpia—"

"Ernst Hoffmann," murmured Josef, nodding sagely. "She was the beautiful automaton in his short story 'Der Sandmann.' Of course, but—"

"She could only say 'Ah, ah.' Think of me as being more like that but much cleverer. A machine made in the image of an adult human female."

"I see." Josef cleared his throat. "Made."

"Half-baked, if you ask me," muttered Gudrun, flicking away imaginary dust.

"Very well," said Josef, pointedly raising one shoulder against Gudrun's interruption. "Since you have no name, I shall call you Lilie." He waited for an objection but none came, though her lips moved. "Now, Lilie, tell us about your task."

Lilie turned the full blue-green of her gaze on him. "I've come to find the monster."

"Ah. And this monster—is it in Vienna?"

"No," said Lilie, "but he's coming. Look." She opened her hand, and to Josef's amazement another of the curiously marked butterflies hung poised for a moment, its black markings reminiscent of the empty eye cavities of the skull, before spiraling up to join the endless dance above their heads.

"Where—"

"This soup will be stone cold in a minute," said Gudrun, and rattled the spoon against the bowl. "Eat. That's what we're up here for."

Josef snatched it from her hand and held it out to the girl. "Will you eat something, *Fräulein*?"

Lilie glanced at the soup and wrinkled her nose in what might have been distaste. "Machines don't need to eat."

"There's plenty in Vienna would be glad of that soup, let me tell you," huffed Gudrun, taking the gesture personally. "I'll give you turning your nose up at good food. Just who do you think you are?"

"Silence, *Frau* Gschtaltner!" roared Josef. "Not another word."

"Huh," said Gudrun, and folded her arms over her chest.

Once again, Josef thrust forward the spoon, handle-first, willing Lilie to take it. "Come, Lilie, eat just a little." He didn't want to repeat history by feeding her, but since she continued to stare at the opposite wall, he supposed there was nothing else for it. By now the girl must be hungry. He stirred the soup and took a small spoonful, carefully avoiding the congealing fat. "Open your mouth, Lilie." It was a very pretty mouth, the lips well shaped and generous, so full of promise that Josef could almost imagine how it might feel to sate his own hunger there. His heart lurched. The spoon juddered violently, spilling most of the liquid.

"Open your mouth immediately, Lilie," he said, more forcefully than he'd intended. "You must eat."

It emerged as an order. And perhaps this was the way it would work, for Lilie immediately obeyed. The thought both alarmed and exhilarated Josef. He could hardly bear to watch the shallow bowl of the spoon pressing down on her lower lip as he fed her. Occasionally the pink tip of her tongue emerged to lick away a glistening trail of soup droplets. Twice Lilie turned her head away, but the insistent spoon pursued her. Josef stopped only when he observed that she was holding the liquid in her mouth rather than swallowing it.

"Good." He surreptitiously ran his fingers beneath his damp collar. "Rest now, Lilie. We will talk again later."

Outside the door Gudrun eyed him severely.

"You should have let me deal with her. Start pandering to her nonsense and there'll be no end to this foolishness."

"The poor child will recover soon enough."

"No fool like an old fool," said Gudrun, taking the tray.

Josef flinched. Had he made himself so obvious? Then it occurred to him that Gudrun would never have dared to speak to him with such disrespect if Mathilde had been there.

"Send Benjamin to me." He omitted the courtesy that would have softened the command to a request. Not that it redressed the balance. "And prepare something more substantial for the girl's evening meal. Cold meat, fruit, cheese—anything she can pick up with her fingers." He couldn't go through all that again.

"And will you be in there talking to her later?" Gudrun flushed crimson before Josef's glare, but she didn't drop her eyes. "If so, I should accompany you."

"Send Benjamin to me," he repeated, without answering.

The boy couldn't have been far away. Josef had barely settled himself before he heard the heavy clump of work boots along the passage from the kitchen stairs. And, newly cleaned or not, that was something else Mathilde wouldn't have tolerated. He opened the door before there was time for Benjamin to forget about knocking.

"What have you found out, Benjamin? Any talk of young women going missing?"

Benjamin shook his head. "Nothing. Well, nothing apart from the Grossmanns' scullery maid. She ran off ten days ago. Their cook reckons she got homesick and went back to her father's farm. Couldn't be Lilie, though." He looked at his hands. "Hedda is much older, and ugly as sin, with a backside the size of a tram. Nothing else. Couple of whores found dead in Spittelberg."

"You'd better keep trying," said Josef after a moment's thought. "Someone must know something. She didn't fall out of the air. For the reasons we discussed, I don't want to involve outsiders unless it's absolutely necessary." He carefully lined up his pens. "So far, Lilie hasn't said anything sensible about her family background."

"A girl like Lilie, you'd think there'd be people out looking for her."

"I don't believe she's from Vienna." Josef replayed her few short answers in his head. There'd been traces of a strange accent. He couldn't place it. "Of course, she may have been brought here, perhaps against her will." He leaned forward, lowering his voice. "That other matter we spoke of . . ."

"I'll try," said Benjamin, "but it won't be easy. I can't just walk in. Fat chance of getting work there—apparently the pay's so good the servants hang on to their jobs. Anyway, I've heard tell they won't take on young men because of all the girls." He hesitated. "*Herr Doktor*, it would be a simple matter for you to join the club."

"No." Josef clenched his fists. "Out of the question."

"They say many of Vienna's top men are members. *Herr Doktor* Schmidt, *Herr Professor* Voss—"

"*No!*" Josef almost choked on the word. Rumors abounded about what went on beneath the Thélème's well-polished veneer of respectability. Foreign women . . . and men . . . prepared to engage in unnatural acts. Sexual coupling turned into theater. Orgies: the loosening of Saturn's restraints as in the ancient temples. Josef swallowed hard. Those who frequented such places were either degenerate, a state surely denoting lack of purpose, or poor, sad creatures having no other recourse to sensual warmth; to be numbered among the latter would be to grind salt into his emotional wounds. He visualized *Frau* Voss with her sharp nose and lipless mouth, *Frau Doktor* Schmidt and her shifty-eyed piety. How would others judge Mathilde if he— No. Besides, a poisonous word dropped here, a venomous nod and wink there . . . even Mayor Lueger wasn't immune: Vienna was growing fast, but salacious gossip traveled faster. He would lay himself open to ridicule, to blackmail. All those that he held dear might be exposed to scandal. "No," he repeated. "No, that place is a pit of depravity."

Benjamin turned scarlet. "I only meant to see if Lilie—"

"It could give certain factions more ammunition than they need."

"Nobody need find out."

Josef looked hard at him. "And how did you discover that the doctor and the professor were members?"

"Well, everyone knows . . . Oh. Yes. Sorry." Benjamin coughed gently. "I'll go back. See what I can find out by hanging around the kitchen door." He was silent for a moment before asking diffidently: "Is she . . . is Lilie all right? One minute Gudrun says she's a thief waiting until we're off our guard, the next that she's a raving lunatic, harping on about being made of clockwork or something. Is that true? Is she really mad?"

"Time will tell," Josef said vaguely. "If I'm to find out what happened to Lilie, she must be questioned extremely carefully. She may not remember yet. She might be hiding something. In either case she must be induced to confide in me."

"Of course, *Herr Doktor*. I understand."

"Patience is called for. Such things can't be rushed." In many ways it was akin to seduction. To his horror, Josef found his imagination was still conjuring up voluptuous pictures of what might be happening even now in the Thélème. The writhing images had Lilie's mouth. Her eyes. Her neck. Those marks on her arm—they were like cattle brands, livestock—an appalling thought. He jumped to his feet and opened the safe, keeping his back to the boy. "You'll need more money since you're going back into the coffeehouses, Benjamin. The taverns, too, I suppose."

"Do you think she's married?"

"Who?" Josef thought of Lilie using the revealing pronoun *he* instead of the neutral *it* for the monster. In his professional capacity, he'd examined her carefully. He knew what he knew. Undoubtedly there was a brutish man in this somewhere, but there was no ring on her finger and no mark where one had been. "You mean Lilie, Benjamin?" He turned to face him. "I doubt it."

"WAIT FOR ME, *HERR DOKTOR*." Gudrun labored up the stairs after him, clutching a workbasket. "I promised to come with you, and come with you I will."

Josef drew himself upright. "There's really no need—"

"I won't utter a word," said Gudrun, shouldering past him. "Not a word. I shall sit by the window and get on with my mending. Quiet as a mouse. In silence."

"Very well." Josef knocked on the door and entered quickly before Gudrun could blunder in. The girl was sitting exactly as before: hands loosely clasped in her lap; eyes wide open and blank. "Good afternoon, Lilie. I thought we might have a chat. How are you feeling now?" He raised his voice when no answer came: "Lilie, you must speak to me. Answer now, please. Do you hear? How are you feeling?"

Lilie inclined her head. "A machine has no feelings."

Josef waited until Gudrun had settled herself by the window with her darning mushroom and was busily jabbing a large needle into the heel of one of his socks. He left the question of emotional response for the moment. There was another, more promising topic that might yield results.

"Tell me about the monster, Lilie." She stared at him for so long without blinking that Josef found himself opening and shutting his eyes at twice the normal speed, as if to ease her ocular discomfort as well as his own. "Tell me about the monster. What does he look like?"

"He is small and dark."

"Small, yes." Unusual. Dark? Josef thought back to children's tales. A picture of a prancing devil presented itself. "And does he have claws or horns? A tail? Huge teeth?"

"No."

"Do you see him in your dreams or in everyday life?"

"No."

Josef frowned. "Where is he then?"

"He is somewhere else."

"Somewhere in Vienna?"

"No, but he will come here soon."

"To find you?"

"No," said Lilie. "He isn't looking for me. I am looking for him."

"Oh? And why is that?"

"He won't recognize me. I'll be able to put an end to it before it begins."

"Ah," said Josef, wondering what Lilie imagined had rendered her incognito. The lack of hair, perhaps: women often attached disproportionate importance to the effects of a different style. "Are you frightened of him?"

Lilie shook her head. "Fear is a human weakness. I have no feelings."

"It's hard to believe you're a machine, Lilie, since you look exactly like a real human woman. And a very comely one, if I might say so." The girl's face remained without expression, but a prolonged clattering of bobbins from the window seat said far more than words and Josef immediately wished the stiff compliment unvoiced. "Like Galatea," he added, "who though not a machine was made by human hands."

"Pygmalion only sculpted one Galatea," responded Lilie. "I am one of many. There are thousands with the face and body that you see before you. Machines such as I are provided with a pleasing female likeness unless otherwise requested. Since we are neither dead nor alive our appearance remains a matter of indifference to us."

Josef leaned his elbows on his knees and made a steeple of his fingers. "Galatea was brought to life by Aphrodite. How is it that you are able to move, breathe, think, and speak?"

"Electrical impulses," said Lilie, rubbing her left wrist, "as in human bodies."

"But," he persisted, "what equivalence exists for the divine spark whereby a human infant quickens?"

"It's the same thing. Nothing but an electrical charge." She looked directly at him. "Such as a bolt of lightning from the *Blitzfänger*."

"From what you say"—Josef's eyes flicked sideways, irritated by the outbreak of huffing and tutting from near the window—"the only difference between a human and a machine such as yourself seems to be the existence of a soul."

Lilie shook her head. "All the soul cares about is experiencing every variety of pain this world can offer. Souls are so greedy for pain they don't care whether the body is natural or man-made. In a natural body it can feel the pain. In a fabricated one it observes the effects."

"But there are pleasures, too," said Josef, profoundly shocked. "Love, friendship, service, knowledge."

"Pleasure is only a pathway to pain because it must always end in . . ." Lilie looked up at the ceiling and Josef's eyes followed her gaze. More of the butterflies must have entered through the partially opened window, for now fifty or more fluttered helplessly against the plaster. Gudrun would have to take a brush to them. The garden must be over-run with the creatures.

"In—?" he prompted.

"Death," said Lilie. "Fear of dying brings humans the greatest pain. Death is implicit in every form of joy. Of course, it also brings the end of pain."

"And what happens when a machine dies? Does its soul return to God?"

"God is a human invention," said Lilie.

"That's enough." Red-faced and trembling, Gudrun thrust herself between Josef and Lilie, still shoving her sewing inside the workbasket. "I'm not listening to any more of this wickedness. What would your father say, *Herr Doktor*? What would he say?" She turned on Lilie. "I'll bring you food later, Miss. Eat it or not, as you please. I refuse to take part in your nasty game. And by the way, don't expect me to get you ready for bed this evening. You're quite capable of looking after yourself."

Josef found himself on the other side of the slammed door without working out how it had been achieved.

"I'm surprised at you, encouraging that sort of talk, *Herr Doktor*," said Gudrun.

"A type of pantheism, perhaps," murmured Josef. "She's a well-educated young woman."

"She can read, if that's what you mean. Every book's been off the shelves in that room. I can tell. I won't explain how. It's enough to say I've only one pair of hands and this is a big house." Gudrun pursed her lips. "Unless, of course, she was looking to see if anything had been hidden behind them."

Two conversations with *Fräulein* Lilie took place today after I discovered that, while gentle persuasion has no effect, a direct order is instantly obeyed. It became apparent that the young woman has been well educated and is of high intelligence. However, whatever occurred in her past has led her to detach herself from emotional response. Lilie avers that she has no feelings, either negative or positive, that she has, in short, turned into a machine. Her elaboration of this fantasy involves a gloomy and joyless view of the world, backed up by simple logic gleaned from atheist literature. Lilie also referred to a man who is likely to have been responsible for the attack on her. She identifies him as a monster and courageously asserts that she will find him in order to see him punished. I am confident that considerable progress has been made and that Lilie is ready to receive treatment.

Two

apa says I should be glad that we've come to live in such a beautiful place. There are many important people here. People who matter. People who will make the future better for everyone. I'm not glad at all, and I don't think he is, either. As we were leaving our proper house, Papa said I must stay in the car with my toys and books while he locked up. After a bit I followed him back inside and heard him walking around talking to Mama, which was very silly because she isn't there anymore.

"What else can I do, Lidia?" he asked the bed. "It's the last thing I want to be involved with, but these are dangerous times." He picked up Mama's hairbrush and ran his hand across the bristles. "How else can I keep her safe?"

I popped out from behind the door. "Keep who safe, Papa?"

Papa got very cross and marched me back outside. "It's about time you learned to do as you're told, young lady."

"Don't want to go." I try to stop him putting me into the car. "No!

No!" I scream so loudly the lady from the house next door throws open her windows to look out. Papa pushes me onto the backseat and starts the engine. He tidies his hair and mops his forehead, watching me in the car's little mirror.

"Be a good girl and we will stop somewhere nice on the way."

"Won't. Don't want to."

"Very well, Krysta." Papa sighs. He sighs a lot more than he used to. I kneel on the seat, watching our house get smaller and smaller until it isn't there anymore.

This new house is big, with fine new furniture and no dark corners to hide in, unlike our real home, which Greet said was impossible for one person to keep clean. A cat with a family of new kittens lives downstairs. Outside, we have a garden with flowers and trees instead of the noisy street. Beyond its walls there's a big zoo, but not the kind that has lots of visitors.

"There are lakes and forests, too," Papa says, raising his voice as I continue to wail and stamp and call for Greet. "When summer comes we'll go for picnics and gather berries. And in the autumn we'll hunt for mushrooms—*Steinpilz* and *Pfifferlinge*. You'd like that, wouldn't you?"

"No. No! *No!*" Who will thread the wild mushrooms on strings now that Greet has gone? Who will tie ribbons in my hair? Who will tell me stories? I throw myself on the floor and kick my legs.

"Stop that, Krysta," Papa says sharply. "You're a big girl now, not a baby." He picks me up and sits me in a chair. I scream and drum my heels against the seat. His eyes dart from me to the door. "Stop! Any more noise and you'll get a smack."

I stick my thumb in my mouth, sniffing and hiccupping. Papa takes out a handkerchief and tells me to blow.

"That's better." He walks to the window and looks out. "I'm only here for your sake, Krysta," he says very quietly. "If it wasn't for you . . ."

He sighs again, and adds in a louder voice: "At least it's safe here. You can play anywhere you like. All the dangerous creatures are behind the walls, and there are guards with fierce dogs to make sure they never get out."

"When will my Greet come?"

Papa frowns. "Greet can't come here. This is a special place."

"Don't like it. Want to go home. Want Greet."

"Enough. Do you know what happens to bad little girls who don't do as they are told? One of these days you'll find out. Then you'll be sorry."

I'M LONELY WITHOUT GREET.

I don't miss her shouting and flicking me with the dishrag, or the way she dragged the comb through my hair and made me drink my milk even when it had skin on it. Even though he sometimes threatens to, Papa never smacks me like Greet did. Instead he sits me on his knee and talks for a long time about being nice and how good little girls are supposed to behave. But he doesn't do cuddles like Greet, either. He holds my hand. Sometimes he kisses the top of my head. Greet gave me big, squashy cuddles and tickled me when she was in a good mood. She kissed me good night and tucked me in—unless I'd made her cross. Then she used to shout: "Get up those stairs out of my sight and let's hope the evil one doesn't carry you off in the night." Papa just stands at the end of the bed and hopes I sleep well.

Most of all, I miss Greet's storytelling. Stories for this, stories for that, stories for everything else—she had new ones for each day of the week, ones that went with most of her jobs. There were puffing, blowing wash-day stories and hot, red-faced ironing stories. There were quick stories for making dumplings or *Apfelstrudel* and extra-long stories for sewing and mending afternoons. People here sometimes read me stories from books. They don't carry them in their heads. They can't do voices like Greet, either. She did little honey-cake voices for princesses, crackly burning-paper ones for the witches, great big roars for the baddies, cheerful voices for the brave heroes. They don't sing. They don't make the right faces. Most stories here are nice and end happily. Some of Greet's were nasty, especially the liver-chopping and fish-gutting ones.

"Once upon a time," begins Greet, grabbing the whetstone from its tub of water, "on a farm near Sachsenhausen, lived a man who let his children watch as he slaughtered a pig." She draws the blade of the largest kitchen knife across the whetstone, tip to heel, with a long quivering *whi-i-i-sh* that sounds like pirate swords slicing the air. Shivers run up my back. Again. Again. "Later that day, when the children went off to play, the eldest child said to the youngest: 'You shall be the little pig. I'll be the butcher.' And with that . . ." Greet reaches into a bucket and slaps a bloody mass onto the table. She brandishes the newly sharpened blade aloft. "The eldest child took a shiny knife and slit his little brother's throat."

I gulp and shuffle backwards, staring openmouthed as her blade slices the offal as easily as a breakfast knife slides through warm butter. I want and do not want to hear more. Greet straightens up, wiping her brow with the back of one hand.

"Now, the mother was upstairs bathing the baby. When she heard the cries of her son, she ran helter-skelter downstairs. On seeing what had happened, she pulled the knife out of the boy's throat and was so angry that she plunged it straight into the heart of the son who'd played butcher—" Here Greet lunges across the table with the kitchen knife, making me scream and run for the door. "Then she remembered the baby and raced back upstairs. But it was too late. He'd drowned in the bath."

By now I'm trembling from head to foot. A small whimper squeezes through my clenched teeth. Greet sweeps the bloody offering into a pan with her bright red hand.

"The woman was so distressed," she continues, her voice mournful, mouth pursed, head shaking, "that she hanged herself from a beam in the barn. And that evening, when the father returned from working in the fields, he took his gun—"

"Margarete!" roars Papa. "What's the meaning of this?"

Greet's mouth snaps shut just like one of the Little Nippers in the pantry, but this time she is the mouse. I put my thumb in. She hangs her head.

"Beg pardon, *Herr Doktor*. She does like her stories."

"There are other stories, Margarete. Pleasant stories. Uplifting ones that tell of the beauty and sanctity of life, of good overcoming evil. You should know better than to frighten an innocent child with such dreadful tales."

Greet glances sideways at me. *Papa, if only you knew . . .*

"Beg pardon, *Herr Doktor*," she mutters. "It won't happen again."

"I should think not," says Papa, his face grim. "Such tales spring from sick imaginations. Childhood is precious. It's where the building blocks of life are laid. We have a duty to protect our little ones from hearing about such atrocities."

EVERY DAY NOW Papa goes to the infirmary. When he comes back he washes his hands. He rubs and scrubs until the basin is full of soap bubbles. His fingers go pink and wrinkly. After he has finished drying his hands, Papa runs clean water and washes them again.

FACES HERE ARE MOSTLY STERN, but Uncle Hraben never stops smiling. He even smiled when he kicked the kittens out of the way. Johanna says he is very handsome but not nearly so handsome as Papa. On my birthday Uncle Hraben gives me a *Negerküsse*. I eat it very slowly, first the chocolate shell, then the marshmallow filling, then the biscuit base. Afterwards I smooth out the wrapper, rubbing the back with my nail until it shines like silver, and he makes it into a ring for me.

"Where is your father taking you this afternoon, pretty Krysta?" asks Uncle Hraben, stroking the back of my neck. I pull away.

"He says it's a secret surprise."

"Ah. I see. But where do you hope you're going?"

I run to the window and point in the direction of the high wall. "To the zoo. Greet's uncle, who's a sailor, went to one in America. He saw a polar bear and a giraffe and . . ." I pause, overcome with excitement and anticipation, before continuing in a hushed voice, *"and they let him ride on an elephant."*

Uncle Hraben bellows with laughter. Some of his friends come over and he repeats what I've said. They also laugh. Eventually he dries his eyes and tells me there are no elephants, bears, giraffes, or monkeys behind the wall.

I take off his ring and put my thumb in my mouth. It's bad luck to cry on your birthday.

"It's not that sort of zoo, *Mädchen*."

"This one's for a different kind of beast altogether," explains the man with straw hair and eyes the color of winter rain. They laugh again.

"What sort of beasts?" I stamp my foot but this only makes them laugh more.

"Animal-people."

There *are* animals that look like people. The old lady who lives next door to our real house has a pet schnauzer, the fattest dog I've ever seen. Greet said over many years they'd grown alike: now both had hair sprinkled with salt and pepper, both with snouts poking into other people's private business, both with bad tempers and yappy voices, both the shape of wine barrels. And once I heard Greet shout, *"Männer sind Schweine!"* at the man who brought firewood. Also, one of Papa's friends had big, yellow teeth that made him look like a rat.

"I still want to see them."

"Too dangerous," says Uncle Hraben. "They eat *proper* little human girls, especially pretty ones. Snip, snap—one bite and you'd be gone."

WHEN PAPA CAME BACK from the infirmary, he still did all the hand washing, even though he'd promised we'd go out straightaway. While he was scrubbing his nails with the little brush, I asked if we were going to the zoo, in case Uncle Hraben had been joking.

"No."

I scowl. "You said I could choose."

Papa dries his hands and looks carefully at his fingers. "Wouldn't you rather come to the toy shop with me? There's something there you might like to bring home. And afterwards we can have ice cream in a café." He runs fresh water and picks up the soap.

"Erdbeereis?"

"Strawberry, chocolate—whatever flavor you like."

The town is bright, with flowers at the windows and many red flags with bendy-arm Xs on them fluttering very gently in the breeze. People sitting outside a café smile at us, some stand up to wave, and when we go into the toy shop, the shopkeeper leaves all his other customers to serve Papa.

"Ah, so this is the birthday *Fräulein. Alles Gute zum Geburtstag!"* He reaches below the counter and brings out two boxes. Each contains a pretty doll. One has dark brown curly hair and a red frock; the other is blonde and dressed all in blue. "Yes, many happy returns from all of us. Here we are. Your papa wasn't sure which you'd prefer."

I look at Papa. He nods. "Which one would you like?"

"Can't I have both?"

Papa shakes his head. "No."

"Want both." I kick at the brass rail running along the base of the counter. I try squeezing out a tear, but it won't come. "Not fair. Why can't I have both?"

"You may have *one*," he says in a tired voice. "If you can't choose, then we will come back another day. Is that what you want? No. Then hurry up and decide before all the ice cream has melted."

"Not fair," I repeat but already know which doll I'll be taking home. The shopkeeper almost imperceptibly pushes the brown-haired doll towards me. She is a bit like Greet except that her eyes are the wrong color, but the yellow-haired doll looks like a fairy princess. "That one." I point and the shopkeeper gives a little sigh and takes the brown doll away. "What's her name?"

"You want the fair one. Good." Papa looks very pleased as he reads the label. "It says 'Charlotte,' but you can give her whatever name you wish."

"I shall call her Lottie, except when she's been naughty," I say, remembering Papa changing "Greet" to "Margarete" when she annoyed him. "Then, she will be Charlotte."

In the café I take Lottie out of her box to look at her knickers. A tiny blob of strawberry ice cream falls onto her blue frock leaving a mark, but I keep my finger over it so Papa won't notice.

JUST BEFORE BEDTIME, Herta brings me a birthday gift, a book called *Der Struwwelpeter*. She says all the stories are about naughty children. I don't like the pictures and neither does Lottie, but Papa reminds me to say thank you. Then I have to sit by Herta, who is hard and lumpy, while she reads me the story of "The Thumb-sucker" in a voice like heavy boots.

"No thumbkins," she says, forcing my thumb out of my mouth and keeping a tight hold on my wrist. "Listen carefully. This story is about a child like you." I pull a nasty face, but Herta doesn't notice.

"'Konrad,' sprach die Frau Mama, 'Ich geh' aus und du bleibst da.'" Herta stops. She taps my leg. "Sit still, child. Now, shall we continue?"

> "See how ordered you can be
> Till I come again," said she.
> "Docile be, and good and mild,
> Pray don't suck your thumb, my child,
> For if you do, the tailor will come
> And bring his shears to snip your thumb
> From off your hand as clear and clean
> As if paper it had been."

It's a stupid story. Nevertheless, I glance anxiously towards Papa when she gets to the part about the tailor. But Papa has his eyes closed. His fingers twist around each other as if they are washing themselves without water.

"Bang!" says Herta, without putting any bang in her voice. "Here goes the door ker-slam! Whoop! the tailor lands ker-blam!"

Seeing what's coming, I quickly pull my hands away and sit on them. Poor Lottie falls on the floor. Herta laughs.

> "Who can tell a mother's sorrow,
> When she saw her boy the morrow?
> There he stood all steeped in shame,
> And not a thumbkin to his name."

Pulling my right hand from under my bottom, she holds the special sucking thumb between two of her big, square fingers, pretending they're scissors. Chop, chop. "Better stop your baby habits in case it happens to you. You've got to be a big girl now."

"Papa wouldn't let the tailor cut off my thumbs."

"He might not be there to stop him." Herta flicks through the pages. "Would you like another story? Look at this one. A very naughty girl is playing with her mama's box of matches, and a minute later . . ."

> *"Consumed is all, so sweet and fair,*
> *The total child, both flesh and hair,*
> *A pile of ashes, two small shoes,*
> *Is all that's left, and they're no use.*

"See? All burnt away. Nothing left of silly Paulinchen but a pile of cinders. Can you imagine such a terrible thing?"

"Greet said she would whip me if I touched matches again." I turn over the page and look at the picture of a black boy holding a big green umbrella. There is a magician in a long red robe and three boys that he turns as dark-skinned as the first by dipping them in a giant inkpot. "Can you read this one?"

Herta frowns as she skims the text. She clicks her tongue.

"Please," I add, in case Papa's listening.

"No," she says, "that is not a suitable story." And with that, she rips out the pages.

AT HOME THERE'D ALWAYS BEEN plenty to do—Greet saw to that. Some days she sat me on the kitchen table to pod peas, and made me count aloud the number in each fat green pod as I snapped them open.

"*Eins, zwei, drei . . .*" If there were more than eight peas, I was allowed to eat the smallest. When the job was finished, there'd be a story, usually "The Pea Test," which I liked until it didn't work. Even with ten peas under my mattress. Or I sorted feathers when she was plucking a chicken or goose—quills in the bucket, down in a basket—and then we'd have "Mother Holle" if I'd done it properly, but "Mother Trudy" if I'd been careless.

Now there's nothing to do except look at my books, draw pictures, or talk to Lottie. The ladies who play with me or read stories only come when Papa's at home. Even the kittens have disappeared. Every so often, Elke, who plaits my hair in the mornings and bathes me at night, comes to check that I'm being good and brings me milk with cake or bread and honey. She talks all the time but never listens. Sometimes the zoo dogs bark or the other animals squeal; the rest of the time it's very quiet. The other people who live in this house are at work all day, some in the zoo, some in the infirmary or offices. Ladies work here, too, but they're far too busy to talk. They dust and scrub and take the mats outside to beat them. Everything is very clean and tidy. Nobody kicks things under the furniture out of sight, and I can't find any of the fluff under my bed that Greet called "lucky sluts' wool."

Lottie says I should go to the kitchen and see if there's a Greet there, so I creep along the passage and look round the door. I see Elke slicing sausage. A big fat lady with a red face is adding up sums; two others are washing dishes. None of them is like Greet. Elke is telling everyone about a film she's seen, about a Swedish girl who falls in love with a rich bullfighter. It's not a new film: the fat woman has seen it before and continually corrects her.

"*La Habanera* was set in Cuba."

The fat woman shakes her head. "Puerto Rico."

"Nobody cares where it's set, Ursel," says Elke. "Not when Ferdinand Marian's the star."

"No, no, Karl Martell was the star. Marian only played Don Pedro de Avila, a wicked foreign landowner, and he died of some filthy disease. Good thing, too, for even though he was her husband, Astrée loved the doctor."

Elke shrugs. "Oh, but Ferdinand—such a fine-looking man." She sighs and presses her hand to her chest.

Lottie is bored now and wants to go into the garden, but something good is cooking in the oven. It might be *Zwetschgenkuchen*—a plum-sugar smell fills the kitchen when Ursel opens the oven door—and Greet always let me eat the trimmings, but the oven slams shut. We decide to wait until the cake is on the cooling rack. Elke hasn't moved. She's still gazing at the ceiling.

"Never mind daydreaming, *faul Nichtsnutz*," barks Ursel. "This isn't the movies, and those sandwiches won't make themselves. As for your Ferdinand, I'm surprised at you. There's something about his appearance no right-minded woman should find appealing. Altogether too dark . . . and that huge nose . . ." She shudders. "In my opinion, Karl Martell's far better-looking. A much better match—you can see at a glance that he comes from the right stock."

"And that's the one who played the doctor?" One of the ladies at the sink laughs as she dries a pan. "Funny thing about doctors, they're either dried-up old sticks or—" She rolls her eyes and laughs again.

"If you're talking about the new one, reckon he's already spoken for," says Ursel. She nods. "Yes, spoken for twice over. It'll come to blows between those two, see if it don't."

Another voice mutters: "He doesn't seem to be in any hurry to get his hands on either. Perhaps he'd rather do without. And who can blame him? Ugly as sin, the pair of them." The speaker's out of sight, but her way of talking reminds me of Greet so I push the door a little farther open. It squeaks, but the clattering and banging as Ursel takes the cake from the oven hides the noise. I'm about take another step into the kitchen but stop when I notice a little old witch sitting in the corner with a black cat on her knee. Her long wand is hooked over the back of the chair.

"You'd be better off keeping that sort of observation to yourself," said Ursel, throwing down the oven cloth and fanning herself with her apron. "Walls have ears. Anyway, each to his own, as the monkey said when he bit into the soap."

"You're right," said the witch, "personal tastes do differ, but do you think the monkey actually enjoyed eating soap, or was it all that was on offer? As I see it—"

"What I think," Elke announced, "is that both the attendants would be getting more than they bargained for if it meant taking on that spoilt encumbrance of his."

Lottie yawns. I edge forward, watching the plum juice bubble around the edges of the cake. Then the witch cackles and I jump back.

"From what I've seen of the daughter," she says, "his wife will take some living up to. And her being dead makes him remember her as seven times more beautiful than she likely was." Her skinny hand keeps stroking the cat and I know she's calling up a storm.

"Pretty she might be," puts in Elke, "but all's not right up here." She taps her head. "Always talking to herself or standing staring at nothing for minutes on end. Won't eat this. Won't eat that. And what a temper! He lets her get away with it, but it can't go on. She needs the flat of someone's hand across her backside. Kicking and screaming and carrying on—in the old days we'd have said she was possessed."

"What can you expect?" Ursel lowers her voice. "They say the blood-line's tainted. Apparently, the mother was an unnatural wife, not to mention parent . . . spent her days playing with paint instead of look-ing after the home. She was a foreigner—a touch of Gypsy there, or per-haps something even more degenerate. This is what happens when folk mate away from their own kind."

"That's the trouble with men," Elke says bitterly. "They choose their wives with their eyes not their brains."

The witch mutters something about trousers and they all laugh. Un-able to wait any longer, I tiptoe behind Ursel and stick my finger in the plum syrup. It's boiling hot, sticky as toffee, and won't come off. I shriek and stick the finger in my mouth, burning my tongue. Elke grabs my hand and plunges it into a bowl of cold water.

"Quiet!" she bellows as I continue to scream. "Stop your noise or you'll have something else to cry about." But my finger is throbbing. It's on fire.

"How long's she been standing there?" asks Ursel.

"Long enough," says the witch, and cackles so loudly that the cat leaps from her knees. She leans forward and taps my leg with her long magic wand. "You can stop now, Krysta." The pain eases straightaway and I stop wailing. She stares at me. "What are you doing sneaking about in here?"

"I want some cake."

The witch raises eyebrows like hairy gray caterpillars. "Do you in-deed? And what else do you say?"

"*Give* me some cake now or I'll tell my Papa."

Everyone looks at Elke. Her mouth turns into a thin straight line and she is suddenly taller. "No, there will be no cake today or tomor-row. I shall speak to your father myself. You are a very rude little girl.

Unless you learn some manners you'll come to a bad end." She points at the door. "Go to your room and don't come in here again without asking permission first."

I kick the table and slam the door. Upstairs, I throw my cup and plate on the floor, squashing the crusts into the mat, and pull my clothes out of the cupboard.

"Bad Charlotte," I say, and stand her in the corner.

The soap tastes nasty. I tell myself the story of poor hungry Hansel and Gretel, left all alone in the dark forest. My gingerbread cottage has a very big oven and I push Elke, Ursel, and the skinny old witch into it and close the door.

AFTER PAPA HAD FINISHED all the hand washing, we went downstairs together. Johanna came to sit beside us. I wished she would go away, but she wanted to talk to Papa. She was puffing a bit, like Greet did after she'd chased me upstairs to give me a smacking. Something had made her cross. Papa listened and nodded, nodded and listened. After a bit he excused himself, saying he had to fetch something from our rooms when really he was going upstairs to wash his hands again.

"Now you and I can have a little talk," says Johanna. She makes a grab and sits me on her knee. "Shall we play Kinne Wippchen?"

She has the same violet scent that Greet used on her afternoon off, but Johanna's got a nasty smell living underneath the nice one. Her nails are painted bright red to match her mouth. There are small brown stains all down one side of her skirt. I don't want to play, but now Papa's gone I'm afraid to say no.

"Brow-bender," she says, tapping my forehead, "eye-peepers, nose-dreeper, mouth-eater, chin-chopper—" Johanna pokes my eyes, pulls my nose, covers my mouth, hits under my chin with the side of her hand. I struggle to get away, but she holds me tight, tickles my chin, and pushes up my nose. "Knock at the door," she says, "ring the bell, lift up the latch, and walk right in—" And with that, Johanna pushes her finger hard into my mouth. It tastes dark and salty. I don't want to play anymore and struggle to get down, flailing my arms and crying for Papa. But Johanna forces me to stay where I am until she's done the *Take a chair*, *Sit by there*, and *How do you do this morning?* Then she begins bouncing me in the air, higher and higher the louder I shriek . . . until Papa returns and she wraps her arms around me, kissing my cheek. "That was fun, wasn't it? Run outside and play now. I want to talk to your papa."

I HAVE PROMISED to be good so that Papa will take me to eat with the grown-ups inside the zoo. Through the big gate we go, and I look everywhere for the animals that look like people, but there are only dogs. When I ask Papa where the cages are, he tells me to be quiet and sit by the window. There is lentil soup with bits of bacon and some omelette. It doesn't look nice and I won't eat it. Papa talks to his friends and I make a family of turtles out of squished-up bread . . . until I notice a naughty boy outside digging in the mud with his fingers. He pounces on something, and I press close to the glass, trying to see if he's found buried treasure. A worm . . . a dirty worm. And he eats it straight down.

"Papa! Papa!" I pull at his sleeve.

"Not now, Krysta." He carries on talking and turns towards me only when he's finished. "Well?"

But it's too late. The boy's gone. I shut my mouth tight and refuse to say anything.

. . .

JOHANNA'S HANDS ARE CLEAN. No one has made her cross today. She pats her knee and opens the new book. "Come, *mein süßes kleines Mädchen*, I have a story for you. Take your thumb out. If the wind changes, it will stay in there forever."

I want to say no, but last time she pushed my thumb into the mustard pot. Papa laughed.

"'*Der Rattenfänger von Hameln*'—have you heard it before? Then listen carefully." Her jacket smells of rusty nails. The buttons stick in my back. She opens the pages and puts on a different voice. "There was once a beautiful town called Hamelin on the banks of the river Weser. The people there were happy, hardworking, and prosperous until the night when a plague of filthy rats crept inside its walls. Big black rats, fat brown rats, greasy rats, lazy rats, dirty rats covered with fleas, rats with huge noses, rats with great hooked claws. Rats do not work or grow their food. Instead they ate every last grain of wheat in the granaries. They stole food from the stores and the homes of the townspeople. They even took bread out of the mouths of the children. They bit the babies in their cradles and sucked their blood. Look, there is a picture.

"Finally the people went to the *Bürgermeister* and demanded that he rid the town of this terrible plague of vermin. What could he do? It was all very well setting traps and killing a few of the beasts, but by the next morning so many more filthy rats had arrived that he might as well not have bothered.

"Then one day a stranger dressed in red and white and black came to Hamelin. 'You will never prosper while your town is overrun by these vile creatures,' he said. 'I can rid your town of vermin. My kind of music will cause every last one to leave and never, ever return.' And of course the *Bürgermeister* agreed."

44

Her voice rises and falls. Other people come and go. They talk and eat and stamp their feet. The filthy rats tumble into the waters of the Weser and are drowned, so the town is clean and bright again.

"See?" She points to the picture of happy, smiling people hard at work. "It will come," she says. "It will come."

Papa returns from work. He nods and takes a drink. Johanna continues to read. She watches him from under her lashes and the story changes, her voice growing solemn.

"'If you do not keep your promise,' said the piper, 'then I must take your children away.' He raised his pipes to his lips and played a different tune. And all the children came running. They followed him through the streets and over the fields." Johanna pauses. She looks at my father. "And there was nothing their parents could do."

My thumb is back in my mouth now. In the picture the children have disappeared through a magic door in the side of a mountain. Only two are left, a boy who had been too busy with his game and the little girl who went back for him. I begin to cry.

"What's the matter?" demands Johanna. "Not crying for the rats, I hope? Are you sad for the poor mothers and fathers?"

I shake my head and weep for the children who could not find their way out.

Three

I n spite of his show of confidence, Benjamin had no concrete idea of where to begin the search for Lilie's identity. He stood, irresolute, outside the house in Brandstätte, still smarting from Gudrun's caustic assertions that his so-called investigations were simply a ruse to avoid real work. Perhaps he'd head south to Graben, find himself a quiet spot by the Plague Pillar to sit and plan his next step . . . and relish, as so many times before, that carving of a cherub plunging its flaming brand into the pestilent old hag at its base. Still undecided, he looked east, towards Stephansplatz. The great cathedral there was dedicated to a Christian martyr whose name, according to the doctor—though it was sometimes hard to tell whether the old man was teasing—could well be derived from the Greek *stephanos*, a crown, but was more likely to have come by devious pathways from *strenue stans*, meaning "laudably standing and instructing and ruling over old women." Benjamin straightened his shoulders. It was undoubtedly a

joke, a sly dig at the reigning kitchen tyrant, for these days even the doctor wasn't immune from Gudrun's sharp tongue, but at least it had nudged him towards a starting point, for there was another "old woman" in Leopoldstadt—neither old, nor female, but awarded the nickname because of his obsession with gossip. Hugo Besser called himself a journalist; others labeled him a scandalmonger . . . and worse . . . nevertheless, very little escaped him.

Benjamin stepped aside for a passing carriage, then hastily—before Gudrun, who had a nose for these things, emerged with a bucket and shovel demanding that he collect the steaming pile of freshly deposited horse shit for the currant bushes—turned north into Bauernmarkt. It was late in the day and the market was over. A few flower sellers lingered, hoping to catch the eyes of young husbands hurrying towards their homes. A solitary street vendor, anxious to sell the last of his pretzels, twirled aloft his carrying pole. Benjamin turned Josef's money in his pocket but wasn't tempted. At least he'd had the good sense to eat before announcing his plans.

The temperature dropped as he approached the canal. Curdled mist rose to devour the sloping banks, swallowing whole trees, licking at the pillars, leaving the bridge damp and slippery. When Benjamin glanced back, the inner city seemed veiled by a gauzy curtain where the mist hung like a lingering ghost of the old defensive walls. As the light faded, the mist advanced, biting great chunks from the earth. Minute by minute the buildings were rendered more ethereal until they were floating free of time, a city not yet fully imagined, a rootless island with the great spire of the cathedral tethered to the clouds. So, in such weather, it must have looked in the distant past; so it would always look, come what may. Benjamin shivered. He blew on his hands and plunged them into the pockets of the warm coat *Frau* Breuer had given him. It had belonged to Robert, her taciturn eldest son, and was only a little out of style so that, Benjamin persuaded himself, as long as nobody's gaze dropped to his boots, he could be taken for somebody.

Thoughts of the warm and fuggy tavern quickened his steps, but as he drew nearer to the familiar landmarks of his childhood Benjamin's pace slowed again. He hadn't been back to this ugly misshapen little island for months, precisely because crossing the Donaukanal felt like plunging back into the impoverished stew of yesteryear. The city's. His own. The face of the Altstadt might be refined, her silks and satins embellished by the most exquisite embroidery, but her undergarments—in the shape of the old ghetto—were threadbare, filthy, unfit to be seen. Moreover, they were bursting at the seams with incomers crammed ten to a room. He'd heard of beds being rented out during the day while their owners worked. And these were the fortunate ones: the rest were forced to settle for the crude shelter afforded by the city's labyrinthine sewers.

Benjamin went on reluctantly, taking shortcuts past shabby street-corner markets where stall holders would continue extracting every last krone from unwilling spenders long after daylight had fled. Unlike the market in Karmeliterplatz, trading was mostly in small change: a gulden was a rarity here, where women fresh from the pawnbroker's agonized over the price of suspect meat and beggars counted out their reckonings heller by heller from sacks hidden among their rags. Quaintly dressed incomers wandered in small groups, intense but purposeless—but it was those clad crown to toe in orthodox black that had the locals looking askance, drawing aside and muttering. Averting his eyes, Benjamin dived into even narrower backstreets, only to be confronted by an ancient building crusted with the scabs of botched repairs, one wall rendered a slimy greenish black thanks to a leaking gutter. Someone had scraped letters into the filth: *Hinaus mit den Juden.* Benjamin grimaced: Out with the Jews. Once again, the stink of new envies and old hatreds had joined that of overboiled cabbage and underwashed bodies.

At the intersection of two alleyways a gaggle of small boys played some incomprehensible game with a spinning bottle. A heated argument broke out and within seconds the group had split into uneven halves, pelting each other with sticks, stones, and fistfuls of mud, and flinging the usual taunts.

"Yid, Yid, spit in your hood, tell your mummy that is good."

"Christ, Christ, g'hört am Mist!"

A woman emerged shouting from a nearby building, throwing a bucket of dirty water in their direction, whereupon the pack reformed and abandoned the place, jostling, clinging to each other's elbows, giggling. As twilight thickened, night creatures emerged from the shadows. They wore masks of flour with brick-dust rouge, caricatures of women, posturing and beckoning in the circles of pea-soup light cast by the lamps. Benjamin thought of Lilie and broke into a run, turning this way and that by routes remembered from his younger years, until he heard the sharp double note of a guard's whistle followed by the harsh *whoosh* exhaled from a departing train. The tavern he sought was no distance at all from the station. He stopped to draw breath before taking the steps three at a time.

The Kneipe was almost full, the atmosphere hovering at changeover point between that of its markedly different daytime and evening clientele. Sedate business meetings, quiet perusal of newspapers, and coffee-fueled discussions were giving way to the livelier bawl and bluster of serious drinking, the wild propounding of extreme political theories peppered with outright sedition. Benjamin was well aware that it wouldn't just be his old friend gleaning information here.

Hugo was in his usual place, crouching so perilously close to the tavern's roaring fire that his clothes were permanently singed. With his massive shoulders and unkempt hair he resembled a vast spider—though he ingested tales rather than spun them. He'd always been stout; now, though, Hugo's backside barely fit onto a settle meant for three—and yet, it was rumored, not a morsel of solid food passed his lips. It was also said that he rarely left this building. In the early hours he ponderously heaved his bulk upstairs; perhaps he never slept, either. Long before midday he was back on his bench, raising his first tankard and dispatching the snot-nosed kid curled on the hearth like one of the *svartálfar*, the dark elves, with a sheaf of closely written articles for his editor. Benjamin grinned and loped towards him.

"*Sittlichkeit und Ernst.*" It was their usual greeting.

"A fart to morality and sobriety," retorted Hugo without looking up. It was the usual response. He seemed no drunker than usual. "And what demon belched you back to Matzoh Island from the fine boulevards? Missing the stench? Last time you graced us with a visit you were after a character reference." One hand slid the magazine he'd been reading out of sight, but not before Benjamin recognized the unmistakable bright red cover."

"*Die Fackel?*"

Hugo grunted. "Beer," he demanded, kicking the dozing boy, who immediately scrambled to his feet and, working his bony elbows against the crowd, went in search of a waiter.

"What do you think of it?" persisted Benjamin, who'd read the doctor's copies.

"Man after my own heart. Says what he thinks. Even about me, the cheeky bugger! And since what Kraus thinks makes sense, he won't last the year out." Hugo leaned back and surveyed him. "Looking good, I see. Life as a servant suits you."

Benjamin's spine twitched. "Not forever," he said stiffly. "I've got plans."

Hugo shrugged. "Dangerous things, plans, my young friend. We're sailing into troubled waters. The signs are all around us. In such times be grateful for small things. And remember, small things are only small when we don't have to go without them. You eat regularly. That's more than most do. You have a warm bed. Well, as warm as it can be when you sleep alone." He raised a wild black eyebrow. "You do sleep alone, I take it, *Herr Doktor* and his *Frau* being so bloody respectable and all that?"

"Beer!" shrieked Hugo's grimy elf, banging his small fist on the table.

A skinny waiter set down six tankards. Benjamin looked to see who else might be joining them, but it appeared the harassed fellow was simply saving himself additional journeys. A mild argument over the alleged piss-poor quality of the brew commenced, during which the scrawny boy retired to his corner, retrieving a hunk of bread and some half-eaten sausage from his sleeve. Saved by the commotion from having to defend his sleeping arrangements, Benjamin closed his eyes, hugging to himself a frenzy of fervid imaginings. When he opened them, Hugo had already emptied one of the tankards; a few droplets still clung to the gingery whiskers that refused to grow into the desired leonine beard despite being encouraged by constant stroking and tugging.

"Fire!" shouted Hugo. The boy scrambled to throw more logs onto the blaze. A thin dog squeezed between Benjamin's legs and attempted to snatch the remains of the bread. It was rewarded with a clout that sent it skidding a man's length along the floor. The boy dipped the retrieved crust in Benjamin's full tankard before devouring it, and then dropped to the hearth, showing his bared teeth to the vigilant dog. Hugo regarded Benjamin, who'd pushed away the contaminated tankard, with incredulity. "Drink up."

"Thanks." Benjamin surreptitiously pulled a different vessel towards him and took a long swallow of beer. Every muscle responded to this unaccustomed pleasure. In an instant, all the tension generated by his never-ending struggle against the plague of rats and caterpillars invading the garden, Gudrun's haranguing, his discomfort at coming back to the area his family had struggled so hard and for so long to leave drained away. Bliss. "Ah."

"Panacea," said Hugo, reaching for a second dose. He peered between the heavy tankards, searching the table's battered surface with its ancient scars and carved graffiti into which spilled dregs gathered in puddles, then frowned and directed a ferocious scowl at the dozing chimney-corner elf. Three extravagantly clad girls walked past, examining the two men closely. After a few yards they turned in a flurry of high-pitched giggles and sauntered slowly back again, plumping up their chests and lingering by the side of the settle.

"Women," observed Benjamin in an attempt to guide the conversation to the desired area.

"Well spotted," sniggered Hugo, throwing back his head to drain his third tankard. He made an abrupt dismissive gesture with one hand. The girls scowled, tossed their heads, and moved on. One turned to spit contempt over her shoulder, her gaze pointedly moving from Hugo to the small boy.

"*Schwul!*"

Hugo shrugged. "*Kneipenschlampe!*" To Benjamin, he said: "Tavern sluts. Whores. They pay a hefty percentage of their earnings to the landlord."

Benjamin scrutinized the three departing rears. "They don't look like local girls."

"Czechs, probably, but since women everywhere are born more or less equal in terms of the attributes demanded by their profession, why would they need to be local? We have twelve nationalities or more crowding into this cesspit end of the city, a veritable Babylon of peoples—Hungarians, Turks, Galicians, Moravians, Bohemians, Bukovinians . . ." He started ticking them off on his fingers, then abandoned the effort in favor of seizing a fresh tankard. "And there's no accommodation for them." Hugo raised his voice. "Decent basic housing, that's what our illustrious Franz Joseph should force the city to spend its money on, not this secession rubbish. Buildings with owls on . . . I ask you. And that *Majolika Haus* covered with flowers and twirly bits. Very nice, I dare say, but who among us can afford an apartment there? Meanwhile, homeless people will freeze to death on the streets this winter." He leaned forward. "It's a scandal. If you ask me, the wrong bloody aristocrat shot his few brains out at Mayerling."

"Oh." Benjamin stared at him, appalled, before glancing quickly at the neighboring tables to see if anyone reacted to this slur on the monarchy. A blond young man on the other side of the fire sat smoothing his chin as he read a book. The dark-haired one sitting a few feet away seemed to be looking straight at them, but a second guilty glance revealed he was dramatically walleyed and could be looking anywhere. The noise level was steadily increasing. With any luck, no one had heard. Benjamin tried to relax.

"Heading for trouble," opined Hugo. "Dazzling riches flaunted cheek by jowl with the most loathsome poverty. It can't go on."

"No," agreed Benjamin, still ignoring the invitation to get political. "As you say, those girls could be anyone, from just about anywhere." He paused. "They might have run away from home. Or been kidnapped. Lost their memories, even."

"Most of them would probably like to, if they're servicing the scum that comes in here." Hugo thumped his drained tankard against the table. He seized another and pushed the remaining one towards Benjamin, belching loudly as he leaned over to clout the boy. "More beer!"

Benjamin quickly finished his own drink. This time Hugo ignored the waiter, who slopped a cloth across the table and slammed down more tankards without ceremony. The boy returned with his ragged shirt folded up to form a sack full of gleanings, bread crusts, sausage ends, some sweaty slices of cheese, a *Salzgurke* with a bite taken from one end. His feet were bare. Perhaps Benjamin grimaced, because Hugo narrowed his eyes and leaned forward.

"The brat does better than most. That's why he sticks around. Think I want him forever hanging on my shirttails? No, I bloody don't. I can hardly hear myself think above his constant chatter."

Benjamin laughed. To his knowledge, the kid had uttered a single word in the last hour. Apart from that he was silent as the grave, barring an occasional bout of sniffing. "Don't know how you put up with the noise. You're philanthropy personified, my friend."

"Can't leave them all to die," muttered Hugo, sending a chill up Benjamin's spine. "We're on the road to Gehenna when the whole world turns a blind eye to children's suffering."

"Gehenna," echoed Benjamin. In the Talmud it was Gehinnom. He no longer adhered to the religion of his forefathers but remembered the terrifying images summoned up by the Book of Isaiah. Gehinnom was the burning place. It was a vile place of child sacrifice, of pitiless live immolation. The passage still brought night terrors that made him glad to be living in a civilized country in enlightened times. "And the king," he muttered, "shall cause his children to pass through the fire."

"Your Gehenna, our Hell," said Hugo, after a short pause to quench his prodigious thirst. "Same bloodthirsty God threatening the same miserable hereafter unless there's a whole lot of bowing and scraping and self-denial. Slave religions, all of them." He glared from the table to the boy chewing on his scraps. "And that's the second time the little sod's forgotten."

"Forgotten what?"

"Obstler!" roared Hugo, aiming a blow. The boy ducked and ran.

"You mentioned missing girls," said Benjamin in an effort to get the conversation back on track. "Anyone in particular? Girls from good families, I mean."

Hugo's bleary gaze sharpened. "I didn't mention anyone missing. What's your interest anyway?"

"Might be a reward," Benjamin said ingenuously. Hugo snorted.

"You're out of luck, then. This city mops up missing wenches. Vienna's lousy with pimps and madams. Little wonder, since every well-heeled *Frau* dismisses her maids when the family leaves for their summer residence. What happens to the poor bitches if they haven't got homes to go back to? Do they care? No. It all provides easy pickings for the *Hurenbock*, the filthy pimps. Summer's the time when raddled old madams trawl the parks and riverbanks harvesting young women— offering sympathy, a meal, a temporary roof over their heads. Next thing they know they've got new careers, flat on their backs in Bulgaria, Turkey, Rumania, and even here." Hugo paused to drink, tipping the tankard at such a precarious angle that liquid spilled from the sides of his mouth, trickling down the sides of his neck and under his collar. He dried his face on his sleeve and produced another spectacularly loud belch. A tall, sharp-featured man glanced down at him, his mouth pursed into a moue of disgust as he passed.

"And are there any records of these maids?" asked Benjamin, shifting uncomfortably. Even kindly *Frau* Breuer had dispensed with plump little Greet before departing for Gmunden. He'd been sad to see the kitchen maid go—she was hardly more than a child, full of songs, old folktales peppered with her own wild inventions—but he hadn't given her subsequent welfare a second thought. The journalist shrugged and spread his hands.

"Why would there be?"

"Just wondered." Benjamin scratched his head. So Lilie might have been somebody's maid—a *superior* maid, of course—who'd suddenly found she was without a job or home. Perhaps she'd been caught in such a trap as Hugo described, and escaped. That would explain the distressing state he'd found her in. Yes, that was it. They'd beaten her. They'd taken away her clothes along with her memory. But to her credit she'd refused to give in. Lilie was too sweet, too pure, to have been involved in any . . . His mind slewed away from the details, though in truth he frequently dwelled on far more elaborate fantasies concerning the two of them. It occurred to him that he'd stand more of a chance with a maid, superior or not, than the runaway daughter of a well-to-do family. A good thought, that. Not entirely fueled by alcohol and warmth. However, he was no nearer to discovering Lilie's real name. And it mattered. How could anyone live without knowing who or what she was? Benjamin blinked and sat up, realizing that Hugo was still holding forth.

"Another few weeks and all the nice big houses in the Altstadt will be opened up again. We'll have a new influx of young girls fresh from the provinces, eager to scrub floors and gut fish. Country wenches. Not, as you say, from *good* families, whatever that might be. Moneyed, I suppose you mean. But innocents, all the same." Leaning his chin on his elbow, he stared narrow-eyed at Benjamin for a long moment before adding: "Why don't you start again and this time try asking the question you really want answered."

"I don't—"

"Fallen for a whore, have you?"

"She's not—" Benjamin stopped dead. The blood rushed to his face. Fool. Shouldn't have had the beer. He wasn't used to it. "No," he said firmly. "There's no one. I was talking hypothetically."

"There's a long word." Hugo raised an eyebrow. "You're still intent on educating yourself, I see."

Benjamin said nothing. The damage was done, so since Hugo was footing the bill, he concentrated on emptying his second tankard and reached for another. His plan of one day entering the university as a student must remain a secret. Nobody, not even *Herr Doktor* Breuer, who had encouraged him to read more widely and even, to Gudrun's disapproval, given him the freedom of his library during the summer, knew about that.

"Sometimes," said Hugo, "more can be learned by people's silences than their words. It's the gaps in the conversation you have to listen to most carefully." He waited, then added: "Here's what I've learned so far. You—" He laughed and took another swig. "I'm joking. Don't look so worried. It's obvious you've come across some pretty wench who claims to be in trouble. She's spun a story that's brought out the knight in shining armor. Am I right?"

"Well . . ." said Benjamin, and stopped.

"Put your cards on the table, Sir Galahad. What is it she needs you to find out? Has she done away with a carping housekeeper jealous of her youth? Fleeing a brutal husband, perhaps? Or is an embezzled employer on her seductive tail?"

"Nothing like that." He gulped desperately at his beer. "She's just—"

A glass of *Obstler* was set before him and Benjamin followed Hugo's example, downing it in one swallow. He choked and was still clutching his throat when the sharp-featured man walked slowly past again, leaning to one side as the room tilted, his nose grown incredibly long, sniffing out trouble. Benjamin attempted to draw Hugo's attention to him, but the effort was too great. Besides, his glass had been miraculously replenished . . . again. The walls buckled, receding and advancing at an alarming speed. The noise of the tavern ebbed, flowed, and finally broke over him like an angry seventh wave. He shook his head hard, as would a dog trying to dislodge a particularly troublesome flea from its ear, and glared at his glass.

"It's only distilled fruit juice," Hugo said reassuringly. "Homegrown schnapps."

Benjamin saw that the journalist's familiar had emerged from his place among the cinders to perch, smirking, on the arm of the settle. "What's he laughing at?"

"Nothing," said Hugo. "Ignore him." One beefy hand wiped the smile off the boy's face. "You were telling me about your young lady."

Benjamin lifted his heavy head and looked carefully round. Suddenly everyone was listening. The three parading girls had paused, ostensibly to warm themselves at the fire, where another tavern slut joined them, her clothes in artful disarray, winking at Benjamin, squeezing his arm as she maneuvered around his seat. The woman's large breasts pushed into his shoulders and she laughed aloud when he politely moved the chair forward, giving her more space. Back came the fellow with the long nose, moving past as slowly as possible. The walleyed man continued to stare. And now the blond man on the other side of the hearth closed his book and sat with his hands folded, waiting.

"She's not my *young lady*," he said very carefully and in a stage whisper. "A friend found her . . . wandering around. She's lost her memory. Can't remember her own name."

"Or so she says."

Benjamin clenched his fists beneath the table in the effort not to spring to Lilie's defense. He nodded. "That's what she says."

"Pretty, is she?"

"Beautiful."

"Uh-huh. And what about her clothing? Rich? Poor? Any clues there?"

"None," said Benjamin, adding, before he had the chance to think better of it: "She wasn't wearing any." He immediately wished the words unsaid. The level of noise in the tavern hadn't diminished and yet a curious stillness seemed to hang over the table.

"You've got yourself—" Hugo laughed. "Or should I say, *your friend* has got *himself*, a runaway whore. And probably a dose of syphilis in the bargain."

"No," muttered Benjamin, knuckling his temples. "She's no whore." An image of Lilie's pretty face danced before his eyes. Conscious that so far he'd achieved nothing on her behalf, he cleared his throat and tried again. "She must have been held prisoner somewhere—"

Hugo laughed; his small familiar dutifully followed suit.

"For ransom, I presume?"

"No. Yes. *Maybe.* Why not?" Benjamin glowered. "This isn't funny."

"Very well." Hugo straightened his face. He pursed his lips as if giving the matter serious consideration. "Many brothels—no, hear me out—many such establishments curtail freedom when the novice is unwilling." One stubby hand drew another draught of beer towards him. "But I hear the inmates of a certain misnamed gentlemen's club are slaves in all but name. Unlikely that she escaped from such a place—from what I hear the security is better than that of many banks—but it's a possibility, I suppose."

"You mean the Thélème club? I thought of that." The words dropped into one of the curious hushes that sometimes fall in noisy, crowded places, and Benjamin felt rather than saw heads turning. His eyes slid sideways and met those of the blond man, who was now sliding his book into a pocket. He noticed for the first time the man's curiously cherubic face, as if the statue on the Plague Pillar had stepped down and, in taking on life, matured a little. One of his cheeks bore a dueling *Schmiss* and Benjamin felt a twinge of envy. Girls couldn't fail to be impressed by such a scar; it was a badge of personal bravery and gallantry. A smile played over the man's lips; he nodded and drew on a cigarette, surrounding himself with a cloud of aromatic Turkish tobacco smoke. Was he offering friendship? Benjamin felt drawn to him, and yet something in the fellow's eyes suggested he would not think twice about plunging the flaming brand into anyone that got in his way.

"Hair color?" repeated Hugo.

"What?" Benjamin looked at him, confused. "Oh, hers . . . it's sort of golden."

"Might be, in that case. Apparently, those at the Thélème have very specific requirements. The stamp of Jerusalem isn't favored there."

What was that supposed to mean? Benjamin tried to get his fuddled thoughts in order, but the atmosphere had changed again and he saw that Hugo's attention was elsewhere. Or rather, it was everywhere, for the journalist had returned to work. His eyes darted here and there, sizing up customers, lingering on one, dismissing another, his head turning this way and that as he homed in on a dozen or more conversations. For the most part his face remained impassive, though occasionally his lips twitched and once he scowled.

Others had now begun pulling chairs and stools up to the table, moving in close with the air of those with weighty secrets to impart. Try as he might, Benjamin couldn't make out a word until a woman joined them, stiff and prim, radiating respectability, tightly buttoned from her high neck to her well-polished boots. Disapproval of her surroundings had compressed her mouth into a thin, reptilian slash. Her refusal of a drink was accompanied by an expression of such intense disgust that the proffered liquid might have already been filtered through somebody else's kidneys. Her eyes were red-rimmed and bloodshot from crying, perhaps even from tears unshed. She drew her shawl more tightly round her meager bosom as she took in the plunging décolleté of the powdered and perfumed woman at the fireside, who was now lifting her skirts to warm her haunches.

Benjamin found the prim woman's presence incomprehensible. He watched her pale fingers nervously screwing a fold of skirt into tight knots as she spoke; he saw Hugo's face become grim and observed that he, like the snot-nosed boy who was now wide-eyed and nervously licking his lips, was hanging on every word. The woman grew steadily more agitated. At one point she stopped and covered her face with both hands as if unable to continue. After calming herself, her voice became harsher, more distinct, and Benjamin caught a single word: Hummel. It was a name that had preoccupied Gudrun over the past weeks, for Juliane Hummel was branded Vienna's most monstrous and unnatural mother. Twelve months ago she and her husband, Joseph, had received a police warning concerning the mistreatment of their four-year-old daughter. A year later, the child was dead. Already the papers hinted at unimaginable levels of cruelty and neglect, but the official cause of death was blood poisoning, and premeditated murder had yet to be proved. Evidence or no evidence, Gudrun wanted to see the pair of them flogged and hanged. Thinking to take home some sensational tidbit, Benjamin dragged his chair farther away from the noisy altercations at the fireside.

"They often left Anna at home all day," the woman said through bloodless lips, "locked in a filthy shed without food or water. I used to push bread and little cakes through cracks in the door. When Juliane caught me, she got him to nail boards over the gaps. I saw her hit the little one's hands with a red-hot poker and laugh while she did it." She looked down at her own hands, as if surprised to find them unscarred. "They tied her, naked, to a tree—like a dog—and put a little dish of food down for her, just out of reach. One bitterly cold winter day they made her stand in a tub of cold water from dawn until it grew dark. And when they beat her, they muffled her screams with rags tied round her head, thinking we wouldn't know what was going on." Every last vestige of color drained from the woman's face as she clutched Hugo's sleeve. "They meant to kill her. It was no accident. Day after day, I went to the police and told them Anna was being starved and tortured to death. Nobody would listen. They won't listen now—I'm nothing, only a gardener's wife. Will *you* listen? Will you tell Vienna what really happened?"

Benjamin swallowed hard. Either the woman was mad or there were unguessed horrors being perpetuated in the backstreets of this city. Hugo met his eyes.

"Gehenna," he said softly. "Hell. Sheol. Hades."

Benjamin nodded. He needed a drink, but every tankard and glass was empty. No, what he needed was to get out of here. Without another word, he stood up and stumbled towards the door, followed by curses and catcalls as he fell into tables and tripped over chairs.

A hand descended on his shoulder as he reached the entrance. Benjamin pulled free, spinning round and bringing up his fists. The size of the man who'd accosted him put an end to any idea of successfully fighting his way out of trouble, but he kept them up all the same. Two steps behind the huge man, tucked into his shadow, lurked the sharp-featured fellow with the long nose. Away from the tavern's lights he resembled a weasel, but his authority became evident when he stepped forward. He flicked his skinny fingers at Benjamin's bunched fists.

"No need for that."

"What are you after?" demanded Benjamin, sobering up fast. "I've got no money."

"Judging by the state of you, any you did have is about to be pissed into the nearest gutter." He drew close enough for Benjamin to smell peppermint on his breath, only faintly masking the odor of fried fish. One bony finger shot forward to prod his sternum. "You're keeping bad company, Benjamin. Don't think I don't know what you've been up to." The finger jabbed again. "Your fat, shit-stirring friend imagines he knows everything, but let me tell you, nothing goes on in this city without me hearing about it. Nothing. I've got my eye on you, boy. Go home, unless you fancy sobering up in the cells."

"You're police," said Benjamin, only now taking in the bulky man's gray uniform, the grenade insignia. "But I haven't done anything."

"Wallow with pigs and expect to get dirty. My advice to you is—keep away from Besser and his kind."

"All right, sir." In spite of the lingering emphasis on *pigs*, Benjamin deliberately kept his voice even, his demeanor reasonable. He reached for the door. "I'll go straight home, sir."

"Give my regards to *Herr Doktor* Breuer."

Glancing back, Benjamin saw that both men had already been swallowed by the crowded tavern. He started to make his way through the maze of backstreets, wondering how much, if anything, they knew about Lilie. After a few hundred yards he came to the lamp where he'd seen the two clown-faced whores earlier. They were still eager for business, but to his surprise both suddenly turned their backs on him. One minute he was upright, staring towards the soft glow of the Altstadt and wishing himself home, the next he was lying on wet cobbles regarding the Seven Sisters high in the heavens. Pain rushed at him, wild as a runaway cart horse. He groaned, reaching a hand towards his aching skull, the movement interrupted by the large boot stamping on his wrist. Benjamin shrieked.

"Keep your nose out of things that don't concern you." The voice seemed to come from a long way off and was accompanied by the distinctive aroma of Turkish tobacco. "Gentlemen's clubs aren't for you or your ilk. Neither are the women in them. Understand?"

"Ye-es." The man released his wrist and what felt like a sledgehammer crashed into Benjamin's ribs. He rolled onto his side, trying to escape. The next blow was unerringly aimed at his kidneys, landing on the side of his back, between his ribs and pelvic bone. Black chrysanthemums flowered in midair and he felt himself falling into a deep chasm. The small hands searching his pockets brought him to himself.

"Get his coat," whispered a voice, close to his ear. "Good cloth. We can sell that easy as anything."

"Clear off." Benjamin struggled onto his knees, pushing them away. "Fucking old whores."

"Fucking drunkard," came their sharp retort as he doubled over, puking.

Gritting his teeth, Benjamin finally got himself upright. His pockets, like his stomach, were now empty; they'd taken every last heller of the doctor's money, his pen, even the used handkerchief.

Four

stand outside the door, listening to Elke complaining to Papa about my naughtiness. She's a big fat liar. I didn't steal any *cake*. And I never said bad words or scratched her *arm*.

"Yes, yes," he says, in his voice that means *No*, "I understand how trying it is for you, but we must take into account—" Elke interrupts him.

"Sad things happen to many children. The girl still needs discipline."

"That's for me to decide." A pause. Then he says: "Was there anything else?" I can tell he wants her to go away, but Elke hasn't finished. She's like my old clockwork sailor. Wind him up and nothing could stop him beating his drum—at least until Greet stepped on him by mistake.

"The Devil makes work for idle hands. Your child needs something to occupy her. Why isn't she at school? It isn't right. You should send her to school."

This time the silence is much longer and full of the sort of crackles that hang in the air before thunderstorms. I hold my breath. If Greet were here we'd be hiding under the stairs so the lightning didn't burn us to cinders.

"My daughter will go to school after the summer." I hear him push back his chair. "Thank you, *Frau* Schmidt, for coming to me. I'll talk to Krysta—"

"Talk? You'll *talk* to her?" Elke's voice rises. "Isn't she going to be punished? That girl needs her backside warmed. If she was my daughter—"

And I hug myself with delight for here comes the thunder.

"Enough!" roars Papa. "She's not your daughter." *Clump, clump,* go his big boots as he paces the floor. His shadow falls across the crack in the door and I step back, holding my breath. "Like any other child," he continues more quietly, "Krysta needs time to adjust to becoming motherless. There may be further minor difficulties. If you feel unable to accommodate them—"

"I can manage," says Elke sullenly.

"Excellent," says Papa. "That will be all . . . *for now.*"

I scuttle back to my hiding place. Lottie wants me to tell her about Hansel and Gretel. It's her favorite story. Last time we pushed Elke and her ugly old friends into the oven. This time we make sure they are nearly dead by forcing them to eat poisoned bread first. Then we blow on the fire until the stove glows red-hot. The noise they make hammering on the door with their fists is like the rattle of the saucepan when Greet made John-in-the-Pocket. She said it was John trying to get out before he was boiled alive, but Papa told me it was really only the pudding basin jumping up and down on the trivet. When everything goes quiet again, we carefully open the oven door and see only scraps of burnt paper. I throw them into the air, letting their words float away on the wind.

Papa asks me later about the things Elke reported to him. "Do you steal from the kitchen, Krysta?" I shake my head. "Look at me when I'm talking to you. Nothing? All right. Now, did you scratch Elke?"

I open my eyes very wide. "No, Papa."

"What about the bad words? She says you called her rude names."

"What sort of rude names?" I ask cautiously. But he doesn't answer and I can tell he doesn't really believe her. "I didn't do anything wrong, Papa. She's being nasty."

"Even so," Papa says, "I'd like you to tell Elke you're sorry for upsetting her. Will you do that for me?"

I scowl and stick out my bottom lip. "Why?"

"Because," he says wearily, "I need her to keep an eye on you while I'm at work."

"Why can't I come to the infirmary with you?"

"Don't be silly, Krysta." He brings out a brown paper bag. "Look what I've brought for you—some lovely black cherries."

Papa only gives me the cherries when I promise to apologize. I take Lottie into the garden, where we count the stones and see how far I can spit them:

> *"Eins, zwei, Polizei,*
> *Three, four, an officer,*
> *Five, six, an old witch . . ."*

ELKE FINDS A KNOT in my hair and yanks it out with the comb.

"Aw! Aw! Don't, you're hurting me."

She starts braiding, pulling so hard that it feels as if every hair is being pulled up by its roots, *ping, ping, ping,* like Greet thinning out the radishes. "Stop that silly noise," she hisses close to my ear, "or I'll give you something to really snivel about." She ties a red ribbon at the end of each plait, screwing up her mouth until it looks like the twisted end of a sausage, and then scrapes the hair away from my face, securing it with matching hair clips.

"Take them out. They're too tight."

"Leave them alone. Finish your milk. Hurry. I've got better things to do than dance attendance on you all morning."

"Won't." I push my cup over and watch the milk run along the table, a big white river carrying with it rocks made of crumbs that disappears over the edge like a creamy waterfall. The cup rolls after it, bounces on the linoleum, and breaks into several pieces.

"You little—" Elke draws back her hand and slaps my leg so hard she leaves red imprints of her fingers. I try to remember the bad words Greet said under her breath when the fire went out or the bread wouldn't rise.

"Hure!" I yell. *"Miststück!"*

Elke is outraged. "What did you call me?"

"Slut. Slut. Slut. Bitch. Bitch. Bastard." I rack my brains for the one Greet shrieked at the maid next door. *"Nutte!"*

Elke's face turns the color of my spilled milk. This time she grabs me, holding my shoulder and spinning me around to land a dozen blows on my bottom. My flailing arms aren't long enough to reach her, but I manage to bite her hand. Screaming and hiccupping with fury, I suddenly need to go to the bathroom. It's too late and I don't care. I'm still kicking and trying to hit her back while the wee runs down my legs.

One of the other witches pokes her head around the door. "Everything all right in here, Elke?"

"See what she's done? Look at this mess. And she's pissed herself. Dirty little creature isn't right in the head. She ought to be over there with the rest of the savages." She turns on me. "Go and wash yourself, you filthy animal."

Lottie says we should find Papa, but the gates to the zoo are closed. Because I fall asleep hiding inside the flowering currant bush, Elke gets to him first. This time his face is very serious.

"Krysta, Elke tells me you did not apologize, even though you promised me you would. To make matters worse, this morning you deliberately broke some crockery. What's more," and here he looks away, so I know what's coming, "she tells me you're no longer clean in your personal habits. Is this true?"

"She kept shouting and hitting me." I start to cry but watch him between my fingers. "I couldn't help it . . . I was so frightened, Papa."

His eyes widen. "Elke *hit* you?"

"Lots and lots of times." I show him the marks on my leg and tell him how much it hurts to sit.

"What started all this? Why was she shouting?"

"She wanted me to hurry and I dropped my cup. D-d-didn't mean to."

"I see."

Emboldened by his grim expression, I add: "I hate Elke, *sie ist ein gemeines Weibsstück.*"

"Krysta!" Papa looks shocked. "Wherever did you learn to use such coarse language?" He waits, but I close my mouth and put my hand over it. "I can only suppose you've overheard the men here talking among themselves. I'll have a word with them. Elke is not . . . *that.* However, she is clearly unfit to look after a better class of child."

Elke is sent away. I stand behind Papa, peeping round him to smile at her. Very early next morning he says I must come to the infirmary with him until a new lady is found to look after me. None of the women here will do it. He sighs over my hair and keeps starting again, but the plaits still come out kinky and uneven.

"I only want Greet to do my hair. Send for Greet."

"Greet can't come here."

"Why not? Why not?" I repeatedly kick the table leg so that the breakfast things jump and clatter. Papa's coffee cup falls onto its side. "I want Greet. I want Greet."

"That's enough," he says. "Carry on like this and I shall start to wonder if Elke was telling the truth." I stop immediately and stick my thumb in my mouth. He sighs. "She was right about one thing. You're far too big to be doing that. What will they say when you go to school?"

"Don't like school. Won't go."

"It's about time you learned to do as you're told, Krysta. Now fetch a book and whatever else you want."

His voice is very tired and I'm sad that he's unhappy again, so I get my things together quickly. Going to the infirmary is exciting: everything's painted white; there are a great many closed doors; and I can hear someone crying. I hope he'll let me wear a nurse's uniform and bandage people up. But Papa takes me into a little room with a narrow bed, a table, and a chair. In one corner is a horrible enamel bucket thing with a lid instead of a lavatory.

"Stay here until I come back," he says.

"But I want to help you."

"You can't, Krysta. Nobody can help me." He does a bit of his hand washing without water. "Promise me you'll stay in here until I come for you. Promise?"

I nod. "Yes, Papa."

"Good girl."

I stand with my ear to the door, listening to his footsteps die away. Then I count to a hundred before opening it a crack. First some nurses swish past, then two skinny old men in stripy overalls pushing a squeaky trolley. When they've gone, I creep back down the corridor to see what Papa's doing. They must cure sick animal-people here, too: something is making a terrible noise that sounds like cats at the end of winter, which is when Greet says they get up to no good. I don't open the door where the noise is in case they escape, but there are only empty beds in the others. At the end of the corridor I find an office with Papa sitting at a desk signing papers. He jumps up, looking cross.

"I am very disappointed in you, Krysta. Very disappointed. Doesn't a promise mean anything to you? We'll have to discuss this later. There's no time now." Grabbing my arm, he marches me back to the little room. "As I can't trust you, the door must be locked. I'll come for you at midday so that we can have lunch together."

I kick the door and beat on it with my fists. "I HATE YOU." Every single one of my new crayons breaks when I throw the packet on the floor.

"Bad Charlotte!" I pick her up by the hair.

When we've both finished crying about the crayons, I notice the bars on the window are quite far apart, very like the ones on the coal chute at home. Getting out is as easy as escaping from the cellar when Greet locked me down there, except that I fall onto the path and graze my knees. I keep close to the wall, bent double so Papa doesn't catch sight of me from his office. I can't see any zoo animals. There are flower beds, and a big aviary in the distance, but the wire's buckled and there are no birds in it. I wonder if the animal-people ate them.

At the back of the building the worm boy is pulling up tufts of grass and scrabbling in the dirt with his fingers. This close I can see that he's very skinny with a sharp nose and big red ears like an imp in one of my storybooks. He has really short black hair that he keeps scratching, and nobody makes him wash his neck.

"Hello."

The boy scowls. "Go away."

"I saw you eating a worm the other day. Yuk."

"So what? I ate lots more this morning." He says his words in a funny way.

"Do you know what little boys are made of?"

"Go away. I'm busy working."

"That's silly. Little boys don't work." After a few moments I chant the rhyme Greet taught me:

> "What are little boys made of?
> What are little boys made of?
> Slugs and snails and puppy dogs' tails—and worms—
> That's what little boys are made of."

"I already told you to go away." He is very carefully pulling a fat pink worm out of the earth. It breaks in half and he quickly digs down to catch the rest of it.

"You can't tell me what to do." I remember what Elke said. "You should be at school. Why aren't you at school?" He doesn't answer. "What's your name?" After I've asked him three times, he tells me it's Daniel.

"I'm Krysta. This is Lottie. My papa's a doctor. What does yours do?"

"He's a professor."

"Oh." I look at his ragged clothes. "You don't look like a professor's little boy."

"Go somewhere else and play with your silly doll."

"What does worm taste like?"

Daniel narrows his eyes and looks fierce. "It's my worm. You're not having any." He opens his mouth, throwing back his head so that the dirty pink worm, both halves still wriggling, goes straight down his throat.

"Yuk. Yuk. Yuk. Are you so hungry?"

"Aren't you?"

"Didn't you eat your breakfast?"

"It wasn't enough."

"They tried to make me eat an egg. I don't like eggs. I wanted ice cream. Papa said no, for breakfast I must eat what everyone else eats. I'm *never* going to do what everyone else does. *Never*. I don't like soft bread or rye bread or pumpernickel. I don't like sausage or cheese or meat or potato."

Daniel keeps digging but I see him lick his lips. "What *do* you like?"

"Ice cream. Strawberries. Cherries. Sugared almonds. Pancakes, but only sometimes. Marshmallow. Greet says I live on fresh air."

He squints at me. "People can't live on fresh air, stupid."

"Don't call me stupid. I'll hit you."

"Stupid, stupid, stupid. You're like a big baby with your stupid doll and your stupid frilly frock and your stupid ribbons." Daniel dives on a worm, a very small one. "Anyway, hit me and I'll hit you back."

"Boys mustn't hit girls. It's not nice."

Daniel stands up. "I don't do what everyone else does, either. Why should I? Hit me and I'll hit you back. I mean it. Just try. You'll see."

He's taller than me but not much. When we've finished staring at each other, he goes back to his digging. I find a small pebble and play *Himmel und Hölle* on the paving stones. The *Erde* square is wobbly. I hop on one foot all the way up to the Hell square, not stepping on a line once, only to find that the Heaven one is broken, so I twist in the air and hop back again. Daniel goes on pulling up clumps of grass and pretends not to notice me.

"Don't you ever get tired of playing worm hunting?"

"I'm still hungry."

"Oh." Perhaps his family is very poor, like the woodcutter and his wife in "Hansel and Gretel." "What would you like best, if you could have anything?"

He stops for a moment. "I would like everything to be back the way it was."

"Yes." I think of Greet and our old house. "I mean—to eat." Daniel doesn't answer. "If you like, I'll bring my breakfast for you tomorrow. I know where they keep the biscuits, too." He shrugs and I can see he doesn't believe me.

"Go away, will you? I've got to find some more worms. They come up when it rains."

"It won't rain today." The sky is bright blue. Not a cloud in sight. "We could jump on the grass. Greet says when she first saw a film with Charlie Chaplin tap-dancing it reminded her of worm-charming. Where she used to live, the birds hop up and down on the grass so the worms think it's raining. They come up to the surface because they're scared of being drowned."

"I know a quicker way of making them come up, but you have to go away."

"Why?"

He scratches his head and fidgets. "Because any water will do." After a moment, he adds: "I'm going to pee on the ground, that's why. They'll think it's raining. Now go away." His hands stray to his trouser buttons.

"I'll turn my back."

"No." He starts to argue, but suddenly some bad magic happens because in an instant Daniel becomes smaller and thinner and paler. He stands like a toy soldier with his arms straight down by his sides and looks at the ground.

"What's the matter?" Then I hear the Earth stone rocking. I jump up, too, and turn around, expecting to see Papa looking very angry. But it's Uncle Hraben and he always smiles.

"It's all right, Daniel. It's only—"

One, two, three big strides—Uncle Hraben is standing over us. He slaps Daniel across the face. Blood pours from Daniel's nose. He falls without making a sound. It's me who is screaming. In the same instant, Uncle Hraben swings me up in his arms and starts stroking my hair.

"It's all right, *kleines Mädchen*, you're safe now. But whatever are you doing here? This is a very dangerous place."

"Papa said I must come to work with him because there was no one to look after me today. He locked me in a little room in the infirmary." I try to see what's happening to Daniel but Uncle Hraben holds my face so that I can't look back.

"Did he, now? And how did you get out?"

"Through the window."

"Naughty girl, you could have caught anything. Does that pretty head of yours ache? Do you itch? Look at these poor little grazed knees. Let's have a peep under here. What's this red mark on your tummy? A bump? Shall I kiss it better?" I struggle to get free, beat his chest, but he doesn't put me down. "Nothing much wrong with you," he says, laughing, and snaps my knicker elastic. "You must tell me if you get any aches or pains or itches. Promise?"

"Yes, but what about the little boy?"

Uncle Hraben looks at me puzzled. "What boy? There is no boy."

"His name's Daniel—"

"There are no *real* children here, Krysta."

I look back and there he is, lying very still on the grass. His eyes are open. He's watching us. Uncle Hraben turns the corner and marches along the back of the infirmary until we get to the open window. I can see my book on the table and the broken crayons scattered all over the floor.

"Is this the place?" He holds me so that I can wriggle back through the bars. "Krysta"—Uncle Hraben catches hold of my wrist as I'm about to slide off the windowsill—"we won't tell your papa about this. It'll be our special little secret. But don't do it again. It might not be your nice Uncle Hraben who finds you next time."

I won't talk to Papa when he comes at lunchtime. I fold my arms and eat nothing, even when he brings me chocolate ice cream. All afternoon I draw pictures of monsters having their heads cut off. On the way home we have to stand aside for a long line of ladies coming in at the gate. I think they must be a ladies' choir like the one at home, because they are all dressed the same, except for their badges, but Papa just grunts when I ask him. I expect they're visiting the zoo. Johanna and some of her friends walk alongside, carrying sticks and whips to make sure the animal-things don't attack them. She stares at Papa.

There are six *Pfeffernüsse* in Papa's box, and I take four of them. If he asks me where they've gone, I shall blame Elke. By the time he goes upstairs to wash his hands again, everyone else is sitting outside, smoking cigarettes and watching the sun go down. I wait until red-faced Ursel locks up the kitchen and then get the spare key from the secret drawer in the hallstand. At night, kitchens are full of goblin shadows, but they don't frighten me. I open the oven door and look inside. It's the same as the one at home: there's nothing to see. Someone has moved the tin of *Lebkuchen* to a higher shelf and I have to stand on the table to reach it, pulling it towards me with a wooden ladle. Greet says it's greedy to take the last one, so I take a small bite and put it back. The rest go into my pocket.

In the morning I wrap some cheese and my breakfast egg in my apron, together with a few bread rolls. For late breakfast there would be meat and *Weißwurst*, but Papa never waits for that. I hide everything underneath my coloring book.

"That's better," says Papa, eyeing my empty plate. "It's good to see your appetite improving." He's also pleased that today I don't make a fuss about being shut in the little room. "It's for your own good, Krysta. There are some things little girls shouldn't know about."

Daniel is already waiting, walking backwards and forwards, kicking at the grass and looking everywhere but in the right place. He didn't know I came out the window. When I call him, he runs towards me, his eyes fixed on the bundle. Today his nose and all along the top of his cheeks are the same color as pickled beetroots.

"Did you—"

"Take that." His hands tremble as I pass it down. "I said I'd bring you my breakfast. Didn't you believe me?" Daniel doesn't answer. He's too busy smelling the food. "Don't just stand there sniffing. Help me down."

Daniel won't let go of the bundle. He sticks out one arm and maybe he's not as strong as he looks because we both fall over.

"*Trottel!*" Yesterday's grazes are now covered with dirt; tiny beads of blood seep through, making my knees look like small flower beds planted with bright red poppies.

"Who are you calling an idiot?" Daniel doesn't wait for an answer. He's got no time for arguments. Two bites and the egg disappears— even the shell—then the cheese and biscuits. Last winter a stray dog sometimes came to our kitchen door; if Greet happened to be in one of her good moods she'd throw it some scraps, otherwise it got boot sandwich. Daniel eats as fast as that dog. He crams the bread in with both hands as though he's afraid someone will take it away. His cheeks bulge. He can hardly swallow. He doesn't even stop to draw breath, so that when he finally empties his mouth he has to gasp for air like I did after Greet held my head under the bathwater for splashing her. He eats so fast that his stomach hurts and he falls down, groaning, holding his belly, trying not to be sick. And then he starts to cry.

"What's the matter, Daniel?" There was nothing to be angry about, nobody trying to make him do anything. He isn't screaming or yelling or kicking or biting—it sounds more like Papa crying after Mama went away. "What's the matter?" I ask again. He points to the empty apron.

"I didn't save any for my little sister."

"We've got plenty of food. I'll bring some more tomorrow."

He dries his eyes. "Will you?"

When his stomach feels better, Daniel helps me to climb back into the room. He doesn't go far: when I look again, he's lying, curled up, at the corner of the building. After telling Lottie about the way he guzzled his food, we decide he must have been lost for a long time, though not in a deep, dark forest like Hansel in the story. It sounds as if Gretel's lost, too. Maybe the witch has already locked her in a cage. Or eaten her. Until Papa comes to take me for lunch, I draw pictures of the gingerbread house after the witch has gone. The roof has tiles made of *Schweineöhrchen*, those twirly little biscuits that look like piglet ears, and the garden is full of more biscuits, *Spitzbuben* and *Zimtsterne*, on angelica stalks, instead of flowers.

Papa likes my pictures so much he doesn't notice my knees. We go into his office and he pins the best one up on the wall. While he's doing that I take a handful of sweets from his assistant's desk. After lunch he gives me a new drawing book and some more crayons. I have another bread roll in my pocket, as well as the sweets, but when I look out the window, Daniel has gone.

Lottie says we should tell the story again. This time a beautiful lady puts her head in the witch's oven to look at something and forgets to take it out again. I am suddenly very sad and frightened. My knees are hurting and I want Papa, but he doesn't come, no matter how loudly I shout his name.

TODAY I ASK PAPA if I can take my bowl of creamed wheat to the infirmary so that I can eat it later, when I get hungry. He says I'm being sensible at last and encourages me to take more bread and butter, too. All morning I sit by the window waiting for Daniel, but he doesn't come, and my newly bandaged knees are so stiff and sore I can't climb out the window to find him. Daniel doesn't come in the afternoon, either. Lottie says he might still have a tummy ache, but I think it's because he doesn't want to be my friend, so I pull the sweets from under the mattress and stamp on each one before throwing them all onto the grass.

After that I do some coloring with my new crayons, but Lottie wants me to finish yesterday's story. I can't do it from the middle, so we have to start again. This time I tell her how bad the witch's kitchen smelled that day—as if a rude person's done some really big, smelly blowing-off—so bad that Gretel's eyes watered and she couldn't stop coughing. The beautiful lady didn't seem to notice. She went on looking inside the oven.

I shout for Papa and kick the wall so hard that new blood comes through the bandages, but the door comes open when I pull on the handle. Something had gone wrong when we came back from the cafeteria and everyone was in such a hurry that he must have forgotten to lock it.

"Papa!" I yell, running down the corridor. "Papa!"

A nurse tries to catch me. I duck under her arm, still screaming. Doors open. Another nurse comes out and grabs my frock. The fabric rips and she's left with the sleeve in her hand. And there's Papa doing his hand washing, only he's doing it with red paint. And someone inside the room is screaming back at me, screaming and screaming, only it's all muffled because of the blanket over their head. And the red paint is dripping onto Papa's shoes. And behind him another nurse is holding something terrible—

GREET OPENS THE DOOR, letting cold night air into the kitchen. From my hiding place under the table I can see the big full moon swimming in a sea of stars. She flicks a dishrag at me and I quickly move out of reach.

"Better do as you're told for a change and go to bed, or you'll regret it."

"Won't."

"Oh, well," says Greet cheerfully, "if you won't, you won't, I suppose. Nothing more I can do. The *Böggel-mann* will be here soon enough and the door's wide open to let him in."

"Papa says there's no such thing as bogeymen."

"Does he? Being an educated man, he's probably right. You and I will just have to wait and see."

A *thump, thump, thump*ing begins and I crawl forward, anxiously watching the back-kitchen steps, almost sure a huge black shadow is pouring down them. Then I realize that the noise is only Greet kneading dough ready for the morning. She clears her throat and sings:

> "Es tanzt ein Bi-Ba-Butzemann
> in unserm Haus herum, bidebum,
> es tanzt ein Bi-Ba-Butzemann
> in unserm Haus herum . . .

> "Er wirft sein Säcklein her und hin,
> was ist wohl in dem Säcklein drin?

Es tanzt ein Bi-Ba-Butzemann
in unserm Haus herum."

I stick my head out. "What *is* in the bogeyman's sack?"

"Oh, this and that." She hums the tune for a bit, then starts again. "There's a bogeyman prowling around our house—"

"Is it food?"

"He thinks so. It's mostly bits and pieces of naughty children—sometimes even whole ones. His other name is *der Kinderfresser*—"

"I'm not frightened."

"Good." Greet makes a grab and I retreat again, shifting position as she shuffles round the table trying to reach me. "Would you like to hear more about the Child-guzzler?"

"No."

"Some people say he's a monster from the planet Saturn. He's dark and squat with a big hooked nose and a long black coat. His bottom lip is so big it flaps against his chest. His arms are very long so that he can reach into doorways and pull little people out. Long ago he did something very bad—"

"What?"

"So terrible that I'm not going to tell you. Anyway, I forget. Because of whatever it was, *der Kinderfresser* was cursed to wander the Earth forever and have no real home. He's been walking for hundreds of years. At night he steals children who are still awake. And *fee fi fo fum* during the day he gobbles them up. *Slurp, slurp,* he sucks out their blood. *Crunch, crunch, munch, munch,* he breaks every bone in their skin." Greet pauses. "Quiet! Did you hear that sound?"

"What sound?"

"*Bumpety-bump-bump,* like a full sack being dragged along the ground."

"N-no."

"If you listen carefully, there's also a *clunkety-clunk* noise, for he's worn out one of his legs with walking and has to make do with a wooden peg." Greet squats down and whispers. "That's what he's really after—a nice new leg." She pats my thigh. "So far none fit, but he keeps searching."

I whimper and start to curl into the smallest ball possible, but Greet has hold of me and is hauling me, feetfirst, out into the light, dispatching me towards the stairs with a sharp slap on my rear.

PAPA SAYS HE has found someone to take care of me during the day. I hold Lottie very tight and don't say anything.

"She's promised to teach you a few handicrafts. Sewing. Knitting." He does a pretend smile. "That will be nice, won't it?"

This time he doesn't try to make me take my thumb out of my mouth. He pulls a roll into small pieces and drinks four cups of coffee before the lady comes. It's the very old witch with the caterpillar eyebrows, the one who was sitting in the kitchen corner the day the plum syrup burnt my finger. There's no sign of the black cat, but she's all in black herself and she's brought her magic wand, leaning on it so people think it's a walking stick. I stare at the floor.

"Say good morning to *Frau* Schwitter." Papa nudges me. "Krysta, where are your manners?" He coughs apologetically. "I'm afraid my daughter is refusing to speak to anyone at the moment."

The witch laughs. "After raising seven children and twelve grandchildren, there's nothing much I haven't dealt with, *Herr Doktor*." She says nothing for a moment, but I can feel her staring. "Are you spellbound, Krysta?"

One quick glance and I see that her eyes are small and very bright blue, shining out from among the wrinkles as if they don't belong there. Her teeth are funny: a very long one on each side and not many in between. As soon as Papa goes, she taps me with her wand.

"There. Now tell me, Krysta, what is your doll's name?"

"Lottie."

"Ah, so at least we know the cat hasn't got your tongue." She produces a ball of gray wool and unwinds a long length. "Come, we must keep ourselves busy. Today I'll show you how to knit."

"Don't want to."

"You can make a nice winter scarf for Lottie." Witch Schwitter pats the seat beside her. "Come and sit here."

"No." I take three steps backwards, but she starts winding up the wool, doing it widdershins, all the time keeping her eyes on my face, and it must be a pulling spell because my feet move forward without asking me first.

"That's better. Sit up straight. Watch carefully. This is how it's done. First we make a loop, so—" She suddenly taps my hand with her little claw. "Are you too stupid to master this, Krysta? Is it true that there's something wrong with your mind?"

"No."

"Then watch and learn."

I struggle with the bone needles and the ugly storm-colored wool, dropping stitches, pulling so tight that the yarn breaks, or not enough so that the knitting looks like a broken spider's web. Three times I throw it on the floor and three times the witch makes me pick the tangle up and carry on. Finally, she lets me put it away.

"We'll do some more tomorrow."

"Won't."

"And why not, pray?"

"I don't want to. It's nasty. I don't want to knit or sew. Only poor people make things. Papa will take me to a shop where I can buy Lottie a prettily colored scarf."

"Is that so?"

"Yes." I watch the witch carefully, for her hand is resting on that stick. "Papa told me I don't have to do what you say, either. You're only supposed to make sure I don't come to any harm."

The witch cackles. She brings up the wand and taps me on the shoulder, making me jump. "Nevertheless, Krysta, all young girls must learn to be industrious. Tomorrow you will go on with what you've started."

"Won't." I rub my shoulder, pinching the skin hard to make sure there's a mark. "I'll tell Papa how hard you hit me and then he'll send you away like Elke."

"*Lügen haben kurze Beine*, my child." She laughs some more. "Yes, as the old saying goes, lies have short legs and usually come back to haunt you. Now read your book quietly. I need to rest my eyes for five minutes."

Lottie and I sit in the corner and listen to the old witch resting her eyes: *schnarch, schnarch* . . . She snores until Ursel brings milk and cake at eleven o'clock. By then I'm not hungry because we've been exploring and bad Charlotte stole some chocolate from a bedroom. After eating it very slowly, we do the "Hansel and Gretel" story again. This time the mother can't make the children go into the forest so she runs away herself.

When the witch wakes she makes me practice my writing while she talks to her friends. I don't mind. When I grow up I shall be a famous author like Carol Lewis or Elle Franken Baum, but the girls in my books will be explorers, they'll fly planes and fight battles, not play down holes with white rabbits or dance along brick roads with a silly scarecrow and a man made out of metal. In the afternoon the witch gives me a little square of printed linen and some brightly colored silks.

"Come along, Krysta." She threads a needle and shows me how to fill in the petals with neat little stitches. "Embroidering pretty things is a good way for young ladies to pass the time."

"Don't want to." I clench my fists.

"You must."

"I won't." Already her hand's tightening on the stick, but this time I'm ready. I shuffle backwards to the other side of the room. "You can't make me."

Ursel, come to collect the plates, clicks her tongue. "Now you understand what Elke had to put up with. It's more than naughtiness. No respect. Never been socialized. Can't imagine what that father of hers thinks he's about." She lowers her voice to a whisper. "Unless there's a change of attitude I wouldn't be surprised if the creature ended up wearing a black *Winkel*." They both look at me.

"Not with her father being who he is," mutters *Frau* Schwitter.

"Indeed," agrees Ursel, scraping up my squashed cake, "but he won't be around forever. She'll have to grow up sometime. And if she doesn't—"

"The money he's paying me," whispers the old witch, with a sidelong glance as if to reassure herself I'm not listening, "she can play up as much as she likes. The worse she behaves, the more I can ask for, so as far as I'm concerned, for the next few weeks she can dance with the Devil himself if she's a mind." She shrugs. "Her future isn't my business."

I get out my drawing book and, until Papa comes back, my pictures are of ugly old witches falling off their broomsticks and smashing into pieces. All of them have *Winkels*, big black striped badges like soldiers wear, but on their faces. I'm in the picture, too, smiling and being very good just to annoy them. When *Frau* Schwitter wants to see what I'm doing, I turn the black crayon on its side and color over everything, making it night, leaving space for a single big yellow star. She's very pleased when I sing "Twinkle, Twinkle" for her:

> *"Funkel, funkel, kleiner Stern,*
> *Ach wie bist du mir so fern,*
> *Wunderschön und unbekannt,*
> *Wie ein strahlend Diamant,*
> *Twinkle, twinkle, little star,*
> *How I wonder what you are."*

Papa scrubs his hands so hard now that his fingers are starting to look as raw and red as *Bregenwurst*. I still won't talk to him, but I help Lottie pass the towel. He sits and shields his eyes, sipping a linden-blossom tisane for his headache while I lie on the floor looking at the pictures in *"Der Rattenfänger von Hameln,"* especially the ones of the rats biting the babies and making nests inside men's Sunday hats. Many of the girls have long yellow hair, like mine. It's only when I get to the last page where most of the children have gone into the mountain that I notice that the boy left behind is dark-haired, like Daniel. I stare at Papa so hard he uncovers his eyes.

"What were you doing to Daniel?"

"Who's Daniel?" he asks wearily.

"He's my new friend."

Papa sighs. "Come here, Krysta." He holds out his hand. But I won't go. "Very well," he says, and knuckles his temples. After sitting a bit longer, he unlocks the little cupboard and pours something that looks like water into a glass.

I can tell he doesn't want to talk to Johanna, but she comes in anyway. Today her mouth shines scarlet. She's wearing a blue, flowery frock and shoes with very high heels.

"I'm glad to see you're enjoying your book, Krysta. Look what else I've brought you." She feels in her pocket and brings out a bright red ball, holding it up for Papa to see before she hands it over. "Of course I made sure it was properly cleaned."

"Very thoughtful," says Papa. "Krysta, what do you say?"

"Does it bounce?"

"Yes." Johanna smiles and tries to pat my head, but I move fast. "Why don't you go outside and try?"

"Not just now, Krysta." Papa shakes his head, adding: "We've had one or two problems. She needs an eye kept on her."

I bounce the ball against the wall and pretend not to hear the first time he tells me to stop.

"We could sit outside," suggests Johanna. "It's a pleasant evening. Krysta can run about and play while we chat."

Papa sighs again but follows us out of the building. He sits and looks at his hands. Johanna's doing all the talking and she keeps touching him, a little pat here and a little stroke there. Sometimes I've heard her roaring like Greet when the butcher brought old meat, but today her voice has become soft and nearly sweet. On and on she talks, every so often glancing at me, while Papa shrinks down on the bench, saying nothing. Finally, Johanna lights a cigar and leans back, blowing smoke rings. She comes inside when Papa decides I must get ready for bed.

"Let me brush your hair for you, Krysta."

Her big hands are clumsy, but I'm still holding the red ball, so I grind my teeth instead of crying out as she undoes the braids.

"Beautiful, beautiful hair," Johanna says as she starts to brush. "Look at it, Conrad, shining like gold."

"It's the same as Mama's hair." For a moment the brush falters. Johanna's hair is as kinky and dull as a back doormat.

"Isn't this nice?" she says. "Almost like a real family. I'll come in the morning and plait it for you, Krysta."

Papa stiffens. "That's very kind, Johanna, but it's not necessary."

"It won't be any trouble."

I'm sent to bed, but I creep back to listen. Johanna is doing most of the talking again, but it doesn't make much sense. I put my eye to the crack and see Papa sitting with his head in his hands.

"It's not a burden you should have to bear alone, Conrad. Of course, if we were married, then it would be *our* secret. Both of us could protect her. Nobody need ever know. Whether the . . . uh . . . irregularity's been passed down or not, surely you can see that the child needs a mother figure."

"Lidia wasn't insane," protests Papa. "It's nothing that can be passed on. It was a difficult birth and she never got over it. And, you know, being an artist she wasn't cut out for domesticity. I blame myself. Too wrapped up in my work. If it wasn't for the other thing—"

"Is that how it will look to the world, though?" Johanna looks at the clock. "It's late. I'd better be getting along, otherwise people might talk." She laughs. "You think over what I've said. I'll see you tomorrow."

PAPA IS WASHING HIS HANDS with red paint. Behind him Johanna is holding something and there's scarlet dripping from her mouth—

I wake up screaming and run to find Papa. He's holding the bottle of water from the cupboard that is always locked. His eyes look funny.

"Papa! Papa!"

"What is it, Krysta? You're supposed to be in bed, asleep."

"What were you doing to Daniel?"

"Who is Daniel?"

"My friend. I told you. I saw you. I saw—"

"Stop shouting." He drinks straight from the bottle. "I've done nothing to Daniel. There are no little boys in the infirmary. What you saw was just a . . . what did I hear you call them? Ah, yes, an animal-person. They're hardly human. That's what we're told. They are rabbits, Krysta: *króliki, Kaninchen, lapins* . . . they're only rabbits."

"No. No. No." I clench my fists. He is being stupid and I want to smack him. "No. Rabbits have little legs."

"Everything I've done is to protect you, Krysta. That's why we came here. Go back to bed now."

"Where's Daniel?"

But Papa's eyes close. The water bottle is empty and it slips from his fingers. "It has to be done," he says. "We have to know what's scientifically possible." He goes on talking but not to me. "Lidia was right—should have gone when we had the chance. Perhaps we still can if we go about it quickly and quietly. Somewhere quiet and peaceful. Far away."

"I KNOW ANOTHER TALE," whispers Greet, "about an evil giant who cut off a boy's legs and stewed them for his dinner with some fine magic beans. He had a harp that played itself and a clutch of golden goose eggs, too. There's a princess in the story. Behave yourself and it all comes out right in the end—the boy kills the giant, grows new legs, and lives happily ever after." She empties a basket of *Stangenbohne*, long green stick beans, onto the table and seizes her knife. An earwig runs out of the pile and *bang!* she crushes it to a brown paste with her fist. "If you want to hear more you'd better hurry up and finish your breakfast."

"Won't."

"Don't you want to hear the rest of the story?"

"No." I push the plate away and cover my ears.

Five

fter instructing Benjamin to avoid heavy work for a few days, Josef sat and mulled over their conversation, wondering how much was being left unsaid. There could be no doubt as to how the boy had spent the previous evening. The sour smell of the Kneipe still clung to him. His appearance was morning-after dejected, and the unnaturally quiet way in which he closed the door behind him said a great deal about the state of his head. All the same, Benjamin had never shown himself as anything but scrupulously truthful, even in the face of Gudrun's wrath, so there was no reason to believe he had lied about being waylaid and beaten and really fallen into some drunken brawl of his own instigation.

On examining Benjamin's back, he'd found evidence of deep and widespread bruising and observed, moreover, that his assailant appeared to have known precisely where to land the kick. Such blows occasionally proved fatal. It was a chilling thought. On the face of it, the attack was no more than a crude warning not to ask questions about the Thélème club, a prosperous institution that—it was rumored—numbered among its members an increasing number of Vienna's elite. It was impossible to know whether Benjamin's mention of a missing girl had also been a factor leading to the attack. If it had been, and Lilie was being sought, then they might be sailing into dark waters.

Josef glanced nervously towards the window. Could Benjamin have been followed? Violence in his home wouldn't be tolerated. He must ensure that every door was locked and bolted tonight.

Rising from his desk, he scanned the street, again standing well back, shielded by a fold of the thick velvet curtains. Nothing out of the ordinary appeared to be happening—maids chattered on the pavement, keeping their mistresses waiting for the packages they carried; an elderly woman hobbled past, towing her overweight and unwilling dog; a respectably clad workingman paused to light a surprisingly ornate meerschaum pipe—and yet each one of these passersby seemed to examine the house for an unduly lengthy time. He shook his head. Perhaps this paranoid peering around curtains marked the onset of querulous old age.

Josef hastily resumed his seat, halfheartedly reorganizing case notes until the elderly clock began its painful wheezing towards the hour when the fragrant aroma of freshly ground coffee beans wafted from the kitchen. After waiting a full five minutes, it became obvious he was expected to fetch it himself. Either Gudrun was taking advantage of the precedent he'd set on those days when he needed company or she was making some new point. Old women developed an almost masculine sense of their own importance, he thought wryly. Not for nothing were witches and hags, those much-maligned antiheroes of children's fairy stories, banished with their brooms, cauldrons, and acerbic tongues to deep, dark forests. Wise, maybe, by virtue of their years, they made for uncomfortable company bent over the kitchen stove, spitting barely disguised curses.

At least today Gudrun greeted him with civility.

"I was just about to bring your morning coffee, *Herr Doktor*. It's ready, but with so much extra work in the house now . . ."

Noting his cup had already been set before the chair he normally chose, Josef waved away her insincere apologies. "No matter." His eyes strayed to the ingredients amassed on the table.

"I'm making a *gulyás*, proper Hungarian goulash, a recipe from Pest—I know it's your favorite and they don't know how to make it here—with *csipetke*, tiny little pinched dumplings, just as they should be. I grew the caraway myself. Fresh seed, not dried, straight from the plant." Gudrun stopped, arms akimbo. "Very time-consuming, of course, but it's a taste of childhood I thought you'd enjoy."

Josef made vague noises of appreciation, wondering what all this buttering-up was in aid of. That goulash was his favorite dish was a fiction—the only thing it conjured up was memories of unwilling visits to orthodox relatives back in Pressburg. Besides, since returning from Gmunden alone, he'd been expected to eat whatever was put in front of him. Something was surely in the wind.

"And perhaps a *rakott palacsinta* to follow? I know how fond you are of sweet pancakes. At this time of year they could be layered with fresh fruit instead of preserves." Gudrun continued chattering on about greengages, late-summer berries, and the exquisite flavor of the new season's chestnut honey from Steiermark. Finally, she poured the coffee, placing a generous platter of cookies within easy reach. "*Herr Doktor . . .*"

Josef smiled behind his hand. *Here it comes.*

"The young woman—"

"Lilie," he corrected gently.

"Yes. She seems much improved today. I have, as you suggested, found her more-becoming clothes, not that she seemed grateful or even interested, but never mind, it was done in accordance with your wishes, not hers. They were in the attic, cast-off garments—Margarethe's, if my memory serves me correctly—girl's clothes really, the young woman being so small."

"Lilie," insisted Josef. "Her name's Lilie."

"Yes. I also provided her with a head scarf, one of my own as it happens, my second best, only a loan, to cover her shorn hair, though it's growing fast, thanks to me and my special oil, my own recipe—"

"And Lilie?" prompted Josef, taking advantage of her pause to draw breath.

"She seems better today, much stronger." Gudrun hesitated. "In my opinion, the girl would now benefit from being occupied. Whatever happened, she needs activity to keep her from simply sitting and brooding. It's understandable that no young woman would wish to be seen in public looking like she does, but I do feel an outing—"

"As I've said, Gudrun, we're keeping her presence here secret. It must remain that way until we know more about who else is involved."

"Yes, yes, but surely she doesn't need to stay a prisoner in that little room? It's not right. Besides—" She broke off to lift a pan onto the table, groaning a little at the weight. "Perhaps you don't realize, *Herr Doktor*, how difficult it is to run this big house single-handed. Some light household duties would both help me and give the . . . give *Lilie* purpose. '*Arbeit macht frei,*' the old saying goes, and it's right. Work would ease her mind—stop her from dwelling on things she can't change."

"What sort of work did you have in mind?" Josef asked cautiously. He pushed his cup forward for Gudrun to refill. She looked away.

"The flowers. Cleaning the silver. Dusting . . . that kind of thing . . .

perhaps a little light weeding in the afternoons to get her out into the sunshine."

"So nothing strenuous or unpleasant?"

Gudrun's eyes narrowed. Her color rose. "Of course not. What do you take me for?" she demanded, back to her usual waspish tone. "Whatever I think of her—or about her part in whatever happened—she's still convalescent. There'll be time enough later for hard work."

"I'll give it some thought, Gudrun. Bear in mind that she may never have helped with household chores before."

"Then it's about time she started!" cried Gudrun. "A woman can't live on her looks forever." She ran her thumb along the blade of the knife and grimaced. "Look at this. All the knives need sharpening and that good-for-nothing idler Benjamin has disappeared."

"He's a little unwell this morning—"

"Self-inflicted," insisted Gudrun.

"He was set upon last night. Some nasty bruises—"

"Yes, yes," she said testily. "I've seen them. Nothing time and a few applications of *Fallkraut* won't heal. There was no reason to bother you with it."

A silence fell, during which they both waited to see if Josef would comment on the use of her much vaunted magical plant. But he held his tongue. Over the years he'd fought long and hard with Gudrun over the use of folk remedies, some of which were downright peculiar but had undoubtedly continued to be used on the children behind his back. Question the use of arnica—*Fallkraut,* leopard's-bane, or whatever name fashion was currently saddling the insignificant flower with—and she'd triumphantly produce Johann Wolfgang von Goethe, his full name rolled out like a red carpet, who had credited the plant with reducing a persistent fever, thereby saving his life.

"I'll talk to Lilie later this morning," said Josef. "Has she taken breakfast?"

"Not a thing. She ate nothing last night, either. Her ladyship looks down her nose at everything I put before her."

He coughed gently. "I hope you wouldn't hold lack of a hearty appetite against her. She's delicately built."

"Scrawny, you mean?" Her hands unconsciously smoothed her formidable front. "Anyone would be skinny living on fresh air."

"Well"—Josef was conscious of choosing his words very carefully—"slender, I would have said. But you think she's stronger today?"

"Strong enough to come downstairs to your consulting room without any of yesterday's carrying-on. No call for us to go pandering to her whims."

"With so much of your own work, there's really no need to involve yourself in this at all," Josef said mildly, picking up the emphasis on *us*. "It's been my practice to receive unaccompanied women as patients for many years."

"I consider it my duty, *Herr Doktor*." Gudrun examined her hands. "One never knows what goes on in these girls' minds—I'm sure you understand me—and I would never forgive myself if *Frau Doktor* Breuer were distressed by even a hint of scandal."

AT THE HEART OF Lilie's hysteria lay, of course, the monster. Josef reproached himself for having considered hers in such simplistic terms as childhood's prancing, horned imp. He briefly considered the word's derivation from the Latin *monstrum*, a portent or unnatural event, a divine omen of misfortune yet to come, before dismissing that as irrelevant. In modern parlance the word could imply physical defect or deformity, even grotesque abnormality. It might also denote gross deviation from normal size. However, while Nature's random rolls of the dice produced creatures infinitely various in form, those monsters who possessed normal human appearance were probably the most dangerous, and it was more likely this man inspired horror, disgust, and fear by his behavior or character. He recalled that Renwick Williams, a mild-looking man dubbed "the Monster," once prowled the streets of London with a double-edged blade, wounding respectable women and slashing their clothes. And, in London again, what of the Whitechapel murderer—Leather Apron—a veritable monster who'd now been at large for ten years committing a series of horrific visceral murders?

In spite of the injuries to her throat, Josef doubted there could be any connection with the attack on Lilie, but he was certainly aware of several interesting parallels between Vienna and London in these final months of the century. Like Austria, England was experiencing an influx of impoverished immigrants. Those who had moved into the East End of London, already a poor area comparable with Leopoldstadt, were mostly Irish, but there were also plenty of Jewish refugees from Eastern Europe, as well as Russia. Racism flourished in the resulting overcrowding and poverty, carried on the incomers' backs with their meager belongings like the boggart from a folktale.

Josef was still wondering how long it would take for such racism to settle into its usual well-worn track when, after a perfunctory knock, Gudrun flung open the door and all but shoved Lilie into the room. He rose to receive them. The older woman's actions suggested unwillingness, but the girl showed no sign of resistance: on the contrary, she took a few steps forward and stood quite still, as if awaiting instructions. Today she wore a saxe blue skirt, a little too long so that it pooled around her feet, emphasizing her slim form and bringing to Josef's mind an image of Aphrodite rising from the waves. The foamy lace of a high-necked blouse concealed the marks on her neck. With his physician's eye, Josef saw that her skin tone had improved and her eyes—the irises really were almost turquoise—looked brighter, more alert. But it was as a man that his gaze lingered on Lilie's beauty, mysteriously so much more than the sum total of its parts, and he was seized by a compulsion to speak of these things, to pass a compliment that might be rewarded with a shy smile. The small grumbles of age that came from Gudrun as she shifted a chair into the full light afforded by the window prompted him to content himself with: "You're looking well this morning, Lilie." And when there was no response, he indicated that she should be seated.

Lilie obeyed, moving from shadow into bright sunlight that made her short curls gleam. A golden lamb, Josef thought, and again he tried to remember the painting she resembled—a modern painting, he was sure, connected to the Secession movement.

"The silly young woman refuses to cover her head," said Gudrun, rummaging inside her sewing basket.

"I am like the emperor's mechanical nightingale," murmured Lilie, staring fixedly at a spot on the wall in front of her. "Machines have no vanity." Her eyes flickered, and Josef, curious to see what had attracted her attention, turned in his chair and saw that more butterflies had found their way into the house. He'd already spoken to Benjamin about them. By now the cabbages must be suffering, their leaves reduced to lacy skeletons; if there were too many caterpillars to remove by hand, it might be necessary to procure a small quantity of lead arsenate.

"Machine?" Gudrun gave a snort of derision. "I've never before come across a machine that needed to visit the *Wasserklosett*. You did. Twice. Did you not?"

"Gudrun, please . . ." protested Josef.

"Huh," said Gudrun. "What goes in must come out." She unreeled a length of elastic from a card, cut a piece, and without embarrassment produced a voluminous undergarment to be rethreaded at the waist.

Josef angled his chair so it faced away from this performance of base domesticity. As was his usual practice, he focused his entire attention on the patient. "How are you feeling today, Lilie? You slept well, I trust?" There was no response, though he'd been encouraged by that quick retort to Gudrun's needling. "Can you recall anything more today? Who attacked you? Where you came from?" He waited. Behind her head, dust motes spiraled in the sunlight. An autumn-dozy fly lethargically climbed a windowpane. "Your real name, perhaps?"

Still nothing. He sighed. Presented with a sympathetic listener, his female patients were usually eager to provide him with information far in excess of what was necessary, glad of an opportunity to air their problems and disparate griefs, tentatively to voice hopes and dreams, to talk and talk, and then talk some more. The "talking cure," he thought, wryly, and then wished he hadn't. With a sinking feeling Josef recalled his stern issuing of orders during their previous session. The role of a parade-ground sergeant did not come naturally. He raised his voice, enunciating each word so clearly he achieved a harshly staccato effect that made Gudrun gasp and drop her mending. "You must answer my questions immediately, Lilie. Tell me *now*—have you remembered your given name?"

Startled, she shifted her gaze to his waistcoat buttons. "I told you, we don't have names. Our numbers are all that's needed." Josef glanced at the smudged digits on her exposed arm but didn't comment.

"Very well. In that case, let's continue to call you Lilie." He leaned back, then changed his mind, bringing himself upright, adopting a more formal tone and a pose more in keeping with the barking of commands. "Your parents, then, Lilie. First, your mother."

"A mechanical girl has no mother. It is constructed, not born." She continued to stare at his chest, at his fob pocket, perhaps. So her mother was dead, or had abandoned her. To a child these things were one and the same. In spite of that, Josef could detect no show of emotion.

"Very well, Lilie. Continue. What profession did your father follow?"

"Father?" The slightest of frowns creased her forehead and her voice became that of one reciting a learned text. "He collected bones from charnel-houses, and disturbed, with profane fingers, the tremendous secrets of the human frame."

Josef blinked and leaned forward, suddenly excited. "Ah, a quote from Mary Shelley—you allude to *Frankenstein*." He hesitated. They were approaching quagmire ground. Dead mother, unnatural father—the very situation warned against in old fairy stories. It was, moreover, Sigmund's territory. "So this is the monster, then? Your father?"

For a fraction of a second, Lilie lifted her eyes to his. "Frankenstein wasn't a monster. He was the *maker* of monsters."

"Agreed." Josef nodded, noting how skillfully she'd evaded his question. He was no longer certain the girl was experiencing any form of amnesia. This was something else . . . something new to him and therefore far more interesting. "And yet weren't Frankenstein's actions monstrous enough to make him one in his own right?"

"Because he used parts of dead human bodies? Or was it because he dared to create life? What he did, others now do better." Lilie made a gesture that encompassed her entire body. "As you can see."

Gudrun had sworn to stay silent, but her rabbinical mutterings could be clearly heard between the weary ticks of the clock. Josef shot her a look of deep reproach, which was ignored. In future, different arrangements would have to be made. To Lilie, he said: "An interesting subject, and one to which we will undoubtedly return. However, now I would like—" He stopped to adjust his voice. "Answer the question, Lilie. Is the monster you seek your father?"

"I have no father."

"Very well. Then we'll talk about the monster. Is he human?"

"He was once."

"How did he lose his humanity?"

"That's what happens to self-made monsters. This one's no exception. And every time he opens his mouth he spawns more monsters."

"Like Zeus?" Josef made a note of this new diversion. He also observed that, as had happened before, once Lilie started to fantasize there was no longer any need for compulsion.

"No, Zeus had his skull split and produced one warrior. *This* monster only spews out creatures like himself."

"Is that so?" Josef tapped the notepad with his pen. "Frankenstein's monster had no name. Does this one?"

"He does."

"And what is it?"

Lilie didn't answer for a long moment. "Adi."

Unlikely, Josef thought, that a monster would have a pet name. In all likelihood she'd invented it on the spur of the moment. Another evasion? Nevertheless, he made a note of it.

"Will you help me to find him?" asked Lilie.

Josef hesitated. He was considering employing the storytelling methods he'd used with Bertha Pappenheim, another one possessed of strong imaginative powers: apparently there'd been an outpouring of little allegorical stories since, some privately published. For a brief moment he wondered if Bertha was involved in this. Could she—*would she*—have planted an actress here as part of some complicated revenge strategy? If so, what damning errand was it that Lilie wanted him to embark on? And why attack him now? Since that terrible night of self-humiliation she'd maintained a dignified silence. Even after his *Studies on Hysteria* had been published and it was possible for anyone in the Pappenheim circle to work out who Anna O. must be—even then she had said nothing. Josef tugged at his beard, forcing his attention back to the present. Lilie was still staring at him.

"Will you help me?" she repeated.

Her eyes met his and Josef felt them working an age-old magic. His gaze dropped to her pretty mouth. A man might promise away his soul rather than refuse a request from such lips. It was his turn to be evasive.

"In a sense, Lilie, yes. Or rather, I will help you to confront what he represents."

"But that's no good. What he represents doesn't need explaining to me. I have to stand before him in the flesh."

"Oh, and what happens when you do?"

"I'm going to destroy him," she said, her voice laced with the slightest tinge of impatience.

"You'll take away this monster's malevolent powers—bring bell, book, and candle against him? Or fetter him like Azzael, the fallen angel?" He smiled. "Or do you mean to simply trap him in a bottle and bury him in the Red Sea?"

"It's no joke," Lilie said, looking at him askance. "I'm going to kill him." She brought both hands together as though wrapping them round an invisible column. Josef watched, fascinated, as she wrung the air. "I shall put the *Unmensch* out of his misery—"

"But—" Josef swallowed hard and decided against mentioning the law. "*Can* such an evil creature as you describe exist in a state of misery? Surely he relishes his actions. They make him what he is. Do you mean there are mitigating factors?"

"They say he screams in his sleep, reliving old terrors. He counts aloud the strokes as the night passes. He—"

"It sounds," said Josef, "as if you pity him."

"I merely state the facts. A machine has no emotions."

"And yet you wish to kill him?"

"That is my task. It's why I'm here. Will you help me?"

It was Josef's turn to be evasive. "To take a man's life is not an easy thing—"

"It's the easiest thing in the world," said Lilie. "It's much easier than giving birth. And considerably quicker."

Josef's hackles rose on hearing such a chilling statement delivered in the girl's sweet voice. For once, Gudrun's huffings and puffings of protest at his back were a relief. He said nothing, simply waited.

"Will you help me?" Lilie asked again.

"I can't be a party to murder, Lilie," he said gently. "And neither can you."

She smiled, as if to herself. "Hanna told me how it would be."

"Hanna?" Josef scribbled the name on his pad. "Who is Hanna?"

"Your granddaughter." Lilie looked away and closed her eyes as if battling with some strong emotion. She gave a long, juddering sigh, like one who'd only recently ceased weeping. *At last*, Josef thought . . . then suddenly took in what she'd said. He looked up, alarmed.

"You've been misinformed, my dear. I have no—"

"Margarethe's daughter," said Lilie, screwing the fabric of her skirt into a tight knot.

Josef laughed out loud, almost drowning Gudrun's tut-tutting. "But she's not even married." He sat back, strangely relieved. And yet a vague disquiet lingered. "Do you imagine yourself able to see into the future?"

"A machine isn't ruled by time. If you stand outside it, past, present, and future events can be viewed as a tableau, so I can see enough." She looked him straight in the face. "What I've told you is the truth. Laugh if you like, but the monster poses a grave threat to at least four women in your family."

Even though he knew this was all part of Lilie's fantasy, a small frisson of fear ran up Josef's spine. "Go on."

"To tell you more would sour your life. But I ask you again, in the light of what I've told you, will you help me carry out my task?"

"I will give the matter more thought." Josef glanced at the clock and found to his surprise that it was well past midday. "*Mittagessen*," he announced, capping his pen and closing the notebook. He doubted Lilie would eat any lunch, and who could blame her if Gudrun served up, as promised, her noxious *Knoblauchcremesuppe*. Garlic soup! Already his digestion was rebelling at the thought of another surfeit of the stuff. "That's enough for now. We'll talk of it again later. Ah," he added, in response to a bout of throat-clearing from the window, "one other thing. I think, Lilie, that you'd benefit from gentle physical activity. Would you be willing to help Gudrun with some light household duties?"

"If you wish," said Lilie. "After all, don't they say work liberates one?"

"The cheeky young *Fratz*!" exclaimed Gudrun, springing to her feet. "Hear that? She's been listening at keyholes. You know what happens to eavesdroppers, my girl? They hear no good of themselves, that's what."

Lilie kept her eyes cast down. But Josef was almost sure she smiled.

LILIE STOOD AT THE TABLE, head averted, eyes closed. Tears streamed down her cheeks. One hand gripped a large knife with which she blindly hacked to pieces a peeled onion held by the other. In spite of her obvious discomfort, Benjamin, peering round the open door, thought he'd never seen a lovelier sight than Lilie clothed in domesticity. After a few moments she mopped her eyes with a corner of apron, sniffing loudly.

"For pity's sake, girl!" Gudrun roughly pushed her aside. "What sort of job do you call that? Think I want finger ends in the stock? Out of my way. You're about as much use as a sundial in a cellar. And don't just stand there daydreaming. There are still the peas to be podded."

"All of them?" asked Lilie, looking at the heaped basket. "There's enough here to feed—"

"We can never have too many. The master is very partial to fresh green peas with spearmint. Also, my own special version of *Erbsensuppe*—"

"So many soups," said Lilie, wrinkling her nose. "Every single day."

"You're the only person who doesn't enjoy them," retorted Gudrun. Still out of sight, Benjamin stifled his mirth too late, for she called: "If that's you at last, slacker, stop your spluttering and coughing and get in here. The knives need sharpening."

"Try using your tongue," he muttered, stepping into the kitchen.

"What was that?"

"Here I am," said Benjamin cheerfully. "Ready and willing." He took the proffered whetstone and lined up the knives. "Good afternoon, Lilie."

"Once upon a time—" whispered Lilie, snapping open the first pod.

"Playacting again," said Gudrun, shaking her head as the onions were ferociously diced and flung into the stockpot. "If you could have heard the nonsense this morning . . ." She made a great show of looking around the room. "And where are the herbs I asked for earlier—the sage, thyme, marjoram, and chives?"

". . . the prince of a far-off kingdom wanted a wife who, in addition to being beautiful and well educated, also had to be a *real* princess. He sought high and low but couldn't find . . ."

Gudrun clicked her tongue. "Hurry up with those peas. We haven't got all day."

". . . a princess who wasn't too old, too ugly, or a peasant in disguise," continued Lilie, head bent over her work. "One dark, stormy night . . ."

"I know this story," put in Benjamin. "Doesn't the prince—"

". . . a beautiful young woman, dressed in rags, soaked to the skin and looking as unlike a princess as you could imagine, knocked at the palace door. She claimed to be the most real of all real princesses. The prince's mother decided to test her . . ."

"The knives," snapped Gudrun. Seizing a metal bowl, she cracked a dozen eggs into it and began whisking vigorously, glaring at Benjamin until he started whetting the blades. Lilie's lips continued to move as the noise in the kitchen crescendoed into something resembling an attack with steel rods on a hornet's nest. It stopped abruptly.

". . . said she'd had a sleepless night," Lilie whispered, into the silence, "for she'd been kept awake by something hard in the bed." Benjamin snorted. Gudrun scowled. "And her entire body was a mass of bruises. The prince rejoiced, for only a real princess would have the sensitivity to feel a tiny pea through so high a stack of feather mattresses. They were married the same day. Which proves"—here Lilie threw the last peas into the basin, the empty pod into a bucket—"you should never judge a person solely by the evidence of your eyes." She folded her hands in her lap.

"You've finished them," Gudrun said, amazed. "So you can exert yourself when you've a mind to."

"Good story," Benjamin said admiringly. Last night he'd persuaded himself she was simply a maidservant, that there was a chance for him. He wondered now how he could ever have thought such a thing. His heart sank. Still, for her sake, he'd put even more effort into ferreting out the truth. He'd visit Hugo again in a day or two. The fat journalist was the nose and ears of Leopoldstadt: sooner or later every bit of slimy gossip slithered within his reach. And, before that, he'd tackle the Thélème, that latter-day Gomorrah. There must be some way of getting inside. He was struck by a sudden realization: when he'd told the doctor the club didn't take on young men because of all the girls, it hadn't been strictly true. Men of a certain type were employed . . . those who had no interest at all in the charms of women. He shifted uncomfortably, wondering what damage it might do to his reputation. Never mind. Others could think what they pleased about him, if only Lilie would look his way.

Just for a minute, Benjamin allowed himself to imagine a future where he was privileged to protect and care for her. It wasn't impossible. Whatever she'd been, Lilie now had nothing: *arm wie eine Kirchenmaus,* poor as a church mouse. He'd picked her up, as his mother would say, in her birthday suit. Where could she go? How could she live? Perhaps the doctor would let him smarten up the small living space over the stables. He could build a partition, making it into two rooms—beg and borrow some furniture from home. It would be a start. By day they'd work, she in the house, he in the garden or taking the doctor on his rounds, seeing each other frequently, smiling at their shared secrets as they passed. In the evening he'd study while Lilie sat and sewed or read or arranged flowers. At weekends, when the carriage wasn't in use, perhaps he'd be allowed to take Lilie for excursions into the countryside, to the Vienna Woods and the castle at Perchtoldsdorf. Maybe even as far as Sankt Pölten, with its Roman remains. When he was qualified and rich he'd rent an apartment in the best part of the city; then they, too, would have a summer retreat in Gmunden—

"Take that gormless expression off your face," bellowed Gudrun, brandishing a wooden spoon.

"What's biting you?" whispered Benjamin. "Someone round here's turning into a she-bear with a sore backside."

"What?"

"Can't help my face," claimed Benjamin.

"I heard what you said. How dare you! We'll have a bit more respect, thank you very much, or you'll be getting marching orders when *Frau Doktor* Breuer returns and hears about your drunkenness."

Behind Gudrun's back, Lilie gave a very small smile. Benjamin returned it with a grin, rolling his eyes for good measure. It was not a wise move.

"Out!" bawled Gudrun.

"Fine. I take it you don't need any fruit picking, then." He stopped in the doorway and winked at Lilie.

"Yes, I'll have— Come back here! How dare you walk away when I'm talking to you? The master will hear about this." She looked at Lilie. "Take this," she said, pushing a large bowl into her hands. "Raspberries. I presume you remember what raspberries are. After that, you can pick fresh flowers for the hall."

"She's getting worse," said Benjamin as Lilie emerged into the sunshine. "Power's gone to her head. Be a good thing when the rest of the family returns. Come on, I'll give you a hand with those raspberries." It occurred to him that nobody could see into the fruit cage from the house.

Away from the gloomy kitchen, her hair shone red-gold. The heat from the stove had left it damp so that the small curls lay flat against her skull like those of a cherub. The blouse was too big for her and gaped open, through which he could see delicate lacework against her white skin. Benjamin carefully angled himself in the hope of seeing more. He twisted a length of raffia between his fingers and moved closer.

"I was afraid you were dead," he said in a low voice. Lilie glanced at him but didn't answer. This close he could see the greenish shadows of the bruises behind her ear, the top of the rough scabs on her throat. His blood seemed to ignite. "Only tell me who did that to you and I'll kill him. I'll kill the bastard slowly, very slowly."

"I'll kill him myself," she answered quietly. "That's my purpose here."

"Was it that filthy club? Were you a prisoner there?"

"One way or another, we're all prisoners."

Benjamin took this cryptic pronouncement as an affirmative. Never mind the doctor's agenda; he now had one of his own. "Let me help you," he said, opening the door of the fruit cage.

After one sideways glance, Lilie stepped inside and stood breathing in the hot raspberry fragrance laced with the sharp tomcat smell of black-currant leaves, while Benjamin seized a stick and drove out a fledgling blackbird that had found its way through the wire. Crickets zithered in clumps of long grass. A couple of white butterflies performed a ritual dance overhead. Benjamin led her along the rows of denuded fruit bushes until they reached the autumn raspberries.

"I planted these." He reached for a particularly large and luscious specimen. "Try it? Have another." Feeding Lilie was something he could have spent the rest of the afternoon doing. But after the third, she turned her head away. "Don't you like them? I prefer apricots myself. What's your favorite fruit?"

She laughed. "Cherries."

"They're finished. Apples and blackberries come next."

Lilie put her hand on his arm. "Daniel, you offered to help me. Can you take me to Linz?" Benjamin looked at her small hand and then looked away, bitterly disappointed she'd not even remembered his name.

"Daniel's my brother," he muttered, his voice flat and dead. "It was Daniel who found you. Daniel and his friend, Bruno."

"Benjamin," Lilie corrected herself, looking up into his face so sweetly that he forgave her instantly. "Of course."

"Linz is a long way, a day's journey, maybe more. We could take the train, I suppose. Is that where you come from?"

She nodded, but Benjamin was not entirely convinced. He looked at her curiously. "Can you really not remember who you are?"

"I said I had no name. That's true. It's not a question of memory."

"Were you running away when you were attacked?"

"No." Her lips trembled. "No, I was running *to* somewhere, not away." She held out the bowl of raspberries. "Surely that's enough. There are only three people in the house."

"We'd better fill it," said Benjamin. "The old hag will gobble up half of them on the sly."

JOSEF, STROLLING THROUGH the garden in search of the first naked ladies, the meadow saffron—*Colchicum autumnale*—that grew in abundance beneath the ancient walnut tree and was for him one of the few compensations of approaching autumn, spotted Lilie and Benjamin among the fruit canes and stopped. The sight of their heads so close together made him uneasy. He took a few more steps, saw Benjamin press a deep red raspberry between the girl's lips, heard her laugh out loud, and turned away, biting hard on his knuckles as sick envy struck him, sharp as a physical blow, dead center of his solar plexus.

An urgent need to regain the sanctuary of his consulting room sent him blundering straight through the herb garden, but with eyes so misted he could barely see the narrow path. His feet strayed, crushing plants right and left, unleashing admonishing fragrances, an unspoken language of culinary flowers: the sharp citrus tang of lad's-love; the evocative scent of mint, alleged by Culpeper—as by the ancient Greeks—to stir an old man's lust; Gudrun's caraway, said to stop husbands straying; and the acrid stink of rue, herb of repentance, of regret. Finally, another, redolent of all things domestic—so strong that it lay like a taste on the air—reached out to claim him, and Josef knew he'd stumbled into the swath of rosemary bushes where the washerwoman spread small articles of household linen to dry in the old-fashioned way. He sank onto the mossy bench nearby and kneaded his calves. Old age was creeping up on him; any more of this foolishness and he'd end up an object of ridicule, or worse, as had the reprehensible pair of elders in Daniel who lusted after the youth and beauty of Susanna. His father had told him the story half a century ago. It was only now, though, that Josef realized that Leopold—who'd always seemed ancient, as fathers often do to their offspring—had been almost fifty, just seven years younger than he was now, when he'd married the beautiful and cultivated daughter of an established silk merchant. A tiny shock ran through Josef as he was struck by a second realization: Bertha Semler, his doomed mother, had only been twenty-two, near enough Lilie's age. It was not unthinkable—

Enough. The situations were entirely different. And as for Benjamin, he was a decent young man who might go far. What better match, questions of faith aside, could there be for Lilie if she were truly lost?

But what if she weren't? The behavior he'd just observed was very different to that exhibited during their informal consultations. She looked perfectly at ease with Benjamin, talking, laughing, and moving without any of that somnolent stiffness or hesitancy of speech. If Bertha Pappenheim had planted the girl in his household, then Benjamin, being so easily swayed by a pretty face, was undoubtedly part of the conspiracy. Josef could hardly believe the boy would betray his generous friendship, but it had happened before. In spite of patronage, the gifts and the freedom of his homes—none of which Josef begrudged—Sigmund now not only cold-shouldered him in public but spoke disparagingly to mutual acquaintances of his timidity, his overcautiousness, his *oddity*, not only professionally but as a man. And all, it seemed, because he was unable to accept in toto his erstwhile colleague's pronouncements on the subject of sexual etiology. If one was not with Sigmund, then one was against him; it had always been that way.

Josef nipped off a flowering shoot of rosemary and held it to his nose. Gudrun had been loud in her praise of this herb, so he was aware it had other qualities deemed superior to its pleasant association with bed linen, towels, and soap. According to her, sprigs under pillows repelled nightmares, Hungary water reduced gout, and an infusion improved memory. *There's rosemary, that's for remembrance*—this time it was Shakespeare backing her claim. It was said to be a love charm, too: tap the intended with a sprig and they were compelled to respond. Josef closed his eyes and allowed his imagination to conjure a blissful moment of fulfillment before letting the rosemary slip through his fingers onto the cold bare ground.

Six

his morning Witch Schwitter spends a long time admiring my hairstyle. The plaits are wound round my head to make a little crown. Greet sometimes did it this way on special days or when we went to the place where they put all the flowers on the ground.

"Somebody did a good job. Not your father, surely?"

"Johanna." I move out of the way so big fat Ursel can push the carpet sweeper under the table to look for crumbs.

"Oh. And when did she do it?"

"Before breakfast. I don't like my hair like this. The hairpins stick in me. It's too heavy. My neck aches."

"One must suffer for beauty," says the witch, tapping me with her wand. "Tell me, did Johanna have breakfast with you?"

"She only has coffee in the morning." The witch and Ursel exchange glances.

"I see. And . . ." The witch starts to ask something else but seems to change her mind and tells Ursel what she wants for lunch instead. When we're by ourselves, she says: "Well, Krysta, you look like a little princess today, so mind you behave like one."

"My great-grandmamma was a real princess."

"Yes, yes."

"She was. She was," I protest.

"A fairy princess?"

"Don't be silly. My great-grandmamma was a *real* princess. In India."

"You're the one being silly, Krysta. If that was so, you'd be black as a Gypsy, and look at you, a perfect little golden-haired *Fräulein*, white as snow, so we'll have no more of your nonsense." I poke out my tongue, but Witch Schwitter is too busy rummaging in her basket to notice. "Come along, now. Look what I've got for you." She holds up a wooden cotton reel. Greet had lots of reels wound with different color threads in her mending box, but this one has four little nails hammered in the top. In her other claw there's a ball of wool.

"What's that for?"

"*Nahliesle*. Some people call it French knitting. This one belonged to my youngest granddaughter, Frederica, but she knits like a grown-up now and she's only seven."

"Is your granddaughter a witch, too?"

"Good gracious, child, what put that into your head?" She twists wool around the nails, letting one end hang down through the hole in the middle. "There, I've started you off. Now watch carefully. This is much easier than working with two needles. Hold the reel in your left hand, *so*, now bring the wool round the nail and pull the loop that's already there waiting over the top of it with your needle." She does a few stitches for me. "And out of the bottom grows a knitted tube, see? It's very quick. You can make pretty winter stockings for your doll."

"Don't want to."

"But you will do some, Krysta." Witch Schwitter's eyes glint and her two long teeth appear. "This is special magic wool. It changes color as you knit. At the moment, the color is blue. Do a few rounds and it will become pink then yellow or green. Now you try."

She watches me work a few stitches. I hate the stupid thing. My fingers feel hot and sticky. I want to play. As soon as she starts looking at her magazine with a picture on the cover of men smiling and waving, I pull all the stitches off so that the silly tube falls to the floor. The witch sighs and clicks her tongue but says nothing. She picks it all up, puts the stitches back on the nails, and closes one of my hands on the reel, the other round the needle.

"Act up all you like, Krysta. I've got nothing better to do and it doesn't bother me one little bit. We'll just sit here together—all day if need be—until you've produced something satisfactory."

"Why?"

"Because I said so. And it's about time you learned simple obedience."

"Why?"

"Quiet now." The witch reaches for her wand. "Concentrate."

I grind my teeth and whisper bad words. This time she keeps watching me until I get past the pink and on to yellow. Then she does a bit more, binds the stupid tube off, and gives it to me.

"That's long enough for one doll's stocking. Tomorrow we'll make the second. Well done, Krysta. Play with your doll now while I finish my magazine."

I sit in the corner with Lottie. She wants to hear "Hansel and Gretel" again but only the part where the witch gets pushed in the oven. Today we make the fire extra-hot and the witch screams so loudly all the windows in the gingerbread cottage break into countless fragments of barley sugar. We sit and eat them while the witch burns. When we look in the oven, all that's left are her nasty yellow fingernails and two long teeth.

Ursel comes in and Witch Schwitter shows her something in the magazine, a picture, I think. They both look at me. I try the silly tube thing on Lottie's leg. She doesn't like it because it's itchy and has no proper foot. I tell her we'll get real stockings from a shop. I want to throw the stupid thing away, but it's difficult to get off and I have to pull so hard Lottie's leg comes loose from her body, leaving a gap. Inside, I can see the cord that holds it on.

I decide we'll play rabbit doctors and borrow Witch Schwitter's little scissors. *Snip, snip, snip.* Lottie makes such terrible noises that I put a cushion over her face. One leg falls off and I hold it up, pretending to be a nurse. Then the other leg falls off.

"What in God's name are you up to?" demands Ursel, standing over me, clutching her duster. She pushes the cushion away with her foot and grabs Lottie. "Look what the little devil's done now. It's ruined. When I think of what this doll must have cost . . . most girls would be grateful." She taps her head. "Not normal, that's what I say. Something's not up to the mark."

The witch waves the magazine. "What did I tell you?" She holds out her claw for Lottie. "Bring the doll's legs here, Krysta. Let's see if she can be mended."

"No."

"Be quick or your father will see what you've done. Come on, now. I've fixed many broken dolls in my time." To Ursel, she says: "Get them for me, please. I don't want to be held responsible for damage of that kind."

Ursel grabs my hands, tearing the legs from my fingers.

"Stop that." I scratch her arm and try to kick her. "I don't want you to fix her. She's being a rabbit."

"It's a doll," grates Ursel, pushing me so hard I fall over. "What's the matter with you?"

"The legs are only held on with elastic," says the witch. "A thick rubber band will do the job. The boys often pull arms and legs off their sisters' dolls—heads, too, sometimes—to play funerals."

"Boys will be boys." Ursel shakes her head but doesn't look cross. "That's only natural. But I never came across a girl who did such nasty things."

They fiddle around with Lottie, taking no notice of her screams. When her legs are back in place again, Ursel puts her on top of the bookcase until I learn to behave myself. They don't put her knickers on.

UNCLE HRABEN brings me a paper cone of jelly babies. I sort them into colors. The black ones taste best. The reds are next, but orange and green and yellow taste of nothing. I used to bite their heads off first. This time I try starting with the legs.

"You're looking very grown-up today," he says, poking my hair.

"I don't like it."

"Nor me. I prefer it loose." Uncle Hraben pauses. "I haven't told anyone about you climbing out the window, naughty Krysta."

"I didn't tell anyone about you hitting the little boy," I say, my mouth full of legs.

"How many more times, Krysta? There was no boy."

"I get smacked if I tell fibs."

"Do you like being smacked?" Uncle Hraben slides his hand under my skirt and pats my bottom. He forgets to take his hand away.

"No." I snatch up the sweets and move to the other side of the table. "Do you?"

He laughs very loudly. "It depends. Not by your papa, if that's what you mean. As for the window, he won't be taking you to the infirmary again." He gives me a funny look. "Not after what happened."

. . .

THE WITCH DIDN'T TAKE her magazine home. It's still on the chair when Johanna comes. This evening she's wearing a blue frock that clings to her legs. Her eyelids have turned blue to match.

"Ooh, is that this month's?"

"Don't know." I ask her to reach Lottie down. "Bad Charlotte." Her legs are floppier than they used to be and she won't sit properly.

"How's your hair? I'm sure everyone liked it. Now, have you been a good girl today?" I don't answer. Johanna has big hands that look as if they're always ready for some smacking. She doesn't want to know anyway. "Let's see what I've got in my pocket for you."

This time she's brought me new hair clips, only I don't think they are new at all because there's a bit of dark hair tangled in one. They smell of the stuff Greet used to pour in the lavatory. Two are like little branches with rainbow-colored baby birds sitting in a row. The others have metal bows, red with white spots.

"Like Minnie Mouse," she says.

"Minnie Mouse is stupid."

"Where are your manners, Krysta?" asks Papa, back from his hand washing but still twisting them round each other. "Say thank you to Aunt Johanna."

"Thank you," I say in my very smallest voice. Johanna smiles.

"Just Johanna will do, Krysta. Which pair do you like best?" I point to the birds. "Good choice." She glances at Papa. "I'll put them in your hair tomorrow morning."

Papa unlocks the cupboard and takes out a new bottle of the special water. He pours a glass for himself and drinks it all in one go. Johanna looks at him, then looks at the bottle. I laugh.

"Where are your manners, Papa?"

"That's enough of that," he says, frowning, but gets a second glass for Johanna. She has a tiny sip, then sits down in the witch's chair and opens the magazine. "Have you seen this article, Conrad?"

Papa stands behind Johanna and looks at the pages she's pointing to. After a moment his face goes funny. He frowns and his lips go away, leaving his mouth like a letter-box opening.

"Why are you showing me this?"

"Aren't you interested?"

"Why should I be?"

I sneak up behind them and look under Papa's arm. There are pictures of ugly ladies and a troll. At the top of the page is a heading in big letters. I spell it out: *Frauen, die nicht Mutter werden dürfen.*

"Why does it say they aren't allowed to become mothers?"

"In case they pass something on," says Johanna. "I mean, look at them. They're hardly human. Sometimes, though, you can't tell what's wrong from appearances—"

Papa snatches the magazine and screws it into a ball. "Go outside, Krysta."

"You said I had to stay in. You said—"

"Do as you're told. Now."

I stamp my feet as I leave, then creep back on tiptoe to listen.

"Remarkably like blackmail," Papa is saying. "I would have expected better of you."

"I don't know what you mean." Johanna pretends to cry. She isn't very good at it. Then she starts telling him over and over again that she's sorry. After a bit Papa says it's all right. He holds her hand to make her feel better and lends her a big white handkerchief with his initials on it. When she blows, Johanna sounds like the coal man's horse harrumphing into his nose bag. Lottie and I go inside the flowering currant bush to look at the powder compact we took out of Johanna's bag. It's round and pale green with a picture of a lady in an old-fashioned gown and bonnet. I powder Lottie's nose and then mine. After we've looked at ourselves in the little mirror, we rub it off and go back inside. Papa is staring at the wall. Johanna is smiling.

"Would you like to play a game, Krysta?" She gets out the *Damespiel* board and pretends to be stupid so I win. It was better when Greet and I played checkers. She hated losing. Once, when she lost six times in a row, she knocked the board off the table and pretended it was an accident.

"What shall we do now? Do you know any poems, Krysta?"

Papa doesn't like Greet's poems, so I shake my head and sing her the *"Alle meine Entchen"* song instead:

> *"All my ducklings*
> *Swimming in the lake*
> *Little heads down in the water*
> *Tails up in the air."*

"Very nice," she says, and begins to clap.

"I haven't finished, stupid."

"Krysta!" bellows Papa. "Apologize immediately." I pretend not to hear.

> *"All my little doves*
> *Settle on the roof,*
> *Klipper, klapper, klapp, klapp,*
> *Fly over the roof."*

DER SANDMANN COMES in the middle of the night. Before, he always had a little flashlight. He leaned over the bed sniffing me and sometimes he felt under the bedclothes while I pretended to be asleep. Greet says he can't steal your eyes to feed to his children as long as you keep them tight shut. Sometimes I have to look, but I only open one eye a tiny bit. In the morning I'd know it wasn't a dream because I'd find a *Negerküsse* or a Pfennig Riesen under my hairbrush. Tonight he's forgotten his flashlight and keeps crashing into things in the dark. When the moon comes out from behind her cloud to see what's going on, Lottie whispers that it's not the Sandman but a *Böggel-mann*. There's a big sack on the floor and he's banging around, opening everything looking for us, and I quickly put my thumb in my mouth to stop myself screaming because it's *der Kinderfresser*, the terrible Child-guzzler, with his sack of arms and legs and sometimes whole children. I slide under the bed, keeping my hand over Lottie's mouth. I'm trembling all over, even worse than the time I hid from Greet after breaking the string of her pearl necklace and she came running up the stairs with the rug beater, threatening to tan my hide.

Then the lights are switched on because Papa has come. *Der Kinderfresser* turns himself into a shadow.

I get up quickly. Papa smells funny. He's emptying the cupboards and drawers, squashing my clothes and books, toys and hairbrush into a bag.

"Papa, what's the matter?"

"Get dressed. We're going on a journey."

"Are we going home, Papa?"

"No. Somewhere else, over the sea, far away—"

"Conrad?" Johanna comes in, wearing only her vest and knickers. They are shiny and pink. She has a floppy bottom and big titties, but not nearly as big as Greet's. "What are you doing?"

"Can't do it anymore. It's killing me. I've got to get out of here."

"Don't be ridiculous, Conrad. You're drunk. Sleep it off. Things will look different in the morning." She tries to put her arms round him. "Come back to bed."

"Leave me alone, ugly cow." Papa pushes her away and starts washing his hands in the air. "Clear off."

Johanna's mouth falls open. "You don't mean that. Not after what we've just—"

"I didn't invite you to stay."

Then Johanna slaps Papa's face and says a very bad word. She beats her fists against his chest, but he pushes her away and stumbles out of the room. Johanna makes me get into bed.

"Go to sleep, Krysta. Your father is very tired. Everything will be all right in the morning."

I lie awake for a long time in case any other bogeymen come. Johanna and Papa shout at each other. Then a door slams. Everything's very quiet. An owl hoots. One of the zoo animals starts howling. A bit later I hear another door close more quietly. I watch a star looking back at me where the curtains aren't pulled properly. If you stare really hard for a long time without blinking, it looks as if the star's falling to Earth. Greet says stars are the eyes of dead people watching us.

"*Funkel, funkel, kleiner Stern*," I whisper into the darkness. "How I wonder who you are."

PAPA USUALLY WAKES ME by shouting, "I won't tell you again," but today it's only the cups and saucers clinking, so I know one of the witches has already brought our breakfast. I pick Lottie off the floor and we see it's nasty fat Ursel with Papa's coffee and rolls and more horrible creamed wheat for me.

"Oh," she says, looking at my nightie, "not even dressed yet? Get a move on, girl. *Frau* Schwitter will be here soon." She picks up the two empty bottles, holding them away from her as if they might bite. "You'd better wake your father. Looks like he made a night of it."

But Papa doesn't want to wake up. He keeps the blankets over his head even when I see his trousers on a chair and feel in all the pockets. Lottie hides the fifty *Reichspfennig* piece she stole under the loose corner of linoleum by my bed. Johanna doesn't come to do my hair. Good. I sit and read my book. After I've finished the story, I wash the bits Papa might notice and put on my very best frock and new white socks. I go to show Papa how pretty I look, but he won't wake up, even when I shout very loudly and kick the bed. I pull his pillow from under his head and still he doesn't move. Lottie and I try some of Papa's coffee with lots of sugar in it, like Johanna drinks it, and eat one of his rolls, spread with butter and some more sugar. Lottie says she feels sick.

Herta comes looking for Papa and tells me to take my thumb out of my mouth. "Where's your father? He's late. There's a busy schedule and we can't start without him."

"Papa doesn't want to get up."

"Really? We'll see about that." Herta stands with her hands on her hips. "Is he on his own in there? Right." She strides over to his door and raps on it with her big hard knuckles before going in. There's a funny noise, a bit like a hen squawking when it's having its neck wrung. Then she runs out and starts yelling so loudly some of the men come racing up the stairs.

"What's the matter?" asks one, grinning all over his face. I've seen him before. He has orange hair and lots of freckles. His voice sounds like fir cones burning. "Chased by a spider?"

"In there." Herta gasps, holding her neck with one hand and pointing with the other. "Strangled."

"Has a spider bitten Papa?" Greet says some spiders hide under lavatory seats and bite your bottom if you sit for too long. "What's the matter with my papa?" No one answers. "What's *strangled*?" The other men crowd into Papa's room, but the orange-haired man only looks from the doorway. His face turns serious. He puts his hands on Herta's shoulders.

"How long?"

"Cold," she says, rubbing her hands up and down her throat. "He's cold. Stiff."

"So it happened last night. One of them must have broken out and come looking for the *Doktor*."

Herta shakes her head. "Even if they could, how would they know exactly where to find him?"

"Animal cunning. You know what they're like."

"But it would take some strength to . . ." Herta goes through her pockets for a cigarette, and the orange-haired man lights it. Her hands are trembling. After a few puffs she says: "Perhaps you're right, Metzger. Yes, that must be what happened."

I stand against the wall in Papa's room. He still doesn't wake up, even though the other men are being very noisy, examining everything— under the bed, in the wardrobe, behind the tallboy. One of them is try- ing the window, opening and shutting it, opening and shutting. Then some go into my room. I follow and watch them find the bag stuffed full of clothes and toys. Herta stares at it.

"Johanna's right. He *was* planning to run away."

A tall, thin man leaves and comes back with Uncle Hraben, who is smiling and looking cross at the same time. He goes into Papa's room and shouts a lot of very bad words. All the other men go away except Metzger with his funny orange hair, who stands across the doorway. When Uncle Hraben comes out and picks me up, I start to cry.

"Why won't Papa wake up?"

"Don't be alarmed, *mein kleines Mädchen*. Your Uncle Hraben will take care of you." He pushes my hair back. "Now, listen carefully. I see one of the maids must have brought breakfast. Was anyone else here? Have you seen any strangers?"

"Only *der Kinderfresser*."

"The Child-guzzler?" Uncle Hraben's smile grows even wider. "No, no, Krysta, I mean real people, after teatime yesterday and before breakfast arrived this morning."

"First Johanna came," I say crossly, "and then *der Kinderfresser*. I thought it was the Sandman, only it wasn't, because he had a big sack. Anyway, the Sandman always leaves me a sweet, and there wasn't one. After that, Johanna and Papa shouted at each other."

Uncle Hraben frowns. "Johanna was here last night?"

"Yes." I struggle to get down. "Let go. I want my papa."

"No, she wasn't," says Herta, giving him a funny look. "Johanna was with me. She was very upset about . . . something. We spent half the night talking."

"That's not right." Uncle Hraben finally puts me down, and I stamp my foot. "She was here with me and Papa."

"Are you calling me a liar?" Herta narrows her eyes and glares. She doesn't frighten me, but I get behind Uncle Hraben just in case. He reaches into his pocket and secretly passes me a licorice wheel.

"Johanna played checkers with me and brushed my hair. Afterwards she took off her frock. She came in my room wearing just her vest and knickers. I saw her titties."

Metzger makes a funny noise and tries to pretend he was coughing. Uncle Hraben puts his hand over his mouth. Herta scowls at both of them.

"The little fool's been dreaming."

"Anyway." I get her powder compact from its hiding place beneath the cushion and leave the licorice wheel there for later. "Look—Johanna left this behind."

Herta shrugged. "Yes, that's hers, but she could have left it at any time."

"Yesterday," I insist, and put my thumb in my mouth.

"You know what happens to children who do that," says Herta, dragging it out with two fingers closing like scissors.

In hobbles Witch Schwitter, leaning on her magic wand so people think it's a walking stick. She opens her eyes very wide when she sees me. "Krysta?" She looks round at the others. "What are you all thinking of? Where's your decency? This is the last place the child should be. Come, Krysta, let's go down to the kitchen. Maybe we can find you something nice to eat."

Ursel comes running up the stairs. Her face is bright red. She's so hot and out of breath she has a mustache made out of little sweat beads. "Is it true? Downstairs they're saying someone's throttled the life out of him. I was up here less than an hour ago. If I'd known . . ." Ursel shudders. "Is he really dead?"

Suddenly I'm scared. I pick up Lottie and hold her very tight. "Who's dead?" Everyone turns to look at me. "Who's dead?" I yell.

"There's been an accident, Krysta," says Witch Schwitter, pulling me out of the room with one claw. I fight her. She has to let go because she needs both hands and she won't let go of her wand. I duck under Metzger's arm and run back into Papa's room.

Papa is still on the bed. Someone has pulled the blankets off his head and he has no clothes on. He looks funny, like a big doll, except dolls don't have hairy fronts. He's asleep with his eyes wide open and has big purple marks around his neck.

.   .   .

"THE HEDGE WAS as high as this house," says Greet as she rubs butter into the flour, "and as thick as the length of this room. In summer it was smothered with dark red roses. So beautiful was their perfume you could smell it five miles away. Their scent was what drew the prince to Sleeping Beauty's castle." She turns the pastry onto the board. "Pass me the rolling pin, Krysta." *Thump. Thump.* The ball is divided in two and rolled into circles. Greet presses the biggest one into a dish. I go on picking stones out of the dried lentils.

"What sort of pie will it be?"

"Kitten-and-*Rapunzel* pie. Waste not, want not: the cat next door had babies and the cook drowned them in a bucket. Do you want the story or don't you?"

"Won't eat kitten pie."

"Then you'll have no pudding."

"Don't care. What did the prince do next?"

"Well, underneath the roses were sharp thorns as big as your little finger and curved like a wicked Turk's scimitar, so he took out his sword and began to chop at the stems." Greet slices the air with the butter knife. "He cut the stems, and the thorns cut him back till the ground was knee-deep in red petals and scarlet blood. It took him a week, perhaps longer, but he finally made a hole big enough to crawl through. And there was the castle, still with the spell on it, everyone and everything fast asleep: cooks, maids, horses, hounds. Dust everywhere. *Schmutz!*" She slaps at the wall with her fly swat, picks the half-dead bluebottle up by one wing, and carries it to the open window. "Even the filthy flies."

"Yes, but what about Sleeping Beauty?"

"She was asleep, too." Greet yawns. "She'd been asleep for a long, long time."

I'm so impatient my feet won't keep still. "Go on, go on."

"Later, perhaps—I'm too tired now. Besides, I've all these kittens to chop up and their eyes to gouge out."

I peer into the basin. "Those aren't kittens, they're the pigeons you bought in the market."

"Are you sure?" Greet laughs and pokes the bloody corpses. "Listen. Do you hear something?" She covers her mouth. *"Miaow, miaow, mia-oooow."*

"That's silly. You're doing the noises. Anyway, I know the end of the story. The prince kisses Sleeping Beauty and she wakes up—"

SOMEONE IS SHAKING ME. Then a hand slaps my face, first the left side, then the right. I blink, and Ursel is standing over me.

"Snap out of it."

Uncle Hraben grabs her wrist. "What was that for? Leave the poor child alone."

"What, let her stand there for another five minutes with her mouth open, staring into thin air? It's some kind of fit. Don't look at me like that—someone had to do something."

Witch Schwitter puts her skinny witch arm round me. "Come, Krysta, time for us to go downstairs."

"No! No! Wait." I throw myself on top of Papa and kiss him. He's a funny color and his cheek feels as if he's just come inside on a snowy winter's night. His eyes stare straight at me but he doesn't wake up, so I kiss him again and again until Uncle Hraben pulls me away. When Witch Schwitter leans over and closes Papa's eyes, I remember him doing that to Mama after he opened all the windows. Everyone moves aside because Johanna has come and her face is a horrible puddle-gray with big dark rings under her eyes.

"Conrad? They told me someone had—" She touches his wrist.

"It's only a spell," I tell her. "You've got to kiss him and then he'll wake up."

"He's dead, Krysta," she says flatly. "Gone."

"No he isn't." I stamp my foot and start kicking the end of the bed. "Papa! Papa! Wake up."

"No great loss, as it turns out," says Metzger, shrugging his shoulders and raising his voice above my noise.

"*Shhhh!*" Witch Schwitter looks very cross and nods in my direction. "Aren't things bad enough without—" She tries to pull me towards her but I won't go.

"Squeamish sod was about to bugger off, abandoning a vital research project, one that might have helped thousands of heroes. More than that, it's an insult to the—"

"I'll kill whoever did this with my bare hands," said Johanna, staring straight at him. "I'll stomp them into the ground."

Metzger sticks his chin out. "Don't look at me. I don't go sneaking around bedrooms in the dark. I'd have stood him up against a wall and shot him."

"It was one of them," says Uncle Hraben. "They must have broken out and found their way in here."

"Don't be ridiculous," Johanna says, glaring at him. "How could the creatures escape? The bloody wall's twice your height with electrified barbed wire on top."

I pinch Papa's toes through the bedcovers. I kick the bed harder so she has to shout to make Uncle Hraben hear. He goes on talking as if he hasn't heard.

"I've already ordered an additional roll call—"

"That was quick." Johanna narrows her eyes. "Exactly when did you do that?"

"Earlier." Uncle Hraben and Johanna stare at each other. "It's better this way." She opens her mouth to say something, but he sticks out his arm and she seems to change her mind. "They're checking numbers right now. Examples will have to be made—two hundred for one. That should teach the murdering swine." He looks around. "We'll keep this an internal matter. *Frau* Schwitter, can we rely on you to do what's necessary here?"

"I'll lay him out, if that's what you mean. As for the little one, she'll need some black clothing." She puts her hand on my shoulder.

"Won't wear black." I don't want to be made into a witch.

"Your days of 'Won't do this,' 'Won't do that' are over," announces Ursel, looking pleased. "No one to baby you now. Girls in orphanages do as they're told without backchat. And they grow up fast."

"For pity's sake, Ursel," says the witch, "no need to be so callous. Her father's just died."

"Papa isn't dead."

"As a doornail," says Ursel. "No good pretending otherwise."

"Stupid fat witch." She raises her hand and I back away. "My papa isn't dead."

Then Lottie asks what we'll do now Papa is dead. Who will look after us? I shake her. She asks again and I pull her hair. "He isn't dead." Lottie starts arguing. She says Papa loves Mama better than me and he's gone away to find her. "Papa isn't dead," I shout. "He isn't, he isn't." Lottie keeps telling me that Papa's dead and we are all alone. She won't stop, even when I hold her by the feet and swing her at the wall, so I scream to cover the sound of her voice and keep screaming until everyone in the room has their hands over their ears except Lottie and me. Uncle Hraben bends down to talk to me. I scratch his face. I run round the room, spitting and yelling very bad words. Lottie's right: now everyone's gone away—Mama, Papa, Greet—and there are only nasty people left. I hit Witch Schwitter and kick Metzger's legs. Herta tries to hold my arms behind my back. Ursel grabs me by the hair and slaps me again. I bite her hand and spit out the blood.

The witch raises her wand and taps me.

It is suddenly very quiet. I am shaking from head to toe. I feel like a blancmange not quite set.

"That's enough," she says, and pushes me into the other room. "Sit down, and if you want to talk or cry, do it more quietly. Ursel will bring you warm milk and honey. I want you to drink every drop. Afterwards you can have a little nap."

"That one's a bloody handful," someone says. It's Metzger. I can tell by his crackly voice. "Still—" He laughs. "I dare say someone will enjoy taming her when the time comes."

Uncle Hraben laughs, too. "Oh, yes."

"The child's backwards. Abnormal. She'll never fit into proper society. She needs putting away."

I think that's Herta talking, but Witch Schwitter has taken out a comb and is pretending to tidy my hair when really she's casting a sleeping spell. When I wake up, it's getting dark and this isn't my bed. Green curtains hang at the window and I can smell polish. There's a big cross facing me with Jesus nailed on it. Below his feet is a statue of Mother Mary, all in blue, beside a box of candles. I'm lying under a quilt, still wearing my clothes, and Lottie is tucked in beside me. I push her away.

People are talking somewhere nearby. I recognize Witch Schwitter's voice, and Uncle Hraben's, but there's another voice of a deep bear-growly man, as well as a lady who bites her sentences into little bits and spits them out in the wrong order. I creep onto the landing to look down, but it's all shadowy below and I can't see anyone. The words squirm out of the darkness like imps in a horrible dream.

"Impossible," the growly man is saying. "Totally impossible. The behavior described to me suggests some mental aberration approaching mania. Psychiatric treatment is indicated."

"Crazy, you mean. We guessed that." That's nasty Ursel's voice.

Growly man coughs. "I believe she could be a suitable subject for convulsive therapy—some interesting work being done in Erlangen—but of course that's not my field of expertise. As it is, the child would need to be kept in total isolation, and we simply don't have the facilities."

"Lack of control. Disruptive. Other girls. No."

"She's had a terrible shock," says Witch Schwitter. "Surely that needs taking into consideration."

"It's not simply natural distress at the death of her father," puts in Uncle Hraben. "There's more to it. According to Johanna—*Aufseherin* Langefeld—the child discovered her mother in the act of committing suicide."

Ursel snorts. "Madness runs in the family, then."

"*Frau* Richter, please." Uncle Hraben is almost shouting. "Surely, as *Frau* Schwitter says, allowance should be—"

"Yes, yes, we mustn't discount the effects of grief—"

"No self-control. Disastrous. Learned early. Essential."

"However, I understand that Krysta regularly exhibits antisocial behavior, and I regret that an orphanage isn't the place for her."

"Where, then?" asks the witch.

There's a long silence, then someone pushes back a chair.

"Stick her with the other undesirables," says Ursel.

"Not that." Witch Schwitter sounds horrified. "She's just a little girl. And Krysta is such a pretty child, too. Isn't there anyone to take her in?"

Behind me, Lottie shouts that nobody wants us. We will have to live in the forest and eat berries and make clothes out of leaves. When the snow comes we'll creep into a cave like bears.

"Wait a minute," says Uncle Hraben. "Perhaps I could be appointed the child's guardian or—"

"That wouldn't be appropriate." A new voice, high and clear: I can't tell if it's a man or a woman. "Particularly as there's also the question of blood. It seems her great-grandmother was an . . . *Untermensch*."

"She was a princess," I shriek, picking up a vase and throwing it over the banister. "And you are all *dumme Schweinehunde*. I hate you."

I run back into the bedroom to pick up Lottie and hold her tight. It's her idea to light candles and set fire to the curtains.

Seven

t seemed to Josef, on waking from another restless night, that he had been wandering in the deep, dark forest of fairy tales, going everywhere but ending up nowhere. Or almost nowhere . . . Aspects of the fractured narrative contained material wholly unsuitable for the bedtime stories of children. In his dreams, writhing in luxuriant foliage or tangled in folds of flesh-colored velvet, his body flagrantly expressed all those secret desires that could never be spoken. Mathilde repeatedly turned from him. Lilie had not, and they lay together among the fragrant spring flowers of a forest clearing.

The cold sausage and tepid coffee of early morning tempered his memories. For a brief time he dwelled on the other occupants of his dreams: his five children filing past the scene of his debauchery, sometimes as infants, sometimes as adults, loitering only to stare in their adolescent forms; colleagues retreating, advancing, with mouths pursed, eyes averted; his father, Hebraic features enormously exaggerated, shaking an admonishing finger, threatening to beat him for the third time in his life; *Großmutter* wielding her wooden spoon of office; and a drifting white shadow exuding melancholy that might have been his mother. And Lilie? Even in her state of abandonment Lilie looked them all straight in the eye and continued to smile. Josef had clung to her lack of shame like a drowning man who clings to a straw through which, even as he sinks below the water into the blackest mud, he imagines it might still be possible to breathe. Now he thought dismally of the creatures of Midrashic literature: *mazakim*, night demons, succubi, fairfaced without exception—

Josef pulled himself up sharply. These were unsuitable thoughts for a modern, educated man, a scientist and an innovator. Thrusting away the delights of his nocturnal fantasies, he reapplied himself to consideration of his patient's medical condition. Lilie's silence, her reluctance to answer questions—unless it was with nonsense or snippets of homespun philosophy—together with the lack of background knowledge beyond the scant facts relating to her discovery, had initially presented an enthralling challenge. Now his inability to move the treatment forward had him pacing the floor and tugging at his beard. With any illness, as with a crime—and perhaps here one followed on from the other—some form of elimination and deduction was called for. Josef smiled. In that, he was not so very different to Conan Doyle's famous detective, in whom Mathilde took such a keen interest. The smile died. He would not think of his wife. Nevertheless, even Sherlock Holmes needed some practical evidence on which to base his deductive reasoning. Here there was nothing, barring the signs of assault and the allusion to a monstrous man, possibly imagined, certainly exaggerated, for how could loveliness like hers be retained where it had been confronted with the trappings of evil? But Lilie hadn't simply dropped from the ether. Of course, if she came from a privileged background she might have been kept at home, her hysteria concealed from the world. Certain factors led him to believe the latter was unlikely, unless she was a young and unfortunate wife. Nevertheless, whether she'd lived in a great house or a modest apartment, been cloistered in a nunnery or a prison—yes, even if she'd been confined in that accursed club—someone in Vienna must know something.

"*Etwas Neues kann man nur finden, wenn man das Alte kennt,*" Joseph murmured. *One can find something new only if one knows at least something of the old.* Yes, it was true. Benjamin would have to redouble his efforts, continue to be his master's eyes and ears in discovering it. Josef was still unwilling to face the world and even more unwilling to analyze why this should be, simply telling himself there would be too many questions if it was known he'd returned alone from a vacation so eagerly anticipated; too many knowing looks. He regarded the breakfast table with distaste and wondered if he could disguise himself well enough to slink, eyes cast down, into Café Museum. Perhaps not: part of the pleasure of sitting in Adolf Loos's new coffeehouse was open perusal of the clean bright design, inside and out—almost aesthetic negation, considering the flamboyance of neighboring Secession buildings—together with the expectation of being in the company of Vienna's foremost artists and intellectuals. Josef stabbed at a slice of sausage and gloomily resigned himself to breakfasting at home.

When the worst of his indigestion had subsided, he went in search of Lilie but found only Gudrun, sifting through piles of old newspapers and pasting cuttings into a large scrapbook, the latest of several volumes. This pastime had occupied her for as many years as he could remember, and her eclectic tastes were a quiet family joke. Pages cut from old comic books jostled for space with religious texts, with *Partezettel*—little could be more fascinating than affectionate obituaries of the loathed departed—and with extravagantly illustrated seed packets, among die-cut scraps featuring cherubs, posies, and mottoes, sentimental girls clutching spaniels, or boys with tops and hoops. Many of his children's youthful drawings—so innocently observant—were pasted here: Mathilde grown comfortably plump; his erstwhile protégé, Sigmund Freud, hardly visible through a cloud of cigar smoke; and poor, bent *Großvater*, bearing a painful resemblance to a croquet hoop. There was even one of himself walking with his good friend, Ernst Mach, proceeded by dramatically jutting beards, hands gesticulating as they discussed some knotty philosophical problem relating the sense of equilibrium in society as a whole to their independent discoveries of how an individual's sense of balance functions by means of fluid within the semicircular canals. Josef remembered that afternoon well. Dora also, no doubt, for she'd ventured too close to a swarm of ferocious bees. Poor girl, though one torture quickly followed upon another—it had taken hours to remove the venomous stingers and give her peace from the poison—stoical to the last, she'd not uttered a sound.

Josef craned his neck to examine on the current double page a snippet of advertisement—some marketing puffery for furniture polish, which showed two trim maidservants shining the face of a beaming full moon—almost obscuring a flyer for the fifth exhibition of the Vienna Secession. Facing it was a reprint of a Max and Moritz cartoon, sprung from the pen of Wilhelm Busch, a man whose intellect Josef considered severely underrated, though his witticisms were fast becoming adages. Ah, the wisdom of the court jester. *"Vater werden ist nicht schwer, Vater sein dagegen sehr,"* quipped Busch—*It's easy to become a father, but being one is rather harder.*

All this, however, served as light relief, for Gudrun's main interest was the compilation of lurid press reports, of snide tittle-tattle about Lueger's Amazon Corps, his so-called harem of female supporters, of intrigues, cases of bigamy, scandals, murders, violent robberies, rapes, beatings, and stabbings, the details occasionally of such beastliness that Mathilde had once forbidden the children to leaf through the pages.

"I see you're still attending to your barometer," he said with a smile.

Gudrun ceased shuffling her findings to glance up at him. "You may laugh, *Herr Doktor*, but within these pages lies a great deal of information about the temperature of Vienna. And it's simmering, I tell you. It's simmering. Heaven help us all if it should ever come to a full rolling boil."

"Indeed," said Josef, replacing the smile with what he hoped was an expression of grave interest. Gudrun turned back a few pages.

"For example, this poor woman, Marie Kindl, who killed herself—"

"Ah, yes, last year, suspended from the window of a *Riesenrad* carriage. A dreadful thing to do in a place where young families—"

Gudrun silenced him with a frown. "When *Frau* Kindl committed suicide by hanging herself from the Ferris wheel she was drawing attention to the depths of her family's poverty, *Herr Doktor*. An act of desperation, I'm sure you'll agree. The rich get richer while the poor get poorer in this city. While some can afford to fritter money on pleasure rides, others have no bread to fill their children's mouths. No good will come of it."

"Indeed," Josef said uncomfortably. "However, Vienna has various benevolent societies—"

"Simmering, I say, and the fire being steadily stoked. If what some of us fear comes to pass, then even respectable households such as this won't avoid the consequences. Especially now that we've opened our doors to trouble." She lowered her voice. "I've seen men loitering in this very street. Oh, yes. There's been a man standing at the corner watching this house for the last twenty-four hours. I swear somebody followed me to the market. And last night I found someone lurking at the side entrance. I went out with the poker to see him off—Benjamin nowhere to be found when he was needed, as usual—and the fellow pretended he'd been sheltering from the rain. Nonsense, of course, a grown man frightened of a light shower. I'm sure there were other things on his mind." Gudrun paused, her mouth twisting with distaste. "Perhaps he was one of Lilie's former . . . *acquaintances.*"

Josef winced at her scathing tone. "And where is Lilie?"

"Picking beans. It's taken her three times as long as any normal person. If she was *my* kitchen maid—"

Josef frowned. "But Lilie isn't a servant."

Gudrun drew herself up. "Indeed, no. Some people don't know the meaning of hard work. Of course it doesn't help that the young fool's dancing attendance on her, as usual."

"Benjamin?" Feeling a sick lurch in the pit of his stomach, Josef crossed to the open door and peered down the garden, shielding his eyes from the sun's glare. "I can't see them." He was about to step outside when Gudrun laughed and muttered something. "I beg your pardon?"

"Climbed up the *Bohnenstängel,* I dare say."

"Beanstalk?" He stared at her. "What on earth do you mean?"

"'Jack and the Beanstalk'—it's a fairy tale, a bedtime favorite of Johannes when he was small—in which an idle child climbs up his magic beanstalk into a world where normal rules don't apply. It seems some folk will believe any fairy tales Lilie chooses to spin, so why not that one?"

Josef drew himself up. "*Frau* Gschtaltner, you forget yourself."

Gudrun lifted her chin and met his outraged glare. "I speak as I find, *Herr Doktor.* Things are not as they were in this household."

"I wish to see Lilie as soon as she returns. Kindly convey my message to her." He turned on his heel, biting back a torrent of offensive words.

. . .

HALF AN HOUR LATER, a tight-lipped Gudrun rapped at his door, flung it open, and addressing Josef with excessive formality, indicated with a curt jerk of her chin that Lilie should enter.

"Come along. Come along. We haven't got all day."

"Good morning, Lilie." He waited while Gudrun settled herself, noting that beyond taking out her thimble—a gift from the children, with tiny needlepoint roses under a glass band at the rim, brandished like a reproach—she made no pretense of working. That done, he turned to his patient, who was standing motionless before him, fresh and sweet in a wide-collared linen blouse. Josef recognized it as belonging to Margarethe, his eldest daughter, worn when she could have been no more than thirteen. Perhaps Dora had inherited it. Maybe she'd even been wearing it during that terrible afternoon. Such things stick in the memory. At any rate, it served to show how small Lilie was, almost as small as Bertha, but more slightly formed, daintier, and . . . *fey*, yes, a good word: fey, fairy-like, not of this world, a creature of the imagination. Murmuring pleasantries as he gestured towards a seat, Josef saw that the blouse formed part of a sailor suit of the sort once made popular in London by the empire-building English queen, who'd invariably dressed her young offspring in variations on the seafaring theme, presumably a nod to the mariners who underpinned her power. He also observed that Lilie was wearing buttoned boots, which seemed several sizes too large judging by her awkward walk. Today her cheeks were flushed, her eyes sparkled, though she kept her face expressionless, and Josef's spirits plummeted as he considered what had so enlivened her.

"You look happier this morning, Lilie." The words had to be forced past his teeth. "Did you enjoy being outside in the sunshine?"

Lilie said nothing. She stared, unblinking, at the wheezing clock.

"I'm told you were picking beans," Josef persisted. "A fine crop this year, I believe." A small shiver ran up his spine as he remembered that in classical times beans were a protection against ghosts and specters; at the Roman feast of the Lemuria the head of the household was obliged to throw beans over his shoulder to redeem his family. "Green beans," he murmured, almost sure the beans that disempowered the lemures were black and wondering why it should matter. "Are there more to come?"

The girl didn't reply. Gudrun clicked her tongue with annoyance. After a moment Josef rose from his seat.

"I need to examine the wounds on your neck, Lilie. Be so good as to undo your top buttons."

Gudrun also rose, moving closer, stumbling in her haste. "Get on with it, girl. Wake up. Do what the *Doktor* says." And when Lilie made no effort to comply, she tugged impatiently at the buttons herself. Lilie flinched and her fists clenched so tightly that her knuckles gleamed white, but throughout the examination she continued to stare towards the laboring old clock.

There was no danger of infection; the cuts had healed. Josef feared they would leave a scar, a shame, though he foresaw that such a blemish might only draw attention to the perfection of the rest. He gently turned Lilie's head, noting that the bruises below her ears were now hardly visible . . . and stiffened as his eyes were drawn to another mark, small, new, livid. A foul taste rose in Josef's mouth and he swallowed hard, fearing this was a mark of passion, but the tender curve of her neck, the soft golden curls clustered at her nape, were so childishly innocent his suspicions melted away. He teased her collar back into place and dropped his hands.

"An insect bite," he said aloud, and thought again of Dora's torment. "With such delicate skin, it pays to take precautions in the open air." Lilie glanced at him but said nothing. "A light scarf, perhaps?" A gauzy affair in rose-colored silk, one that he'd bought for Mathilde in Venice, sprang to mind. It was a pretty thing, but as with so many of his gifts, his wife had never worn it: too overt a statement of femininity, possibly. It would look well on this fragile young woman.

"The beans could have been picked in half the time," complained Gudrun, "without the chattering and laughing."

"Sunshine and laughter are often the best medicine," Josef chided her. "As you've said many times."

"Huh," said Gudrun, returning to her workbasket.

Josef also reseated himself, conscious of her smoldering resentment. If Vienna was simmering, then so was she. It wasn't hard to find the cause, though it was odious to make comparisons between the two females. Remembering certain incidents in the nursery, he flinched at the thought of Gudrun's rage unleashed and wondered how Mathilde managed her employee's bad moods. "We must talk later about finding some extra help in the house," he said in an effort to mollify her. "Clearly there is too much work for one." Gudrun, turning the thimble between her fingers, her attention ostensibly fixed on the minuscule petit-point stitches, barely acknowledged his words. Josef allowed himself a mental shrug, focused on Lilie, and tried a new approach, though in truth it was old ground he was covering.

"Is there anyone you'd like us to contact, Lilie? Someone must be anxious to know you're safe and well." Lilie didn't answer. "Talk to me," he said, speaking more forcefully. "Tell me who we should notify. Where does your family live? Distant relatives? Friends? There must be somebody."

"Answer!" roared Gudrun. "You chatter incessantly when you're with that fool of a boy, so have the courtesy—"

"I won't talk while the old woman's here," said Lilie very quietly.

Gudrun gasped. "Old woman?"

"And why is that?" Josef inquired.

"She mocks me. Every word I say to you is ridiculed later. You should have heard her this morning—*'Make sure you return that knife to the rack, Fräulein Namenlos,'* she said. *"'We don't want to retrieve it from the monster's chest later, do we now?'"* Lilie had managed a fair imitation of Gudrun's accent. Now she sat in silence with downcast eyes.

"I see." Josef tugged at his beard.

"You believe her?" Gudrun demanded, scarlet with outrage. "You think that of me after all the years I've served the Breuer family?"

Josef cleared his throat. "My dear woman, no one doubts your loyalty—"

"I won't say another word until she goes," Lilie murmured without looking up.

Josef could hardly conceal his delight. "Perhaps, *Frau* Gschtaltner, in the circumstances—"

Gudrun stood and marched towards the door with her head held high. It shut with a sharp click, and Josef waited until he heard the sound of retreating footsteps.

"Now, Lilie, there's just you and me. Everything that passes between us will remain confidential." He hesitated. "As between priest and penitent."

"But I've done nothing that requires absolution."

"Ah," said Josef, picking up on her understanding of individual Confession, "then you are of the Roman Catholic faith?" Lilie shook her head.

"I know of it." She pushed back her sleeve, displaying the inked digits as if to remind him of her renunciation of her humanity. "But I don't need such rites."

"You have no conscience?"

Lilie shrugged. "Does your clock? Does the gramophone? Or an automobile?"

Josef rearranged his pens, squared up the blotter. "And what of other feelings, Lilie—love, loneliness, longing?" A lump rose in his throat. When no answer came, he added: "What about hate, or anger, or despair?" Lilie still didn't answer, and with his emotions back under control, he peered over his spectacles at the girl who was staring into the middle distance, abstracted, as though she were listening to far-off music, or eavesdropping on an elfin conversation inaudible to him. "Lilie," he barked, "you were angry with Gudrun, weren't you?"

"She's a bully."

"Oh." Josef hesitated. "She doesn't ill-treat you, surely?"

"Are you asking if she strikes me? Not yet. She doesn't need to. She pinches and pushes. Her elbows are sharp, and so is her tongue."

"Oh."

"Perhaps I'll kill her. Afterwards."

"Now Lilie—"

"Gudrun's a weakling at heart." Lilie's voice was quiet and matter-of-fact. "Killing her would be easy. A few seconds is all I'd need."

"Really, that's enough—"

Lilie looked pensive. "Perhaps I'd enjoy it. Some do."

Was that a clue? Josef leaned forward eagerly. "Some of whom, Lilie? Tell me where." After a moment he repeated the questions, but her eyes had closed, her expression had turned abstracted. It was almost as if she could at will detach herself from the present and slip, like some medieval wanderer, into the otherworld. Or was it subterfuge? This was so like Bertha: he'd never been entirely sure she wasn't indulging in amateur dramatics. What if Lilie was her student? This train of thought brought back his previous concerns. What if the pair of them were colluding in some act of revenge? "I did nothing," Josef whispered. As for his fear of a conspiracy, sooner or later Lilie would give herself away. Deciding to ignore the girl's murderous fantasies, he rapped on the desk. "Lilie, concentrate, please. We were talking about your dislike of Gudrun."

She blinked and nodded. "I've known women like Gudrun before."

"Tell me about them. Tell me about what they did to you."

"Nothing. Silly beasts. All bark and no teeth."

"Were they connected to your monster?"

"Perhaps," she said dreamily, pulling at the ribbon hanging from her collar, "since they all go, *chop, chop, chop*, hundreds of goats and sheep, one after the other, into his charnel house. You can smell their blood and smoke on the wind."

"Explain," he demanded, his voice rising again. Josef scratched his head. Wherever she'd been incarcerated it wasn't a religious institution. And no prison doled out judicial executions on the scale she was suggesting. Of course, a century ago she might have been describing the Narrenturm when it still functioned as the madhouse. *Ah, of course that fit. . . .* In those days the mentally ill were treated as less than human . . . as dangerous lunatics, chained like savage beasts to the walls, with nothing but straw mats to sleep upon. And who knew what threats of death were heaped on their poor, befuddled heads? Perhaps such institutions still existed in some quiet backwater of the provinces. "Explain," he repeated, this time more gently. Lilie clasped her hands.

> *"Ene, tene, mone, mei,*
> *Pastor, lone, bone, strei,*
> *Ene, fune, herke, berke,*
> *Wer? Wie? Wo? Was?*

"You're next."

"You have a pretty singing voice, my dear," Josef said. He frowned.

"Eeny, meeny, miny, moe"—what was the significance of a children's counting-out game?

> *"Two little sinners left their work undone,*
> *One paid the price, and then there was one.*
> *One little sinner left all alone . . ."*

Lilie's voice tailed off. She turned in her chair and looked straight at him. A very small smile appeared. "Don't let's talk about that, *Herr Doktor.*"

Josef blinked. He was almost sure . . . but, no, it couldn't be. And yet . . . Had Lilie really batted her lashes at him?

"I'm told you're the cleverest man in Vienna."

Josef smoothed his mustache. "Well, I—"

"And you mend broken souls."

"I wouldn't put it quite like that." He frowned, thinking that what she'd just said was as good a way as any to describe the unraveling of patients' multifarious emotional pains. Josef straightened. "Lilie, we must—"

"Help me, *Herr Doktor.* I must cleanse the Earth of this fiend. It would be the greatest service to mankind you could ever undertake."

"Lilie—" Josef gave a small laugh, but the rejection stuck in his throat as she rose from her seat and placed one slender hand on his.

"And save your beloved descendants from terrible misfortune."

They both looked down. Josef compared the sagging skin of the age-blotched opisthenar resting on his desk—for it was hard in this moment to own it as the back of his own hand—with her firm flesh, her perfectly formed nails. He sighed, oppressed by a moment of defeat, for a man is old for far longer than he is young. Perhaps he'd become youthful again in last night's dream. He glanced at the door, alerted by a small sound, and then became insensible to everything but the fact that she'd moved away to sink gracefully back into her chair. He casually covered the loathsome flesh where her hand had lain, waiting for the moment when it could be surreptitiously pressed against his cheek. Suddenly very tired, he decided to let Lilie elaborate on her violent preoccupations; after all, spinning stories had brought Bertha relief.

"Very well, Lilie. What do you propose?" Josef wondered how he could continue treating her after the rest of his family returned. She couldn't stay here. Perhaps he'd take a small apartment for her, somewhere fashionable, with a young maidservant—fresh up from the country and not too bright—to act as chaperone. Not that a visit from an eminent physician should cause tongues to wag. He moistened his lips. As with Bertha, a course of massage might be beneficial.

"We must kill him now, before he gets too big."

"Exactly." Josef blinked, and replayed her words. "He's small, you say. Like a *Kobold*? An imp?"

"No," said Lilie, with a touch of impatience. "Like a boy."

He stared at her. "You mean the monster is the size of a boy, or *is* a boy?" His mind raced. Were they dealing with an abusive brother rather than the father? It wasn't unknown.

"He's a boy now," she said sharply.

"Indeed. And does he have a name?" asked Josef, interested to see if any details of her story had changed.

"I told you. It's Adi."

"So you did." Josef nodded, glancing at his notes. If the monster was a brother, then the diminutive made more sense. "And the rest of his name?" He looked up, hoping Lilie would hereby supply her patronymic. "Come, Lilie, he must have a family name."

"*Herr* Wolf."

"*Herr Wolf*—is that his real name?"

"Yes," said Lilie with a small frown.

"Good." There were many families with the surname Wolf in and around Vienna. With a start Josef recalled the composer Hugo Wolf, said to suffer from mental instability. No, it was more than that. The man had insisted on being institutionalized; there were rumors of syphilitic insanity.

"No," she said a moment later, terminating that line of inquiry. "It's not. I remember now. His real name is Gröfraz."

"Ah." It sounded like another nickname. "Any others?"

"Some people call him the Manitou. It's an evil spirit."

Josef laid down his pen. "How did he hurt you, Lilie?" he asked quietly. In response, she hummed a familiar snatch of tune, moving her fingers in time.

"Have you collected the musical box yet?"

"I beg your pardon?"

"A Stella, isn't it? For Margarethe."

"No . . . *yes*, that is, it's still being engraved." He stared, confused. It was a secret. A surprise. "Who told you about this?"

"*Geschichten aus dem Wienerwald.*"

"But—" Josef stopped abruptly. "*Tales from the Vienna Woods.*" Exactly so. The clockmaker must have talked. He'd think about that later. "You were telling me about the monster."

"No. We need to talk about how we're going to kill him."

"Very well."

"It doesn't take long to kick someone to death—" Lilie stopped in the face of Josef's involuntary gasp before continuing: "*Squish, squash.* But the boots need to be very large and very heavy." She glanced at her tiny feet.

"Lilie!"

"Yes?" Her expression was so sweetly puzzled that Josef found it hard to believe she'd uttered such a speech.

"Lilie, you can't have seen anything so dreadful. It isn't a normal part of life."

"Isn't it?"

"These are peaceful times, my dear." She'd closed her eyes, wilting like a flower, and Josef hastily brought their interview to a close. "That's enough for this morning, Lilie. Out you go into the sunshine. And no more kitchen work today. Rest. Relax. We'll talk again later."

As she left, Josef jotted down the girl's suggested method for killing her abuser. Such bloodthirsty ideas could only have come from sensational novels. It might be as well to curtail her reading material severely. That, in turn, presupposed that he'd play a part in Lilie's future, and he sat for a while picturing himself visiting her in a small apartment somewhere off the Ringstrasse. Some care was needed, for Sigmund took a daily constitutional walk around the Ring, and Mathilde didn't need further ammunition. With that in mind, proper case notes must be kept. Josef filled his pen and wiped the nib, tapping his teeth with the barrel, resisting the urge to chew the end like a schoolboy.

Fräulein Lilie X

There has been considerable improvement in the patient's physical condition. She has a poor appetite, but this may change now that a modicum of exercise is being taken. The patient appears contented, in spite of wildly extravagant claims during informal conversations relating to personal observation of murders or executions. She appears to possess a curious detachment from the reality of death and her own humanity. As yet, no treatment has been prescribed. Some tension appears to exist in the back and shoulders. A course of massage may be advisable.

He jumped, and his pen skidded across the page in response to a furious knocking upon his door. Fearing some calamity, Josef ran to open it, but Gudrun was already in the room, red-faced and breathing hard, in a state of great excitement.

"Look at this." She flapped a thin column of newsprint in his face. "Was I right? I was. No more mysteries. That girl's an escaped lunatic. We're not safe in our beds. Here, read for yourself. I came as soon as I spotted it. Well, go on."

"You'd better tell me," Josef suggested, since Gudrun made no move to relinquish her hold on the paper. She took a deep breath.

"Last year. In Lambach—"

"Lambach?" It was a small market town in Upper Austria, a major stop on the old salt route. Josef remembered visiting the place many years ago with his father, but couldn't recall why such a long journey had been made, only that an ancient Benedictine monastery decorated with broken-armed crosses dwarfed the other buildings. It contained wall paintings dating from the early twelfth century reputed to illustrate the biblical Jesus being expelled from the synagogue in Nazareth, though to his young eyes the beauty of the frescoes had diminished any hint of an anti-Semitic message. Now that he thought about it, they could only have been in Lambach because of the illness of some relative or a friend of his father. That would explain why the many representations of healing in the frescoes had taken on such weighty significance: St. Andrew advising—

"At the *Volksschule*," Gudrun added impatiently. "A young woman attacked a small child for no reason. She tried to strangle the little innocent, which is exactly what that Lilie creature did to our poor, dear cat."

"How is the cat?" inquired Josef, crossing the room to straighten his father's portrait. Gudrun followed him.

"Who knows?" she said carelessly. "It'll turn up when it's hungry. The point is—it's her. The crazy woman: it's Lilie."

"Ah, and what does the article say became of this woman after the attack?"

"They locked her in the madhouse—"

"We're safe enough, then."

"Not so," said Gudrun grimly. "Ten days ago, she escaped—"

Josef laughed. "And walked for several days, naked and wounded. Come, come, Gudrun, this is nonsense. Only a fool could think that way. Your dislike of the girl is clouding your reason."

"Nonsense, is it?" Her mouth tightened. "So now I'm a fool."

"I apologize." Already Josef regretted his choice of words. "I phrased that badly. But please understand that I have a responsibility to Lilie. After all, I took her on as a patient."

Gudrun carefully folded the slip of newspaper. "And you won't even consider that she might be the escaped lunatic?"

"Of course not. Lilie's a gentle creature. In spite of her curious way of expressing herself, she could no more attack a child than fly."

Gudrun drew herself up. "I disagree. She's a devious and cunning wench, a liar, constantly playacting and capable of anything. All men are fair game to such a female. She's certainly got you and Benjamin wound round her little finger. Fluttering her lashes. Touching your hand." Her color darkened and she looked away.

"Is that so?" Casting his mind back, Josef suspected she'd spied on his entire conversation with Lilie. He'd been meaning to get that door catch mended for months. "I wish to see Benjamin immediately," he said coldly. "Ask him to bring tools. It seems some repair to the door is necessary. As for your accusations, *Frau* Gschtaltner, I repeat: they are unfounded. Perhaps Lilie is not the only one suffering delusions."

"Is this my return for all these years of service to *Frau Doktor* Breuer, to the Breuer household, to the children? To be mocked like an old woman in her dotage? To come second to some chit of a girl brought in off the streets?"

"That was not my intention."

Gudrun wasn't listening. "So be it. But I have responsibilities, too. I don't often take my afternoon off, there being so much work, but today I will. And we'll soon see whether or not my suspicions are nonsense."

"Where are you going?" demanded Josef, but she pushed past him without another word, holding the folded newspaper before her like a talisman.

THE SMELL OF FISH well past its prime came at Benjamin like a smack on the nose, even before he crossed the threshold. In the kitchen corner, Lilie stood looking down at a pair of large brown trout, dull of eye and oozing slime. Their stomachs had been hacked open; blue-gray entrails spewed onto the chopping board and she stirred them with the point of her knife.

"There should be a golden ring. Where's the ring?"

"What's that?" enquired Benjamin, taking the knife from her hand.

Lilie continued to peer at the slowly spreading pile of guts. "If only we can find the ring, then everything will come right. I told you before—nobody can fight Fate."

"Go outside, Lilie," Benjamin said, glancing at her pale face. "Get some fresh air." As the girl slipped out into the sunshine, he turned on Gudrun. "I thought the master said no unpleasant jobs."

"Unpleasant? Preparing some nice salmon for our dinner? Not that she's making a very good job of it."

"Perhaps she needed instruction."

"In a simple task like cleaning fish? Don't talk nonsense."

"Apart from anything else, these aren't fresh," declared Benjamin. "They stink to high heaven. Where did you get them from?"

Gudrun shrugged. "Someone came to the door. I haven't got time to go trotting backwards and forwards to the market every day. And why should I, with two youngsters in the house?" She lifted the lid of a pan and peered at the simmering contents.

"I'll bury these." Benjamin scraped the offensive mess into a basin. "You can't serve muck like that to the *Doktor*, and I'm certainly not eating them." The pan lid was replaced with a resounding clatter. Gudrun faced him, arms akimbo.

"Is that so, Lord High-and-Mighty? Running the kitchen now, are you?"

"If I was, Lilie wouldn't be given the nastiest jobs . . ."

Gudrun's anger seemed to drain away. She laughed. "So poor Cinderella's got you both jumping to her defense. Perhaps the two of you will have to jump a little higher sooner than you think."

Benjamin scowled. "What's that supposed to mean?"

"Never mind. When you've finished poking your nose into things that don't concern you, the front-door brass needs polishing."

"I've got potatoes to lift. Why can't you—" He stopped, noticing that Gudrun was unusually well dressed beneath the huge, somewhat grubby apron. "What's going on?"

"See to the door," said Gudrun. "Here's the salt and flour." She seized a flagon. "Out of my way. I'll mix it with just enough vinegar to make a paste. After you've applied that, you'll need plenty of elbow grease. When it comes to the nameplate, *Frau Doktor* Breuer likes to see her face in it." She glanced at the clock. "And if there should happen to be any visitors, ring the bell and show them into the hall."

"What visitors?"

Gudrun's mouth shut like a trap. Since nothing could induce her to say more, Benjamin took the proffered cleaning materials with a bad grace and stationed himself on the front steps. This was women's work, and although he approached the task in his usual manner—attempting to carry it out cheerfully to the best of his ability—he was acutely conscious of a pair of young maids giggling and nudging each other as they passed. The hastily contrived brass polish did little to shift the blotched veil that was the forerunner of verdigris clinging to each letter of Breuer's name and title with malicious tenacity. Benjamin swore softly as he gouged and scraped and rubbed. His thoughts revolved around small matters of domestic revenge before drifting into a future so illustrious that all such grievances were forgotten.

The sound of a throat being cleared behind him made Benjamin jump violently, spilling the remainder of Gudrun's vile compound. It spread over the step like the dirty white droppings of a giant pigeon, reaching almost to the toes of the visitor's well-polished boots. On raising his eyes, Benjamin was dismayed to recognize the sharp-featured policeman who'd sent him on his way after the evening spent drinking with his old friend Hugo Besser in Leopoldstadt. At least there was no sign of the grim-faced giant who'd loomed over him so menacingly; instead the weasel was accompanied by a stout young man in spectacles and another who was short and red-haired with a multitude of freckles, hardly older than Benjamin and awkward in his blatantly new uniform.

"*Inspektor*," Benjamin muttered. "What can I do for you?"

"*Chefinspektor*," corrected the stout young man, his expression severe. "*Chefinspektor* Kirchmann." He took out a pocket watch and nodded approval. "We're here to see *Frau* Gschtaltner and *Herr Doktor* Breuer, precisely on time, as arranged. Kindly announce us."

His superior raised a neat little paw. "One moment, Brunn, if you please. Young Benjamin here and I are old friends. Perhaps he can tell us something about this mysterious girl."

"What girl would that be?" inquired Benjamin, attempting to look profoundly puzzled. "Ah," he said, as if suddenly enlightened, "you mean *Hedda*, the Grossmann's missing scullery maid. No mystery there, as far as I know. The cook said she went home. Didn't like Vienna. Missed the pigs, I dare say."

Kirchmann narrowed his eyes but made no comment. Stepping over the spilled mess, he stationed himself pointedly before the door, and, as instructed, Benjamin tugged at the bell before ushering the visitors inside. The *Chefinspektor* about-faced on the threshold, thrusting out an arm to exclude the youngest officer.

"You, Stumpf, will remain outside and observe. And perhaps with a little more questioning our young friend will recall the *Fräulein* in question." Kirchmann turned away in response to Gudrun's effusive welcome. "Ah, *Frau* Gschtaltner, we meet again. Is *Herr Doktor*—"

Stumpf twitched with annoyance as the door closed in his face with a dull thud. He drew himself up but still hardly reached to Benjamin's shoulder.

"I've got work to do," announced Benjamin, seizing his cleaning rag.

"So have I," said Stumpf, taking out a notebook. He smirked. "I thought doorsteps and brass polishing were the scullery maid's job."

"And I always understood collecting gossip was left to old grannies," retorted Benjamin, observing with silent mirth that the ginger-haired officer was now standing in the puddle of spilled cleaning compound, and that where the stuff stubbornly refused to shift tarnish on brass plate, it made short work of boot polish.

. . .

JOSEF WAS SURPRISED when Gudrun ushered Lilie into his presence, insisting the girl had asked to see him . . . especially as it soon became obvious she'd done no such thing. Not that Lilie resisted—at least there was a crumb of comfort there, and he welcomed it—but her air of bewilderment, the sense that she'd been snatched from another place holding her interest more completely, was evidence enough. A small frisson—of apprehension rather than fear—spiraled the length of his spine. This was Gudrun's doing; something new was afoot. So far he was at a loss concerning its nature, but in her present mood any departure from usual practice warranted investigation.

However, such tedious concerns must wait. Lilie was here. And since she'd come without being summoned, this seemed an appropriate time to broach the subject of therapeutic massage. Josef moistened his lips. He flexed his fingers under cover of the desk and avoided looking at his father's portrait while mentally asserting that this discomfiture was unwarranted. His intention was simply to hasten the healing process and was in no way self-serving. From his experience with Bertha . . . and with others . . . Josef knew the laying on of hands had a profound effect on the emotional state of the fairer sex, intensifying the patient–physician bond in ways that were below and beyond mere speech. Hence, he continued with his methods no matter what calumny was heaped upon massage by disdainful colleagues—who likened it to the sweaty procedures of the gymnasium—aware that it had been practiced for more than two millennia, its efficacy recognized by Hippocrates, the father of medicine, and by the ancient physician Claudius Galen, who wrote extensively on its benefits in *De Sanitate Tuenda*.

But in spite of any amount of self-justification Josef continued to struggle with a sense of unworthiness that tangled his words and thickened his tongue. He'd hardly got further than generalizations when the clatter of boots on the hall tiles provided him with an excuse to abandon his efforts. He rose quickly and strode to the door. Here Josef was confronted by Gudrun, resplendent in her second-best gown, holding herself unnaturally upright. Without being invited, she ushered two men over the threshold.

"*Herr Doktor*, you have visitors—"

"So I see." Josef noted with a sense of foreboding that one wore the storm-gray of the city police. The foremost man extended his hand.

"*Herr Doktor* Breuer. A pleasure to renew your acquaintance."

"The pleasure's mutual, sir." Josef struggled to put a name to a face that, with its sharply chiseled lines and extraordinarily long nose, should have been memorable. Vague recollections of some civic occasion surfaced, but the name itself continued to elude him. The thin face was transformed by a smile that redeemed the man's unfortunate features.

"Thank you again for your kindness that dreadful night, *Herr Doktor*. My wife often speaks of it." His eyes dropped. "And we both appreciated the care with which your boy, Benjamin, drove us home."

Ah, that was it. Josef nodded. The man's wife, as plump as he was thin, had succumbed to the heat and a surfeit of wine. He'd put his carriage at their disposal. Benjamin had later regaled him with tales of loud and persistent scolding, crowned by the fat woman's inability to negotiate the carriage steps. It had ended in a pavement debacle. "*Chefinspektor* Kirchmann. This is an unexpected pleasure." He inclined his head as Kirchmann introduced his colleague, *Inspektor* Brunn, and waved the two men towards chairs, frowning when Gudrun made as if to follow them. "*Frau* Gschtaltner, some coffee for our guests, if you would be so kind."

"It's already prepared," said Gudrun, sailing majestically towards the kitchen.

Turning his attention back to the policemen, Josef found both men staring at Lilie, who seemed oblivious to their presence. He cleared his throat. "How may I be of service?"

"*Frau* Gschtaltner—" Kirchmann broke off as Gudrun returned with a tray. Placing it on a side table, she prepared to pour.

"Thank you," said Josef, noting that a pair of the piebald butterflies had fluttered in after her. The damnable things got everywhere. He would have to instruct Benjamin again. "We can manage."

"But . . ." Gudrun protested.

"That will be all, *Frau* Gschtaltner, thank you."

"Is she staying?" Gudrun demanded, darting a vitriolic look at Lilie.

"Thank you," Josef repeated, accompanying her to the door and closing it firmly, waiting for the satisfactory clunk of Benjamin's replacement latch. As he settled behind his desk, Kirchmann caught his eye and grimaced commiseration. Since Josef's only acknowledgment was the slightest of nods, the *Chefinspektor* continued with an explanation of his presence.

"We're assisting the Wels-Land authorities in their attempt to recapture a dangerous criminal."

So that was Gudrun's game. Josef clenched his teeth but nodded calmly enough, his expression one of detached interest. "The Lambach case, I presume?"

"That's correct. There's a possibility that the fugitive found her way to Vienna—"

"A long journey," said Josef, "and not an easy one. I believe the average walking speed is five kilometers per hour. To travel almost two hundred and fifty kilometers suggests a degree of purpose unusual in someone judged insane." He rearranged his pens and neatly squared up a sheath of notes. "Were you seeking an opinion on the fugitive's state of mind?" He noted that the *Chefinspektor* looked increasingly embarrassed and that his colleague was laboriously writing down every word.

Lilie, who had been sitting in silence, stretched out her hand, allowing one of the butterflies to alight there.

"How lovely they smell." She looked at Kirchmann. "Don't you think it's a pity the scent drives everyone mad?"

Kirchmann's mouth opened and shut. "Er, indeed, yes."

"It is a fact," said Brunn, in a flat, gray voice, "that butterflies have no smell."

Lilie continued to look at Kirchmann. "Not butterflies. Flowers."

"Flowers, are they? Very well." The *Chefinspektor* managed a weak smile and directed a pleading glance in Josef's direction. "Flying flowers. A delightful idea."

"Lepidoptera." Brunn shook his head and wrote rapidly, ending with a full stop so vigorous that it must have marked several pages.

"Stupid," said Lilie. "*Dumm wie Bohnenstroh.*"

"Thick as two short..." muttered Brunn, dutifully recording the insult before realizing it was addressed to him and viciously scoring through the words.

"More coffee, gentlemen?" As Josef set down the pot, he motioned Kirchmann to continue. "Do you seriously believe this wretched woman has come to Vienna? Are you here to inquire whether she was previously a patient of mine?"

"*Frau* Gschtaltner drew our attention to the unorthodox way in which..." Kirchmann paused, his eyes flicking sideways to indicate Lilie, "in which a certain young woman entered your household. Apparently, there was an alarming domestic ... incident. She is convinced that they are one and the same." He coughed apologetically. "*Frau* Gschtaltner was very insistent."

"One and the same?" Josef looked down his nose. "Who? I don't understand."

"The violent fugitive from Lambach and this young woman, *Herr*

Doktor," Brunn said with a touch of impatience. Josef looked at him in amazement.

"Quite impossible. Now, unless there is anything else you wish to discuss . . ." He rose and took a few steps towards the door. The *Chefinspektor* intercepted him. Taking Josef's arm, he steered him towards the window.

"Your pardon, *Herr Doktor*, but *Frau* Gschtaltner tells me the young woman was discovered near the Narrenturm in a very distressed condition. Beaten. Unclothed." He lowered his voice. "There was a suggestion of sexual foul play. The *Frau* even intimated the girl might have been working as a prostitute."

"It is what one would expect," added Brunn, "of a female criminal."

Josef shook off Kirchmann. "Let me be plain," he said quietly. "*Frau* Gschtaltner has reached a difficult time. Women who've lived out their lives in service get to an age where any youth and beauty they once possessed has gone. To view such a life in retrospect—a life without a lover, a husband, without children, without even a home of their own—must be a bitter thing."

"Indeed," concurred Kirchmann. "A life affording security, I suppose, but perceived as full of missed opportunities. Yes, there must be regrets."

"And then," Josef said, "to be confronted by this pure young woman in the flower and beauty of her youth . . ."

As one, the men's eyes turned to Lilie, who sat in silence, her eyes cast down. Sunlight played through her hair, turning it to gold. The butterfly still perched on her hand, its wings quivering gently. Its mate fluttered nearby.

"Exactly," Kirchmann said with a sigh. "Yes. Impossible to avoid jealousy." After a moment's reflection, he nodded sagely. "I understand all too well. My wife has a maiden aunt of just that age who took up writing anonymous letters to men in prominent positions. Some particularly poisonous ones"—he coughed and fidgeted—"full of claims relating to a fictitious love child and detailing astoundingly bizarre . . . er . . . practices were sent to Mayor Lueger. All very embarrassing." He glanced at Josef. "We placed her in Bellevue. The family decided it was in her best interest."

"An excellent choice," said Josef. "It's a particularly enlightened sanatorium for those with nervous problems, and Kreuzlingen is no great distance from Vienna. I know *Herr* Binswanger, the director, well. Like his father before him, Robert pays great attention to engaging the patients' intellects—educational activities, outings, crafts, and gardening."

Kirchmann looked dubious. "No doubt. We were concerned only with placing the old bi—*woman* where she could do no more harm."

"Precisely so," Josef said smoothly. So long a silence followed that he felt obliged to fill it. "I've often thought females are unfortunate in that, as it were, they die twice. Once when they become devoid of youthful charms and cease to be desirable; later, in actuality. Between the two is a curious time, of family warmth in those lucky enough to be so blessed, but often of sheer peculiarity when this isn't so and where such women are left to their own devices . . . well." Nobody commented. It suddenly occurred to Josef that being left to their own devices might not be considered a misfortune for women, but rather a period of great liberation if such a gift could be accepted. He considered what it must be like to be judged on physical appearance, to be desired on looks alone—and then, with the passing of time, to be not. He thought of Bertha's solitude. He tugged at his beard.

"Three times." The voice was so small, issuing from such a deep pit of silence it took Josef a moment to register that it belonged to Lilie.

"What's that, my dear?"

She looked up. "She has another death—as a mother—when her child dies."

"*If*," Josef said comfortingly. "It doesn't always happen."

"*If*," echoed Lilie, "and when." She blew gently on the butterfly and it fluttered into the air.

"Very perceptive," said Kirchmann, nodding vigorously. "Very true."

"Imagine what it's been like for those women with large families," whispered Lilie. "Death after death after death." Her head drooped. "There's no end to the dying. That's why there are so many flowers."

"All right, Lilie," Josef said quickly. He glanced at the others. "Gentlemen, as you can see, this talk of dying has disturbed my patient. If there is nothing more, might I beg you to excuse us?"

"One moment," said Brunn. "Where do you come from?" he demanded of Lilie. "Where have you been living?"

Her forehead creased. "I'm in Germany."

Brunn frowned. "This is Vienna."

"Vienna's in Germany," said Lilie, without looking at him.

"No, no, my dear," Kirchmann said in soothing tones. "It's in Austria."

"But Austria's in Germany, so Vienna must be, too."

Brunn smirked and surreptitiously waved his hand in front of his face. She caught the gesture and her lips trembled. "Perhaps we're somewhere else."

"Please direct all further questions to me," Josef said sternly.

"Of course." Kirchmann awarded Brunn a stony stare.

"I hope I can count on your discretion, gentlemen," murmured Josef. "Lilie's family are anxious that her treatment remains a private matter."

"Oh," said Kirchmann with a wry smile, "it's secret. As with the young Pappenheim girl." Under Josef's direct gaze, he added: "I follow these things, *Herr Doktor*. I've always been interested in the tangles of the mind. Mostly in connection with matters criminal, though. I am unable to say more."

Eight

he sun's warm on my back and I keep bumping into Greet's shadow. She says it will thunder this afternoon; all the scarlet pimpernels and blue bird's-eye have opened wide to watch the big black cloud sneaking over the horizon. I want to stop and poke a stick into the ants swarming up between the cracks of the path, but Greet has tied a length of string around my waist and fastened it to her apron so I have to run to keep up. Hot weather makes her cross and nasty. My leg still smarts from the slap she gave me after I escaped this morning.

When we get to the washing line she unties me and hands over my *Stoffpuppe.* "Stand there. Don't drop your dolly. Move an inch and it'll be back in the cellar for you, Miss, do you hear me?"

"Look." A ladybird has landed on my arm. It opens and shuts its wing cases while I try to count the spots.

"*Marienkäfer,*" Greet says, frowning. "Don't hurt her, for that would bring disaster. Say the rhyme and then blow gently until she flies away."

"What rhyme?"

"You know perfectly well which rhyme, *Dummkopf.*" Greet huffs and puffs as she struggles to lower the clothes prop. "*Marienkäferchen, fliege weg!* That one. Remember now?"

"No. Anyway, I don't want her to fly away home."

"Unless she does, our house will burn down, especially with a thunderstorm promised. Say the rhyme. Quick.

> *"Marienkäferchen, Marienkäferchen, fliege weg!*
> *Dein Häuschen brennt,*
> *Dein Mütterchen flennt,*
> *Dein Vater sitzt auf der Schwelle:*
> *Flieg in Himmel aus der Hölle!*

"And watch which direction she flies off in, because that's where your future husband will come from."

"Don't want a stupid husband."

"You'll get one whether you want one or not, Krysta. Some of us do"—Greet sighed, and reached for Papa's shirts—"and some of us don't." She looked at me. "Now say the rhyme."

> *"Ladybird, ladybird, fly away home!*
> *Your house is on fire,*
> *Your mother is crying,*
> *Your father sits on the doorstep:*
> *Fly into Heaven from Hell!"*

I blow, but the ladybird won't move.

"There we are then," Greet says, folding pillowcases. "We're done for. Probably be roasted in our beds like suckling pigs in an oven. Covered in crackling. Served up with gravy. What an end." I blow harder.

The beetle opens its wings midfall and flies directly upwards. Greet shakes her head. "Oh dear. Looks like your own true love will die before the wedding day."

"Don't care." I've got my eye on something better than husbands: the earth between the vegetables is newly dug, rich, dark brown, the color of chocolate. Greet insists it tastes nasty, nothing like candy, but I'm not convinced. Behind her back I scoop up a whole handful and shove it into my mouth.

"Idiot child!" Greet bawls above my shrieks. "*Das war dumm.* Only worms eat dirt. It's a taste of the grave. When will you learn to do as you're told?"

I scrape at my tongue and spit and howl and stamp. My entire mouth is coated with the thick, cold, gritty stuff. It's between my teeth and slipping down my throat. Greet holds my hair out of the way as I bend over, retching. Even vomit tastes better than dirt.

"Perhaps that'll teach you a lesson, Krysta." Greet wipes my face on a corner of her apron. "Your dolly's done for—covered in sick—perhaps we all are, for the blasted ladybird's come back to sit on your shoulder— it's Our Lady's messenger telling us there'll be nothing left of the house by morning except a pile of cinders. Don't take on so. I'll try cleaning her." She picks my rag doll up by one foot and pushes me up the garden path. "And I see that ladybird still hasn't gone. Wriggle your shoulders. Maybe that'll shift it. No. Well, I fear it's all over for us. And look at those ants swarming. Flying ants, too. They bite. I'll come out with a pan of boiling water in a minute. That'll get rid of them. Did I ever tell you the tale of the poor boy in the grave? It's very sad. All about a mean and nasty man whose house burns right to the ground."

She goes on talking, but I can't hear the poor boy's story above the sound of my wailing. The taste of dirt and disappointment lingers. My lips feel dry and cracked. Occasionally a bit of stone finds its way onto my tongue, but I have no spit left.

I DON'T REMEMBER FALLING OVER and yet I'm facedown in a patch of mud by the side of a road. It's raining. There's dirt in my mouth. Everything hurts. My fingers hurt most of all, but they're underneath me so I can't see what's wrong with them. It's night but the whole place is lit up. There are two bright lights somewhere in the distance, moving all the time, sweeping backwards and forwards like the eyes of a giant owl watching rats running from side to side in a trap. The big aviary with its empty perches is in front of me. I must be inside the zoo because there's the cafeteria and the infirmary's farther along. I want to run and find Papa, but he isn't there. I try to remember where's he's gone—

Then I see Lottie lying in a puddle and crawl towards her. She's ugly now. Her skin is bubbly and cracked and there's a hole where her nose used to be. All her lovely blond hair is black and crispy. Her legs hang loose. I hold her tight and say it doesn't matter, but we both still cry.

Why my fingers hurt is because they're covered with blisters—like the ones Greet got after she dropped the fish kettle on her foot—and there's no one to rub butter on them. Lottie asks why I'm wearing nasty dirty clothes and where my shoes have gone. I don't know. I can't work it out. Greet will roar and Papa will shout—then I remember Greet has gone away and Papa—Papa . . .

My screaming brings the animal-people creeping from their sheds to look. They beckon and make noises. They try to talk.

"*Chodź tu*. Come here. Come with us."

Some of them stroke my hair and hold my hands, but I push them away.

"Get off, dirty animal-things. You're not eating me."

"*Chodź z nami, dziecko.* Come with us, little one."

When the rain starts pouring down, two of them pick me up and carry me into their shed even though I scream much louder, hitting them and kicking. They only have two candles inside, but I can see rows of beds stacked up with more of the animal-people sitting and staring. I put my thumb in my mouth and stare back until one of those who have learned to talk properly comes forward and squats by my side, putting her arm around me.

"Don't be afraid, my little one. You're with friends now."

I stick my elbow into her. "Go away, stupid animal-thing."

She takes no notice. "I'm Erika. What's your name? Not going to tell me? Very well, perhaps you will later. Right now we need to find you somewhere to rest." She shows me a bed where a skinny animal-person is already fast asleep. "Share with Lena. There's enough room if you lie head to toe."

"Won't."

Erika looks at me. "There's nowhere else."

"Won't sleep there." The mattress looks thin and lumpy. Lena has the single blanket wrapped round her, but I can see she isn't wearing nightclothes. "I want my *Federbett* and my nightie with the pink flowers."

Someone laughs. Erika hushes them. She shakes her head.

"We are poor people now," says Lottie. "Papa's gone. Everyone's gone. Everything's been taken away. Nobody will look after us."

"A BODY CAN ONLY PUT UP with so much," says Greet, picking up my scattered clothes. "Any more of your 'Won't do this' and 'Won't do that' and I'll pack my bags and go. See how you get on then. Now that your mother's dead—God rest her misguided soul—men being what they are, it'll be a wicked stepmother for you before the year is out. She won't want you."

"My papa—"

"Oh, she'll have ways of turning your father against you. Or maybe she'll just poison him. And what happens next? You know what happens next. Into the wild forest with an empty belly and nowhere to lay your head but a bed of leaves with stones for a pillow—"

"It's not too bad," says Erika, and pats my head. "Make do for tonight. We'll see what tomorrow brings."

"No," I say round my thumb. "Want to go home. Want my papa."

"Papa's dead," whispers Lottie. "Dead-as-a-doornail dead."

"No," I bawl, even though I know she's right. "Take me to my papa. I want Papa."

IT'S DARK AND THE HOUSE is silent until a car goes by with a scraping of gears as it turns the corner. Its headlamps momentarily light up the room and I see goblin shadows creeping along the baseboards.

"Mama! Mama!" No one comes. I carry on shrieking her name, making myself small as possible while the shadows finger my bed. Finally, Greet throws open the door and picks me up, giving me a hug that squashes the air out of me.

"Hush now, Krysta. That's enough."

"Go away," I gasp. "Want Mama."

"Mama has gone to a better place. You'll have to make do with me."

"Don't want you. Take me to Mama."

Greet puts me back into bed and sits beside me. "Your mother is dead, Krysta, dead and buried. She chose to go, and no one can bring her back."

. . .

"Lie down now," says Erika. "Try to rest. The day starts early here."

"Mama! Papa!" I howl, and as an afterthought: "Greet! I want Greet."

"Shut her up," mutters a harsh voice. "I need my sleep."

"Want Greet," I shriek again. "Take me to Greet."

Erika shakes her head. She says nothing, but her face is sad, and suddenly I find myself weeping without trying to, a new kind of weeping, one I can't stop. It feels as if my whole body is crying, from deep inside right out to the ends of my fingers and down to my toes. I throw myself on the floor and crawl under the beds until I get to a corner. Lottie and I curl into a tight ball. We cry until we fall asleep.

A noise like a long scream wakes me. It's still dark and all the animal-people jump up and rush around. When the noise comes again, they file out of the shed. Lottie says we should leave and look for Greet. Neither of us knows where she went after Papa sent her away, but it must be somewhere on the other side of the forest by the lake.

"As you know," says Greet, while she fills the jars with big black cherries, "Hansel and Gretel were abandoned in the dark forest. But do you know why? Well, I'll tell you—it was the final solution for their parents, not just because there was no food but because the children were wild and naughty and would not do as they were told. They also threw their clothes on the floor and answered back. Deep, deep into the forest the parents marched the little sinners. Each child was given a dry crust. No butter. No honey. Then the parents went away, first the mother, then the father. The minute they were out of sight, all the wild beasts of the forest gathered round. They're always hungry, those wild animals." She stands the jars in the preserving pan and turns up the heat. "What do you suppose happens next?"

I don't answer. In the spring Greet put Peter in her shopping bag and set him free among the bushes in the park. She said he wanted to go and anyway she'd no time for cleaning out smelly rabbit hutches. Next time we walked that way there was white fur all over the grass. Greet found his tail and brought it home for good luck.

LOTTIE AND I stay in the shed all day. When it's beginning to get dark, the animal-people return, dragging their feet and hardly making a sound. After they light the candles, the one who can talk comes to find me.

"Krysta, it's me, Erika. Up you get. It's time to wash and to comb your hair."

"Won't. Go away." I back into the corner, holding Lottie in front of me and making myself small. I spit at her, a very little spit, much less than usual, but it still lands on her skirt. Erika looks at it. Then her hand comes towards me. "You can't smack me," I yell. "You're only an animal-person. If you hit me, my papa will—" I stop. Lottie reminds me that if there is no Papa, anyone can hurt me.

"None of us will strike you," Erika says quietly. She drags me to my feet. "But there are things about living here you must learn very quickly, otherwise you will be punished by the others. Be a big brave girl now. No more tears. Wash your face and"—she fumbles in her pocket for a gap-toothed comb—"tidy your hair." She puts an arm round my shoulders. "Are you ready to tell us your name?" I shake my head and pull nasty faces at the other animal-people watching and listening.

"Krysta," one of them says. "At least, that's what she told Daniel."

Daniel's a real boy, even if he does eat worms. Erika is a bit like Greet, but much thinner and quieter. "Are you an animal-person, Erika?"

"Are you?" She does a very tiny smile that looks as if it hurts, and then gives me a little push. "Hurry up now, Krysta. It's almost time for lessons."

"Won't go to school."

"Everyone here goes to school."

"Papa says I don't have to go until after the—"

"You *will* go to your lessons," Erika says fiercely. "And you will learn. Life is hard, but knowing about other people, other civilizations, other ways of living, other places—that's your escape route, a magical journey. Once you know about these things, no matter what happens, your mind can create stories to take you anywhere you want to go."

I dry my nose on my sleeve. "Anywhere?"

"Anywhere and any-when."

Daniel stares at my nasty clothes. "What are you doing here?" He doesn't wait for an answer. "Have you got any bread or eggs?"

I shake my head. "You didn't come back."

"Sometimes people don't." He looks away. "That's what happens here."

Because I wouldn't say please or thank you, Papa put the candy into a glass bowl on the sideboard and said it would stay there until my manners improved. I poke out my tongue behind his back. While Greet is busy bringing in the washing, I climb onto a chair and pull the bowl towards me. It's a very pretty bowl held up by a fish and with dragonflies and flowers all around the top. The candy is right at the bottom, next to the fish's eyes, and I have to balance the leather pouf on top of the chair so I can reach inside. Greet opens the door as I'm putting all the empty candy wrappers back.

"You little devil!" She flicks my legs with the wet dishrag. "Your papa will give you what-for when he comes home. Get down this minute." But the shock of the cold water makes me slip and I fall, taking the bowl with me. It breaks into a thousand pieces; there's glass everywhere. Greet's face goes white. "That was your mama's!" she shrieks. "Your papa treasured it. *Du schlimmes Mädchen!* You wicked, wicked girl. How shall I ever be able to tell him about this?"

"Didn't mean to." Scarlet beads blossom from my fingertips. There's a gash on my leg. I start to wail.

"Stand perfectly still. Don't move a muscle." Greet fetches a pan and starts picking glass from my hair and clothes. "And don't expect sympathy from me," she says. "You brought this on yourself. Heaven only knows what will become of such a naughty, disobedient creature."

Snuffling and miserable, I stare at the floor, counting the shards of glass lodged in the rug: *eins, zwei, drei, vier, fünf . . .*

EACH MORNING, even if it rains, we have to line up outside the shed and wait, like at school. Erika is being my mother, just for now, and I hold her hand until the name-calling starts. Then I stand up very straight and count the bits of gravel around my feet: *eins, zwei, drei, vier, fünf . . .*

One day Johanna comes. The name-calling goes on for even longer than usual, and when it doesn't come out right she gets very cross and walks between the rows, slapping the back of everyone's heads. I try counting the slaps: *achtzehn, neunzehn, zwanzig . . .* Then—twenty-one— Johanna is right by me, so near I can smell her violet scent. I remember

the lovely red ball and the hair clips she gave me, and the book we sometimes looked at together with the pictures of the filthy rats stealing food
and biting babies in their cradles. She played games with me, too. And
braided my hair. When Papa was here Johanna wanted to be my new
mama. Forgetting all Erika's warnings, I step out of line.

"Hello, Johanna."

"No," Erika whispers, and claws at my clothes, frantically trying to
pull me back. So does one of the other women in my shed, Annalies, who
is standing on my other side. Johanna turns and looks at me, but I can see
from her face she doesn't want to be my mama anymore. I shuffle back
into my place and go on counting slaps: *sechzig, einundsechzig* . . .

Then Johanna is behind Annalies, *slap*, and now me—

UNCLE HRABEN ISN'T LIKE JOHANNA. He seems very pleased to
find me and takes me to see the rabbits. I tell him about Peter, but not
about him being set free in the park.

"These are big rabbits, Krysta, much bigger than ordinary ones.
Enormous. And they're very beautiful. You will never have seen such
rabbits."

The rabbits have their own shed with clean pens and lots of fresh
straw. At one end there's a room with tables where ladies are carefully
brushing their coats and putting the loose hair in trays. Most are white
like the rabbit in *Alice in Wonderland*, but one has black spots on his
nose and another is very pale orange.

"Their fur is used to line hats and jackets," Uncle Hraben tells me.
"Wonderful stuff, rabbit fur. Keeps the cold out better than most
things."

I remember Papa talking about doing things with rabbits, but they
must be different ones because the legs of these are too small.

"Where are the really big rabbits, Uncle Hraben?"

"You want even bigger ones?" He laughs. "There will be, in time. You have to plan these things, pretty Krysta. For example, if you wanted only golden-haired baby rabbits you would choose the parents very carefully. It's no good expecting to get beautiful offspring if the mother or father is dark or has a huge nose, nor big healthy ones if either parent is stunted."

Next to the combing place there's a kitchen with food being measured out. Someone who looks like Witch Schwitter but not so old is scrubbing huge piles of carrots. On the floor are baskets of tomatoes, celery, greens—broccoli, lettuce, kale, parsley, spinach, and endive—and bunches of dill, basil, mint, and tarragon. The witch cuts the carrots into small chunks before starting on bowls of apples and plums. I steal a plum. Uncle Hraben laughs again when he notices my cheek bulging.

"Are you hungry, Krysta? Come with me, in that case." We climb three flights of stairs to a room that is nearly all windows. "This is my tower. Do you like it? Now let's see." He gives me cake and an orange. I remember the way Daniel crammed food in his mouth and make myself peel the orange very carefully. "Better?" he asks. "What else have we got, I wonder?" He opens a little drawer and takes out a Pfennig Riesen, holding it just out of reach. "How about a little kiss to say thank you?" His cheek is scratchy. "Poor little Krysta with no papa." He pulls me towards him. "Sit on my knee. A bit closer . . . cuddle up, that's right. Now, what if I was your new father?" He runs his hand up and down my leg. "Would you like that?" The toffee clings to my teeth and I can't say no. After a few moments Uncle Hraben sets me on my feet. "I must work. Come back tomorrow. Your new papa will bring some delicious food. What would you like?"

"Cherries."

"Too late for cherries."

"Ice cream."

"Perhaps."

We are almost at the door when Uncle Hraben doubles back and stops in front of a cupboard. "I expect you're missing your nice things, Krysta. Don't worry. They're safe." He opens a door, and my frocks, my skirts and jumpers, socks and knickers and shoes are inside, even my handkerchiefs, all stacked in neat piles.

"Give them to me."

He shakes his head. "You can't wear nice things out there, little one. They'd get spoiled, or stolen. You wouldn't like that, would you? You can have it all later on. Until then, put them on when you come to visit your new father."

GREET SAYS PAPA TOLD HER to make sure I eat lots of vegetables, especially green ones, but I don't believe her. He never eats them. They look like sick.

"Won't." I move the carrots and cabbage around my plate, squashing them smaller and pushing bits onto the table. When she gets up to fill the kettle, I drop some of the mess onto the floor.

"Stop that," Greet says without turning round. "I know what you're up to. Finish your food now while it's hot. It'll be much worse when it's cold."

"Don't like it. Won't eat it."

"Never mind 'don't' and 'won't.'" Greet scowls, placing the teapot between us. "You're going to sit there until every last bit has been eaten."

"It tastes nasty. Give me some cake."

"Give me some cake, please."

"Please," I mutter, squeezing the words between my teeth.

"No," Greet says with a smug smile. "Not until that plate's empty.

Then you may have a very small piece. Do you know what happens to girls who only eat cookies, candy, and cake? For a start, they never grow up into young ladies. First, their skin starts looking raw as new meat. Next, their hair drops out, and then their teeth. After awhile they are so weak they can hardly walk. Their bones turn to rubber. Soon they are crawling everywhere on their hands and knees. And"—she leans across the table, fixing me with her eye—"before too long they are begging strangers in the street for proper food—meat and cheese, bread, potatoes, and greens."

EVERYONE HERE IS ALWAYS HUNGRY. They never stop talking about food. When someone tells a story—even if it's a proper story about princesses or wolves and not one about how things used to be—no one ever wants to know about the beautiful dresses and jewels or how big the palace was, just what they had to eat. Zsofika and her friends play a little game over and over again. "What are you cooking today?" one of them asks. The answer is always the same: "Wait a minute. First I have to get the roast out of the oven before it burns." When I take Lottie from her hiding place, she agrees with me that it's a very stupid game.

Some nights, instead of stories or singing, there are pretend feasts in the dark. Each person has to bring a special dish they used to make at home. Weronika brings green borscht.

"It tastes of spring in this place where it is always winter. Tonight we'll eat it with black bread and plenty of creamy butter."

Lottie would turn up her nose if she still had one, because the soup's made of sorrel and potatoes and you eat it cold. Nobody says a word for a moment, though there are a few sighs and I feel Lena screw up her toes by my head. Someone calls out: "It's delicious, Weronika. Please let me have the recipe."

Mirela also brings a soup. When she says hers is called *Legényfogó Káposztaleves*, everyone laughs. Lena tells me this is because it means man-catcher soup, but she doesn't explain the joke. Everyone laughs some more when Mirela tells us it's served with soft bread and kisses. She's also brought *Ürgepörkölt*, which is squirrel stew. Lottie says she feels sick. So do I when Riika starts telling us about roast reindeer with rowanberry jelly. Everyone knows only witches eat rowanberries. While we're waiting for the puddings to come, I whisper some more "Hansel and Gretel" to Lottie. She didn't know about the gingerbread cottage's secret back garden full of nettles and *Rapunzel* and rowan trees, or about the black mandrakes, which scream when the witch pulls them out of the ground for her dinner. Where real people grow cabbages, she has rows of purple toadstools in between the red-and-white-spotted ones. The witch also keeps slugs in little cages and eats their eggs instead of tapioca. In place of hens she keeps crows that fly off each morning looking for battlegrounds where they can harvest eyes. All around the garden there are hunchbacked willow trees that snatch tiny birds from the air with their knobbly claws and squash them into holes in their trunks.

Lottie is so scared we almost miss the first pudding, *Makowiec*, which is poppy-seed cake. We take an extra-large slice. Nobody brings any ice cream.

THERE ARE MANY CHILDREN besides Daniel, but he is my special friend. As autumn turns into winter, we play games to keep ourselves warm: catch, tag, and What's the time, Mr. Wolf? Hide-and-seek is our favorite, though we often find things we don't want to. There's more counting now, though everyone has a different way of doing it.

Jeden, dwa, trzy, cztery, pięć, sześć, siedem, osiem, dziewięć, dziesięć . . .

En, to, tre, fire, fem, seks, sju, åtte, ni, ti . . .

Un, deux, trois, quatre, cinq, six, sept, huit, neuf, dix . . .

Yek, duy, trin, shtar, panj, shov, efta, oxto, en'a, desh . . . Coming!

Sometimes, however hard we look and however long we seek, some of our friends hide themselves so well we can't find them and never see them again. One after another they disappear. It's like a game of Ten Green Bottles.

> *"Zehn grüne Flaschen, hängen an der Wand,*
> *Ten green bottles, hanging on the wall,*
> *And if one green bottle should accidentally fall—"*

I stop because Daniel pulls faces and doesn't join in with my singing. "I had a book about a magic door into a mountain," I tell him. "The Pied Piper took other children there. Perhaps Casmir and Aisha and the others have found the way on their own. We should look for it, because there's a wonderful place behind that door."

Daniel shrugs. "They've gone, like my little sister did. They won't come back. I told you already, that's what happens here."

SOMETIMES WHEN I'M VERY SAD, I visit Uncle Hraben in his tower. He lets me put on one of my nice frocks and gives me paper and crayons so I can draw pictures. Once, he brought me ice cream, but usually it's cake or *Apfelstrudel*. I don't mind so much anymore. One Sunday, he came to the shed to find me because there were new baby rabbits. Daniel ran away when he saw him. All the others shrank back and made themselves look very small. When I come back, Erika and Cecily make me tell them everything.

"Were you in a room alone with him?"

"Not today." I tell them about the baby rabbits. They don't seem very interested. "When I go to his special tower, he gives me nice things to eat. And I can change into my other clothes."

They look at each other. Erika shakes her head. "From now on, you will come to work with me. At least I can keep an eye on you there."

"Why?"

"So that he doesn't lure you into his tower again. You mustn't go there."

"Why not?"

"Because he's not a nice man."

"But Uncle Hraben knew Papa. They were friends. He *is* nice. He says he wants to be my new father."

"You and I must have a long talk about . . . certain things," says Erika. "Innocence is not the same as ignorance."

"Keep out of his way," advises Cecily. "Hide when you see him coming. Take nothing. If you do, there will be a high price to pay."

"He's fattening you for the kill," says Lena, who'd been pretending to be asleep.

"That's silly," I say. "He's not a witch."

Lottie thinks Uncle Hraben might be a witch in disguise because he pinches my bottom and squeezes my legs and arms exactly like the witch did to Hansel when she put him in the cage. We argue then, because I know why Lottie doesn't like him. He says she's ugly and he'll buy me a new doll if I throw her away. In the end, I call her Charlotte and put her back in her hiding place.

Nine

n his haste to catch up with interrupted chores, Benjamin overfilled the baskets and while hurrying towards the kitchen tripped on uneven stones, spilling potatoes and scattering mud all over the newly swept path. Fear of Gudrun's wrath made him kick as much of the soil as possible into the herb garden before running to the stables for a yard brush. Here he found Lilie perched on the old bench where he usually sat to polish tack, her eyes wide open, staring straight ahead, hardly blinking.

"Lilie?"

"You all think I'm mad. That horrible fat policeman waved his hand in front of his face, like this, as if my mechanism's faulty, one of my springs has come loose. I see what I see. There's nothing I can do that would make them understand."

"Don't worry. It'll be all right." He rubbed his palms clean on his trousers and then tentatively took her hand in both of his. Lilie looked at it and smiled.

"It's nice when you do that."

Benjamin regarded her warily. "But I've never—"

"Not often enough," she said. "Did you ever think I was mad? There were times when I thought I might be."

Suddenly unsure of himself, Benjamin relinquished her hand. Poor girl. What could he say? Lilie was obviously still more fragile than he'd realized. Perhaps it would be better if she went indoors. A storm was brewing. Somewhere a dog howled, and dense flocks of starlings flung themselves screaming from one rooftop to the next. Even the stoical old carriage horse had become restless, whinnying softly, constantly fidgeting, its shoes striking sparks on the stable floor. The playful breeze that had been tugging leaves from the walnut tree all afternoon was now gathering strength, growing into a knife-edged wind, making the mass of foliage above their heads shift and sway. Looking up, Benjamin caught sight of a single pink rose far enough back to be protected from the weather, and he thrust his hand deep into the thorns to pick it.

"For you," he said, cradling the flower against the wind. "It's an old-fashioned rose: an Old Blush China. *Frau Doktor* Breuer says this variety has been cultivated in China for over a thousand years."

"The Last Rose of Summer." Lilie cupped it in her hands, breathing in the sweet fragrance. "There's a poem written about it. I learned some of the words in . . ." She looked confused. "I once learned it:

> *"Die letzte der Rosen steht blühend allein;*
> *All ihre Gefährten, sie schliefen schon ein."*

She sighed and repeated the few lines:

> *"'Tis the last rose of summer,*
> *Left blooming alone;*

> *All her lovely companions*
> *Are faded and gone."*

"A sad poem, by the sound of it," said Benjamin, wishing he'd ignored the flower, which he had hoped would lighten Lilie's spirits and not plunge her into further melancholy. He felt his own spirits plummet. "Summer will come again, Lilie, and so will the roses. More, with care." He'd prune the bush at the earliest opportunity, heap so much fertilizer round its roots that next year's display would astound her. "It will be a glorious new century, with more roses than ever before."

Lilie turned her head away. "Not for us."

"Why not? What do you mean?"

"Haven't you remembered yet?"

"Remembered what?" Benjamin took a swipe at yet another pair of black-and-white butterflies riding the wind currents around his head. The garden was overrun with the damn things. Nothing could shift them. And really, the autumn should have finished them off by now. "Lilie, what are you talking about?" He reached out and laid a hand on her shoulder, hoping his touch would provide some comfort.

She smiled sadly. "The last verse of the poem goes like this:

> *"When true hearts lie withered*
> *And fond ones are flown,*
> *Oh! who would inhabit,*
> *This bleak world alone?"*

"You won't be alone, Lilie," Benjamin said staunchly. "If you'll only allow me, I'll stay with you forever."

"Get up then!" shouted Lilie, her entire body tensing. "On your feet! Walk! Now!"

"What?" He rose slowly, looking down at her in dismay. "Come, Lilie. Time to go into the house and rest. Everything will be fine."

"Only if you can keep moving," she said, her face unutterably weary. "We're getting nowhere and I no longer have the strength to support you."

"Just look at that," said Gudrun, standing, arms akimbo, at the kitchen door. "Now the young fool's got the cheek to pick your wife's roses for her."

Josef, who'd come in search of a linden-blossom tisane to ease his throbbing headache, moved unwillingly to stand at her shoulder. She jabbed the air, pointing to where Benjamin and Lilie were sitting together on the tiny bench. His view was partially obscured by a bush planted against the stable wall, but he saw enough—his touch, her smile—to gauge their growing closeness, and turned away, his cup juddering violently against the saucer. "Two young people thrown together by circumstances. One can expect little else."

He swallowed the tisane in one go, scalding his throat, and immediately poured more boiling water into the cup, drinking the pale green liquid before it had a chance either to infuse or to cool, as if it might cauterize a raw wound deep in his chest. "I will eat alone in my study this evening. A light supper, if you please."

Josef lurched back to his sanctuary, where he paced the floor, kneading his temples, almost weeping with misery. His father's eyes followed him, his portrait radiating disapproval, until finally Josef turned on it, shaking his fist. "Your wife was no older than Lilie, *Vater*, so if I'm an *älter Wüstling*, what does that make you? Two old lechers together then—it must be a family trait. As for me being married, do you know how long it has been since Mathilde and I—?"

He sank into a chair, gripping his head with both hands as the dream of the wild forest was replayed before his closed eyes, only now it was Benjamin lying with Lilie in the soft ferns, Benjamin's work-worn young hands on her smooth white body. . . .

How would he dispatch the boy? Poison? The knife? No, he'd dismiss him without a reference. Throw him onto the street. Let him starve. He'd—potassium bromide. That was the answer. A hefty dose of the anaphrodisiac would soon put an end to Benjamin's interest in Lilie. Josef groaned. That way lay madness: any more and he'd end up in a worse state than the poor muddle-headed creatures he passed on to the sanatorium. Some days he woke convinced Lilie was simply a creature of his imagination, a beautiful fantasy born of loneliness and despair, and he was forced to rush downstairs to assure his senses of her flesh-and-blood reality. However had things come to such a pass?

He straightened, clutching the edge of his desk as he fought for self-control, but in spite of his efforts, the image of Lilie's pale body against the dark trees lingered. Then another creature stealthily interposed itself on the scene and Josef gasped as he visualized the painting that for days had remained so tantalizingly out of reach. A picture of Lilith, a fairly recent work by one of those passionate Pre-Raphaelite painters, an Englishman who'd studied at the Munich Academy. Lilith but with Lilie's face, barefoot and naked in a lonely forest, happily entwined with her familiar. What was the painter's name? Perhaps he'd read about the work in the *Zeitschrift für bildende Kunst*: the magazine for fine arts seemed a likely place. Josef's eyes strayed to the cabinet where he kept back copies.

Collier, that was it! John Collier.

Collier's Lilith was supremely beautiful, with a voluptuous body and a torrent of red-gold hair. There was no trace of the storm witch, the bringer of illness and death, in her calm and peaceful expression. As for the serpent, it was huge. Josef could imagine Sigmund making much of Lilith's contented smile as she cradled the creature against her body, its head lying over one shoulder like a caressing hand, its flickering tongue pointing to her pert right breast, its sleek coils encircling her hips, fettering her ankles . . . apart from that one sly coil parting her knees and traveling up the back of her thigh.

Josef swallowed hard. He'd studied the painting at length when a copy had first come into his hands. Now he wondered whether his naming of Lilie had been in response to the erotic sensations he'd felt at the time, rather than with reference to a garden flower whose symbolism was chastity and innocence . . . although the quality of innocence that it denoted, if he remembered correctly, was associated by the Greeks with ignorance of approaching danger. Perhaps, if Lilie was Lilith abbreviated, she was to blame for his present confusion, since her demonic namesake was the incarnation of lust, causing the most proper of men to be led astray. Rabbinical myth decreed: one may not sleep in a house alone, for whoever sleeps in a house alone is seized by Lilith. In the Zohar it claimed she roamed by night, vexing the sons of men and causing them to defile themselves in the manner of Onan.

At this point Josef caught his father's eye. He took a deep, calming breath.

Leopold Breuer, an educated and progressive Jewish scholar, had poured scorn on such beliefs, pointing out that—far from deriving from any rabbinic legend or Midrash—most of the superstitions about Lilith the she-demon originated in a medieval work known as *The Alphabet of Ben Sira*. He'd considered the book scurrilous, possibly anti-Semitic, an impious digest of risqué folktales with a protagonist born of an incestuous union between the prophet Jeremiah and his daughter; it was to the shame of uncritical Jewish mystics in medieval Germany that such nonsense came to be accepted as truth. An echo of his father's sardonic laughter floated down through the years. Josef subsided. He permitted himself one scowl at the laboring clock, which had so gleefully counted away all the days of his youth, and attempted to fix his thoughts on the purity of a white lily.

For a while he was successful, then other suspicions returned to gnaw at his good intentions—about Lilie's possible collusion with Bertha, or Freud, other estranged colleagues, political activists, perhaps even Mathilde—and Josef knew that if he was to retain his equilibrium, never mind his sanity, these must also be confronted. For if Lilie was an actress planted here to discredit and shame him—

It was impossible. To reason along those lines was as ludicrous as linking her with a she-demon. "Forgive me, sweet child," he murmured, smoothing his beard. "I had to start somewhere." One thing was certain: for both their sakes he must persist in seeking clues to the girl's background. Benjamin had been unsuccessful. Josef had already discounted the escaped-criminal story—apparently the police weren't taking it seriously, either—and it irked him that Gudrun showed no sign of contrition. Perhaps he should avail himself of the services of a private detective . . . but, contrary to popular fiction, such men were mostly drawn from the lower strata of society and might be induced to talk in their cups, however much they were paid.

Josef recommenced his pacing. And stopped dead.

Nothing had changed. If he had to continue searching for information, it should be here, in Vienna. The little he did know suggested that Lilie had been kept somewhere against her will. She'd been beaten and, he feared, worse. The horror of the experience had affected both her memory and her thinking processes.

Once again he came back to it: failing a monstrous family home, there was only one place in this city that could be likened to the seraglio, a place where, it was rumored, young foreign women were held captive for the pleasure—sadistic, or otherwise—of any member with enough money to hire the use of their defenseless bodies. Outrageous. Criminal. Bestial. Josef loosened his collar. He would insist that Benjamin find a way of getting inside the Thélème to make inquiries. It would almost certainly be dangerous. The boy might come to serious harm.

Josef avoided looking in his father's direction. A thrashing never killed anyone. Benjamin was young. He would mend.

AT FIRST GLANCE, the place seemed ordinary enough: a respectable house at one end of a terrace of similarly respectable houses. Benjamin walked slowly the length of the street and back again, unobtrusively examining its façade as he passed, wondering if the building really was Vienna's prime den of iniquity or whether the friends who'd assured him of this were even now doubled up with mirth as they anticipated the voluble indignation of the below-stairs maids. Earlier, he'd passed a few street vendors en route to the main thoroughfare—a broom squire laden with every manner of brush in creation, a shoeshine woman, a scissors sharpener. Now the street was empty apart from two soberly dressed matrons who passed by on the other side and darted quick, contemptuous looks in his direction. Benjamin examined his hands. The doctor's insistence that he set out immediately had hardly given him time to scrape the dirt from under his nails. He'd never known his employer so frosty, so abrupt. They'd both remained standing throughout the interview. The coins the doctor had tipped onto his desk for expenses were generous, but the gesture seemed almost contemptuous and his mouth was grim as he watched Benjamin laboriously pick them up. There'd been no good-bye, none of the usual pleasantries.

"I'll do my best, *Herr Doktor*," he said, and meant it, but the doctor merely turned his back and walked to the window, throwing it open to allow half a dozen of the black-splotched butterflies to escape. Benjamin decided he'd better check the cabbages again. The things were getting everywhere—garden, stable, even into the kitchen, where Gudrun spent half the day swatting them with dishrags. They were turning into a veritable plague, though the Talmud had never mentioned butterflies. "I'll go round with the chemicals again tomorrow," he promised, and left when the doctor still didn't respond.

In retrospect, Benjamin thought to himself, the policemen's visit was troubling the doctor. After all, he'd wanted his return to Vienna to remain a secret. What chance of that now? Gudrun had betrayed him, the poisonous old hag.

He reached the end of the street, about-faced, and ambled back, whistling under his breath. This time he steeled himself to stop on the pavement outside the final house and look more carefully at the entrance. His face suddenly flamed. The tiled panels to each side of the front door were decorated with scantily clad dryads—nothing wrong with that— but below them were curved stone benches, each supported by a pair of leering satyrs, or perhaps representations of Priapus, all possessed of such huge and enormously engorged *shvantz* that they must surely fall flat on their faces should they attempt to walk. This was the place all right, the Thélème. And there was the side entrance—

His nose twitched as it detected a faintly remembered smell, pleasant enough and yet bringing with it some associated fear that set his heart pounding and the hair at his nape prickling. Benjamin spun round, fists clenched, to find himself facing another character from that drunken evening with Hugo. No policeman, this. The flaxen hair and sweetly serene choirboy face belonged to the man who'd sat by the fire eavesdropping on their conversation and, Benjamin was now convinced, followed him through the back alleys in order to administer that savage beating. He winced. The deep bruising caused by his assailant's feet and fists were not yet fully healed. This afternoon, the fellow was sporting a warm smile contradicted by the wicked glint in extraordinarily pale blue eyes; the dueling scar on his cheek seemed even more pronounced by daylight.

Benjamin swallowed hard and took two steps backwards. "Good afternoon," he said, hoping the tremor in his voice wasn't obvious.

"Clear off."

"I beg your pardon?"

"Go back where you came from. You're not welcome here."

"Very well." Benjamin politely inclined his head. "Then I'll wish you a good—"

"If I catch you sniffing round here again," whispered the other, coming horribly close and gripping Benjamin's coat lapels, "I'll take great pleasure in breaking every bone in your filthy body. Do you understand?" He was still smiling.

Benjamin's throat closed up. He nodded mutely and began walking back towards Stephansplatz, stopping only when he faced the great cathedral. Eyes cast down, he sneaked inside the Christian stronghold and found a quiet corner from where he could sympathetically view the public agony of Vienna's *Zahnweh-Herrgott*, Lord of the Toothache. An hour later he returned to the Thélème. Benjamin knew, for a fact, that Lilie would do as much—more—for him. This time there was no hesitation: striding down the side of the building, he made straight for the servants' entrance.

The rear of the house lacked the well-polished respectability evident at the front. Blistered and peeling boards—similar to theater backdrops depicting Venetian palace interiors, imperial ballrooms, bucolic landscapes, seascapes—partially screened grounds so badly neglected they suggested the proprietor's complete lack of interest in anything outside the building's four walls. Benjamin cast his eye over the grim tangle of brambles and nettles, the battalions of damson suckers massing for a final onslaught on the foundations, and decided his most sensible option would be to offer his services as a gardener. A few steps more and he saw two men smoking and playing cards on an ornate cast-iron table lacking one leg and supported instead by a wooden block. The men were in their shirtsleeves, despite the chill wind sending rags and tatters of black cloud scuttling across the overcast sky. A carafe of wine and crumb-strewn plates stood between them, and he noted with interest the fine-quality glasses being used. Nobody here, it seemed, passed on the cracked and chipped tableware for use by the servants. Both men looked up as he approached.

"What you after?" growled the nearest.

Benjamin hesitated. At close range neither fellow looked as he'd expected such men to look. There was nothing womanish about their appearances. On the contrary, both were broad-shouldered and well-muscled. He shrugged. "Heard tell this was a friendly place to those who don't fit in with the rest of the world."

"Might be," said the nearest, with a low-pitched grunt of laughter. "What's it to you, pissling?" He stood, lazily stretching, and Benjamin hastily shuffled backwards. The man was huge, the biggest man he'd ever encountered, considerably taller than him, probably not far off seven foot. Ugly, too, with an upper lip twisted and scarred—perhaps indicating a cleft palate clumsily repaired. His frank appraisal alarmed Benjamin. It must have showed: the giant grimaced ferociously before bellowing with laughter. He winked, turning towards the open doorway. "Perhaps I'll see you again, *Zwerg*. Right now, there's work to do."

"You go on, Kurt," said his companion. "I'll sort this out." He put his hand on Benjamin's arm. "Sit down, my young friend. Take a glass. What's your name? I'm Wilhelm."

Wilhelm's hands were clean, well cared for, and Benjamin self-consciously hid his own beneath the table edge. He realized this hadn't been thought through well enough; on the other hand, near-enough honesty was probably the best policy, and he plied Wilhelm with simple questions about the club. "I've heard so many rumors about this place." This was true enough. "I could never work out what was real and what was tavern talk." He lowered his voice. "Is it true they sell foreign girls to the highest bidder? Is it true you have beds big enough for ten?"

Wilhelm smiled. "You shouldn't listen to such tittle-tattle, my young friend."

"What about orgies that last seven days and seven nights?" Benjamin asked hoarsely. "Is that true?"

"This is a very discreet club," said Wilhelm, pulling at his left ear. "It's not for run-of-the-mill folk who follow dull rules and restrictions handed down from above. Only the better sort of gentlemen are invited to become members."

"Rich, you mean?"

"That, too," agreed Wilhelm. He gathered up the playing cards, shuffling and splitting the pack before replacing it in its box. A small chill ran up Benjamin's back as he caught sight of the topmost card. Gudrun often amused herself with cartomancy on the kitchen table after their evening meal. Her readings were usually on behalf of people she'd only read about in newspaper headlines while cutting and pasting into her scrapbooks: Luigi Lucheni, Mark Twain, Szczepanik (the crazy Polish inventor of what he called the *Fernseher*)—and, more recently, Carl Schlechter and Philipp Meitner, in an effort to predict the outcome of their eagerly awaited chess tournament. While he took very little notice of her solemn pronouncements, Benjamin did know that the ace of spades was the card indicating misfortune, sometimes associated with death or, more often, a difficult ending. "This is an interesting place to work," Wilhelm added, watching Benjamin's face. "Rarely a dull moment."

"Where I work, there's an old woman who makes my life hell. You know what they're like—always at you. 'Fetch this.' 'Carry that.' 'Buck up.' 'Get a move on.' Don't know how much longer I can stand it." Benjamin sighed deeply. "Anyway, I'd rather be among people who understand me."

Wilhelm sat back in his chair and took out another cigarette. "Benjamin," he said, with an air of triumph, "you can stop beating about the bush. I know exactly what you're after."

Benjamin gulped. His throat muscles contracted, but he forced a bashful smile. "Do you indeed?"

"Well, one of the things, at least." Wilhelm laughed. "You want a job here. That's it, isn't it?"

"I thought you might need a gardener." He nodded towards the unkempt garden.

"The yard's better left as it is. Digging large holes in smooth turf is too noticeable. Anyway, you'd be wasted on such work."

"I don't have much experience in other—"

Wilhelm waved that aside. "From time to time, we take on custodians. There are no vacancies right now, but I could make it happen." He looked speculatively at Benjamin. "Yes, I could be very helpful."

Benjamin met his eyes. "I'd be grateful." He hesitated. "If I worked here, what exactly would I be expected to do?"

"Oh, simple enough work. All an *Aufseher* really does is enforce order . . . keep an eye out for trouble, nip it in the bud. We've a couple of hundred"—again he glanced at Benjamin—"odalisques in residence. They aren't always peaceful creatures."

"Odalisques?"

"The females." Wilhelm sniggered. "That's what we're told to call them. There are many less dignified terms."

"Oh."

"Thing is, my young friend, all animals have certain characteristics in common. Put too many rats in a box and they fight, or try to break out. We're here to make sure everything runs smoothly."

"And do they? Break out, I mean?"

"Occasionally." Wilhelm's eyes strayed to the garden. "They don't get far." He was silent for a moment, then touched Benjamin's arm again. "We'll be a man short soon, and it strikes me, Benjamin, that you'd fit in here very well. If you like, I'll recommend you for the position—"

"I would indeed!"

"You are eager." Wilhelm laughed and ruffled Benjamin's hair. "Must go now. There's a lot to get done before this evening, but I'll have a word with . . ." He picked up the glasses and made for the door Kurt had entered earlier. "Come back tomorrow. I may have good news for you."

CONSCIOUS OF WILHELM'S EYES on his back, Benjamin strode towards the street as boldly as he dared. Luckily, there was no sign of the fair-haired man who'd threatened him earlier; nevertheless, he increased his pace, anxious to lose himself in the crowded thoroughfares of Vienna's center, only slowing as he reached Stock-im-Eisen-Platz, site of the ancient horse market. He stationed himself near the nail-tree, catching his breath and listening to a burgher's wife—obviously dressed in her *Sonntagskleider*, her Sunday best—showing her drably attired country cousins the countless nails hammered into the tree over more than four centuries, turning it into the famous staff in iron. The tree was guarded by the Devil himself, she assured them, her voice hushed. Benjamin hid a smile as each of the women looked askance at the façade of the Palais Equitable as if expecting the Prince of Darkness to leap from the shadow of one of the American eagles.

When the women departed in the direction of Stephansplatz and the sanctity of its cathedral, Benjamin also moved away from the niche housing the tree trunk and stood deep in thought before the bronze reliefs of the legend on the building's door. Someone had sworn one of the locksmiths depicted here had six fingers, a sly reference to the nimble digits possessed by members of that guild. He'd never found it, was almost sure they'd invented the story, but he continued to examine the figures closely even as he assessed his visit to the Thélème. Granted, he'd done well, established a contact within the club who'd even dangled the promise of a position there . . . yet he felt no real sense of achievement. The prospect of returning to that place of dark undercurrents and secrets made him uneasy, though he must for Lilie's sake. Remembering her sweet face bent over the rose brought a rush of longing, and Benjamin turned for home. However, the prospect of being interrogated by the doctor in his present sour mood stopped him in his tracks; instead he headed towards Stephansplatz, cutting through the line of buildings that divided it from Stock-im-Eisen-Platz so that he arrived minutes before the burgher's wife and her easily impressed entourage. Ignoring their suspicious glances, he stopped by a street seller's brazier to buy the first *Maronen* of the year, chestnuts, plump and sweet, fresh from the southern forests. Something about the man's scrawny and ill-fed assistant, furiously blowing on the glowing coals, nudged at his memory. After a moment the picture of Hugo Besser's barefoot protégé crouching by the Kneipe fire gnawing at kitchen scraps presented itself. Benjamin nodded; he'd meant to go back. With so many contacts, Hugo would undoubtedly have discovered something about Lilie. Juggling his last hot chestnut to rip off the peel, Benjamin tossed it into his mouth and crossed Stephansplatz in the direction of Leopoldstadt.

As he approached the Donaukanal, two men fishing from the bank glanced briefly in his direction, frowning as if the sound of his footsteps might frighten away any chance of dinner. Their anxiety was unjustified: moments later both lines twitched and, from his vantage point on the bridge, Benjamin watched the men land a fine pair of carp. He lingered awhile, watching the late-afternoon sun illuminating the south tower of the cathedral; as the sun set it would also shine on the Giant's Door on the western side, where Gudrun swore the bones of a gigantic man had hung in days gone by. Benjamin thought of Kurt and shuddered. Though he seemed good-natured enough, the fellow's massive fists could pulverize him as easily as any other man might swat a fly. A knot of fear tightened below his ribs. He took a deep breath to calm himself, staring into the winter-gray depths of the water before again lifting his eyes to the Innere Stadt. For now all was serene: there was no mist today, the sky was still bright, the air clear and crisp; not even the slightest suggestion of a breeze ruffled the line of bare trees penciled against the inner-city walls. Why then this lingering sense of foreboding? He frowned, rubbing his eyes in disbelief, as a vast black cloud swelled from the cathedral roof, swirling, rising and falling, rapidly increasing in size as it approached the bridge. Storm hags? A demon? Perhaps he was asleep, caught fast in an *Alptraum*. Benjamin pinched himself, grunting at the sharp pain. This was no nightmare. Then the cloud was directly above him and he laughed aloud, for his demon was nothing but a mass migration of starlings, probably including the same ones he'd noticed while talking with Lilie outside the stable earlier. Still smiling at his own folly, Benjamin turned his back on Stephansdom. With a swift glance towards the slowly revolving Ferris wheel, he took a second deep breath before plunging into the malodorous underbelly of Mazzesinsel.

At first the shouting seemed no more than a falling-out of neighbors—common enough in this part of Vienna, where growing hardship repeatedly caused a witch bag of old grievances to burst asunder. Only a few days had passed since Benjamin's last visit, but he noticed a dramatic increase in graffiti. In some squares *Judenfrei* had been hastily scrawled on almost every wall, even occasionally the more ominous *Judenrein*, cleansed of the Jews, an impossible claim by those the doctor angrily referred to as simple-minded members of the Christian Social Party. From the base of each letter, bright red paint trickled through the soot and filth, resulting in a curious color, one Benjamin could hardly put a name to but was nevertheless familiar with, something once seen or dreamed, reminiscent of old blood. The sense of foreboding returned. Benjamin shrugged it off. These things went in cycles; next month it would probably be the Czechs' turn to be persecuted because of their demands for a bilingual Vienna. The noise grew louder: to the shouts and yells were added the sounds of breaking glass, dull thuds that could only be falling masonry, the pounding of many boots. Though it shamed him, Benjamin had no wish to get involved in any local skirmish, no matter who was involved. His sole aim was to satisfy his employer's need for information about Lilie's background . . . and Lilie, too, he supposed, not that he cared. Where she came from, whatever she'd done, it would never matter to him. That she'd survived and stayed at his side would always be enough.

Benjamin moved away from the uproar, slipping through gaps between buildings, down alleyways running with fetid water, and across neglected squares, his route taking him in a wide arc round the site of the trouble. After a breathless few minutes, he stopped, confused: either the disturbance was rapidly moving outwards or his memories of childhood haunts had faded, for now the noise seemed right on top of him—in front, behind, above, below—and yet the streets were almost deserted. He whirled, unsure of which direction to take, headed towards the Casa Sefardi, and immediately regretted the decision: Schattenplatz was also deserted but clearly something had happened here. Shop windows were smashed, shutters ripped from their hinges; goods and fittings lay scattered over the cobbles. His nose detected the smell of scorched fabric. Wisps of smoke drifted aimlessly. Benjamin took a few steps across the open square, conscious of unseen eyes watching from the windows of the apartments above. On the east side, a baker's shop had been attacked, tins and trays, scales and weights, thrown into the gutter—recently, too, for one of the large brass weights still rolled from side to side as if trying to right itself—and Benjamin stooped and began collecting them before realizing his action might be misunderstood. He was no looter.

Others had no such qualms. Small movements, at first hardly more than the stirring of the buildings' shadows, quickly became a horde of scavengers. A bowed old man stumbled forward, attempting to spear a new-baked loaf with his cane, only to have his prize snatched by a rack-ribbed cur. Ragged children spewed from dark crevices, snatching up bread—even when it had been fouled by the gutter—tearing it with their teeth as they melted back into their hiding places. Women came running, darting fearful glances behind them, gathering even the smallest morsels of what remained and carrying them away in their skirts. Benjamin ran alongside them. "What happened here?" Nobody answered. He might have been invisible.

The smoke increased. A dull glow in the ragman's shop threw into relief a line of outmoded coats, investing them with a semblance of life as they twitched and contorted. Moments later, the fire took hold. The front of the shop became a curtain of flame belching forth foul-smelling smoke that crept along the ground before rising in phantasmal columns, filling the square with ghosts and muting every sound. Into this silence erupted the roars and cries of a multitude of voices, the slap of running feet, and behind them, countermelody to this cacophony, a steady double beat of marching boots. Benjamin turned to run, but it was too late. The fleeing crowd blundered through the smoke, seeking exits. Their pursuers relentlessly pressed them on, their arms rising from the smoke to fall on heads and backs. Benjamin thought there were gray uniforms but couldn't be sure, for it was the loathing on the faces that held his eye. The panic was so great that entrances to the narrowest streets were rapidly blocked. People started falling round him, choking, disappearing beneath the smoke; Benjamin fell, too, managing to scramble upright only by hauling on the boot of one of the attackers. Coughing and gasping, his eyes streaming, he fought against the crowd, elbowing, punching, kicking—a guilt-ridden process, whatever was necessary to survive—making for the opposite side of the square, reasoning that the attention of the aggressors would be focused in front rather than behind.

He was out of luck: a small knot of reinforcements waited there, perched on tumbled stones better to observe the proceedings. Some were laughing uncontrollably. Another was counting aloud, gripping the collar of a great black dog whose bared teeth and attempted lunges were more terrifying than any amount of barking. One man sat apart, enthroned on a section of wall higher than the rest, polishing a gold Hanukkah lamp—an exquisite thing with a design of prancing stags—with his pocket handkerchief. He was intent on his work and his head remained bowed, but Benjamin's mouth was suddenly dry. That crown of flaxen hair coupled with the dueling scar was unmistakable: he'd come straight to the one person in Vienna he'd been trying to avoid. He quickly turned back towards the square, thinking to hide in the smoke and the madness. Behind him, the laughter stopped. He was suddenly surrounded.

"What have we here?"

"Well, well, where you from, boy?"

"H-here," quavered Benjamin. "I'm Viennese, like you. I live in Brandstätte."

"Hear that, *Herr* Klingemann? This rat thinks he's like us."

"I heard." The fair-haired man slowly descended, passing the lamp to a companion for safekeeping. Benjamin flinched at Klingemann's smile, guessing what was coming. And he was right: a sharp blow to each ear sent him reeling, first one way and then the other. Someone forced him to his knees and he fell heavily, small stones pressing into his shins. Klingemann leaned over him, coming so close Benjamin could smell the scent of his cigarettes, the undertones of stale tobacco, his hair pomade and a musky perfume that he knew but could not place. "You're nothing like us, boy. You and your ilk aren't wanted in Vienna. Get that?"

Benjamin's anger temporarily overrode his fear. "I was born here. I've got as much right—" The blow knocked him sideways onto the cobbles, banging the side of his head.

"You've got no rights, rat."

"Let's see what the creature's made of." It was Klingemann's voice.

Benjamin shook his head violently, trying to marshal his thoughts into order. "I'm just the same as you," he began, before realizing he was not the creature referred to. Two paces away, the huge black hound was snarling and yipping, biting at the air, fighting to get free. Gritting his teeth, Benjamin struggled to rise. He was almost upright when someone kicked his legs from under him. A heavy boot landed between his shoulder blades, pinning him to the ground.

"You are not the same as us," barked Klingemann. "The time will come when we'll prove it to you. Crawl back to your rat hole . . . No, back down on your hands and knees. Be thankful I've more important things to deal with." He kicked Benjamin in the ribs. "And remember this—you've had two warnings about being in places where you're unwanted. No more chances. The next time I see you, you'll be wherever your lot goes when the life's beaten out of you."

reet feeds Papa's shirts between the mangle rollers, turning the handle so energetically her words come out in small rushes along with the water. "You'll come to a bad end, my lady, unless you change your ways. Do you know what happens to girls who tell lies?" I roll my eyes and kick the laundry tub. She elbows me. "Stop that. Now, for the last time, did you steal the cake?"

"No. I don't like *Spuckkuchen*."

Greet narrows her eyes. "And why's that?"

"I only like sweet cherries, not sour ones with the stones left in."

"There we are then. You've given yourself away nicely. How would you know whether they're sweet or not without tasting?" Greet holds up one of my dresses, squashed thin as paper by the wooden rollers. She shakes it alive again; one arm waves good-bye as it drops into the hanging-out basket. "I know a story about a girl who couldn't stop telling bigger and bigger lies until finally the nasty little creature claimed she could spin straw into gold."

"Stupid."

"Of course it was. Straw's good for nothing but old cows to chew on."
Out through the rollers come Papa's doctor coats, so long and flat they
remind me of a picture of Wendy sewing Peter Pan's shadow back on.
Greet seizes each before it touches the ground. She examines them
carefully, making sure they're white as spilled milk, every trace of the
sick people boiled away. "Trouble was—the emperor happened to hear
about it. He was very wealthy, but such men always like the idea of being even wealthier. That's the way of the world. Always has been. Always will be. The rich get richer while the poor get poorer. Fairness
never comes into it. If I had my way—"

She goes on talking to the washing so I pick a dandelion clock and try
getting it to tell me the time: *eins, zwei, drei, vier, fünf* . . . Greet once told
me if you puffed away every seed, your mother would no longer want
you. It doesn't matter anymore. I keep blowing until we get up to seven,
but it's already past eleven, which means the dandelion isn't telling the
truth, either.

"What did the emperor do?" I ask when Greet finally stops muttering.

"He ordered his guards to lock the little liar in a cellar with a cartload
of straw and her spinning wheel. And there she had to stay in the dark.
Alone. Not even a dry crust to chew, never mind stolen cherry cake.
Spinning for her life, until the day wishes could come true and all his
treasuries were overflowing with gold."

"Why didn't she climb out of the coal hole?"

"Emperors don't use coal. They burn banknotes."

"What happened to the girl in the end?" I dance from one foot to the
other, impatient for the rest of the story. "Didn't someone come to rescue her?"

"No," snaps Greet, snatching up the peg bag. "This time the wicked
girl had to learn the hard way not to tell lies. She's probably there still if

she hasn't been eaten alive by hungry rats. Out of my way, I've got work to do."

"But . . . but before, you said a little man called Rumpelstiltskin spun the straw into gold and I . . . she became queen." I suck hard on my thumb. This is no time for tears.

"Stories," says Greet, "are fast travelers, always moving on." She empties the bucket of mangle water over the stones, making me jump out of the way as soap bubbles tinted ultramarine by the *Waschblau* bag rush towards the drain. "Oh, yes, stories change with the wind and the tide and the moon. Half the time they're only plaited mist anyway, so they disappear altogether when daylight shines on them."

"When I make up stories I'll write them down so they won't disappear or be changed."

Greet shrugs. "Then they won't be proper stories, will they?"

THE BUNDLES OF STRAW where we go each day are taller than Erika and very heavy. There's no spinning wheel so she twists it into long ropes, which she braids to make shoes. Her hands get covered with little pricks and scratches. Sometimes they bleed. Afterwards her fingers swell up and hurt but still she must continue twisting and braiding, going on and on like the girl in the story who couldn't stop dancing. Other people here use straw to make bags and sun hats.

Every morning I try to hide, but Erika always knows where to find me. I don't like coming here. It's cold and the air is full of dust. Straw doesn't taste nice, and you can't swallow it however long you chew. I don't believe cows eat it. There's nothing to do but sit under the bench and tell Lottie straw stories, "Rumpelstiltskin," "The Three Little Pigs," and the one about the straw bull with the tarred back. I tell them a hundred different ways, but they all end happily. The nastier ones I keep in my head to tell Daniel later. Sometimes I creep into a nearby room and watch mats being woven from reeds. They're damp and smell like a riverbank, reminding me of *The Wind in the Willows*. Papa started reading it to me the Christmas before we came here, but he was too busy to finish and Greet said the small letters made her head ache.

When the weather gets really cold, more people vanish. Sometimes they fall right down in the snow like the Little Match Girl. And others melt. Or stay where they're told and turn overnight into Snow Queen statues. Erika makes me a vest out of an old pinafore laced up with string at the front.

"It's ugly."

"Put it on. An extra layer will help."

"Uncle Hraben still has all my nice vests and jerseys in his cupboard."

"Stay away from him. Remember what I told you?"

I stick out my lip and say nothing. Erika's story about what bad men do to little girls was nasty and stupid, like some of the things Greet said when she was cross. But Greet's stories were always about someone else a long way away, and Erika only talked about what might happen to me. Lottie keeps reminding me about Uncle Hraben's pinching and prodding; I still don't believe the rest of it. These days, Erika and Annalies watch me even harder than Greet did, but when they forget, I'll sneak through the rows of tents and run to the tower to get some of my winter things.

Soon it becomes so cold Lena's nose turns bright red and has a dewdrop hanging from it. At night she lets me sleep cuddled up to her back, which is nice, until she cries in her sleep. The snow makes her sad.

"Another year coming to an end," she says. "Another year stolen."

Annalies doesn't plait straw anymore. Now she goes into town to clean houses. Sometimes she brings back crusts, ends of sausages, or magpie bits and pieces, hidden in a special pocket sewn inside her skirt. Erika says this is madness and not worth the risk, but Annalies won't stop.

"They've taken everything from me. Everything. Taking something of theirs, however small and insignificant, is the only thing that makes life worthwhile." Annalies steals apple peels and single earrings, bent spoons, cloves and toothpicks, jar labels, keys to unknown doors and lost boxes, scent-bottle tops, hairpins, spent matches.

One day she comes back with a handful of beans. They're dry and very hard, wrinkled like fingers that have been in bathwater too long. "Here, Krysta, a little present. It's almost Christmas." She gives me four, counting them out as if they were gold coins. "And who knows, they might turn out to be magic ones."

"We can eat those." Daniel holds out his hand. I close my fist round them.

"What if they really are magic beans?"

"Don't be stupid."

Now he's said that, I won't give him any. I won't eat them either because, in the story, Jack's mother said he was stupid to exchange their old cow for a handful of beans, but look what happened when he planted them. Greet used to plant beans like these in a double row, saying: one to rot and one to grow, one for the pigeon, one for the crow. And when they came up every plant had lots of pods, with five or six smooth green beans in each.

"HURRY UP WITH THAT PODDING." Greet rattles the pan. "We haven't got all day."

"Don't want to. Won't. Don't like beans."

"Well, you should. Beans make you grow up big and strong."

"I don't care."

"You've been told before"—Greet stoops to pick up the beans I've pushed onto the floor—"what happens to people who say they don't care. Remember?"

"No." I fold my arms over my chest.

"Don't care was made to care," she chants, snapping open the pods:

"Don't care was hung,
Don't care was put in a pot
And boiled till he was done."

"That's stupid. Nobody boils people. The pots aren't big enough. Anyway, beans are nasty. They taste like caterpillars. I won't ever eat them."

"Let's hope you never have to, then." Greet gathers together the empty pods. "Did I tell you the story of the poor old woman who had nothing in the world to eat but a few dried-up old beans at the back of her cupboard?"

"Don't want to hear." I put my hands over my ears, leaving a tiny gap between my fingers for Greet's voice to squeeze through.

"Of course," continues Greet, chopping dill to go with the beans, "the old woman wanted to cook them. So she gathered sticks for a fire, using a handful of straw as kindling. While she was waiting for the fire to grow hot, she emptied her few beans into a pan. Now it so happened that a single bean fell, unnoticed, to the floor, where it lay beside a piece of straw. Soon afterwards a burning coal from the fire leapt down between them. Then the straw said: 'My dear friends, how did you get here?'"

"Stupid. Straw doesn't talk."

"I thought you weren't listening." Greet begins scrubbing the kitchen table. "Anyway, the coal replied: 'Luckily, I sprang out of the fire, otherwise I'd be dead by now, burnt to ashes.' At that the bean joined in, saying: 'I, too, escaped with a whole skin. If the old woman had got me into the pan, I'd have been made into broth without any mercy, like my comrades.'"

I take my hands off my ears. "Why can't we have a proper story?"

"Why couldn't you pod those few beans for me?" retorts Greet. "Stories shouldn't be left in the middle, so let me finish now I've started. Well, like someone else I know, the straw turned up his nose at the mention of broth—"

"Straws don't have—"

"'I also came close to death,' said the straw. 'The old woman destroyed my entire family. She seized a hundred at once and burnt them alive. Luckily, I slipped through her fingers.' Well, the bean, the coal, and the piece of straw decided to run away and seek their fortunes together. They hadn't gone far when they came to a stream. Since there was no bridge, the piece of straw stretched himself across the water so the others could walk over him. But the hot coal stopped halfway, frightened by the sound of rushing water, at which the straw started to burn, then broke into two pieces and tumbled into the stream. The coal fell, too, hissing as she touched the water and breathed her last. The bean, still watching from the bank, laughed so much she split her sides. By good fortune, a tailor had stopped to rest by the stream, and being a kind-hearted fellow, he sewed her together again. But he only had black thread—which is why all beans have a black seam running up their middle."

"Let me see."

"No." Greet holds the pan out of my reach. "You'll have to wait until you've learned to eat up your beans without complaint."

. . .

ONE SUNDAY AFTERNOON, Lena comes back smiling and happy because she's been offered a new job. "There's a sun bed, just imagine . . . and I'll be able to wear makeup."

Erika gets very angry. "Are you crazy? Isn't everything bad enough without losing every last shred of self-respect?"

"Don't be like that. I just want to have pretty clothes again, clean clothes—"

"If you ever get to wear them," Erika says, her mouth twisting.

Lena shrugs. "It's only for six months, Erika. Then they'll let me go home."

"Since when did their promises count for anything?"

"At least I'd feel like a woman and not an animal."

I sit on the end of the bed, pretending to be mending Lottie's arms and legs again but listening hard. Perhaps I've become an animal without noticing, because now I have to bite my nails off to stop them being claws. When Erika and Lena start shouting bad words at each other, I creep outside and run to the empty aviary with my beans. Each one really does have a black seam along its tummy, so if that story was true, why shouldn't the others be? After choosing a place next to a metal pillar—so the magic beans have something to climb up—I start digging. The ground is frozen hard. My holes aren't as deep as Greet's, but I heap snow over the disturbed earth. "One to rot and one to grow, one for the pigeon, one for the crow"—I say her planting spell three times just to be sure.

Afterwards, I think about visiting Uncle Hraben in his tower. There would be cake, and toffees, and I could cleverly steal one of my vests and the red gloves embroidered with little snowmen that Greet made for me. Too late: Erika has come looking for me, hunched against the wind and with her eyes red from crying. Without a word, I follow her back to our hut. When I sleep, I dream of climbing up and up a bean-stalk, on and on, sunrise, sunset, winter after winter. Finally, I reach the top and step into the magical country of giants, harps playing lullabies, geese laying golden eggs big enough for six breakfasts, only to find someone has been left behind. But the beanstalk has withered and died. I can't go back.

I wake sad, and when we trudge past the aviary, there's no sign of any beanstalk, though in the story Jack's grew overnight. Perhaps it won't grow because I forgot to say thank you for the beans. It's too late now. One day Annalies doesn't come back. On Christmas Eve, Erika gives me a little bed made of plaited straw for Lottie to sleep in.

GREET GETS NASTY every time Papa comes back from a hunting trip. Her face turns red. She burns my breakfast and throws plates into the sink.

Blood trickles under the door of the little outside room where the game is kept. The door is locked, just like Bluebeard's; when I look through the keyhole, I see a sad-eyed young deer, some pheasants, and a hare hanging from great hooks in the ceiling. Every night, cats clean away the blood, which grows darker as the days go on. Next Sunday, Papa's hunting companions will come for dinner and there must be roast venison, and *Hasenpfeffer* with potato dumplings and *Blaukraut*.

"I've only got one pair of hands," Greet tells the ceiling, as she sharpens her big cleaver and lines up the knives. "God knows there's enough to do in this house without playing butcher." She glares at me. "Out from under my feet, Miss, if you please."

I run outside and only creep back when the old man and his boy have been for the heads and feet Greet doesn't want. The kitchen smells of rusty iron. A few flies circle the huge pans of meat.

"Waste not, want not." Greet quickly stuffs some money into her pocket. "These days, plenty of people are being reduced to eating blockade mutton again."

"Mutton's sheep."

"Dog, I mean. That's what blockade mutton is: dog." I can tell by her voice she's still angry. Sometimes Greet uses *Pfeffernüsse* in the *Hasenpfeffer*, and though I won't eat hare stew I want some of her ginger cookies before they all go to thicken the gravy.

"Shall I pick the herbs for you, Greet?"

She blinks. "That's an improvement, I must say. Yes, I'll need some thyme, Krysta, and a few sprigs of rosemary. Ah, and two bay leaves from the tree at the end of the garden."

As a reward, I get a handful of cookies. When I ask for a story, it's full of bangs and crashes.

"There was once a pretty young maiden promised to a wicked bridegroom. One day she went to visit him, following an ash path to his lonely black house in the middle of the darkest forest that ever was. Nobody was at home except an old woman, who told her the bridegroom was a robber and warned her to run home as fast as she could. But this silly girl—" The cleaver falls and splinters of bone fly into the air. Greet wipes the sweat from her forehead with a red-stained corner of apron. She sniffs mightily. "This silly girl, like so many others, took no notice at all until it was too late, for the wicked bridegroom and his friends were at the door. Just in time, the old woman hid her behind a barrel. In came the evil men, *betrunken wie Herren*, dragging after them a young girl. First they forced her to drink wine with them: a glass of red, a glass of white, and a glass of black. After that, they pulled off her pretty clothes and put them in a pile ready to sell in the market. And then they—" Greet stops abruptly. She clears her throat and glances towards the door.

"What?" My voice has shrunk to a croak. I've heard enough but still I have to know what happens next.

"And then they . . . uh . . . after they'd finished doing evil things—"

"What sort of things?"

"Things so bad I can't tell you. All I'll say is that it went on for a long time, and she screamed and cried and called on God and all his angels to help her." She dives into the deer, ripping out its liver and lights. "And when they'd all finished what they were doing over and over again, she was dead, so after chopping off her fingers to get her rings, they cut her up small and sprinkled the pieces with salt."

"Did they eat her?"

Once again Greet looks at the door. "Of course. And afterwards they threw the bones on the fire to make more ashes for the path through the forest."

"W-what happened to the bride?"

"She ran home and told her father, who had the robbers brought to trial. They were flayed alive and beheaded with axes." Greet stares into the basin of entrails. "Yes, that day there was so much blood it ran from the courthouse in Altona right down to the Elbe."

IT'S ERIKA'S TURN to get a new job—sorting big piles of dressing-up clothes in a place much warmer and cleaner than where she plaited straw. There are long tables heaped with pretty silk dresses like Mama used to wear, shoes, handbags, and mountains of fur coats. Sometimes I try things on, but there's no looking glass to see myself in. We find funny things mixed in with the clothes—soap and toothpaste, false teeth, spectacles, photographs, combs. The person in charge here does not shout or slap. His name is Schmidt; he makes sure the soup at midday is hot and lets everyone have a proper rest. After a bit he gives me a job, too: my fingers are small enough to help unpick the fur coats so the tailors can sew them into new ones.

It's hard to find the tiny stitches in the fur. Whenever it's easier I know someone has unpicked them before and there will be money and jewels hidden inside the collars and cuffs. This is a big place, with many rooms, and yet every time it happens I look up to find Schmidt standing over me. In the end, I realize he's another sort of witch. There's an ugly old ginger cat here that watches us with eyes the color of Greet's nastiest pea soup; it runs to tell Schmidt the minute my fingers feel something lumpy beneath the seams. One day a pretty gold brooch falls from a hem even before I snip the stitches. It's tiny, in the shape of a flower, with blue stones for petals, and I'm about to hide it inside my shoe when Schmidt turns up, holding out his big red hand. The cat weaves through his legs, looking at me and smiling by narrowing its eyes. It disappears into thin air when I swing my foot. Erika tells me to leave it alone or I'll get sent to work in the bad room full of dirty, smelly clothes covered with blood and bugs, but I don't care.

A few days later, I pretend to make friends with the witch's cat and get it by the neck, squeezing so hard its eyes bulge as it claws empty air. Suddenly Schmidt appears and I have to stop. Next time it won't be so lucky.

WHEN WE WANT to make up stories, Daniel and I go to our special place behind one of the sheds. "It's your turn," I remind him. He shakes his head.

"Your stories are better than mine. Nastier things happen to the bad people."

"All right. Who shall we kill today?" We decide all the zookeepers must die. Since they're so much bigger than us, first we need to put a magic spell on them. This makes us huge and turns them into dwarves. Then we make them line up like children in the school yard. Daniel has a large whip, and when they won't do as they are told quickly enough, he snaps their legs with it. They have to stand there a long time while we run between their legs very fast, playing the game Cecily taught us in order to keep ourselves warm:

> In and out the Bluebell Windows,
> In and out the Bluebell Windows,
> In and out the Bluebell Windows,
> I am your master.

When the verse comes to an end, we are supposed to choose someone and sing:

> Pat the one you've chosen on their shoulders,
> Pat the one you've chosen on their shoulders,
> Pat the one you've chosen on their shoulders,
> All day long.

But by then we're tired and giddy, so we leave that part out and march them through the dark forest until we get to the gingerbread cottage. We have to hurry because the magic doesn't last long and they'll soon grow back to their real sizes. This witch keeps an enormous oven, big enough for elephants and giraffes or a thousand ordinary animals, hidden behind her bathhouse. The zookeepers must know about it because we have to prod them with pitchforks and fire guns into the air to make them move. They shuffle forward, blubbering and wailing, pretending they're sorry and saying someone else made them do the bad things. We force them all in, even Uncle Hraben, though he begs me not to. "I knew your papa, Krysta. I gave you toffees."

Daniel slaps his head. Once. Twice. Three times. "Isn't everything bad enough without losing every last shred of self-respect?"

When we have bolted the door, we cover it with mud so we can't hear them howling, and gather fir cones and dead branches for the fire. The witch has to light it. She's very frightened and makes secret signs with her fingers. Then she gets on her knees and tries to remember how to pray. A lot of smoke comes out of the tall, tall chimney. Today it smells of violets and burnt caramel. The ashes are black and the trees shrivel and die as they fall on them.

OUTSIDE THE TAILOR'S FACTORY we can see the tops of forest trees over the wall. Most are ink-black firs, but one is a spiteful chestnut that wouldn't throw us a single nut in the autumn, though now spring's come it lets the wind carry heaps of yellow-green catkins into the yard. Two of my bean plants have grown, though they're not very big yet.

A whole lot of new people come. One of them is an ugly old woman, who stares very hard at me and clutches her chest, croaking: "It's my girl from the cabinet!"

I poke out my tongue and run away, but she hobbles after us, dragging one foot and wanting to touch me. Daniel says she's not right in the head. He waves his hand in front of his face.

Uncle Hraben has been away for a long time. One day he reappears to tell me the cherry trees are blossoming. "I've missed you, Krysta. I used to look forward to our little chats. Come and see me one afternoon. There are new baby rabbits. Your pretty clothes are waiting for you."

I look at my feet and say nothing.

"Come soon." He looks so sad that it's hard to believe any of the things Erika told me. Later on, when he says the first cherries of the year have arrived, Lottie warns me to stay away from him, but her voice has grown very faint. There's not much left of her now.

All that day and the next while I am unstitching the big coats, I try to remember the taste of cherries. There will be cake as well. Or even some bread . . . with butter. On Sunday I creep towards the tower, slipping from one building to the next so that Erika can't see me, racing up the steps. "Where are the cherries?"

Uncle Hraben sits back in his chair and lights a cigarette. "Now, pretty Krysta, you know there are things you must do first."

I wash my hands and take out my best frock and clean white socks. Although Uncle Hraben pretends not to watch, he starts laughing when I can't do up the buttons.

"You're getting to be a big girl now. Never mind. Come here anyway."

I sit on his knee, but today it feels bony and uncomfortable. When he hands over the cherries, they're unripe and tasteless. I eat them anyway. Uncle Hraben pats my head. He squeezes my arms and legs and tickles inside my unbuttoned dress while telling me about his new puppy, which is called Fürst.

"Is he called Prince because he's a king's son?"

"No, silly little thing. He's *der Fürst der Finsternis*, the Prince of Darkness."

Uncle Hraben says nothing for a while, then slowly puts his hand where Greet said nobody ever should.

"Stop that!"

"Don't you like it?"

"No." I quickly jump up and pull on my ordinary clothes.

He laughs again, but it's not a very nice laugh. "Time to get rid of that dirty old toy," he says when I wrap Lottie in her carrying rag. "Big girls have better things to do with their time than play with broken dolls. Come back tomorrow, Krysta. There'll be more cherries . . . other nice things, too."

I want to talk to Erika about what happened, but she's busy with a whole crowd of new people. It was probably one of them who stole my plants with the tiny bean pods. She doesn't finish telling her new friends things until it's almost dark. Then she goes to the lavatories and disappears. When I can't find her, Cecily holds me tight and says she's in a better place. For a little while I hope Cecily might be my new foster mother, but she prefers being a teacher to telling people to wash their necks. "You must do these things for yourself now, Krysta. It's time to stop letting people treat you like a baby simply because you're so very small. Don't forget, I know what a clever girl you are." She hesitates. "However strange this may sound, Krysta . . . No, listen to me, this is important . . . Sometimes, even when it's impossible to get the things you want—love, security, attention—it's still possible to give them. Do you understand?"

I shrug. "That's stupid."

"Look around you at all the children with mothers too sick and weak to care for them. Perhaps you—"

"Don't look at me. I don't want to look after them. Why should I?"

Lena comes back soon afterwards. She's ill and won't even share my bed. Now there's no one to look after me. Nor is there anyone to make me waste long days in the fur place, so Daniel and I spend most of our time together when I'm not doing my lessons. In the spring he suddenly shoots up in height; now the ladies in my shed tell me I'm doing the same. Lena wants me to cut my long hair off.

"You be careful," she says, between coughs. "They'll come for a pretty girl like you if we survive long enough."

I stay away from Uncle Hraben but often see him at a distance, walking with the Prince of Darkness. One day, I almost bump into him and another man with a full-grown dog as they inspect the shed where the madwomen press their faces against the glass. The Prince of Darkness growls at first, then tries to jump up and play. Uncle Hraben slaps the puppy's nose very hard with his leather glove. The other dog snarls, showing huge yellow teeth dripping foam, until the owner orders it to stop. Then Daniel comes racing round the corner.

"Found y—" He stops dead. The color drains from his face as the big dog lunges forward, straining at its leash, twisting and turning, growling and snapping at the air as it tries to reach him. Uncle Hraben roars commands at the Prince of Darkness, encouraging it to do the same. Very slowly, very gently, Daniel begins backing away. I see Uncle Hraben mouth something to his companion, who nods and yanks the bigger dog so hard that for a moment it's up and dancing on its hind legs. Meanwhile, Uncle Hraben has slipped the Prince of Darkness's leash. The young dog leaps forward and Daniel is on the ground screaming, rolling in the dust as he tries to break free.

"Stop him!" I yell, and beat at Uncle Hraben with my fists.

"Don't worry, Krysta," he shouts above the noise, "nothing much will happen—just a few bites, unless the mutt's better than expected. This is just a little practice for young Fürst. All dogs have to start somewhere." He waits a moment or two longer, holding me back so that I can't run to help Daniel, then bends and says, very close to my ear: "I'll call the dog off now, Krysta, as long as you promise to come and see me tomorrow. From now on you'll have to be a good girl and do as I say. Otherwise . . ."

I nod without saying a word. Uncle Hraben kicks the Prince of Darkness, roaring commands until he has it back on the leash.

When he goes, only Daniel's weeping and the soft drumming of the madwomen beating on the glass break the silence. I've been turned to stone, a statue with eyes fixed on the sky, watching the smoke and the clouds changing places above me.

Eleven

enjamin's yelp, as icy water from the outside pump stung his grazed face and hands, was loud enough to bring Gudrun from the warm chimney corner.

"Who's there? Oh." She lowered the heavy pan. They both stared at his legs. "Look at the state of you. And what's happened to those trousers? They were a good pair, years of wear left in them, and now you turn up with the knees out."

Humiliation had its own sour taste. It rose like bile in Benjamin's throat as he relived that never-to-be-forgotten crossing of the square, inching forward on his hands and knees like a penitent, ridden like an ass, cursed like a dog, kicked and buffeted, spat on, the smoke threatening to choke him. A fresh round of insults and blows rained down every time he tried to rise. They'd made him crawl, face hardly raised an inch from the filthy cobbles, until new victims presented themselves. Finally released, he made for a wall, blindly groping for finger holes in the uneven stones in order to pull himself upright. One stealthy glance over his shoulder showed his attackers tightening around a group of poverty-stricken, ringleted *Ostjuden*. What could he do? Benjamin had lurched away full of self-loathing. He was a coward.

"You've been fighting," crowed Gudrun. "Oh, just wait until the master hears about—"

"Leave me alone," snarled Benjamin, dabbing at his bleeding legs with an old rag. "Run and tell him if that's what you want. I really couldn't care less."

"You're no better than a guttersnipe. Scrapping and brawling—"

Benjamin glared at her. "There were hooligans running riot in Leopoldstadt. I was one of those attacked."

"Oh." Gudrun subsided. "In that case . . ." She held open the door. "I suppose you'd better come into the light. Stand right there. Don't come any farther. That floor's been washed."

"I can't . . ." The kitchen momentarily turned black. Benjamin stumbled forward and clung to the table. Lilie, who'd been polishing silver, leapt up to support him.

"What's he done? Let me see."

"Out of my way, girl." Gudrun pushed her aside and seized Benjamin's head between her two hands to peer at the broken skin. "This needs cleaning and some of my marigold poultice slapped on it to draw out the dirt. You could have picked up anything in that filthy place." She pulled forward a stool. "Sit down."

"No." Benjamin shrank from her show of rough compassion. "It's all right. I'll see to it myself."

"Please yourself. What's another scar on a face so ugly?"

"Benjamin isn't ugly," protested Lilie. Ignoring Gudrun's snort of derision, she stroked his cheek and he leaned into her. "It was him, wasn't it? I should have known he wouldn't keep his promise. I did everything he—" She fell silent as Josef appeared in the doorway.

"What's going on?" His eyes widened as he took in Benjamin's wretched state. "How did this happen? No, don't answer. Come with me. Not you, Lilie—I need to speak with Benjamin alone."

"He can't go anywhere in that state," protested Gudrun.

"I dare say it will all clean up." Josef took Benjamin's arm. "Bring hot water and see about finding fresh clothing. Benjamin is of a size with Robert."

"How many pairs of hands do people think I've got?" Gudrun asked of the ceiling. "It seems the more I do, the less consideration I get."

Benjamin found himself seated in one of the worn leather armchairs in the doctor's consulting room without being able to remember how he arrived there.

"Don't try to talk," said Josef. "Let's have a look at you first." He peered into the boy's eyes. There followed an extremely uncomfortable process of cleaning and removing grit from his raw knees, after which the doctor applied various compounds, all of which stung but probably no more than Gudrun's dubious potions would have done. At least Josef was gentle.

After he'd finished, Benjamin experienced another blank spell. Perhaps he dozed. This time, when he opened his eyes, Josef stood over him with a soft white shirt and a pair of trousers.

"These should fit you." He pressed a glass of wine into the boy's hand. "Drink this. It will help."

"Thank you, sir. I'm sorry to cause so much trouble." Benjamin's head sank onto his chest again. Holding it erect seemed more trouble than it was worth.

"Never mind," the doctor said urgently. "What happened? You went to the club. Was someone there responsible for this?"

"No. That came later." Benjamin took a few sips of wine. The peppery *Weißgipfler* revived him a little, but he was too tired to tell the full story. "I made a . . . friend at the club. I'll need to go back tomorrow to find out more. After leaving there, I went to see Hugo Besser, you know, the journalist—thought he might know something. I never got that far. There's been trouble in Leopoldstadt, sir, really bad trouble this time. Some ruffians were wrecking shops, setting buildings afire, and attacking people. From what I could see, the violence was directed"—he hesitated—"against our people, sir, against Jews." His head drooped again.

Josef reached forward and turned Benjamin's face up. "Any blows to the head?" The boy nodded.

"When they got hold of me, they . . . they pushed me around a bit."

"I see." Josef stood up and began pacing the floor. "I couldn't help overhearing something Lilie said." He took a deep breath. "She said—these may not be her exact words—*I should have known he wouldn't keep his promise. I did everything he asked of me.*" Josef straightened a picture. He ran his finger along the top of the frame and checked it for dust before whirling around and staring hard at Benjamin. "To whom is she referring? What is the name of this man? What promises? And why have neither of you spoken of this before?"

Benjamin sighed. "I don't know what she's talking about." But there was something. It hovered right on the razor's edge of memory, and the harder he tried to catch hold of it, the more it retreated. "I don't know," he repeated. "Was it more of her . . . you know, fairy stories . . . like that nonsense about being made of clockwork, or never eating?"

"Hmm," said Josef. "Perhaps." He sat and refilled their glasses. "Tell me more about what happened in Leopoldstadt. Who were the instigators? Christian Socials? Lueger's men?" Without waiting for answers, he continued: "It's been four years since that foolish man started issuing warnings to us."

Benjamin sat in silence for a moment, remembering their late-night conversations. During the 1895 elections the mayor had threatened to start confiscating property. An empty threat, of course: Lueger was merely trying to ensure the Jews didn't support his political opponents. And naturally he was addressing the better-off, assimilated Jews— merchants, professionals, and academics—not the pathetic creatures who fled their homes to seek shelter here. Even so, it was Karl Lueger who'd started calling the Hungarian capital *Judapest*—a jibe gleefully seized on by the mob.

"Lueger's a troublemaker," he said at last. "He says whatever will get him popular support."

Josef nodded. "And never mind the consequences. So far it's all talk— some utterances more poisonous than others. Mark my words, sooner or later some madman will take his ramblings seriously. And then what? *The Jew is guilty*, goes the slogan. Of what, we ask? The eternal question. Of whatever the Gentile multitude decides, naturally. We are always the scapegoats, no matter what." He cleared his throat. "So how did you escape from his thugs?"

"I crawled," mumbled Benjamin, and wished the words unsaid. He felt his cheeks flame and stared at the floor. There'd been dog shit on his palms and nowhere to clean it off until he came to the canal. He'd crouched on its banks in the fading light, biting back tears. Even after prolonged scrubbing the stink had clung to his broken skin. How could he ever touch someone as pure and lovely as Lilie again? When he'd finally risen, stiff and aching, the smallest movement opening his partially scabbed wounds, he'd looked back in the direction of Schattenplatz. Two columns of dark smoke rose, so thick and straight they might themselves have been chimneys, each with a cloud-like finial flattening itself against the sky. Benjamin could not get the image out of his mind.

Josef patted his shoulder. "Go to bed, lad. Sleep's the greatest healer. Everything will seem better in the morning. Those knees may take awhile to mend, but the graze on your cheek is superficial." He smiled. "There won't be a scar."

"Just a minute," Benjamin said wearily. "There is something—"

"It'll wait until tomorrow, I'm sure."

"No, it's important. This man—"

"The one who attacked you in Leopoldstadt?"

"I'd seen him before." Benjamin paused, fighting to get his thoughts in order, the process impeded by his reluctance to revisit a series of abject humiliations. "Today he was passing the club—or at least I thought he was passing, but maybe there's more of a connection. He's a striking-looking fellow, very fair-haired, almost white, and with a scar here." He drew a finger across his cheek. "Well spoken and immaculately dressed. There's something about him . . . he smiles . . . all the time, but only with his mouth, if you understand what I mean. His eyes"—Benjamin gave a small shudder—"they're pale, like a fish's eyes. Cold as ice."

"An unpleasant character," commented Josef.

"There's more. He was in the tavern the other evening, sitting near Hugo and me while we talked. The club was mentioned—"

Josef leaned forward. His eyes gleamed. "Was Lilie?"

"Not by name," Benjamin said quickly. "Well, we don't know her real name, do we? No, I talked about missing girls in general." He coughed. "Hugo gave me *Obstler*. I'm not used to anything so strong."

"You let your tongue run away with you?"

"We . . . uh . . . spoke more about the Thélème and . . . uh . . . whether it was possible for a girl to escape. The blond man probably heard everything. I thought all along that he was the one who came after me when I left. If he works at the club, it would make sense. I wasn't going to risk another kicking, so when he told me to clear off today, I didn't need telling twice." He raised his head, meeting Josef's eyes. "I went back later, though."

"But there he was, waiting for you in Leopoldstadt."

"Yes. I hope never to see him again."

"His name?" prompted Josef.

Benjamin frowned, struggling to remember the period before the men had knocked him to his knees. He closed his eyes and saw the fair-haired ringleader perched on his tumbled-stone throne, polishing not a stolen crown but a golden lamp. He heard again the jeers of his companions. "Klingemann. The others called him Klingemann."

"Not a name I know." Josef grimaced. "So it revolves round him."

"Perhaps." Benjamin looked at him curiously, fancying a note of relief in the doctor's voice. He was unable to pursue that suspicion, for the doctor had urged him to his feet and, the half-empty bottle in his hand and his son's clothes over his arm, was guiding him through the kitchen toward the stables.

JOSEF BREUER AWOKE from a sleep so deep and dreamless he wondered briefly how nearly it resembled the untroubled slumber of the dead. Eyes still closed, he scratched and stretched, flexing each muscle as if by this small effort he could assure himself of his own corporality. When his thoughts turned to the events of the previous evening, Josef experienced repeated waves of irritation with Benjamin for getting embroiled in something that must surely interfere with their investigation. The boy was a fool. What else could he do now but instruct him to desist from the proposed return to the club? An eminent physician couldn't be seen to be responsible for sending his manservant to serious injury or death. If the worst happened, questions would be asked. The truth would be out. Evil interpretations would be put upon the innocent purpose of the visit. Finally, he, *Herr Doktor* Josef Breuer, would be judged guilty. He'd be pilloried. Become a laughingstock. His entire life's work would count for nothing and the whole Breuer family would be held in contempt.

His blood boiled. His eyes snapped open.

The room was full of butterflies: white wings, black-dappled, twisting, turning, rising, and falling as softly as petals dislodged by a gentle breeze. Their apparently aimless movements made them as much creatures of dreams as was Lilie, with her beauty and fragility, her mystery. Josef swung his legs over the side of the bed, anxious as always to find her, touch her . . . prove to himself she wasn't an apparition spun from his yearning for lost love. Feet still dangling, his eyes were drawn to two butterflies settled on the bed rail, intertwining their antennae like a pair of lovers. Psyche and Cupid, he thought sourly, though in the present case it was Psyche and not Cupid whose true identity remained hidden. Oh, Lilie, Lilie . . . what dark purpose brought you here? He tapped the bed frame and the butterflies rose, weaving a courtly dance above his head. A strange, sweet fragrance, evoking memories of the countryside in spring, filled the room.

Josef's thoughts returned to Benjamin. While it was true the boy was incompetent, couldn't even get rid of a few garden pests, at least his battered state had provoked a telling response from Lilie.

"I should have known," Josef said aloud, savoring each word. "I should have known he wouldn't keep his promise." He frowned. "I did everything he asked of me," he added, though he wasn't absolutely sure she'd finished her sentence.

The butterflies danced nearer, circling his head, and he irritably swatted them away. What did Lilie's words signify? Why should she, quite out of the blue, assume she knew the identity of the person responsible for the attack on Benjamin? Did it mean she was acquainted with this fair-haired man, this—what was his name?—ah, yes, *Klingemann*? And why so little surprise at the boy's injuries?

He went through the meager facts again, sifting words and silences, weighing nuances, looking for hidden meanings. It brought no comfort.

The answer was simple enough: they were in collusion. Josef's fists clenched. His temples throbbed. Their plans, whatever they were, thrown awry, the ungrateful pair had betrayed themselves. All that remained was to discover their purpose. He sprang up, uncomfortably aware of the clicking of his joints, and just as quickly sat down again.

Of course, there was another way of looking at things. If this Klingemann was connected with the Thélème, and if it was through such a base place that Lilie knew him, then she was already a . . . his mind slewed away from the term "fallen woman" and alighted on the delightfully evocative "bad girl." One who, Josef thought, suddenly elated, did everything asked of her. Such a wench could easily be induced to change allegiance. She could have whatever her heart desired. For surely nothing would stave off old age more effectively than a girl looking like an angel, possessing the legendary sexual appetites of Lilith and yet remaining biddable as Eve. Elated at his resulting tumescence, Josef threw open the door of his armoire, selected his second-best waistcoat and prepared to take on the day. Once he'd persuaded Lilie to admit her antecedents, it would be necessary to leave the house in search of a charming little apartment.

He took the stairs two at a time, dwelling on the pleasure of furnishing a place for her with all the folderols and fripperies most women—not Mathilde, though she once had—liked to surround themselves with. And then his Lilie would simply disappear. Gudrun would be glad she'd gone; a simple story of sending the girl back to her newly discovered family would suffice. As for Benjamin, he'd offer the boy a reward for his silence—and for relinquishing any ridiculous hopes where the girl was concerned—better pay, a grander title, even a rudimentary education. If that didn't work, he'd have to disappear, too—sudden illness, a fever or an unfortunate accident with some poisonous gardening compound. Copper acetoarsenite, Paris green, the current weapon used by Parisians against the plague of rats in their sewers, was easily procurable. And patently necessary: the boy had been as ineffectual in ridding the property of rodents as he had of these damned butterflies.

Today Josef's appetite for breakfast was not as pressing as his need to preen his amour propre. Making his way to his study, he cast his eye over the shelf bearing back volumes of the *Wiener Medizinische Wochenschrift*, to which he'd been contributing from 1868 onwards: *"Zwei Fälle von Hydrophobie," "Das Verhalten der Eigenwärme in Krankheiten," "Über Bogengänge des Labyrinths."* Other periodicals, too: he'd almost lost count of the number of learned articles. It was not for nothing that five years ago he'd been elected a corresponding member of the Imperial Academy of Sciences in Vienna. And then there was his work at the military medical school demonstrating the role of the vagus nerve. At the time he was hardly older than Benjamin, nevertheless his findings revolutionized professional understanding of the link between the breathing apparatus and the nervous system. How could a penniless gardener–cum–odd job boy presume to compete with the physician who'd demonstrated the mechanism of the Hering-Breuer reflex? Josef poked thoughtfully at his scale model of the inner ear. He'd also laid bare the secrets of fluid in the semicircular canal. Balance and breath: these were the fundamentals of human existence; those they held in common with God. He was not, after all, nothing, whatever Freud and his sycophants professed to believe. Neither was he the spent old man Mathilde perceived him as. Furthermore, he was master in his own house. Gudrun and her nonsense would get short shrift today.

AFTER HOLDING Lilie's chair for her, Josef perched on the edge of his desk and smiled, hoping both to put her at ease and to hide his own anxiety. Not only were butterflies clinging to the curtain rail, but some seemed to have taken up residence in his stomach as well. He smoothed his beard. "You look lovely today, my dear. As always, of course, as always."

Lilie plucked at the folds of her skirt. "I told the old woman I wouldn't wear stripes, but she said I must."

"Never again," Josef said quickly. "In the future, you will select your own cloth—silks, satins, velvet, calico, with trimmings of lace or feathers, whatever meets with your approval. We shall find a seamstress—"

"I don't mind what I wear, as long as it hasn't got lines pointing to the ground."

"Very well." Josef doubted Lilie's professed disinterest in apparel would last long. "Perhaps some jewelry, then."

"I already have a bracelet." Lilie pulled up her sleeve to reveal a circlet of plaited grass studded with the dried heads of common daisies. "Benjamin made it for me."

Josef's mouth tightened. "Oh."

Selecting one of the flower heads, she pulled off its petals, one by one. "He loves me, he loves me not . . ."

"Diamonds and pearls would settle the question faster. Or perhaps you'd prefer sapphires?" When Lilie didn't respond, he returned to his chair and shuffled papers. One way or another, the boy would have to go. "Now, my dear, I have a few more questions for you. I hope you'll answer frankly." She looked up. "Do you know a woman called Bertha Pappenheim?" He strained forward, watching her expression intently.

Lilie shook her head. "People often lose their names. Names fall into holes or get eaten by wild animals. Sometimes they're carried away by the wind."

"Just so, just so." Josef chose to ignore this nonsensical statement. "It is possible *Fräulein* Pappenheim may have been using another name." He hesitated, then added softly: "Anna, for instance."

"Did she fall in love with you?"

Josef gasped. "How—" He recovered himself. So Lilie did know Bertha. He must tread carefully if he was to find out whether the girl was here to make trouble on his ex-patient's behalf. "Is *Fräulein* Pappenheim well?" he inquired. "The last I heard, she'd gone to Munich with her mother."

"I never met her. Just heard about it somewhere," Lilie said vaguely. "Didn't she become a writer? Or was it a slave trader? I don't believe she's still alive."

"I think she is." Even as Josef contradicted her, he was dismissing the idea. She knew too little. "And what about *Herr Doktor* Sigmund Freud?"

"*Ficken*," said Lilie.

Josef's eyes bulged. "Go on."

"Someone told me he had *Geschlechtsverkehr* on the brain," she said, with an impish smile he'd not seen before.

"You've met him?"

"Oh, no. How could I have?"

"He only lives a short walk from here," Josef said, again watching her carefully. "Berggasse 19."

"In Vienna?" Lilie's brow furrowed. "But I thought he . . ."

"Yes?"

"No, that's right. I was confused."

Josef waited, but Lilie had turned her attention to the butterflies. One alighted on her outstretched hand. Her lips moved and he became convinced she was spinning either a spell or a tale, though he couldn't catch a single word. He cleared his throat. "Have you seen Benjamin this morning?"

"He's in the garden, eating bread and honey. Down came the blackbird and pecked." She glanced in his direction and the butterfly immediately took flight. "It's our favorite food next to apricots and cherries. And we both hate soup—especially the old woman's."

"His injuries were quite severe." Josef paused. "I believe you know the man who inflicted them."

"The white crow."

Josef made a note of this. He rather thought a white crow pointed mankind to its final journey in the mythology of some obscure race. It could be checked later. Then he remembered Benjamin's description of Klingemann: fair hair, almost white. "Tell me about him." And when she didn't respond: "Has he also hurt you, Lilie?"

"One for sorrow," she murmured.

"Two for joy," he countered, picking up the thread of the children's song. He walked over and placed his hand on her shoulder, squeezing gently. He let his fingers travel down the side of her neck towards the sweet hollow just visible above the lace edge of her bodice. "One may be for sorrow, but two makes for joy—"

"Nine for a secret—"

"Tell me your secret, Lilie. Is it about the Thélème? Were you a prisoner in that accursed club? What happened there? How were you mistreated? It will never happen again. These things won't be forgotten." He bent closer, his lips grazing the short curls on the crown of her head. "Come, you can trust me. Tell me everything."

"So many secrets never to be told," whispered Lilie. "Can I really trust you?"

"Of course, my dear. You have no better friend . . . and indeed, I would like to become far more—"

"But I trusted you before and look what happened."

Josef's hand dropped to his side. He straightened, looking at her questioningly. "I don't—"

"What about your promise to help me destroy the monster?"

"Only tell me his name and I'll see him brought to justice."

Lilie shook her head. "His name is the most secret of the secrets.

Only one other person knows. He doesn't remember yet." Josef noticed her fingers creep under her sleeve to fasten onto the plaited-grass bracelet. "I'll tell you this"—she lowered her voice—"the monster's hiding in the safest place on earth."

"Oh? Where's that?"

"In the past."

"I see." Josef hid a smile. "And can we travel there?"

"You don't need to. He's there, all right. The past protects him so well that anyone who finds him by chance won't lift a finger to harm him. But I know. And because the monster doesn't know that I know, I'm the only one who can . . ." She paused to blow away the butterflies hovering before her face. "Yes, I'll take him by the left leg and throw him down the stairs."

"Run along now, my dear." Josef sighed. "We'll talk again later." For now he would keep their sessions short and sweet. Short and bittersweet, he corrected himself, with another sigh, for little progress had been made. At least she hadn't flinched from his touch. He straightened his shoulders. It was time to tackle his rival.

JOSEF CORNERED BENJAMIN in the *Küchengarten*, digging up carrots with a surprising reverence, tapping free loose earth, twisting off the yellowing leaves and laying the roots in his basket as if they were delicate blooms. He watched in silence for a few moments, his mood lightening as he was beset by schoolboy thoughts regarding their phallic shapes, for large and small, thin or stumpy, the roots were as knobbed and twisted, knotted with veins, or curiously kinked as any human organ.

"You like carrots?" he asked gruffly. Benjamin glanced at him, nodded and continued to dig.

"I've developed a healthy respect for every kind of food, sir. We've had a good crop—enough to see us through the winter, however long. Others are not as lucky." He pushed the fork into the earth and straightened. "Things are getting worse in Vienna. Meat's hardly affordable. Bread prices are rising. Vegetables are expensive, even now in the autumn when they should be cheap and plentiful. We've talked of it before, *Herr Doktor*, and agreed such things breed trouble. I've heard the incomers are selling everything of value they still own in order to buy bread."

Josef nodded, discomfited by the boy's display of social conscience. He felt the need to re-establish his position while softening it with a compliment. "You manage my garden very well. We've never had such splendid crops." And felt rebuffed when Benjamin simply responded with another nod and returned to his harvesting. Perhaps the misguided young fool was selling garden surplus to feather a nest for the two of them. How far had it gone? Had the boy's hands traveled more of Lilie's body than had his? Did they already have an *understanding*? He gritted his teeth. "I require you to go back to the Thélème."

Benjamin's back tensed. "I can't."

"From what you said, the fellow is expecting you to return," Josef persisted, ignoring the boy's white face. "You must. We still don't know for sure if Lilie was held there."

"Sir, I was taken on to look after the garden and stable—"

"You were taken on as a favor to your father," retorted Josef.

Benjamin glanced towards the ancient walnut tree. He opened his mouth as if to speak but appeared to change his mind, for his lips tightened.

"As an odd-job man," continued Josef. "To do whatever is required of you."

"In the Breuer house and garden, with the greatest respect, sir," argued Benjamin. "No mention was made of roaming the city acting as private detective being part of my job . . . or getting beaten up for my pains. Besides"—he colored—"the man is a . . . he is a sexual deviant, a *Schwul* . . . I fear he may have other expectations."

Josef looked at him askance. "Which no one is obliging you to fulfill."

"And there's the other man, Klingemann. If he should turn up . . ." Benjamin shook his head. "No," he repeated, "I don't consider going to such a dangerous place to be part of my job."

"It is when something impinges upon the safety of this household, young man. Having brought a stranger into my household, you have a certain responsibility. Questions remain unanswered. Who is she? Where did she come from? Is she really what she seems? Could someone have . . . Well, that apart, the point is, we may not be safe until we've discovered the truth, which I am convinced will be found in that club. This is why I must insist you return." Josef paused. "Naturally, I would not expect you to carry out this task without generous recompense." Again he saw Benjamin stiffen. "Leave the gardening and look to your appearance, if you please. You will go back to the Thélème today, as arranged." He turned away, indicating that the discussion was closed.

Lilie stepped from behind the tree and stared at Josef's departing back. "What does he want you to do?"

"Same as before." Benjamin shrugged. "He's still trying to find out who you are. Where you came from. Your . . . your . . . How you made your living." He sank onto a mossy root and took two apples from his pocket. One he polished on his sleeve before offering it to Lilie. "He wants me to go asking questions . . . somewhere."

"Don't go," she said urgently. "It feels dangerous. Promise me you won't go."

"I'm not. Why should I? None of it matters to me. In time the past fades and becomes like a half-remembered dream."

"Or a nightmare."

"All that matters is that we are alive. Here. Now." After a moment's hesitation, he added: "Together."

"We've been in worse places," said Lilie.

Benjamin glanced at her, perplexed. "Be that as it may, Lilie, I . . . I hoped we could live here peacefully and quietly."

Lilie turned to face him. "Today he tried to . . ."

"The doctor?" A tingle ran the length of Benjamin's spine. His fists curled into tight balls as he guessed what she was unwilling to say. "He tried to what?" he asked, more sharply than he intended, anxious not to misunderstand.

She looked away. "He wants . . ." Lilie shook her head. "You know we can't stay here, Benjamin. We have to move on. Up you get."

He scrambled unwillingly to his feet and stood very close to her. "Where could we go? What can we do? How would we live without my job?"

"Someone will help us, I promise you. Anyway, I'm supposed to be helping *Frau Drache* in the kitchen."

"Breathing fire," said Benjamin. "That's what dragons do best." He watched her go, flitting through the shrubs as lightly as an elf, then picked up the fork and doggedly continued digging along the row.

JOSEF, STANDING OUT OF SIGHT, watched the small drama unfold. He saw Lilie come to the kitchen door and stand on the threshold, lips moving as though in silent prayer, until Gudrun turned from the stove and noticed her.

"Hah, there you are at last."

"What would you like me to do?" asked Lilie, and Josef thought he'd never heard a sweeter voice. He shifted a little, craning his neck for a better view.

"Here," said Gudrun, swinging two fowl by the feet. "I want to make Paprikash." She dropped them on the central table, folding her arms across her plump abdomen as Lilie stared at the scrawny, yellow-scaled legs. "Pluck and draw those, will you? I presume you know how."

Lilie wrinkled her nose. "I've seen it done."

"Well, get on with it, girl. We haven't got all day." Gudrun suddenly noticed a butterfly clinging to the underside of a pan. One quick flick of a kitchen rag consigned it to the floor, and a moment later it was reduced to a grayish paste beneath the sole of her boot. The girl whimpered. Josef grimaced. Gudrun narrowed her eyes. "Perhaps we'd be free of pests if that fool of a boy wasn't continually distracted."

Lilie seized the first bird's head and yanked at its neck feathers, struggling to divide the quills and down into separate piles. Soon there were feathers everywhere—on the table, floor, stove, shelves. Handfuls of down floated around the room, borne on cold blasts from the outside door. "Mother Holle," she said. Josef stifled a sneeze.

"What's that?" demanded Gudrun, turning, red-faced, from the stove.

"Don't you know the story of Mother Holle?" Lilie laughed. "Cock-a-doodle-doo! My golden maid, what's new with you?"

"I've no time for that nonsense. And neither have you, my lady. Just look at that mess. At this rate, you'll be spending the rest of the day cleaning up."

"There's always time for stories, Gudrun. Someone once told me that stories lighten any task. Anyway, look at the feathers whirling against the ceiling. It's like in the story when the beautiful hard-working girl shook Mother Holle's bed."

"It will snow soon enough," said Gudrun.

Lilie smiled. "So you do know the story? The one about the girl dropping her spindle in the well—"

"Sooner or later, everyone gets to know the Dark Grandmother." Gudrun gave a dismissive snort. "As I remember the tale, the slow and useless daughter ended up covered in black *Pech*. Haven't you finished yet?" She peered at the carcasses. "You're not going to leave them like that, surely? I can't cook birds with half their plumage still on."

There followed a long silence while Lilie bent over the goose-pimpled poultry, working stray feathers out of the skin. A small noise alerted Josef to the fact that he wasn't the only secret observer. Benjamin stood at the kitchen door, as yet unnoticed by the women. His eyes were fixed on the girl and there was an expression of such longing on his face that Josef felt he might choke on his upsurge of white-hot rage.

Gudrun nudged Lilie aside for another inspection of her work. "That'll have to do." Taking a cleaver from the wall, she chopped off the birds' heads with two decisive blows. Lilie stepped back too late, and the gore splashed her skirt. The heads lay on the scrubbed pine, combs trailing, eyes wide, staring at each other, until they were scooped up and consigned to a bucket. "Come on, get on with it—livers in the basin, gizzard in the stock pan."

Lilie screwed up her face, looking away as she steeled herself to plunge her slender hand into the cavity of one of the fowls. "I just can't do it," she said, after the third attempt.

"Let me," offered Benjamin, choosing this moment to announce his presence. Josef also judged it time to show himself and strode into the room, pushing open the door with such force that every jug and plate on the dresser rattled.

"That's enough. Finish off for her, if you would, *Frau* Gschtaltner. This is not the sort of task I had in mind for a convalescent. And find her different clothes. Surely there are more stored in the attic." When the girls had been growing up, not a week seemed to go by without the dressmaker calling. "Something dainty in pretty pastel shades. I believe we've spoken about this matter before."

"I do my best, *Herr Doktor* Breuer," said Gudrun with elaborate formality. "This very morning I brought down a fresh selection of garments. And what did Madame do but turn her nose up at them—"

Lilie seemed to freeze. "I told you I didn't like stripes."

"Beggars can't be choosers in my opinion."

"Don't speak to Lilie in that—" began Benjamin, turning red with anger. Lilie silenced him by laying her hand on his arm, gently pushing him aside to face Gudrun. Josef's eyes narrowed at the gesture, for not only did her hand remain there far longer than he deemed necessary, but the boy had the effrontery to place his own dirt-stained paw on top of it. And instead of tearing herself free, she smiled at him. *She smiled.*

"I'm not a beggar. I have asked for nothing"—she looked at Josef—"except *Herr Doktor* Breuer's help in a certain matter."

"Hoh, yes," scoffed Gudrun. "Of course—having done with 'Mother Holle,' we're back to the slaying of ogres and monsters."

"*Frau* Gschtaltner!" roared Josef.

Gudrun took a step backwards, raising her ladle defensively. "I speak as I find, sir." Josef looked through her, addressing the wall behind her head.

"*Frau* Gschtaltner will accompany you upstairs, Lilie. She will find you more suitable apparel and she will do so without comment or criticism. What you are wearing can be discarded."

"Now?" demanded Gudrun, indicating the pans bubbling on the stove.

"Now." Josef held open the door, taking long, slow breaths in an effort to restore his equilibrium. With the prospect of a new life before

ELIZA GRANVILLE

him, he'd no wish for a death attributed to apoplexy. The women departed in silence, Gudrun's head held high, her face a mask of displeasure, and Lilie with backward glances that were mostly directed at Benjamin. Josef closed the door after them, raising his hand to halt the boy's hurried departure. "Not you." He sat down, angling himself away from the blood-speckled feathers. Benjamin remained standing. "I'm surprised to see you still here in your working clothes, young man. I requested earlier that you keep a certain appointment."

"With the greatest respect, sir—"

"Spare me your mealy-mouthed excuses," spat Josef. "I'm your employer. I expect my orders carried out."

"As they always have been, *Herr Doktor.*" The color drained from Benjamin's features. "But this time you don't realize what you're sending me into."

"It's hardly more than a social engagement," Josef said dismissively. He stood, drawing himself up to his full height, momentarily disconcerted to find his gardener had grown and now stood a head and shoulders taller. The two men faced each other down the length of the table.

"No," protested Benjamin. "You don't understand. That man . . ." His voice trembled; he closed his eyes, as if to steady it. "You are sending me into the lion's den."

"Then you must acquire the faith of a Daniel."

"I'm no—"

Josef raised his voice. "It's a condition of remaining in my employ that you carry out this task. It's simple enough. All I need to know is whether Lilie was previously an inmate. This is the key to unlocking her memory." He jutted his chin. "Bear in mind that you'd be hard-pressed to find another position without a character reference. Remember your humble beginnings, young man. Remember how I helped your family in their time of trouble. And then spare a thought for how your relatives—your mother and father, your brothers, sisters, grand-mother, aunt—would exist without that portion of your wage you're able to send home each month." He hesitated, shocked by how far his rage and jealousy had taken him. But there was no going back. Neither of them had a choice. "You will, as I said before, receive very generous recompense."

"I'll do it," announced Benjamin, "but not for money, nor for you, *Herr Doktor* Breuer. Whatever becomes of me, however badly things turn out, I'll go through with this for Lilie. And when I return, *if* I return, Lilie and I—"

"Don't imagine—" began Josef, but stopped the torrent of venomous words in the nick of time. Far better to let the foolish boy believe in a future with Lilie until the truth about her had been unearthed. Afterwards, one glimpse of his lovely girl in the exquisite clothes and jewelry he'd provide would disabuse a humble gardener of any hopes in that direction. "Don't imagine the worst," he finished, in response to Benjamin's fixed stare. "It is, after all, only a club concerning itself with pleasure."

TODAY WILHELM SAT ALONE at the three-legged table, head tipped back, drawing languorously on a cigarette as he stared at the sky. There was no sign of the gigantic Kurt, for which Benjamin was grateful. Neither had the vicious Klingemann put in an appearance; with any luck the fair-haired man's connection with this place existed only in his fearful imagination. Nevertheless, he hung back a moment or two longer, anxiously checking every nook and cranny, peering into the darkened doorway to the interior, before making his presence known.

"Welcome back, Benjamin. I was afraid I'd never see you again." Wilhelm rose, threw his cigarette to the ground, and clasped Benjamin's hand, keeping hold of it as he gestured to the other chair. "Sit down, sit down. Oh, dear, whatever happened to your face? And look at your poor hands." He finally released his hold, grimacing at Benjamin's damaged palms. "Looks like you've been playing rough games, young Ben. Can't have that. Work here and you'll have to keep your nose clean." He paused to light another cigarette. "Tell me about it."

"It's nothing."

"No need to be brave. Not with me."

"I was attacked," mumbled Benjamin. "Thieves. They were after my money. I didn't have any . . ."

"So the blaggards gave you something to remember them by," finished Wilhelm. "Well, Vienna is becoming a dangerous place. You clearly need someone to protect you."

Benjamin made noncommittal noises, unsure of how to respond. For want of anything better to say, he asked: "Where's Kurt?"

"Kurt?" Wilhelm looked down his nose. "Why would you want to see that *Gscherda*?"

"I don't," replied Benjamin, with such emphasis that Wilhelm beamed and nudged him.

"Kurt's all right in his way. All brawn and no brain. Country boy. He'd be handy in a fight, though. Not that anyone one would touch you with me around." Wilhelm peered at Benjamin through a cloud of cigarette smoke. "I fancy you'd be happier with someone a little more . . . hmm"—he pursed his lips—"let's say, *refined*." He held out his cigarette case, which was silver, embossed with an eagle's head rising from a cornucopia also containing flowers and ferns. "Smoke?"

Benjamin hesitated before taking one, and bent his head as Wilhelm pushed the button and opened the lid of his shining cap lighter. He sucked hard, taking in a lungful of smoke, and immediately started coughing and choking. The world spun. He clung to the crippled table, felt it rock unnervingly, heard his companion's laughter above his own

rasping and groaning. Wilhelm reached over and snatched the cigarette, sticking it between his own lips.

"First time, huh? Why didn't you say?"

Benjamin grunted. His bowels felt loose. Maybe he'd throw up.
"Thought I'd try." He took a few deep breaths and massaged his throat.
"Never again."

"It gets easier." Wilhelm smiled knowingly. "As does every acquired
pleasure. Some coffee will help." He disappeared and returned with
two steaming cups. Once again Benjamin was taken aback by the fine
quality of the china. His work-worn fingers seemed too big for the delicate handle. The rim was so thin it hardly seemed to exist. As for the
saucer, it was no more substantial than a flower petal. These things
must indicate good living. Perhaps there was something to be said for
working in a place like this.

"You were going to ask about the possibility of a position here, Wilhelm," he asked, revived by the hot drink. "Any news?"

Wilhelm set down his cup. "Is that all you came back for?"

"No," said Benjamin. At least that was true. "Not at all," he repeated,
feeling the color rush to his cheeks.

"In that case, yes. You may start on the first of the month."

"What? Really? But that's only a few days away."

"There's just one thing." Wilhelm leaned forward, lowering his
voice. "I've said you were a cousin, my older sister's child, newly arrived
from Burgenland. It was the best way. Nobody likes strangers here." He
straightened. "They don't ask too many questions, either. Anyway, I'll
see nobody bothers you."

"I don't know how to thank you," stammered Benjamin, taken aback
by the speed at which everything had been arranged.

"Oh, Ben, I'm sure we'll think of something." Wilhelm patted Benjamin's knee and didn't take his hand away.

"What will my new duties be?" Benjamin asked to cover his discomfort.

"Fancy a quick look round? It'll be easier to explain as we go."

Benjamin jumped to his feet. "I would, indeed."

"You're eager," exclaimed Wilhelm, picking up the coffee cups and making for the shadowed doorway. "You're supposed to see the boss first, but why not? After all, you'll be working here next week. Come along then, Ben, follow me."

They emerged from a short passage into a vast kitchen, four times the size of the one in the Breuer house, where silent youths in striped overalls scoured pans, chopped meat, or prepared vegetables under the eye of the cook, a woman as wide as she was tall, her massive bosom jutting like a ship's prow. She wore a starched apron and her braided hair was almost concealed by a white cap, but her cheeks were painted magenta, giving her the appearance of an oversized Dutch doll. One large and raw-knuckled hand gripped a cleaver. On the block in front of her lay a carcass—a pig, Benjamin thought, though it was extremely lean and lacked both head and trotters. She snickered as Wilhelm and Benjamin edged past her.

"Found yourself another one already, Wilhelm?"

"Leave off, Heike." Wilhelm frowned, but Benjamin stared open-mouthed, for the woman's voice was so deep, so gruff, that it could surely only belong to a man. And now that he looked again, although there was a woman's silk blouse above, there were trousers and very large boots below. He waited, hoping for more conversation, but the cook had already lost interest in them. The cleaver fell. Splinters of bone flew across the room. Red chrysanthemums flowered on Heike's apron. Yes, it must be a pig. As he drew alongside the stove, Benjamin glanced into a gently bubbling cauldron of liquid, noting it was almost clear, except for a few beans together with strands of finely chopped onion and cabbage.

Wilhelm wrinkled his nose. "Soup for the odalisques. It's all they need. Mustn't get fat, on any account. Don't worry, my young friend, you'll find the staff here eat rather better."

"Was that a pig being butchered?" Benjamin asked anxiously. It wasn't the question he wanted answering, but there seemed no polite way to approach the subject of whether the cook was male or female. Wilhelm looked at him askance.

"Don't you eat pork?"

"Of course," lied Benjamin. "It's just that I've never seen so much meat in one place before."

"We get all sorts of meat here. Doesn't do to be fussy."

"I'm not. Get fussy and go hungry, as my *Großmutter* used to say."

"That's the spirit." Wilhelm put his hand on Benjamin's shoulder and guided him out of the kitchen and through a vestibule lined with a dozen or so jardinières filled with flowering jasmine, each supported by a naked marble nymph. Every wall, the ceiling also, had been painted with easily recognizable themes from French fairy tales—with flowers and plants trailing and undulating to form borders—hardly a straight line anywhere. Such emphasis on natural forms always pleased Benjamin. He looked back as his companion opened the far door and, as with the front door, realized what he'd missed at first glance: the paintings were obscene. It was as though a team of smutty-minded schoolboys had rewritten each tale, portraying the simple stories in the most indecent way possible. The entire court, their faces bright with lasciviousness, watched the prince awaken the Sleeping Beauty with far more than a kiss. Cinderella—

"Come on." Wilhelm nudged him. "Plenty of time for that later." He shepherded Benjamin into a passage broken up by countless doors, between which hung full-length gilt-framed mirrors.

"This is a very long corridor," said Benjamin, perplexed. "It's strange—the house seems bigger inside than from outside."

"That's because it takes up near enough the entire south side of the street. Each house leads into the next. You haven't seen anything yet. Wait till we go upstairs." Wilhelm briefly examined their reflections in the glass. "Quite a contrast, you so dark, me so fair. Look good together, don't we?" He patted Benjamin's cheek. "Anyway, this is where they take their exercise. Twice a day, ten at a time, forty turns each. Your job would be to make sure there's no squabbling. They fight like alley cats, given half the chance."

"And then what? Do you punish them? I'm not sure I like the sound of that." Perhaps this was the key to Lilie's condition. Benjamin found he was holding his breath.

"Nothing to it." Wilhelm pressed the molding at the side of one mirror. A panel slid open and he beckoned. "I'll show you." The stairs were dark and narrow; a dank, green smell Benjamin associated with caves rose to meet them. When they reached the bottom, he saw they were standing in a cellar far more ancient than the house built over it, lit only by means of an air vent close to the ceiling. In all the years since, nothing had been changed—the floor was damp and uneven, the walls dappled with mildew—except the arched recesses that had once accommodated barrels had been turned into crude cells. The smell was more intense here. It was the stink of the midden. Wilhelm took out a handkerchief and covered his nose, muffling his words. "A spell in here with the mice and spiders soon sorts out their temper tantrums."

"So no whipping?" said Benjamin. "No shaven heads?"

"Of course not. We wouldn't want to spoil their looks." Wilhelm turned away, making for the stairs. Benjamin was about to follow when a small movement caught his eye. A young woman, hardly more than a child, rose from a pile of rags, feeling her way along the wall until she managed to support herself on the bars. The girl's eyes were enormous in a face so painfully thin her cheekbones protruded like knobs. A mass of fair hair, tangled and dirty, reached almost to her waist. There was something familiar about her and Benjamin feared she must be the daughter of family friends, or perhaps a neighbor, come to a bad end.

"You shouldn't be here," she whispered.

"How can I help you?" he asked, darting a quick look at Wilhelm's departing back. "Who shall I contact?"

"You shouldn't be here," she repeated, and melted back into her pool of shadow.

Benjamin ran after Wilhelm. "What's she done?"

"Who?"

"The girl in the cell," he said impatiently. "From the look of her, she's been there far too long. What did she do?"

"The cells are empty, my young friend. We only use them as a last resort. As for being there too long, an hour is usually long enough to break them of bad habits. First sight of a mouse's tail and they're screaming to be—"

"I saw a girl," insisted Benjamin. "Come back down. Look for yourself."

"Either you've got a good imagination," said Wilhelm, as he demonstrated that each cell was unlocked and decidedly empty, "or you wanted to get me down here alone with you. Not that I mind, you understand"—he squeezed Benjamin's biceps—"but there are more salubrious places."

Benjamin said nothing. As a child, he'd baited Rabbi Blechmann with claims that he'd seen ghosts trailing behind him on the way to the synagogue. The old man had retaliated with a two-hour lecture assuring him that, according to traditional wisdom, lingering spirits did exist; to see one might be considered a blessing, for in life these had often been pious Jews, but they must never be consulted. Later he'd wondered if this meant that the spirits stood outside time and were able to see the whole of human history unfold like a tableau. The rabbi had gone on to explain, with copious references to the books of Samuel and Kings, that although these *ovoth* were almost detached from earthly desires, there also existed dybbuk, evil spirits who might be looking for a body to possess. The girl had been neither, he was sure. By the time he'd followed Wilhelm back into the corridor, Benjamin was almost convinced he'd imagined her. As for her words of warning, they were probably self-generated, too. If this was what one puff of a cigarette did, he wanted none of it.

"I'll show you a nice, cozy spot for private . . . conversation," declared Wilhelm, lowering his voice. "Only a few of us get to see this, but since you'll be working alongside me to start with, why not? Not a word to the others." Linking arms with Benjamin, he ushered him back into the vestibule, where the sweet scent of the jasmine seemed curiously at odds with the paintings, for although at first glance the subjects had appeared to be an innocent maiden triumphing over adversity, closer inspection revealed the threat of corruption closing in on her. Entwined with each border, in a parody of illuminated manuscripts, were misshapen imps and gnomes, apes and bestiary creatures peering at her from behind leaves and flowers and stinkhorn fungus, either gesticulating towards their outrageously swollen members or savagely ingesting their companions. Benjamin found it hard to tear his eyes away, and he was still looking over his shoulder as they started to climb the thickly carpeted stairs leading to the upper floors, where he caught glimpses of even more explicit paintings and statuary.

Without a word, Wilhelm hurried him up another flight, and then another, narrower but still as luxuriously carpeted, until they came to a bolted and padlocked door. Here he relinquished Benjamin's arm and, first glancing from left to right, took a key from the bunch on his belt, using it to open a small cupboard containing a further pair of keys, one for the padlock, the other for the door itself. Beyond lay a dimly lit space. The air was stale. Faint whispers coiled from above. Wilhelm wordlessly drew Benjamin inside, locking the door behind them.

Benjamin took a step backwards. "What's this?"

"*Shhh.*" Wilhelm laid a finger over his lips and shook his head. "This leads to the tower," he added, his lips brushing Benjamin's ear. "Never speak to anyone of what you are about to see."

As his eyes grew accustomed to the poor light, Benjamin saw steps as narrow as those allowing access to the cellar. This one, like the main staircases below, was carpeted, though in white; the walls were covered in some thick fabric that muted every sound and had thick silken ropes instead of handrails. He was suddenly afraid—of what he might see, of what might be about to happen. Fighting the urge to run, he dragged himself up the stairs, heart thumping, head aching, and with Gudrun's foul *Kürbissuppe mit Salami* churning so violently in his stomach, there was a very real danger of him throwing up. Benjamin's only relief was to beam rage at Gudrun. She knew he hated her homemade salami and loathed pumpkin; if he never ate another spoonful of her pox-ridden, resentment-seasoned witch's-brew soup again it would be too soon.

"*Shhh,*" Wilhelm repeated as they stepped into an aerie with several plush sofas forming a circle facing the walls. The walls themselves had narrow openings reminiscent of the arrow loops of ancient castles but covered by gilded wooden shutters. Wilhelm silently indicated he should open one. Benjamin stepped forward unwillingly, fumbled with the fastening, and found himself looking down into a room where a score of small girls lay sleeping in a row of little wooden beds. Each had a thumb firmly in her mouth, some the left, others the right, sucking gently, as if dreaming of feasting on breasts snatched away too soon. Everything in the room was white, from their lace-trimmed dresses to the delicately ornate furniture. A scatter of toys and books littered the floor. In the center of the room a toothless old granny sat in a rocking chair, furiously knitting a piece of work so long it coiled around her feet.

"Nap time," Wilhelm breathed at his shoulder. "It won't be so quiet by and by."

"But they're children," whispered Benjamin, profoundly shocked. "Surely you don't . . . they don't—"

"Don't be disgusting. What do you think we are?" Wilhelm grimaced. "No, certain gentlemen with equal amounts of patience and money pick one out for the sheer pleasure of watching it grow." He smirked. "Like a flower. And then, perhaps, if they're still able when the time comes, they pluck it."

"It?" repeated Benjamin. He looked again, noticing the children were without exception light-skinned and with long hair in every shade of blonde, from chill moonlight to hot sun-gold. "So much yellow hair."

"Yes, there's a lot of call for fair types." Wilhelm touched Benjamin's glossy hair. "Me, I prefer dark." He waited, expectantly, but Benjamin was so deep in thought he hardly noticed and didn't respond.

"Where do they all come from?"

"Everywhere, anywhere: school yards, backstreets, ghettos, farms, forests, and mountains. We harvest them for their looks—yellow hair stands out in a crowd—and carry them off like cattle rustlers. No good looking like that, my young friend. Harden your heart and ditch your conscience if you want to work here." Wilhelm closed the first shutter and indicated Benjamin should open the next. Again, he hesitated. And again, he steeled himself to look.

These were older girls, some drawing or reading, others playing together under the eye of a stern-faced matron. There were pet animals running around, too. Cats, Benjamin thought, then he saw that they were large rabbits. His vision blurred. The aerie seemed to spin. He rubbed his eyes. Perhaps he was dreaming. "There are far less of these . . ."

Wilhelm nodded. "Pretty at seven isn't necessarily pretty at ten. They don't always turn out as required in other respects, either. It depends on the parents, and the parents' parents." He looked over Benjamin's shoulder. "Seen enough?"

"What happens to the ones you don't keep?"

"What do you think?"

Benjamin said nothing. The fear returned. Pushing past the other man, he flung open the third shutter and, to his alarm, saw only one young girl in this room. She sat before a looking glass, combing hair that reached past her waist. He was overwhelmed by a need to see her face and stood with his own pressed against the opening, willing her to turn. Wilhelm pulled him away and stood in front of the aperture, shutting off his view.

"Her sponsor's about to get a return on his investment."

"What do you mean?"

"You saw for yourself."

"But she's only—"

"Old enough," said Wilhelm. "Why should it matter to you? From what you've said, you're not that way inclined." He pulled Benjamin towards him, placing one hand firmly on his hip, the other at the back of his neck. His lips grazed the boy's cheek. Benjamin immediately tore himself free and Wilhelm's hands dropped to his sides. "Kurt, is it?"

"What?"

"Go for the big fellows, do you? Even that oversized *Schluchten-scheisser.*"

"No!"

"Then what is it? We came up here to be alone. Don't I please you?"

"It's not that," said Benjamin, thinking furiously. "It's just that I can't stand being rushed."

"Ah." Wilhelm nodded and squeezed Benjamin's shoulder "Not only the smoking you haven't tried before, then. You're new at this game, too. Why didn't you say? I'm in no hurry." He sank onto the sofa, smiling reassuringly. "Close the shutter, my young friend. Come and sit beside me."

Benjamin took one last look into the room below and stifled a gasp. The girl was standing now, staring straight at him. The looking glass lay on its side, her hairbrush was on the floor. Inside the curtain of bright hair, her face was guant as that of a young witch. Her whisper was hardly more than the thin piping of a bird in winter reeds. "You shouldn't be here."

"So you're really not interested in Kurt?" inquired Wilhelm.

The girl's lips moved again. "You shouldn't be here."

"No." Benjamin quietly secured the fastening, his mouth suddenly dry. He sank onto the seat beside Wilhelm. The other man moved closer, wrapping his arms around him. His wiry strength alarmed Benjamin far more than the enforced intimacy. When a kiss was demanded, he closed his eyes, imagining the finely stubbled cheek was his brother's. Wilhelm laughed softly.

"Not quite what I had in mind, Ben, but time's on our side." He started towards the stairs. "There's nothing else to be up here for. We'd better go."

Benjamin pointed to the last shutter. "What about—"

"Empty."

"No." Terror washed over him. "No, it can't be." And when Wilhelm kept going, Benjamin threw himself towards the final spy hole, only to find that the room was indeed a dark void, although he was almost sure the faint sound of weeping circled the space below. Above it came the click of Wilhelm unlocking the door onto the corridor. The sobs grew louder as Benjamin continued to peer through the opened shutter. "Where are you?" he breathed into the gloom. The weeping ceased. A girl's face emerged from the pitch black, pale and hazy, ill-defined as a photographer's crayon portrait. Her lips moved but no sound reached his ears. Slowly her features melted back into the darkness. The hopeless weeping recommenced. Benjamin rubbed his eyes. This time he really had seen a ghost.

"Ben!" came Wilhelm's urgent whisper from below.

"Coming." Benjamin quickly closed the shutter and hurried after him. It was only when he reached the bottom that he realized he might have discovered something of importance: the ghostly girl's hair had been chopped off; she was almost bald. There was no opportunity to question his companion further. Wilhelm's face was creased with anxiety as he took the stairs two at a time.

"We were up there longer than we should have been," he muttered. "There are a million things I should have been doing. I only hope the boss . . ." He paused as they reached the penultimate flight, peering carefully up and down the corridor. "All right, my young friend, I'll take you as far as the kitchen. It's easy enough to find your way out from there." He was hurrying across the vestibule when the main entrance door was flung open and Benjamin's worst fears were realized.

"What the hell's he doing in here?" roared the flaxen-haired man, tearing off his coat and flinging it to the ground.

"This is the young cousin I spoke to you about, *Herr* Klingemann," said Wilhelm, moving to stand between them. "My sister's boy, from Burgenland. You very kindly said he could work alongside me."

"Cousin, my arse, you lying toad." Klingemann's smile was sweet and deadly. "Any fool can see what he is." He ran at them, deliberately knocking over jardinières, so the marble nymphs lay chipped and broken among shards and earth and crushed flowers; Benjamin thought of the broken iron table outside and trembled. "He's also a spy for that filthy hack, Besser. And if he's a friend of yours, you can clear off, too."

Wilhelm looked at him and then moved aside, his expression contemptuous. "I was mistaken, sir. He's nothing to me."

"I'm not Besser's spy," cried Benjamin, backing until he could go no farther. Kurt arrived from nowhere to tower over him, and whether male or female, the cook's stout form blocked any hope of exit through the kitchen. Other men were crowding into the vestibule now; not a friendly face among them. Only Klingemann continued to smile as he cracked his knuckles.

"Always in the wrong place at the wrong time. I warned you what would happen, *Judenscheisse*."

Twelve

or days I keep close to the hut, making myself invisible. I try talking to Lena, but she's sick now and does too much crying. Nobody else wants to talk. When they aren't at work, they sleep or stare, though there's nothing to look at. Lottie is worn-out and it's no good looking for Daniel: he'll stay out of the way until the marks don't show anymore. Cuts and bruises only bring more cuts, worse bruises.

Now there's only school in the evenings to look forward to. Cecily says I'm her best pupil, but she doesn't allow babies in so I have to stop sucking my thumb. She calls me her little polyglot and teaches me about Greeks and Romans and geometry, showing me how Pythagoras's theorem works by drawing it in the mud with a stick. She started showing me his tetractys, too—I like these because they're magical—but it was raining too hard and the triangles of numbers kept washing away before I could add them up. Instead we sat in the doorway and talked about Pythagoras and his beans. When I said my magic bean plants had been stolen, Cecily patted my hand and told me about two green fairy children who came out of a forest in England and ate nothing but bean-stalks. I can get her to talk about English kings burning cakes, hiding in oak trees, or cutting off the heads of their wives, but she doesn't do real stories, only history. When I tell her how boring everything is, she reminds me of the other children, and in the end I force some to sit down and listen to me.

There's another person doing stories but not very good ones. Hers come out *bang bang bang* like thin slices of plain dry bread falling onto a plate. Mine are fat, oozing caramelized sugar, bursting with currants and spice. When the other children are really hungry, I can take them into even darker forests, do away with the witches in horrible ways, and let them eat gingerbread. The other storyteller is called Hanna.

"Now, children," she says, "today I have a new tale for you. It's about two men who were squabbling over an old plum orchard. Each man claimed he owned it. Each said he could prove it was *his* father, and no-body else's, who'd planted the plum trees many years earlier. The quarrel went on for months. In the end, their wives made them agree to put the case before the rabbi. The rabbi listened to everything they had to say. Even then he couldn't come to a decision, because both seemed to be right. Finally, he said: 'Since I can't decide to whom this orchard belongs, the only thing left to us is to go and ask the land.' And so the wise old rabbi walked very slowly out of the village until he came to the plum trees. Here, he put his ear to the ground and listened. After a moment the rabbi straightened up. 'Gentlemen,' he said, 'the land says that it belongs to neither of you. On the contrary, both of you belong to it.'"

A woman mending her skirt nearby smiles, but the children sit and wait, even though anyone can see the story's come to an end. It was a stupid story and I want to say so, but Greet always warned me to be careful with people who look funny.

Hanna must be the ugliest-looking woman in the world. She's even uglier than the hunchbacked Gypsy woman who came to the door with baskets of daffodils in the spring and *Steinpilz* every autumn. Perhaps she was a witch, too. Greet always bought something from her. It was unlucky not to. The flowers she put into a jam jar, standing them on the windowsill so the Gypsy could see if she happened to pass by. The mushrooms were buried deep in the garden; even though they looked like ordinary cèpes, they could just as well be poisonous toadstools. Hanna drags one foot behind her when she walks and wears dirty old rags knotted around her fingers. Her face is as twisted on one side as a wrung-out dishcloth, and where her hair has grown, it's striped to match her skirt. When she isn't telling stories, she talks to anyone who will listen . . . and if there's no one, she mumbles to herself.

THIS TIME DANIEL comes to find me before the dog bites have a chance to heal. He doesn't say he misses me, but I know he does because I miss him, too. Some children are hanging around wanting more of my stories and I have to chase them away. One of them keeps close to Daniel and won't go, even when I pick up a stick.

"What's this? Your shadow?"

"Let him stay," says Daniel. "He's not hurting you."

"Why should you care? Get out of my way."

Daniel stands between us. "Don't be like—"

"I want to talk to you on your own. I don't want her listening."

"He's a he, not a her," insists Daniel, but both of us look doubtfully at this new arrival.

"All right, then. What's your name?" The creature says nothing, only stares at me with its big frog eyes. It's as thin as paper and just as pale. I'm not sure it ever had any hair. "Well?" I demand, pinching its arm.

I take my hand away quickly. The arm feels funny, as if the bone were made of rubber. "Are you a boy or a girl? Say something." I lift my foot, ready for a kick, just a small one, to see if the leg is rubbery as well.

"Don't," says Daniel.

"What's it got to do with you?" He sounds upset, so I just do a little tap with my toe. I hardly touched. It can't possibly have hurt and yet tears and snot start pouring down the creature's face. "If it won't say what it is, there's only one other way of finding out. Are you going to look, or shall I?"

"You can forget that!"

I've never seen Daniel so angry. His face turns beetroot color. For a moment you can hardly see the bruises and teeth marks. "Neither of us will. Not ever. You hear me? What's up with you? Haven't you learned anything from being . . ." He throws up his arms. "What does it matter to anybody? *Verschwinde!* Go on, clear off! I'm not talking to you."

"Good. See if I care. I'm not talking to you either, stupid." I walk away without looking back. Lottie is yelling something from inside my vest, but she can shut up, too, because I don't mind if I never see Daniel again. For all I care, he can disappear in the night, like the others. Good luck to him, if he likes that gristle-bone thing better than me. Anyway, Daniel can say what he likes, but he needn't think I won't find a way to get rid of it.

HERE I AM BLINKING at the zigzag of light unzipping the black sky. There's a distant rumbling that sounds like the sleepy dog over the road growling when I poke it with sticks. A mistle thrush is singing in the apple tree—I can see its speckled belly from here—and Greet is rushing to bring in the washing before the storm breaks. One moment she's hauling down a billowing sheet, the next she has me under her arm, muttering bad words under her breath as she drags me back into the kitchen.

"I told you to stay there, you naughty girl. Do you want to be burnt to a crisp by a bolt of lightning? I don't want you following me every-where, hanging on to my apron. Why can't you ever do as you're told?" Taking a length of string, she ties me to the leg of the table. "There, that'll put an end to your disobedience."

I scream and kick, but Greet takes no notice. Without another word, she darts outside again. However hard I tug at the knot, it won't come undone, so I begin pulling the table, inch by inch, towards the door. It's too big to go through. One corner jams on the frame. Another flash comes. And another. Finally, there's a huge crash overhead and the sky opens. Rain buckets down. I crawl under the table and Greet has to do the same, puffing and blowing as she pushes the laundry basket in front of her.

When she's finished drying her hair and shouting at me, Greet gives me my milk, without cake, and starts on the ironing. There's usually a story to go with it. I can tell from her face it won't be a nice one.

"Once upon a time," she says, spitting on the iron and making it siz-zle, "there was a stubborn child who never did what her elders and bet-ters told her to do. Naturally, God grew displeased with this little sinner and before long she became so sick that no doctor could save her. The sexton dug her grave and the stubborn child was carried to the church-yard. After she was lowered into her grave and covered with earth, one of her little arms emerged and reached up in the air. They—"

"Why didn't they put her in a box? Mama went in a box with brass handles and flowers on top."

"Well, they didn't."

"Why?"

"Who knows? Perhaps they were too poor. Maybe she was too

wicked. I don't know. They just didn't." Greet slams down the hot iron and a smell of scorching fills the kitchen. "Anyway, they pushed it back down and covered the mound with fresh earth, but again the little arm popped out. So the child's m—. . . so *someone* had to go to the grave and beat the disobedient child's arm with a switch for a day and a night. Only then did the arm withdraw and go down into the earth as it was supposed to."

I push away my empty mug. "That's stupid. Dead people don't stick their arms up."

"Are you sure? If you don't want to find out, you'd better start doing as you're told. And in future, when I say, 'Stop following me around,' stay where you're put."

MORE PEOPLE ARE DISAPPEARING. It's mostly the very old ladies and the sick people who are taken to the hospital to be made better. Some of the children go, too. Lena scrubs her cheeks to make some color come. Last night we heard a lot of noise. This morning the aviary is full of ravens, all hard at work. I try not to look.

Hephzibah says there was a king in the Bible called Oreb, which means "raven." "One raven used to raid the Israelites—and look, now they're all at it."

GREET'S BEEN IN A FUNNY MOOD all week, sometimes banging and crashing, sometimes twisting the corner of her apron into tight knots as she stares into thin air and sighs. This morning she's cleaning the yard with the big stiff-bristled broom, making pale dust devils rise from the corners.

"Leave me be." She elbows me aside. "I've no time for idle chatter today."

I stamp my foot. "Want a story."

"You can want away, young lady. It's too bad, really it is. Cast out onto the street with hardly a week's notice after working my fingers to the bone for your father. And naturally everything must be left in perfect order for when the great lord and master decides to return home. It'll take me all afternoon to cover the furniture with dust sheets." She straightens, kneading the small of her back. "And how will he manage you, I ask myself? How will he manage you?"

"Shall I sprinkle the flagstones with water, Greet?"

"It's no good trying to get round me that way," she says. "Besides, all my stories are used up. You've wrung me dry."

I do it anyway, scooping handfuls of water from the bucket and throwing them over the stones to lay the dust. Little pockets of mud form to be played with later. "Where will you go, Greet?"

"Home," she says mournfully. "I've nowhere else. What else does an old maid do at these times but take herself back to the hens and the geese, the fields and the forest? With my parents gone, it's my brother's farm now. Of course he'll be glad of another pair of hands at the moment, but the old maid won't be welcome after this is all over." She sighs very loudly. "His boys will return—if, God willing, they're spared—to take over the work. And what then? Nobody wants another mouth to feed if they don't need the hands attached to it."

"Where did the boys go?"

Greet snatches the bucket and slops water round the yard. "To be soldiers." She marches back into the kitchen. "After the way I've been treated, I deserve the best coffee in a fine cup on my last day." She brings one of Mama's from the dining room. It has pink roses all round and a tiny rosebud decorating the handle. The saucer is so thin the light seems to shine through it. My milk comes in the usual stupid baby mug.

"There was once an honest and hardworking soldier," she begins, cutting us both extra-large slices of gingerbread before I get a chance to complain, "who was set upon by robbers. After stealing everything he had, they poked his eyes out and tied him to the nearest gallows tree."

I'm so busy covering up my own eyes I forget to swallow, and I choke, spitting crumbs into my lap.

Greet slaps my hand. "Any more of that and I'll throw your cake to the birds." She refills her cup. "The poor blind soldier heard a fluttering of wings as three ancient ravens settled onto the gallows—"

"How did the soldier know they were ravens if he didn't have any eyes?"

"By their voices, silly."

"Ravens don't have—"

"Do you want to hear this story or not? Well, then. Now, the first raven told its sisters that the king's daughter was near to dying and the king would give her hand in marriage to any man who could save her."

"What if it was a lady—"

Greet tightens her mouth at me. "'And yet,' said the raven, 'curing her is the simplest thing in the world. All you have to do is catch the toad from that pond over there, burn it alive, and make it into a potion with a little water.' Then the second raven said: 'Oh, if only people were as wise as us. Listen to this, sister ravens. Tonight, dew with miraculous powers will fall from Heaven. If a blind man should wash his eyes with it, he would regain his sight.' The third raven croaked loudly. 'Oh,' she said. 'If only foolish Man was half as wise as us. You've no doubt heard about the great drought in the city? And yet if the stone square in the marketplace was removed, water would gush out, enough for the entire population.' With that the ravens flew away to roost, but the soldier, who'd overheard every word, washed his eyes in the precious dew. His sight was instantly resto—"

"But you said the robbers poked his eyes out, so how did he find—"

"Quiet!" roars Greet.

"Stupid story." I kick the table leg and fold my arms tight over my chest.

Greet eyes me over the rim of her cup. "Time for me to make a start on the dust covers."

"Don't care. I know the rest. The stupid soldier does all the things and marries the silly princess."

"Ah, but there's more." Greet starts to get up. "Still, if you don't want to hear . . ."

"What?"

She settles back down again, pours a third cup of coffee, and cuts us more gingerbread. "It so happened that one day the soldier, who was by now married to the princess, met the robbers who had attacked him so violently. Of course, he was wearing such fine clothes, they didn't recognize him immediately. When he told them what had happened, they fell on their knees, begging forgiveness. Instead of having them executed, the soldier let them go. If it hadn't been for them, he said, he wouldn't have his present good fortune. And so, the robbers decided to spend the night under the gallows tree to see if the ravens would reveal any more secrets. But the ravens were furious. They knew someone must have overheard their conversation, for all the things they talked about had come to pass. They went in search of the eavesdropper and found the robbers sitting under the gallows tree." Greet hesitates. She leans forward, lowering her voice. "The ravens fell upon the robbers, sitting on their heads and pecking their eyes out. *Peck! Peck! Peck!*" She wets her finger and—jab, jab, jab—uses it to pick up the scattered crumbs of gingerbread. "*Peck! Peck! Peck!* They kept hacking at their faces until no one could have recognized them, not even their mothers."

At that moment a pair of birds falls flapping and squabbling from the tree outside the window. I know they're only blackbirds, but I run upstairs and hide under my bed anyway. In the middle of the night when I tell Papa about my nightmare, he gets very cross.

"That woman wants locking up."

I DON'T SEE DANIEL AGAIN for two whole days. In the end, even though I want to stay out of sight, I have to go and find him. The skinny creature is still keeping close to him, saying nothing, but Daniel won't look at me. Something's wrong with his face. Every time I get in front of him, he turns away.

"What's the matter?"

He's got his hand over his mouth, so his voice is muffled. "I fell over. All right?"

"Don't be stupid. What really happened?"

"Mind your own business."

I pull at his hands.

"Get off."

His mouth is bloody and he's lost a couple of teeth. I suddenly feel very sick. "It was Uncle Hraben, wasn't it?"

"You mean that *Arschloch* with yellow hair and the big black dog? The one who's always smiling—even when he's kicking you? He's not your uncle, so why do you call him that?"

"That's what Papa told me to call him." Somehow, putting "Uncle" before someone's name used to make me feel safe. "What did he say?"

"Nothing." But he gives the game away. "You mustn't go there. Please don't go. Promise me you won't."

"I won't."

Daniel grabs my arm. "No. I mean it, Krysta. Swear you won't go back." He's trying not to cry. His nose starts to run and he wipes it on his sleeve. "Swear! *Swear!* Everyone else has gone. Left me. If you should . . . go away . . ."

He's staring at me now, and I hope he can't see what I'm thinking, because I know I'll have to go to Hraben's tower for exactly the reason he's asking me not to. Daniel's my only friend. I think of the Prince of Darkness, his great teeth and wicked eyes. He does exactly what his master commands. I don't think Uncle Hraben would tell the dog to bite me, but he wouldn't think twice about letting it eat Daniel.

"Don't be stupid. I'll never go away."

"Promise?"

In the house outside the zoo where Papa and I used to live, there was a shelf of cowboys-and-Indians books by a lady writer called May Karl. Some of them were about Old Shatterhand, who became the blood brother of Winnetou, an Apache Indian. They had many adventures together and bravely fought their enemies side by side. I pull up my sleeve. "We could be blood brothers."

Daniel shakes his head. "That's just for kids. Anyway, we haven't got a knife." He turns up his nose when I find a sharp stone. "Just promise you won't go back there."

"Promise," I agree, but don't say to what.

"QUIET!" ROARS GREET. "My poor head aches with your constant *why*-ing and *what*-ing? Some things just are and that's the end of it. It's as well you aren't the maiden whose six brothers were turned into swans by an evil witch. The only way to break the spell was to remain silent about this terrible secret for seven years while she sewed magical shirts from flower petals. Never a word fell from her lips during that time. Not a word, nor a sigh, not even a squeak."

My FEET HAVE BECOME big heavy rocks that I have to drag up the stairs to the tower. I walk right in without knocking, and Uncle Hraben seems very pleased to see me. He gives me two *Negerküsse* on a little plate. I eat the first one whole and then carefully nibble the chocolate off the marshmallow of the second. Afterwards, we go to the cupboard. I take out one of my special frocks and hold it against me; Lottie reminds me that it's the one I wore the day she came home with me. Anyone can see it's far too small now.

Uncle Hraben sits at his desk and lights a cigarette. "I want you to do something very special for me today, pretty Krysta."

I back away. "What?"

"Can't you guess?"

I shake my head. "No." But my voice is so small and faint I'm not sure he hears the first time. "No."

"I'm sure you can. Try." He leans back in his chair, smiling at me and puffing smoke rings. "I asked you to do it once before. Surely you haven't forgotten?"

"You want me to sit on your knee?"

"All in good time, Krysta. Something else comes first." When I don't answer, he says, very softly: "I asked you to call me something. Do you remember now? I asked you to call me Papa."

"Won't."

"Ah, but you must."

"Won't," I repeat, taking another few steps backwards. There is a chair behind me and I can go no farther.

Uncle Hraben laughs and throws me a Pfennig Riesen. "Sit there,

Krysta, and think about it while I finish this little lot," he says, pointing at a pile of paperwork. "Soon it'll be time to take *der Fürst der Finsternis* for his afternoon walk. I'm sure you'll come to your senses before that."

There's a small table to one side of my chair with writing materials in a half-open drawer. After I've crammed the toffee in my mouth, I quietly take out a pen, together with a tiny bottle of permanent blue, and write the same numbers that Daniel has on his arm all down mine. If we can't be blood brothers, then we'll be ink ones. My numbers aren't as neat as his: the nib's crossed and the ink runs a bit. Some of them are blurred—

"What in God's name are you doing?" shouts Uncle Hraben, seizing my wrist. "What's this?" He doesn't wait for an answer, but rubs my arm so hard with his handkerchief that the skin turns red. Even so, the numbers don't come off. Catching me smiling, he snatches Lottie from my lap and throws her out the window before slamming it shut. "It's about time you grew up, Krysta. I've examined the records and found you are quite a bit older than you appear to be. Big girls should be thinking about something more interesting than filthy old *Spielzeuge*."

I bite back the rage and tears. "Things like Pythagoras?"

Uncle Hraben gives me a strange look. "It's easy enough to remember the things young ladies should be concerned with—certain pleasures, then *Kleider*, of course, and after that, *Kinder, Küche und Kirche*. Sometimes the old ways are best." He takes his dog leash from the wall. "Is that understood?"

"Yes."

"Yes, *Papa*." He smiles at me, coiling the leash around his hand.

"Yes, Papa." I squeeze the words out through my clenched teeth. Uncle Hraben lets out a long sigh.

"That's better." He pats my bottom. "Off you go, Krysta. Come back tomorrow. I won't feed Prince, just in case you forget. He's a fierce dog now, a little dangerous. He has to be, to keep everyone safe."

Daniel is waiting at the bottom of the steps. There's no sign of the creature. "You promised not to go there," he says reproachfully.

"No, I didn't. Why are you following me?"

"I always do. Promise you won't go back."

"All right." I begin searching the ground underneath the window.

"If you're looking for your doll, then I've got her here." Daniel opens his hands. All that's left is a jumble of grayish pink pieces. One hand. One foot. No face. Even her eyes have gone. I swallow hard.

"Lottie kept all my stories safe for me until I could write them down. Now they're lost."

"You can make up new ones."

"No. I'll never do another story again. Not ever."

"Don't say that." Daniel looks horrified. "How else can we get our revenge?"

I shrug. "Why bother? It isn't real."

"It might be if we want it badly enough."

"We'd need magic for that." I decide to bury Lottie in the aviary, where I planted the beans. "And magic isn't real, either."

I'd already asked Cecily about that. "Magic is all in the imagination, my dear," she'd said, as if that was an end to it.

"You mean, if I imagine hard enough, it might happen?"

Cecily laughed. "Perhaps," she'd said, but I could tell she meant no.

Daniel is looking around nervously. "We shouldn't hang round here."

"Come on." I trudge towards the aviary, where we put all the bits of Lottie into the cold, hard earth. "Dust to dust," I say. It's all I can remember. They've all gone: Mama, Papa, Greet, and now even Lottie.

"At least we've still got each other." Daniel squeezes my hand. I hadn't noticed he was holding it. "We'll never be parted."

"If you won't ever forsake me," I say, comforted a little by realizing I can still remember Greet's stories, "I won't forsake you."

. . .

"BELIEVE YOU ME, there were plenty of other children abandoned in the wild dark forest," says Greet. "And like a certain person not six paces away, some of them were very bad indeed, never doing as they were told, getting their clothes dirty, answering back. No good always blaming the parents. Take the story of Fundevogel—"

"Stupid name." I wipe my sticky hands down my front to see what Greet will do, but she's busy slicing onions and her eyes are running too much to notice.

She sniffs. "He was called that because his long-suffering mother let a hawk carry him off. Anyway, a forester found the boy and carried him home as a companion for his daughter, Lina. As these two children grew up, they became inseparable. It so happened that their household had a very ill-tempered cook—some people don't know how lucky they are—who was also a witch. She decided to roast and eat Fundevogel, but Lina found out. The pair ran away together. Of course the cook came after them. When Lina saw her coming, she turned to the foundling boy and said: 'If you won't forsake me, I won't forsake you.'

"'Never ever,' replied Fundevogel."

"NEVER EVER," SAYS DANIEL. "I'll always stay with you."

I can't tell him it's just me standing between him and the Prince of Darkness.

"THIS IS QUITE NORMAL," says Hraben when I can't stop crying. "Next time will be better. Come back tomorrow." He looks at my face. "You must come back. If not, your young friend . . . already he's not welcome here. I allow him to live . . . for now. That's my gift to you. And this." He puts cake on the table, but I don't want it. My mouth is swollen and sore. The tears sting my cheeks. Everything hurts.

EVERY AFTERNOON now I must visit Hraben in his tower. Today he has a group of friends with him. They're in the middle of a noisy game of Skat, so he tells me to sit in the corner and wait. Another pack of cards lies scattered on the floor. After a bit I pick them all up and look at the photographs on the backs. They're all of places in Germany: Berlin, Munich, Innsbruck, Kraków, Vienna . . . The Skat game is very noisy: *geben— hören—sagen—weitersagen*; Papa once tried teaching me the rules, but I liked Quartett with Greet better. One of the men wants to play Doppelkopf instead, but the others won't agree. They're playing for money, I think, and passing round bottles of the stuff Papa used to keep locked in a cupboard. They are talking about something called the Hellfire Club. It was started in London many years ago, but Cecily has never mentioned it.

"Do what thou wilt," mutters one of the men, and looks at me. "No friars, but at least we have a little nun." They all laugh.

"Find your own," says Hraben. "Think how long I've had to wait."

"More fool you."

"Has the deed been done? Then what does it matter?"

"We'll see how the game goes," says the first man, smoothing his chin and staring at me.

After awhile, Hraben leaves.

GREET WIPES THE SWEAT from her forehead with a red-stained corner of apron. She sniffs mightily. "This silly girl, like so many others, took no notice at all until it was too late, for the wicked bridegroom and his friends were at the door. Just in time, the old woman hid her behind a barrel. In come the evil men, *betrunken wie Herren*, dragging after them a young girl. First they forced her to drink wine with them: a glass of red, a glass of white, and a glass of black. After that, they pulled off her pretty clothes and put them in a pile ready to sell in the market. And then they—" Greet stops abruptly. She clears her throat and glances towards the door.

"What?" My voice has shrunk to a croak. I've heard enough but still I have to know what happened next.

"And then they, uh . . . after they'd finished doing evil things—"

"What sort of things?"

"Things so bad I can't tell you. All I'll say is that it went on for a long time, and she screamed and cried and called on God and all his angels to help her. And when they'd all finished what they were doing over and over again, she was dead—"

THE TOWER DOOR IS UNLOCKED and I creep inside, groping my way along the furniture until I stand in front of Hraben's desk. Taking out his scissors, I cut my hair as short as possible, hoping being bald will make me ugly as sin. When I can't feel any more long bits, I search for his broken silver cigarette lighter, the one embossed with an eagle's head rising from a bunch of flowers and ferns. It takes twenty tries before I get a little spark from it. First I set fire to Hraben's papers, then the playing cards, and after that all my frocks and pretty things so they can't be taken to the sorting hut to be sold with the rest of the clothes. Getting the furniture to burn takes longer.

I'm unlucky: Johanna spots the flames before any real damage is done. She hauls me out by my neck, shoves a knife to my throat, and spits on me. I don't care what happens. I'm already dead. My arms and legs move mechanically. But since Hraben hasn't finished with me, my only punishment is to be confined in the bunker until I come to my senses.

"*Miststück!*" Johanna throws me inside so hard I hit the far wall. I lie in the darkness, all the breath knocked out of me, surrounded by echoes of the slamming door and grating key. As those sounds die away, I realize I'm not quite alone. It's pitch-black and the air's stale, but I can hear something moving.

"**What did the emperor do?**" I ask when Greet finally stops muttering.

"He ordered his guards to lock the little liar in a cellar with a cartload of straw and her spinning wheel. And there she had to stay in the dark. Alone. Not even a dry crust to chew, never mind stolen cherry cake. Spinning for her life, until the day wishes could come true and all his treasuries were overflowing with gold."

"Why didn't she climb out of the coal hole?"

"Emperor's don't use coal. They burn banknotes."

"What happened to the girl in the end?" I dance from one foot to the other, impatient for the rest of the story. "Didn't someone come to rescue her?"

"No," snaps Greet, snatching up the peg bag. "This time the wicked girl had to learn the hard way not to tell lies. She's probably there still if she hasn't been eaten alive by hungry rats."

Whatever it is comes nearer. It isn't rats: too big, and too much heavy breathing.

"Keep away," I snarl, putting up my fists.

"Don't be frightened. I won't hurt you. You're the little girl who tells stories."

I know that voice. It's ugly Hanna with the white-striped hair. "Go away. Leave me alone."

"Your name's Krysta, isn't it?"

I don't answer. Everything hurts too much. All I want is to be quiet, but Hanna starts talking and doesn't stop. I put my fingers in my ears; when I take them out she's describing her family's garden. There's a big walnut tree under which a huge patch of meadow saffron grows, so palely pink, so apt to quiver in the slightest autumn breeze, that her *Großpapa* called them naked ladies.

EVERY TIME I CLOSE MY EYES in come the evil men, *betrunken wie Herren*, dragging after them a young girl. "First they forced her to drink wine with them: a glass of red, a glass of white, and a glass of black. After that, they pulled off her pretty clothes and put them in a pile ready to sell in the market. And then they—"

NOW UGLY HANNA'S TELLING ME about the stable where a white owl lived, sleeping by day and hunting mice by night, annoying the old cat who thought it was her exclusive territory. They were constantly at war: he'd shriek and she'd caterwaul until the scullery maid threw buckets of water at them.

AND THEN it's Greet's voice again: "And then they, uh . . . after they'd finished doing evil things—"

"What sort of things?"

"Things so bad I can't tell you. All I'll say is that it went on for a long time, and she screamed and cried and called on God and all his angels to help her."

I DOZE AND WAKE to Hanna still talking. Now it's about her grandfather's study with a mangy deer's head on one wall and a picture of *his* father in funny, outmoded clothes. On the desk sat a huge model of the inside of an ear. It terrified her. What if an earwig climbed inside and got lost in the labyrinth? There were hundreds of books: *Groß-papa* was a great thinker, conversant with the writings of eminent philosophers—Plato, Kant, Mill, Spencer—but he never lost his eye for a pretty face. Sometimes she and her brother, Erich, would look through his portfolios of pictures, copies of famous paintings depicting beautiful women. There was one in particular, of Lilith by John Collier.

"I used to dream of growing up and looking like that," said Hanna. "Of course, it could never be, since I was so dark and strong-featured. And one day I saw the painting brought to life. Do you remember how I stared? Collier might have been painting you, pretty Krysta—"

"Don't call me that."

"With your long golden hair—"

"I've cut it off."

"Oh no! Why?"

"I don't want to be beautiful. Now I'm just a machine." Nobody can hurt a machine. Greet starts whispering her story inside my head. But now it's Uncle Hraben's tower I see, rather than the robber's house in the forest. And Greet's voice turns slower and deeper.

"A glass of red, a glass of white, and a glass of black. After that, they pulled off her pretty clothes and put them in a pile ready to sell in the market. And then they—"

I realize Hanna has fallen silent for the first time since I was pushed in here. Then she whispers: "Poor child. Come here." Even a dead person needs comfort. Even a machine. Hanna winces when I find her hand, and I shudder, for the rags have fallen off and now I can feel she has no nails on her fingers. "You're cold. Spring will be here soon. Then it'll be warmer. In Vienna we would walk to Stephansplatz in good weather. You must go there after this is over, but don't stand too close to the towers in case the cathedral bells deafen you. It's said that Ludwig van Beethoven discovered he was stone-deaf when he saw pigeons taking off from the towers as the bells were rung but could hear nothing at all. Yes, every one of them is a working bell, so they all have names, just like people. There's Feuerin, whose job is rousing the city in case of fire, and Bieringerin, the beer ringer, who warns the tavern keepers it's time for last orders. Poor Souls only tolls for funerals. Kantnerin calls the cathedral musicians, while Feringerin tells the people it's time for High Mass on Sundays. As for the Pummerin—Old Boomer—that hangs in the south tower; it's so big and heavy it used to take sixteen men pulling on the bell rope to get the clapper to strike. But the weight was so great the tower started to suffer. It can never be swung again, it's forbidden, for fear of bringing the whole edifice crashing down. People forget how heavy the Pummerin is. It was cast from more than two hundred melted-down cannons captured from Turkish invaders over two centuries ago and is nearly ten feet across. The bell's very important to the Viennese; some say the city might fall if anything happened to it." Hanna pauses to draw breath. She touches me in the darkness. "Are you still awake, Krysta?"

"Why do you talk so much?"

"Because soon I shall go from here and everything that I have seen or heard, felt, smelled, tasted, enjoyed, loved, will be extinguished and forgotten. There will be nothing left of me but a number on some ledger.

And so, I give the Earth my memories." She laughs. "It's my talking cure."

"Cure for what?"

"Fear, perhaps. Nobody wants to be just a number."

Hanna doesn't know she's talking to a dead girl. "I do."

"That will pass, Krysta. It will pass." She hardly pauses before plunging back into the streets of Vienna. "Things being as they were, Father didn't like us to go inside the cathedral, though Elisabet and I crept in many times to see the *Zahnweh-Herrgott* and nobody ever said a word. I've thought back to that figure many times recently: poor man, face contorted by such human pain; I've seen that expression on countless faces here. But then, how could two little girls know what was to come? Anyway, the story goes that three medical students, a little the worse for wine, decided he was suffering from toothache and tied a bandage round his jaw. Their mockery was rewarded with severe toothaches the very same night. Back they had to go and publicly apologize. Their toothaches were immediately cured. Father thought people believing such nonsense were hardly better than primitive heathens, but *Großpapa* disagreed. 'Son-in-law,' he said, 'the power of the human mind and its susceptibility to suggestion is truly amazing.'" Hanna rises and walks around for a few minutes.

Greet's voice tiptoes into the silence. "After they'd finished doing evil things—"

"What sort of things?"

"Things so bad I can't tell you."

Hanna comes back to sit beside me. "You'll find things of interest on the outside walls of St. Stephan's, too. There are two bars an ell long on the wall outside for measuring fabric. An ell is the length of a man's arm, but 'which arm?' we used to ask. For the arms of Herr Gruber, the butcher, were very short and fat, while those of old Herr Böker, the piano tuner, reached way below his knees. And whatever you do, don't miss *der Fenstergucker*. He's beneath the stairs: a stone self-portrait of the unknown sculptor gawking through a window. Perhaps the same man was responsible for those carved lizards and toads biting each other all along the handrail. At the top of the stairs, there's a stone puppy. Aunt Dora told me about the puppy. Poor Dora." Hanna is silent for a moment and I slide in a quick question.

"Why did they put you in here, Hanna?"

"We heard a rumor. They're saying he's dead. I said very loudly that I hoped it had been a long, painful, and totally humiliating death with the knowledge that all he'd striven for had failed utterly."

"But who are you talking about?"

"The monster, Krysta." Her voice is almost impatient. "*Herr* Wolf. *Der Gröfraz. Der Teppichfresser.*" She spits out the names. "The fiend responsible for all of us being contained here, the black-hearted Pied Piper who deals in *Massenausschreitungen*. That's all it is, mob violence. If only I'd been able to see into the future, I would have crawled to Linz—that's where he was raised, the area around Linz—yes, I would have crawled there on my hands and knees. I would have done what Yahweh did as he passed through Egypt at Passover, though I wouldn't have limited myself to the first-born."

I ask her to explain, and she does, but immediately afterwards she's off again, guiding me round her city, to Stock-im-Eisen-Platz, describing the nail pillar and the bronze sculpture of locksmiths with their nimble fingers—she swears some are depicted with six on each hand. Now on to the Secession building with its gilded dome consisting of three thousand gold-plated leaves and seven hundred berries; to Graben and the Plague Pillar; over the canal to ride on the big Ferris wheel. I'm only half listening because I didn't know there were more people to wreak vengeance on than the keepers here.

It seems a long time later that Hanna tells me her grandfather was a doctor. That makes me sit up. "My papa was a doctor."

"Ah, then you will know what special people physicians are. But of course when I was a little girl the eminent *Herr Doktor* Josef Breuer was simply my grandpa, who used to take us out and buy forbidden sweets and ice cream. '*Na, Opa, nun mach mal schneller!* Come on, Grandpa, hurry up!' we'd shout. He would do anything for anybody. If anyone asked him for help, he'd give it unstintingly. He was renowned for it." She chuckles. "He had his little weaknesses: *Shlishkes* with freshly roasted and ground coffee, *Germknödel* with extra poppy seeds and vanilla sauce . . ." Hanna laughs again. "Once, he fell in love with a patient. It was almost a scandal. None of it matters now."

Her voice rises and falls. Neither wholly asleep nor totally awake, I follow her around Vienna's markets and pastry shops, and back to the old Breuer house in Brandstätte to rummage for dressing-up clothes in the attic, or to eavesdrop on the old housekeeper squabbling with the groom.

THE MINUTE I FALL ASLEEP, into my dreams come the evil men dragging after them a young girl. First they forced her to drink wine with them: a glass of red, a glass of white, and a glass of black.

A NOISE ALERTS ME. It gnaws and scratches at the wall. This time it must be a rat, but I don't care until a thin shaft of moonlight the color of pea soup points across the floor. Someone has made a tiny hole between the bricks.

"Hanna, look."

"Krysta. Krysta."

I hear the whisper before she gets a chance to respond. The light is extinguished. Someone has covered up the gap. "Daniel? Go away. You shouldn't be here."

"I had to see if you were—"

"Go. *Now!* You shouldn't be here. Go. Quick! You shouldn't be here."

"Where will I go if you aren't with me?"

I can't answer that. And, anyway, Daniel's gone. Snatched away. He doesn't say another word. The moonlight continues to finger through the gap he's made.

"Was that the young boy I saw you with?" asks Hanna. "Your *Zvug* perhaps?"

"What's that?"

"The one you are meant to be with. Your one-day husband."

"I don't want a stupid husband."

"Grandfather said even the great Plato taught that each of us is only half of the whole. Our lives are spent seeking the person who will make us whole. We know it as *bashert*—that coming together with the lost half. They say when it happens the pair is lost in an amazement of love and friendship and intimacy. Afterwards one will not be out of the other's sight even for a moment."

I shrug in the darkness. There's nothing to say. It's just another of Hanna's stupid stories. A minute later she's telling me about holidays with her grandparents.

"They always took their summer vacations in Gmunden. It's a town surrounded by mountains, the Traunstein, the Erlakogel, the Wilder Kogel, and the Höllengebirge—*Großpapa* made us learn all their names—and there are beautiful views over the lake. It's peaceful now, though it had its moments in history. In 1626, a General Pappenheim put down a peasant rising in Gmunden. It was round about the time battleships were made there. These days, it has a large maternity home."

She laughs. "Of course they only employ storks that deliver blue-eyed, fair-haired babies."

I'M BACK IN THE KITCHEN. Greet's cleaver falls and splinters of bone fly into the air. She eyes me, hesitating over punishing me with the rest of her story.

"What?" My voice has shrunk to a croak. I've heard enough but still I have to know what happened next.

"And then they, uh . . . after they'd finished doing evil things—"

"What sort of things?"

"Things so bad I can't tell you. Things so bad I can't tell you. Things so bad—"

I CAN ONLY MEASURE TIME PASSING by the light creeping through the tiny chink that Daniel made in the wall. Morning comes at last. The day passes. Another night. Hanna is too busy remembering to bother with sleep. When they come for her on the morning of the third day, she quickly whispers instructions to me before walking to meet them, still spinning her story after her like Clotho—one of the old Greek ladies Cecily says measure out our lives, long or short, nice or nasty, depending on what mood they're in. I do what she says, making myself small in the corner, hoping I've been forgotten. The door slams. I don't hear the lock turn, but I stay very still, waiting and waiting until the tiny beam of daylight fades and everything's completely dark. Once outside, I slink between shadows, dodging the giant eyes of the lights as they sweep backwards and forwards, missing nothing in their path. Our hut is strangely quiet: far less whimpering and moaning, hardly any snoring.

Lena's bed is empty. I crawl underneath and wait for morning. My voices slide in after me.

"And then they, uh . . . after they'd finished doing evil things—"

"What sort of things?"

"Things so bad I can't tell you. Things so bad I can't tell you. Things so bad—"

"Bad things," says Erika. "Things that make you wish you'd never been born."

"Thirty times, some days," whispers Lena, and weeps.

"Listen to us," urges Annalies. "We know. We know."

TODAY THERE'S NO SIREN, and no standing outside having names checked, because nobody's going to work. It's not like an ordinary day off, though. Instead of resting, everyone is stuffing rags in their shoes and tying blankets round their shoulders. We are going for a long walk round the lake and towards the northwest. The first people have already gone. I can't see anyone I know.

Billows of smoke rise to meet the clouds. Soft feathers of ash fall and a cold little breeze comes out of nowhere, whipping them into pale ghosts that accompany me as I run here and there looking for Daniel. If it hadn't been for the creature crouching over them, shaking its bony white fists at the sleek ravens, I'd never have looked twice at the heap of bloodstained rags near the aviary.

Daniel fights me when I try getting him on his feet. "You go, Krysta. Take the Shadow. Get out of here."

I feel like smacking him. "You know I won't leave without you."

"I'll be all right. I shall go into the magic mountain with the others. It leads to a better place—an old woman told me so."

"Are you mad? You've got your stories mixed up. That's not the Pied Piper's mountain. It's the way to the witch's cottage and her oven."

Daniel groans. "I don't care anymore. They're saying it's a long way to where we're going. Many days' walk. I can't, Krysta, I can't."

"You think I'm heading where they tell me to? We're going to escape," I say fiercely. "I'll cast a spell and make a great forest spring up, or a magical mist rise, and turn us invisible. That's when we disappear. Besides, help is coming. They all say help is coming."

The Shadow hooks its rubbery arm under Daniel's and I haul on his jacket. Together we manage to drag him into the ragged column that's already shuffling towards the gates. One of the zookeepers is clouting people at random as they pass; the Shadow stumbles and almost falls as the blow from a whipstock lands on the back of its head. We keep our eyes averted from the buses lined up like ravenous vultures, albino ones this time, waiting to pounce on the weakest, the sickest, and the old, to stoke their burning appetites. Soon we are alongside the lake, which is covered with a gray scum of ash, like the budding trees and the clumps of yellow iris and kingcups at its edges. And the pale ghosts march with us: Papa, Erika, Annalies, Lena, Hanna . . .

"*Me hot zey in dr'erd, me vet zey iberlebn, me vet noch derlebn,*" they sing. "To hell with them, we will survive, we will yet survive."

Thirteen

 large boot nudged Benjamin back into consciousness.

"*Blau wie ein Veilchen*," said a voice. "That's how it happens. First they get drunk as lords, then they start brawling, and finally this."

"Looks like one of the rats from Matzoh Island," growled a second man. "Beats me where they get the money for hard drinking."

"There's always money for booze. Well, at least his troubles are over. Now he's just another long-term resident for the *Zentralfriedhof*. Get him carted away."

"Sure he's dead?" This was a younger voice. Benjamin was almost certain he recognized it. He tried to speak, but his mouth felt as though it had been rammed full of rags. Nor could he open his eyes: something had glued them shut. By repeatedly working the muscles of his right cheek he managed to get one eyelid free. He was lying on his stomach on grass. Not a lawn. It was studded with dandelions and crisscrossed by dusty tracks. Morning, he thought. Tiny drops of dew hung from each blade and petal. And there was running water nearby, its smooth song interrupted by splashes and gurgles as though against some partially submerged object.

"We'd better pull it farther up the bank," suggested the first voice. "Ready? One, two, three . . . *heave!*"

A pair of startled ducks took flight, shrieking imprecations as their wings broke the water's surface. Benjamin was aware of hands grasping his shoulders but felt nothing else. His body no longer belonged to him. Now he could see the river, close by. Between the reeds, two moorhens were shoveling in the mud with their beaks. More dangerous was the large black raven strutting a few yards away. *Hraben* went for the eyes. He groaned. "I'm alive." The words emerged as a rusty croak.

"What was that?" The youngest voice was much nearer now. Benjamin perceived a hazy black shape bending over him. Perhaps it was Death itself. And two more dark-clad figures. Witches . . . Finally, he realized they were policemen.

"D-don't take me to the cemetery."

"Told you he wasn't dead!"

The boot nudged him for a second time. "Turn him over."

Again Benjamin felt nothing but the hands pulling at his shoulders. From the corner of his one good eye he saw the sky above, storm-gray with black striations.

Someone gave a short bark of laughter. "You're right. Not a corpse. Not a pretty sight, either."

"I'm not a corpse," protested Benjamin. The last thing he'd care about was being a pretty one. Something funny about this idea, but he couldn't reach it. "I'm alive."

"See?"

"Very well, Stumpf. In that case, arrange for him to be taken to the

Allgemeines Krankenhaus. If he lives, well and good. If not, they'll be dissecting him the minute he's cold. The students have to practice on something. We'll be obliging them, contributing to the *Leichenbücher.*"

The thought of ending up as a numbered cadaver for the teaching hospital terrified Benjamin. "Not the AKH," he croaked. "I work for an important physician. He'll look after me." He suddenly was able to put a face to the name. Stumpf was the small ginger-haired officer who'd been left to question him on the front doorstep the day Gudrun had run to the police with her crazy suspicions about Lilie. "Remember me—Benjamin? I work for *Herr Doktor* Josef Breuer, in Brandstätte. Tell them, Stumpf." There followed a short silence. He could feel their eyes peering at him.

"Hard to tell," said Stumpf.

"Collecting gossip," mumbled Benjamin. "Like an old granny."

Stumpf sniggered. "And you're the oversized scullery maid." Benjamin heard a creak of leather as the young policeman straightened. "Yes, I remember him now, though I wouldn't have recognized him in this state. He's definitely *Herr Doktor* Breuer's servant. Shall I take the prodigal home?"

Sensation was slowly creeping back into Benjamin's body, starting at his neck and inching downwards. It wasn't a pleasant experience. He felt like the boneless meat of a schnitzel vigorously tenderized by a mallet. Rough hands raised him into a sitting position. One of his arms swung loose, but he didn't wish to look at it. Not yet. His lips were swollen and sore. Salty taste in his mouth. Pain. And he suspected the small hard objects lodged under his tongue were broken teeth. As Benjamin was pulled upright, his gaze rested on Stumpf's boots. He hoped the young officer had forgotten the disastrous effects of Gudrun's improvised brass cleaner. He'd been incandescent with fury at the time.

Fortunately, as he helped him towards the waiting carriage, it seemed Stumpf had set aside past grievances.

"You're in a bad way, scullery maid. How did you get into such a state?"

"Six of them," mumbled Benjamin. He tried to say the name of the club, but the initial *th*-sound proved beyond him. Liquid poured from his mouth, but he lacked the energy to wipe it away. "Small girls," he said urgently, "prisoners there. Stolen like sheep. Rabbits. An old granny knitting something so long it must have been socks for the giant." His legs crumpled beneath him and he fell into pitch darkness. Benjamin felt himself lifted. Then a door slammed, followed by the slow double *clop* of horseshoes against stone. "Is this the hearse?"

"We're taking you home." Stumpf's voice seemed to come from a great distance. "Almost there now. Wish you'd tell me who did this to you."

"Giant," breathed Benjamin, as nightmare images started crowding back. He shuddered. "A cook, half man, half woman. The one with white hair held me down in front of the picture. Sleeping Beauty. They hit me with a broken nymph."

Stumpf sighed. "Oh, well, never mind."

"All the girls came out to watch."

"By the way," inquired Stumpf. "How *is* the mad girl? I hear she's a real looker."

JOSEF HAD BEEN AWAKE for most of the night, making frequent trips to the stable to see if Benjamin had returned. Finally, he fell asleep over his desk. This was where Gudrun found him. Her face was lined and gray; she clung to a chair while attempting to impart her news.

"The boy—Benjamin—"

"What is it?" Josef sprang to his feet.

Gudrun emitted a long, low wail. "How will I tell his mother? For pity's sake, *Herr Doktor*, she mustn't see him like that."

"Dead?" An iron fist seemed to punch Josef hard in the solar plexus. *"Baruch dayan emet,"* he muttered automatically. "Blessed be the one true judge." Then he added: "This is all my fault."

The housekeeper stared. "According to the police, the young idiot had been drinking and fighting. How can the foolishness of youth be laid at your door?"

"No, no." Josef kneaded his temples. "You don't understand. I sent Benjamin on a fool's errand. If it hadn't been for me . . ." He looked at her. "Where have they taken the body?"

"They've brought him home to die," said Gudrun. "I told them to carry him to his room above the stables. Shall I see to his injuries? Give him something to lessen the pain? Perhaps I could make his passing easier. My—"

"No!" cried Josef. "Stop them. Benjamin must be brought into the house. I'll care for him myself." He noted her sharp intake of breath. "With your help, of course, Gudrun, if you would be so kind. We'll both care for him. The boy won't die if we have anything to do with it."

"Very well," she agreed, apparently much mollified. "We can do our best." She turned and hurried from the room, leaving Josef to gather whatever might be necessary.

Even Gudrun's warning didn't prepare Josef for Benjamin's sorry state. He examined the boy carefully, each discovery bringing a new rush of remorse. On three occasions, the boy had suffered violence because of his actions. This time Benjamin hovered on the precipice of death. Even if he lived he'd probably bear scars for the rest of his life. And all resulting from his employer's lust. Josef fought to regain his professionalism. If he was to win this battle with the Angel of the Abyss, it was vital to set aside his emotions.

"He's a tough customer," Stumpf had said when they carried Benjamin in. "It's a wonder he didn't drown. God knows how he managed to crawl out of the river following a beating like that."

Josef had merely nodded. God did indeed know, for He saw everything, including the shameful desires in the filthiest locked and bolted recesses of a man's heart. He helped Gudrun cut away Benjamin's sodden garments, recognizing with a sick lurch of his stomach that these were his son's clothes, the ones he'd handed the boy after the previous beating. Mentally, he willed Stumpf to leave, but the young fool lingered. Josef guessed he'd never ventured this close to a man's final moments before. Stumpf's next blurted question confirmed this.

"Will he die, do you think? He was raving earlier about nymphs and shepherds, and a sleeping beauty. He's quiet enough now." Stumpf had stared doubtfully at Benjamin's still and bloodied form. "I suppose that could be a bad sign." He jumped back as Gudrun pushed past him with a bowl of bloody rags. "I'd better go."

"More hot water, please, Gudrun." Josef continued to investigate Benjamin's wounds, realizing it would be necessary to shave the boy's head. A clot of blood had formed in his left ear; closer examination revealed it came from an internal injury. The condition of the left eye gave Josef equal cause for concern. He'd never seen such hideous swelling.

"He'll lose that eye," announced Gudrun. "Mark my words."

"Hush." Josef feared she was right. "The boy isn't deaf."

"I'm surprised he isn't dead," she said, though a fraction more quietly.

Benjamin stirred. "I'm not a corpse." A froth of red bubbles formed on his lips. "Don't let them give me to the students to cut up. Don't give me a number . . ." With that he sank back into unconsciousness.

"Fuchs is the man we need," said Josef, drawing the housekeeper to one side. "Gudrun, you must take a message to *Herr Doktor* Ernst Fuchs, head of the ophthalmic clinic at the university. Ask him to be so kind as to call on me urgently. There's no better ophthalmologist in Vienna. If anyone can save Benjamin's eye, he can." He turned back to the battered body lying on his son's bed. No need to worry about being used for teaching practice. Benjamin's body was too broken to be of much use. Almost savaged. Whoever tossed him into the river had clearly thought it was over for the boy.

Josef continued to work when Gudrun departed after hastily donning her best coat and hat. Wrapped in the room's silence, intent on his stitching and manipulating, it took him awhile to realize that hot water and fresh cloths continued to arrive, that another pair of hands was deftly placing his instruments within reach. When the last bandage had been secured, he carefully rolled the boy onto his side to remove the bloodstained draw sheets. It was not a job to attempt alone and he was grateful for the two slim hands working alongside his. Then realization dawned.

"Lilie!" He hastily covered Benjamin's naked form. "You shouldn't be here, my dear." He hesitated. "It isn't seemly—"

"Poor Benjamin. What did they do this time?"

"Knife wounds. Bruises. Some nasty breaks." Josef refrained from spelling out his worst fears. He guessed from Lilie's expression that this wasn't enough of an explanation and was grateful when Gudrun returned, bustling proprietorially into the room and setting things to rights. "He'll be bedridden for some time, I'm afraid."

"More work," sighed Gudrun. She caught Josef's eye. "Though I am sorry for the boy, naturally."

"Did you deliver my message?"

Gudrun nodded. "*Herr Doktor* Fuchs is attending to patients all afternoon. He will come at his earliest convenience." Sighing again theatrically, she seized the bucket of soiled dressings and made for the door. "I'd better move this since nobody else has bothered."

"You forced him to go," said Lilie suddenly.

Josef looked at her, astonished. "What do you mean, my dear?"

"I begged him not to. I knew it would be dangerous. What did you say to make him go there?"

"What do you know of the place?" he countered. "If you could have told us more about the club, he wouldn't have had to put himself in such danger."

"I know nothing about it," she answered quietly. "I've never been there, but anyone could see how frightened he was."

"You've never been there." He swallowed hard. "Oh." After a moment he said: "Then where *did* you come from, Lilie?"

Her eyes slid away. "Look, the flowers are in here, too."

"They're butterflies, my dear."

"Are you certain?"

"Lilie," he said more urgently, "where were you before you came here? Last month, say? What about last year? Where did you live? What about 1898? And what were you doing in 1897? Were you in Vienna for the 1895 elections—"

"I told you. I didn't exist before. At least, not like this. I was created to come here and—"

"Stop it!" Josef sank his forehead onto his palms. "Don't." When he'd calmed himself, he added more quietly: "Yes. You came to destroy the monster. I'm supposed to help you. Then tell me who created you, Lilie." He reached out with both hands. "Who is responsible for your beauty?"

"Perhaps you are."

Josef sighed heavily. "I think not." If it was possible to create objects to meet one's deepest longings, then nobody would need God.

"Perhaps I invented myself. You, me, Benjamin"—she waved her arm around the bedroom—"all of this." The light was fading: in that instant she looked smaller, somehow younger, infinitely more vulnerable. "Do you think that's possible?"

"No." Josef continued to look at her. "No, Lilie. No."

Lilie pointed to Benjamin. "The butterflies are being drawn to him."

Josef detected that a new edge of fear had crept into her voice. She seized his arm.

"What does that mean, Josef? What does it mean?"

THERE WAS A MOMENT OF PANIC as Benjamin realized he was in a proper bed with pillows and linen. He'd begged not to be taken to the hospital. If you were a poor man, the price for medical attention was to be stamped with a number immediately after death and shunted into the dissecting room. Managing to get one eye open, he saw this wasn't in fact the AKH. Nor was it his ramshackle lodging over the stables. Instead of warped boards with gnawed holes marking the abodes of rats and mice, the floor was highly polished, spread with a Turkish rug. The ceiling was smooth and white with an ornate central boss, totally lacking the familiar mud-daub nests of swallows tucked under rough-hewn beams. And it was in vain that Benjamin searched for the companionable barn owl that roosted by the unglazed window during the day. By raising his head a fraction he made out a mahogany wardrobe and matching chest, bookcases with volumes whose titles he was unable to read, and a large pair of ankles that he recognized all too well.

He sank back, feigning sleep. Too late: the movement had already been spotted. Gudrun advanced.

"Well, well, this is a fine how-to-do, my lad." When he didn't answer, she took her vexation out on the pillow, lifting his head to thump the feathers back into shape. "After this, I warrant you'll be sticking much closer to home." She shook the quilt. It settled back on his body as weightlessly as a cloud and Benjamin wondered why there was so little sensation in his limbs.

"I can't feel my legs—"

"You will, soon enough. We gave you something to ease the pain."

"Thank you," he said weakly.

Gudrun gave the pillow a final thump. "You're lucky to be alive. If it hadn't been for me—and the doctor, of course—"

"Thank you," he repeated. "Where's Lilie?"

"Oh, you'd have been in a sorry way if it had been left to her," retorted Gudrun. Her lips carried on moving, but Benjamin was already slipping back into the warm black silence.

When he woke again, Lilie was sitting nearby. She pulled the chair close to the bed.

"Well, neither of us has much hair now. And what's happened to your poor eye, Benjamin? I told you to keep away from him. Why didn't you listen?"

"The doctor said I must. We were trying to find out who you were, where you came from."

"But you already know everything about me."

He said nothing.

"You always have. It's time you started remembering."

"I don't understand." What did she mean? Although he'd tried, Benjamin had no memory of them being together ever before.

In one of their late-night discussions, enlivened by copious wine, the doctor had claimed the Greek god Zeus sliced the souls of humankind in half, leaving each half yearning for the other.

"Love," he'd said, pulling at his beard and with a slight sneer, "is simply a pretty name for the pursuit of the whole."

When Benjamin had laughed, the doctor went on to quote a philosopher, Plato. The original human form was not as now, but three in number: man, woman, and a third being the perfect union of the two. A sudden vision of the huge cook who was neither male nor female and yet improbably both made Benjamin shudder. To his mind, there was nothing perfect about that kind of monstrosity. But who could argue with such an illustrious name as Plato?

"My people call it *bashert,*" he mumbled, realizing he was drifting again.

"What's that?" Lilie bent closer.

"Plato's divided soul. *Bashert*—the reunion with the lost half." He tried to reach out to her, but the effort was too great. "They say when it happens the pair is lost in an amazement of love and friendship and intimacy. Afterwards you can't leave the other's sight, not even for a moment."

AFTER THE PREVIOUS NIGHT of broken sleep, Josef was grateful not to have been woken by Gudrun. It revealed unexpected kindness. She had a soft place in her heart for the family, despite her brusque manner. Then he realized not being called might have a more ominous cause. Throwing on his clothes, he hurried along the corridor to Robert's old room, where a series of rasping breaths from the bed assured him that Benjamin still clung to life. The room seemed as full of echoes as an empty theater or concert hall between performances. "All the world's a stage," the English bard would have us believe. . . . A physician played his part in more dramas than most, even though his bargaining with the Norns remained, for the most part, silent. Here it was as though a great saga, partly told, hung on the air. Dismissing the thought, Josef approached the motionless form.

"Any change?" he asked, reaching for the boy's wrist. The pulse was irregular but less weak than before. There was yet hope. "Has he spoken?"

The faintest whisper emerged from the shadows: "A little."

This was the front of the house. The curtains were thick, designed to keep out both street noises and the light from the gas lamp immediately outside; the room was still in darkness apart from the feeble glow emitted by a night-light that did little more than illuminate the head of the bed. As his eyes grew accustomed to the gloom, he saw not Gudrun but Lilie curled in a chair drawn up to the bed. She was wrapped in a robe several sizes too large; when she stood it trailed on the floorboards, forming a pool of pale silk around her bare feet. Aphrodite rising, Josef thought, captivated. It wasn't the first time he'd caught a glimpse of the goddess in her. Oh, to wake to such a sight each morning. Perhaps he should consider more permanent steps. With Bertha he'd even considered fleeing to America. It was not too late. Then he noticed the dark circles under the girl's eyes.

"Why are you sitting with the patient? I instructed Gudrun not to disturb you."

"She's old and needed to sleep." Lilie shrugged. The robe slipped from one shoulder, revealing a nightgown of the finest lawn. "Besides, I wanted to be here." Josef tore his gaze from the soft swell of her breasts. He saw she was holding Benjamin's hand and removed it from her grasp.

"You say the patient spoke. Was he lucid?"

"Perfectly."

Josef hesitated, afraid of what Lilie might say next. He was conscious of a change in her. Of something incalculable. Suppressed excitement, perhaps. She looked tired, yet her eyes shone. "Did he tell you what happened to him?"

"No, we talked about Plato."

He stared. *"Plato?"*

"Yes. He said men and women were once a single being. That we spend our lives looking for the other half of ourselves."

Josef ground his teeth. "No, no, Lilie. As I explained to Benjamin when we discussed this very idea, it is merely an allegory to explain the biological need of the male for the female. Be so kind as to draw back the curtains, my dear."

Pale sunshine flooded the room. He heard Lilie catch her breath. Glancing over his shoulder, he saw the windowpanes were covered with a multitude of the white butterflies, gently fanning their wings. This morning their black blotches looked like death's-head eye cavities. He couldn't tolerate their empty, baleful stares a moment longer. Since the boy had failed to rid the house of this plague of insects, he'd have to bring someone in from outside. Some modern Pied Piper, suitably equipped, armed with vial rather than flute. He felt Benjamin's forehead and began to examine the visible wounds. The boy stirred and muttered as Josef lifted the edge of a dressing, checking for early signs of infection. Even a short spell in the Wienfluss had proved fatal in past years when the flooding waterway brought cholera to the city.

"We'll let him sleep." Josef put one arm around Lilie's shoulder, guiding her towards the door. "I suggest you return to bed for a few hours, my dear."

She pulled away from him. "No, I want to stay with Benjamin."

"You'll disturb his rest. Come back later, when Gudrun has assisted me in attending to his wounds."

"You don't understand," said Lilie. "Benjamin will die unless I stay to keep him going. He must hear my voice—"

"Quite unnecessary," interrupted Josef, breathing in a greedy lungful of her scent. Floral, though he could not place the bloom. "Benjamin is almost certainly out of danger."

"We were never in more danger," whispered Lilie, glancing from side to side. She took a few steps backwards.

Josef was suddenly afraid. For the second time, his sweet girl's outline seemed less distinct. It occurred to him that if he didn't act immediately, Lilie would slip away and be lost to him for all eternity. He reached forward to take her in his arms, but found she wasn't where he expected her to be. All he caught hold of was her wrist. He raised it to his lips, showering her hand with kisses. "My dear, did you think over what we spoke of yesterday?"

She looked at him, so clearly mystified that Josef realized he hadn't been plain enough.

"We talked of being more than friends. Do you understand me?" He persisted, emboldened by her slight nod. "Could you learn to love me? Will you live as my dear companion?"

Lilie shook her head and pulled her wrist free. "That can never be."

His heart sank at the blunt rejection. The sunlight fled, leaving the room gray and desolate as life without her.

"I beg you to reconsider." Josef threw himself onto his knees. "See how your beauty makes a complete slave of me, my dear. All I ask is to be allowed to care for you. My marriage is a sham. My life was empty before you came. I'm not a poor man. I can provide for you generously." He clutched the hem of her gown. "I'd give you—if I thought one day you might return my feelings . . ."

"But I don't want anything."

"Don't say that." Josef threw his arms around her thighs and started to weep. "I'll take an elegant apartment in the best part of the city. We'll fill it with stylish furniture, graceful clothes, jewelry, furs . . . all the things young women want. All I'm asking is that you think about it. I'll wait for an answer."

"My answer won't change. Please get up."

He looked at her. "I never suspected you could be so cruel." Josef pulled himself upright awkwardly, using the bed rails for support. "Is it Benjamin? Are you and he—" The question choked him. He turned away, mopping his eyes before rounding on her and demanding harshly: "Does Benjamin tell you how beautiful you are?"

"Benjamin has never seen me beautiful."

"Other men, then—"

"Why should they care? You saw the policemen." She waved her hand in front of her face. "All they see is madness. It's the same with the other men. They see my situation, not me."

"There are other men then?" Oddly, his hopes revived a little when she didn't deny it. He moved boldly towards her. "Wouldn't you prefer one man who would love and cherish you, rather than many who do not?"

"You're dead," said Lilie.

He swallowed hard. "Older than you, perhaps, but—"

"No." She looked at the window, where the shadows of the clustered butterflies formed shifting patterns reminiscent of newly unfurled leaves on the window seat. "You're dead."

"Think it over carefully, Lilie. As I said, you'd want for nothing. I'd settle a portion of my estate on you, enough to provide for the rest of your life should I . . . should we be parted in an untimely fashion." Once again he drew strength from recalling the large gulf of years between his own parents. "Isn't there anything I can do or say to change your mind, Lilie?"

Instead of answering, she moved towards the butterflies. They hovered around her like falling blossoms, clinging to her hair, her shoulders. Filling her cupped hands.

"Anything at all," said Josef, watching as she was transformed into another goddess, this time Flora, personification of spring flowers, youth and beauty, both of which might be his again by proxy.

"Take me to Linz."

His mouth dropped open in astonishment. *"Linz?"* Why Linz? Was this finally the clue to Lilie's origins? "Of course, my dear. If that's what you want, we'll go the minute Benjamin is sufficiently recovered to be left in Gudrun's care. My sweet child, I'll take you everywhere—Paris, Florence, Venice, Rome, London . . ." He paused, breathless, hardly able to believe she'd finally acquiesced. "But tell me why you wish to visit Linz?"

"There are beautiful views of the Alps."

"Dearest Lilie, we'll visit Switzerland if it's mountains you want—" Josef flung wide his arms.

"It must be Linz," she insisted, neatly avoiding his embrace. "That's where it all started. The monster will be too big by the time he comes to Vienna. Just take me to Linz and I shall make sure it ends before it can begin."

By MIDAFTERNOON the boy's condition had worsened. Clearly, his internal injuries were even more serious than suspected: Benjamin was feverish, raging, speaking in tongues. A tight-lipped Gudrun strewed herbs and poked curiously shaped amulets beneath the pillow. Josef, already driven to distraction by impatience, sent Lilie away, claiming possible contagion, and paced the floor of his study to avoid meeting her anguished eyes.

"Oven," shrieked Benjamin. "I'm burning in it. Let me out."

"His parents must be summoned," insisted Gudrun as they sponged the boy's burning body with cool water. "Mark my words, he'll leave us tonight."

"There's still hope," countered Josef, dreading the thought of Benjamin's family arriving. "I don't want them to see their son in such a terrible state."

"I'm sure they'd prefer to say their farewells when he's alive than dead."

"Gingerbread roof," yelled Benjamin. "Break a piece off."

"More ice," said Josef. "We'll wait a little longer. The fever may break soon."

Gudrun compressed her lips. "Very well."

Josef turned back to the bed and saw Benjamin's functioning eye open, the pupil moving as though watching something invisible to Josef floating about the room. The boy's cracked and swollen lips parted.

"Madness. Finish. Flowers. Story."

"Yes, yes." Josef saw these more or less coherent utterances as a good sign. He noted that Benjamin's heartbeat had also slowed. With any luck the boy might still recover. If he did not, how could the responsibility for his death be borne? And would it ruin the bargain he'd struck with Lilie? He sat down heavily.

"I'm so very sorry for my part in this, Benjamin. What can I do to make it up to you?" He thought for a moment, recalling their late-night debates in happier times, then added: "When you're better, we'll have to see about your education. It would be a pity to let a mind like yours go to waste." Benjamin said nothing. His gaze was now fixed on the ceiling. Glancing upwards, Josef saw hundreds of butterflies clinging to the edges in something like a hastily drawn frieze. "Psyche," the doctor murmured, hoping their presence wasn't a sign of the soul's imminent departure.

. . .

GUDRUN TOOK THE FIRST WATCH. After a snatched supper, Josef sat
at his desk, one eye on the clock, waiting for her call. A little before
midnight he took down the portrait of his father, turning it to the wall,
leaving him free to set aside his responsibilities and imagine instead the
joys of traveling accompanied by Lilie. After Linz, he'd suggest continuing westwards to Munich, or perhaps—since she hankered after an Al-
pine setting—turning south to Salzburg. He hoped the sweet child
wouldn't insist on waiting for Benjamin's recovery. It was hard to ascertain whether she'd formed a serious attachment to him. He doubted
there'd been time. Of course, she owed the boy a certain debt of grati-
tude for rescuing her from outside the Tower of Fools. Josef rubbed his
eyes and yawned. A proper education would be more than adequate
reward for that, as well as compensation for the injuries he'd suffered.
Alas, one thing was certain: Benjamin would never fully recover from
what he'd suffered. His arm was shattered, the leg that was broken in
three places would probably mend shorter than the other, resulting in a
limp that would accompany him for the rest of his life, and Fuchs had
not yet examined that damaged eye. Josef knew that, whatever the
young man's afflictions, they'd be a permanent reproach, a small but
constant blight on the happiness that was to come with Lilie. It must be
endured. Perhaps she'd realize in time that even an older man was pref-
erable to a cripple.

He dozed for a while, waking with his forehead pressed against the
blotter. His dream had been vivid, sun-kissed, warm, full of spring
sounds—a wood pigeon's vibrato croon, a cuckoo's call, the drone of
honeybees—and beneath them all the rise and fall of a quiet voice. The
sounds of nature faded with the dream. The voice did not, though he
still couldn't distinguish the words. Instead it grew louder, a melody of

few notes that relentlessly drew him into the corridor, up the stairs, along the passage, until he came to the sickroom. Josef pushed open the door and saw Gudrun asleep in a chair by the window.

"He started to make his way through the maze of backstreets."

The voice was quite distinct now and easily identifiable as Lilie's. Josef took a step nearer the sickbed before recoiling. The two were lying wrapped in each other's arms. With shaking hands he pulled away the quilt. Lilie was all but naked, her skin dappled with the blood that had seeped from Benjamin's dressings. Gudrun shifted at his cry of anguish but didn't wake.

"After a few hundred yards, he came to the lamp where—" Lilie continued. Josef seized her arm, tearing her from the bed.

"Let go of me at once!" she cried. "I must stay with him. Don't you understand? He'll die if I leave."

"Do you love him?" Josef glared at her.

"We've been through so much that we're bound together forever."

"But do you love him?"

"Yes," she answered simply.

Josef clenched his fists. "And what about you and me?" His expression darkened. "What of your promise?"

"I'll keep my word." She shrugged. "You can do whatever you want to me. I'll endure anything. Just take me to Linz so that I can—"

"Endure?" Josef felt the blood drain from his face. What she was proposing was worse than nothing. "You will return to your room immediately," he said through clenched teeth.

"No." Lilie clung to the bed. He was forced to rip her hands free and drag her towards her room.

"Tomorrow I'll have you interred in an institution. Let them listen to your fantasies. As for your paramour, the hospital can have him. If he survives, he'll never work for me again." Throwing her inside, he locked the door. "You can go to Hell, the pair of you, as far as I'm concerned." He turned away, screwing up his mouth as though chewing a bitter fruit.

"I will be with Benjamin," said Lilie, her voice small but resolute as Josef saw her figure walk away down the corridor.

He stared at the door. It was still locked. There was the key. He flung it open and ran after Lilie, seizing her arm and pulling her backwards, forcing her into the darkened space. When she began to dissolve on the threshold, he pushed at the air, slamming the door so hard that the entire wall shook. This time the key grated as it turned. And Lilie was again walking down the corridor away from him, already made small by distance. Josef began to run, his footfalls heavy against the polished wood, but every step widened the gap, until she was little more than a pale shadow, a phantom, an illusion, a creature spun of moonlight.

THIS TIME THE KNOCKING was so loud and so persistent that Josef finally lifted his head from his hands. He'd been sitting at his desk for a very long time, had hardly moved since returning heartsore from Gmunden. He was chilled to the bone and his legs were stiff from lack of use. Plates of untouched food surrounded him, and there were more trays on the floor. A carafe of wine lay on its side, spilling dark liquid onto his papers. Groaning with effort, he rose and shuffled over to unlock the door.

"I know you told me not to disturb you, but I must." Gudrun waved a telegram in his face. "It's for you, *Herr Doktor* Breuer. It's from your wife. She'll be home by nightfall." She blushed. "Normally, I wouldn't open other people's correspondence, you understand, but in the circumstances . . . not speaking or eating, never venturing out. . . . You haven't been yourself, sir." She waited, her eyes raised expectantly.

"You did the right thing," Josef said with an air of resignation. He glanced at the flimsy paper. "Nightfall, you say?"

"If not sooner." Gudrun flung wide the curtains, rubbed dust from the sill with a corner of apron, and started piling up plates in the crook of her arm, clicking her tongue in exasperation. "At least now everything will go back to normal. How I'm to get the house straight before then, I don't know. Were these important?" She draped the wet papers along the back of a chair and awarded the model of the inner ear a desultory polish. "That's a little better."

"The girl . . ." Josef began, knowing Gudrun would overwork her, given the chance.

"Yes, but where can we find one quickly?"

He tried again. "Lilie's—"

"I know, I know, there must be fresh flowers for the house, too. Someone will have to go to the market."

"But I didn't—"

"We can't wait. With everything topsy-turvy I need immediate help. *Frau Doktor* Breuer mustn't see her home in this state. What a *Schlampe* she'd think me!" She sighed. "Heaven knows, I tried, but—"

"You did your best, Gudrun. No blame will be apportioned to you. When you were left to look after the house, it was never intended that you'd have me here, never mind the others."

"Others?" Gudrun's brow furrowed. She frowned as if trying to remember elusive faces, before making a dismissive gesture with her free hand. "It was always too much for me, *Herr Doktor*, even when the house was empty. The truth must be faced: I'm not as young as I once was."

"None of us is." Josef padded towards the window and stared into the street. "Older but no wiser. Alas, our dreams continue to haunt us."

Gudrun looked at him doubtfully. "About the house, *Herr Doktor* . . . I have a niece, a very willing and hardworking young *Frau*. With proper direction, she'd help me set things to rights in no time at all. And perhaps one of her young brothers could tidy up outside." She waited for an answer, adding, when none was forthcoming: "*Frau Doktor* Breuer will not be pleased to see her garden so neglected."

"Do whatever you think best, Gudrun. I will see to it that he's generously recompensed." The words were oddly familiar. They sent a small chill up his back, though he could see nothing in them that should cause the least alarm. Perhaps this sensation was what the French scientist Émile Boirac meant by the term *déjà vu*—he'd never really understood the concept, and his erstwhile friend Sigmund had dismissed such eerie feelings as simply *das Unheimliche*. The uncanny. What did it matter? It meant nothing.

For the first time in days, Josef managed to rouse himself from his apathy and plodded outside. He stood breathing in the frost-tinged autumn air. Gudrun's comments were justified: the garden was unkempt. Docks and nettles were winning the eternal battle between Man and Nature in Mathilde's herb patch. Even the bushes on which the weekly washerwoman spread laundry to dry had become leggy and looked dead at the crown. He nipped off a single remaining flower spray and breathed in its fragrance.

"There's rosemary," he muttered, "that's for remembrance." The smell awoke in Josef a troubling sense of something too soon forgotten, but whatever it was continued to elude him. He wandered farther along the path and saw bindweed choking the fruit cage. Couch grass and moss had invaded the vegetable plot. And beneath the old walnut tree the fragile autumn crocus struggled for life and light through a heap of moldering nuts. Everything was falling into decay.

The outbuildings were also in poor shape. Mathilde had, of course, retained the carriage for her daily excursions around Lake Traunsee, and without the horse the stable was a chilly, sour-smelling place. He braved the crumbling stairs to reach the attic where the children once played. Now it contained only a half-empty feather mattress inhabited by mice. Two ancient saddles hung from the rafters. A mildewed book lay abandoned on a window ledge, an ancient copy of *Kinder- und Hausmärchen*, and he paused to flick through the pages. It fell open at *"Hänsel und Gretel."* Josef smiled. It had been Margarethe's favorite childhood story, the volume no doubt hidden here because Mathilde so strongly disapproved of the Brothers Grimm. She considered their tales quite unfit for children. Witches, ovens, talking animals, small frissons of fear—he'd never really understood her objections to these things, which seemed so natural a part of childhood. Josef glanced over his shoulder, then turned the pages until he came to his own favorite, *"Der Froschkönig."* "In the good old times," it began, "when wishes often came true . . ." He smiled rather sadly, for "The Frog King" was a story where true love looked beyond mere outward appearances. The book closed with a dull thud that sent a cloud of dust spiraling upwards.

There was nothing to do but return to the house, its rooms shrouded in dust sheets. He went upstairs, visiting each bedroom in turn, lingering when he reached the one at the back of the house, reserved for guests. A solitary white butterfly beat its wings against the windowpane; released, it fluttered towards the stable and clung to the old rose tree growing over the entrance. Josef could not bring himself to leave this room, where a faint, sweet smell brought to mind those months when he'd cared for Bertha Pappenheim, her eager wit, that storm cloud of dark hair, those smoldering eyes, her small and delicate form. What could life have been, if he hadn't forsaken his little Anna O? He'd justified his decision by speaking of responsibilities, his marriage, his work, his children. . . .

She'd spoken only of love. "Love will not come to me again. I'll vegetate like a plant in a cellar without light."

Fourteen

t is many years before the Pied Piper comes back for the other children. Though his music has been silenced, still thousands are forced to follow him, young, old, large, small, everyone . . . even the ogres wearing ten-league boots and cracking whips, even their nine-headed dogs. We are the rats in exodus now and the Earth shrinks from the touch of our feet. Spring leaves a bitter taste. All day, rain and people fall; all night, nixies wail from the lakes. The blood-colored bear sniffs at our heels. I keep my eyes on the road, counting white pebbles, fearful of where this last gingerbread trail is leading us.

Has the spell worked? I think so: coils of mist lap at our ankles, rising to mute all sounds, swallowing everyone around us whole. When the moment comes, we run blind, dragging the Shadow behind us, stopping only when my outstretched hand meets the rough bark of pine trunks. One step, two, and we're inside the enchanted forest, the air threaded with icy witch breaths. The day collapses around us. Phantom sentries swoop from the trees demanding names, but our teeth guard the answers so they turn away, flapping eastward in search of the cloud-shrouded moon. Roots coil, binding us to the forest floor, where we crouch in silence punctuated by the distant clatter of stags shedding their antlers.

We wake, uneaten. Every trace of mist has been sucked away by the sun. The landscape seems empty. We haven't come far: I can see where the road runs, but there's no sign of anything moving along it. It's quiet until a cuckoo calls from deep within the trees.

"Listen."

"*Kukułką,*" he says, shielding his eyes as he searches the topmost branches.

"*Kuckuck,*" I tell him. He still talks funny. "She's saying '*Kuckuck*'!"

He gives his usual jerky shrug. "At least we're free."

"Only if we keep moving. Come on."

The Shadow whimpers, but we force it upright and support it between us, moving slowly along the edge of the trees until we come to fields where more ravens are busy gouging out the eyes of young wheat. Beyond, newly buried potatoes shiver beneath earth ridges. Cabbages swell like lines of green heads. When we kneel to gnaw at their skulls, the leaves stick in our throats.

We carry on walking, feet weighted by the sticky clay, until the Shadow crumples. I pull at its arm. "It's not safe here. We must go farther. If they notice we've gone—" Keep going. Sooner or later kindly dwarves or a softhearted giant's wife must take pity on us. But fear has become too familiar a companion to act as a spur for long. Besides, we're carrying the Shadow now. Its head lolls, the wide eyes are empty, and its feet trail behind, making two furrows in the soft mud. It could be the death of us.

"We should go on alone."

"No," he pants. "I promised not to leave—"

"I didn't."

"Then you go. Save yourself."

Daniel knows I won't go on without him. Besides, I'd never have found him if it hadn't been for this miserable creature. "No good standing here talking," I snap, hooking my arm under the Shadow's shoulder and wondering how something thin as a knife blade can be so heavy.

Another rest, this time perched on the mossy elbow of an oak tree, attempting to chew a handful of last year's acorns. Only the sprouted ones stay down. The Shadow lies where we dropped it, facing the sky, though I notice its eyes are completely white now. Without warning it gives a cry, the loudest noise it's ever made, followed by a gasp and a long juddering out-breath. I finish spitting out the last of the acorns. The Shadow isn't doing its usual twitching and jumping; it doesn't even move when I push my foot into its rubbery chest. After a moment I gather handfuls of oak leaves and cover its face. Daniel tries to stop me.

"Why are you doing that?"

"It's dead."

"No!" he cries, but I can see the relief as he pulls himself onto his knees to check. "After enduring so much, still we die like dogs . . . *pod płotem* . . . next to a fence, under a hedge." He closes the Shadow's eyes. "*Baruch dayan emet.*" It must be a prayer: his lips go on moving but no sound emerges.

"But we're not going to die." I tug at his clothes. "Shadows never last long. You always knew it was hopeless. Now we can travel faster, just you and me."

He shakes me off. "The ground here is soft. Help me dig a grave."

"Won't. There's no time. We must keep going. It's already past midday." I watch him hesitate. "Nothing will eat a shadow. There's no meat on it." When he doesn't move, I trudge away, forcing myself not to look back. Eventually he catches up.

The path continues to weave between field and forest, and once we catch sight of a village but decide it's still too near the black magician's stronghold to be safe. Finally, even the sun starts to abandon us, and our progress slows until I know we can drag ourselves no farther. By now the forest has thinned; before us stretches an enormous field with neat rows as far as the eye can see. We've pushed deep between the bushy plants before I realize it's a field of beans.

"What does it matter?" Daniel asks wearily.

"Cecily said you go mad if you fall asleep under flowering beans."

"No flowers," he says curtly.

He's wrong, though. A few of the topmost buds are already unfurling white petals, ghostly in the twilight, and in the morning it's obvious we should have pressed on, for hundreds of flowers have opened overnight, dancing like butterflies on the breeze, spreading their perfume on the warming air.

"Let me rest for a bit longer," he whispers, his cheek pressed against the mud, refusing to move, not even noticing a black beetle ponderously climbing over his hand. "No one will find us here."

His bruises are changing color. Where they were purple-black, now they are tinged with green. When he asks for a story, I remember what Cecily told me about two children who came out of a magic wolf pit. They had green skin, too.

"It was in England," I tell him, "at harvesttime, a very long time ago. A boy and a girl appeared suddenly, as if by magic, on the edge of the cornfield. Their skin was bright green and they wore strange clothing." I look down at myself and laugh. "When they spoke, nobody could understand their fairy language. The harvesters took them to the Lord's house, where they were looked after, but they would eat nothing at all, not a thing, until one day they saw a servant carrying away a bundle of beanstalks. They ate those, but never the actual beans."

"Why didn't they eat the beans like anyone else?"

"Cecily said the souls of the dead live in the beans. If you ate one you might be eating your mother or your father."

"That's plain silly."

"I'm only telling you what she said. It's a true story, but if you don't want me to—"

"No, go on," he says, and I notice in spite of his superior tone he's looking uneasily at the bean flowers. "What happened to the green children?"

"After they ate the beanstalks, they grew stronger and learned to speak English. They told the Lord about their beautiful homeland, where poverty was unknown and everyone lived forever. The girl said that while playing one day they'd heard the sound of sweet music and followed it across pastureland and into a dark cave—"

"Like your story of the Pied Piper?"

"Yes." I hesitate, remembering that in Cecily's story the boy died and the little girl grew up to be an ordinary wife. "I don't remember the rest."

He's silent for a moment, then looks at me. "What are we going to do? Where can we go? Who can we turn to? Nobody has ever helped us before."

"They said help was coming. They said it was on its way."

"Do you believe it?"

"Yes. That's why we must keep walking towards them." Beneath the bruises, his face is chalk-white again. His arm doesn't look right and he winces whenever he tries to move it. There's fresh blood at the corners of his mouth. And suddenly I'm so angry I might explode. "I wish I could kill him." My fists clench so hard my nails dig in. I want to scream and spit and kick things. He continues to look questioningly at me. "I mean, the man who started it all. The monster. If it hadn't been for him—"

"Didn't you hear what everyone was whispering? He's already dead."
Again, the small shrug. "Anyway, my father said if it hadn't been him
there'd have been someone else just like him."

"And maybe then it would have been someone else here, not us."

He smiles and squeezes my hand. "And we would never have met."

"Yes, we would," I say fiercely. "Somehow, somewhere—like in the
old stories, we would meet, because we must. Still I wish it could have
been me that killed him."

"Too big," he says weakly. "And too powerful."

I knuckle my eyes. "Then I wish I'd been even bigger. I would have
stepped on him or squashed him like a fly. Or I wish he'd been even
smaller. Then I could have knocked him over and cut off his head or
stabbed him in the heart." We sit in silence for a while. I think about all
the ways you could kill someone shrunk to Tom Thumb size. "We
ought to go now."

"Let me sleep."

"Walk now. Sleep later."

"All right. But first tell me a story—one of your really long ones—
about a boy and a girl who kill an ogre."

I think for a moment. My stories are slowly coming back to me, but
none seems bad enough until I realize there were other circumstances
in which an ogre really could be killed. It was easy enough. I'd seen it
done. And now the smoke ghosts catch up, settling round us and coating every leaf and flower with anonymous ash. Erika, Annalies, Lena,
Cecily, Hanna . . . Only their voices identify them, frantically repeating
what messages they must before we breathe them in, using them up by
making their dust our own.

"Yes, life is hard," whispers Erika, "but knowing about other people,
other civilizations, other ways of living, other places—that's your escape route, a magical journey. Once you know about these things, no

matter what happens, your mind can create stories to take you any-where you want to go."

I sit up. *Anywhere?*

"Anywhere and any-when."

"My grandfather would do anything for anybody," adds Hanna. "If anyone asked him for help, he'd give it unstintingly. He was renowned for it." And almost as an afterthought: "He never lost his eye for a pretty face."

All of a sudden, I'm excited. Daniel is still holding my hand. I give it a sharp tug. "Get up. From now on I shall only tell you my story while we're walking. The moment you stop, I shan't say another word." But his shoulder hurts. He won't move, so I start my story anyway, letting him rest, while all around us the bean flowers flutter and dance in the sunshine like butterflies about to take flight. If Cecily is right, it could be in these very ones that the vanished people have taken refuge. There are thousands, millions—one for every stolen soul. Already there are too many to count and yet all the time more are opening their frag-ile petals to the soft breeze.

We try chewing beanstalks, but they're stringy with juice like pale green blood. The tender young leaves at the top of the stalks are better, even though their taste reminds me of *Bohneneintopf*, the nasty bean stew Greet forced me to eat.

When night comes, it's almost too cold to sleep. We curl close to-gether and I continue whispering my story into the darkness, only stop-ping when Daniel's whimpering tells me he's dreaming. At first light we stumble on until we reach a cattle trough at the edge of the next field. Both of us drink in spite of the squirming insects and the water boatmen bugs skating along the surface. The earth beneath the trough is soft and wet. Daniel kneels, digging for worms with his good hand. I try to eat one, but it wriggles at the back of my throat, making me retch.

"You've got to put your head back, like this," Daniel says, and demonstrates with a fat pink one. He swallows hard and rubs his throat. "See? Then they go straight down."

I wipe my mouth on my sleeve. "I'm not hungry for worms."

He shrugs and digs some more. After another rest we move faster for a while, following a cart track across a stretch of rough land bordered by more forest and broken up by enormous bramble bushes humped like sleeping whales. We argue about my story: Daniel thinks I should make Benjamin taller and cleverer.

"That's stupid. He's only a gardener."

"I don't want to stay a gardener all my life," he says indignantly. "I'm going to be a professor, like my father."

"Who said you were Benjamin?"

He rolls his eyes. "I must be. You're Lilie, aren't you? You've made her beautiful *and* clever."

"She has to be, stupid, so Josef helps her find the monster in Linz before it's too late to change everything."

"Well, at least you could stop the old hag pushing Benjamin round."

I scowl at him. "It's *my* story. If you don't like it, I won't tell you anymore."

We walk in silence for a while. The land dips into a valley with a road running alongside a small river, both making for a distant lake with a village on its far side. I look at the sun and wonder if we're still going the right way . . . and who it is we are seeking.

As we reach the road, Daniel says: "I wouldn't mind being a gardener. At least you'd always have plenty to eat. Potatoes, carrots, peppers . . . apples, apricots—"

"Cherries," I say, closing my eyes to bring back the taste. "Strawberries."

"Cabbage. Beetroot."

"Ugh."

"You wouldn't say that if you'd tasted my grandmother's *gołąbki*." Daniel smacks his lips. "It means 'little pigeons.' They're parcels of meat and onions wrapped in cabbage leaves. And we'll need to grow plenty of beetroots for making *barszcz*—"

"I'd rather have ice cream." But I feel sad, remembering Mirela, Lena, Riika, Zsofika, and all the others whispering recipes in the darkness for their pretend feasts. Erika called it cooking with the mouth. I suddenly want to put my thumb in.

"We'll try every sort of food there is," declares Daniel, and is about to say more when we hear the rumble of an approaching vehicle. I grab at his bad arm, making him yelp with pain. His face turns white, he's shaking, and I think his legs collapse under him even before we throw ourselves into the ditch. Thick green water sloshes over us as we peer through the fringe of plants. A white bus—exactly like the ones lined up by the gate as we were marched out—lumbers slowly past, letting out explosive farts, filthy black smoke pouring from its exhaust pipe. We wait, hardly daring to breathe. Snails cling to the undersides of stems and a large frog clambers awkwardly over Daniel's ankle. Greet said French people only eat snails or frog legs and that I should be grateful for proper food. But snails are made of snot, and when I think about catching the frog it takes an enormous leap onto the bank.

We stay in the ditch for a long time, until the only sounds are faint church bells above the soughing of trees. When we finally climb out, the bleeding's started again and I've lost a shoe, but there's no time to fish in the thick mud, so my feet will have to take turns wearing the one that's left. Daniel trudges on, bent double. He doesn't even notice. Dripping green slime, we hop, stone to stone, across the river, and pass deep into the forest until the tree canopy becomes so dense it's almost dark. Each trunk is the same as the one next to it, lined up in rows as straight and black as bars of a cage. The ground is springy and covered with pine needles that absorb every sound.

"Go on with your story," whispers Daniel, and I whisper, too, almost sure that we're being watched. When my eyes grow accustomed to the dim light, I see someone has scattered white quartz pebbles between the trees. A few minutes later there's a loud fluttering above our heads and we look up to see white birds fighting among the branches. I think they're albino ravens, which are even more dangerous than black ones. When I tell Daniel this, it cheers him up.

"They're only doves," he scoffs. "Look how small they are. And their tails are like fans." He sniggers until I flick his hurt arm to shut him up.

Here I am trying to wriggle inside my own story in order to get rid of the monster and it looks as if I'm being pulled into a different one. A white dove sat on the roof of Gretel's home. Hansel marked the way to the witch's oven with white pebbles. Both were scared and hungry. Did the tale really end as well as grown-ups told us? Greet changed her stories whenever she felt like it. I throw a handful of pebbles into the branches and the doves fly away. After this, I tell my story in a much louder voice.

The fir trees start to give way to birch and oak. The forest floor becomes mossy, studded with small flowers—violets, primroses, and little pinky-white ones nodding their heads as we disturb the air in passing. It's a good sign. My story has flowers. There's no mention of any in "Hansel and Gretel."

Then we come to a wall. It's high, almost completely covered with ivy hanging like a thick curtain and full of squeaking and rustling that might be little birds but could just as easily be ferocious rats. *Big black rats, fat brown rats, greasy rats, lazy rats, dirty rats covered with fleas, rats with huge noses, rats with great hooked claws . . .*

Daniel nudges me. "What's up?"

"Nothing."

"You looked a million miles away." He nods towards the wall, looks to each side and behind him. "Which way do we go now?"

"We'd better walk round," I say, though really I've no idea of direction because we haven't seen the sun for a while. "Quietly, until we know what's on the other side." Still he hesitates, so I lead him clockwise, treading carefully. According to Greet, going widdershins invites disaster. We stop where half the wall has collapsed, leaving a wide gap that the ivy has been trying to darn. Daniel works a hole in its crisscrossed runners and peers through.

"I think it's a garden," he says, angling his neck for a better view. Above our heads, a flock of white doves skims the phantom wall, only to be absorbed by the bright light beyond. All my anxieties return. If it's a garden, there must be a house, perhaps even the witch's cottage.

"Let me see." I shove him aside and climb onto some tumbled stones.

Daniel's right. I'm looking at a garden, though it's wildly overgrown with battalions of docks and nettles advancing through tangled rose beds. The house it surrounds is huge and must once have been grand, almost a little *Schloss*. Now it's a blackened ruin with broken chimneys standing against the sky like rotten teeth. The charred roof timbers resemble the gnawed rib cage of a wild beast brought back from Papa's hunting trips. But there's something else . . . something standing to one side of the ruin, half hidden by a tree . . . that makes me catch my breath, leap down from my perch, and start fighting with the ivy.

"Help me!" I shout at Daniel. "Quick! Don't just stand there staring. We need to get to the other side." He doesn't move, so I snap off shoots and runners, pulling and tugging until I've made a space big enough to squeeze through. When the ivy tugs at my remaining shoe, I kick it off without a backward glance.

After the hushed forest, the garden is noisy. Crickets zither in tussocks of dry grass, jackdaws squabble over the chimney pots, and the air throbs with the incessant cooing of countless doves. Above them rises the strident alarm of a blackbird as I run across the sunlit wilderness to where a long walkway leads to a pond in front of the house. It's like those in parks—a wide stone rim for sitting on—with a marble fountain in the shape of a forlorn mermaid. Once, she poured water from a huge conch shell; now there's nothing left for her to do but stare at dragonflies darting above water-lily buds sticking up through the green scum in the shape of clenched fists.

Still running, I veer left, pushing through a hedge almost as thick as the one in "Sleeping Beauty." And stop. I have come to the tower.

It's just as Hanna described: a perfectly round tower with row upon row of slit windows, and a spike on top that must be the *Blitzfänger*, the lightning rod naughty boys throw stones at. Hanna told me the building had been out of use for more than a century when she was a little girl; that must be why it's covered with bird droppings and has saplings growing tight against the walls. Three steps lead up to a door made narrow to match the windows. There's a key in the lock, and I'm on the point of going inside to see the chains where they shackled lunatics when Daniel finally catches up with me.

"What is it?" He's gasping and knuckling his side. "What did you see?" He seems unimpressed when I point to the tower, and looks round as though expecting something more. "Is this where we find people to help us?"

"Don't you understand?" I gabble. "This is the Narrenturm . . . the Tower of Fools. We're inside my story. This is where it all . . . It's where you—I mean Benjamin—found me. We've walked all the way to Vienna."

"Don't be stupid. That's impossible."

"I'm not the one who's stupid," I roar. "What's wrong with your eyes? Isn't that a tower?"

"Yes—but Vienna must be a thousand miles away. And you're the fool because that tower's only a *gołębnik*."

"A what?"

Daniel scratches his head, screws up his face, and finally comes up with the right word. "A *Taubenturm*." His tone is superior. "It's just a very big dovecote."

"It's the Narrenturm, you idiot!" I'm so enraged I throw myself at him. Daniel screams and crumples, falls to his knees, clutching his shoulder and crying.

"I hate you," he squeals.

"Good. See if I care. I'm off."

Behind the tower I slip through an arched opening to find a walled garden nearly as overgrown as the area in front of the house. A glasshouse choked with vines runs along one side. On the others, gnarled trees, tied against the warm bricks with stout wires, are covered with blossoms and busy with insects. Beneath them straggle some of the herbs Greet liked to grow: *Fenchel*, *Thymian*, *Rosmarin*, and *Salbei*. Beans have seeded themselves between the weeds and their black-and-white flowers are more fully open than those on plants out in the field. A long length of the garden has been completely taken over by the big shiny leaves of disgusting rhubarb plants. I sit on a stone, picking thorns from my feet and trying to remember Greet's nasty puddings—which never got sweet enough, no matter how much sugar you added—to stop myself being ashamed of what I did to Daniel. Even though I don't like him anymore, he's my only friend.

Doves land on the top of the walls, preening their feathers, showing off their tails, all flying off at once, even when my stones are miles away from them. I glance at the tower. Now that I've stopped being cross it's easy to see I might be wrong, because there are doves at nearly every window opening and more on the roof. From this angle I can see that the spike on top is only a weather vane; as I watch, the weathercock gently swings towards the west.

I'm also starting to worry that Erika was wrong, too, when she promised my imagination could take me anywhere and any-when. But if that isn't true . . .

No. I won't even think about it.

Instead I make for a small building tucked into the corner end of the glasshouse, a shed holding gardening tools, clay pots, and sieves with different sizes of mesh. An old straw bee skep hangs from the ceiling, along with strings of withered onions that crumble at the slightest touch, and there's a pile of dry sacks beneath the workbench. I pull them out to make a bed. We can't go any farther today, and this seems a better place to sleep than in the open air.

Daniel's still in front of the tower, though he's toppled onto his side, his bad arm sticking up at such a peculiar angle I feel sick looking at it. His face has paled even further so that now it's a horrible grayish white and covered with a film of sweat. His breathing's fast and shallow; it's as if he's silently panting. I push at his leg with my bare toes, but he keeps his eyes closed.

"I'm sorry," I mumble. It's the first time in my life I've apologized and really meant it. Not that it makes any difference to him.

"Go away."

"Get up, Daniel. Come with me. I've found somewhere to shelter. A gardener's shed. It's a bit like Benjamin's room over the stable."

He manages a very small smile. "Oh, yes, in Vienna."

"Ha-ha."

After a bit more pushing, Daniel rolls onto his knees. I help him up, letting him lean on me as we limp towards the shed. It's difficult to walk like this and avoid sharp stones cutting into my bare soles. My shoulders ache. I want it over with. At the entrance to the garden he stops altogether.

"Don't leave me," he begs.

"I've already told you I won't."

The only answer's a faint grunt. He's scaring me now. His eyes have rolled up into his head, just as the Shadow's did before . . .

"Daniel! Wake up!" He starts and looks around him, as if surprised to find himself here. "Stay awake, Daniel. I don't want to be left here all alone."

"You won't be alone, Krysta." Even as he speaks, he's slowly collapsing, dragging me down with him, his knees buckling, head drooping, as if drawn towards the earth. I'm fighting so hard to keep him upright I almost miss his whispered "If you'll only allow me, I'll stay with you forever."

"Get up, then!" I shout, knowing that if he lies down here I'll probably never get him moving again. "On your feet! Walk! Now!"

"What?" Daniel rallies again, straightening his back and shuffling forward. "Don't worry. At least we're free. Everything will be fine."

"Only if you can keep moving," I retort, suddenly unutterably weary. "We're getting nowhere and I no longer have the strength to support you."

I THINK IT'S THE NEXT DAY when the *Hexe* returns home to find us. We seem to have slept for a long time. Daniel wakes and moans as she throws open the door. I'm already up on my feet and reaching for the long-handled hoe. Silhouetted against the bright sunlight, the witch looks twice as wide as she's tall, but when she steps forward I see that she's wearing a nurse's uniform with a bulky greatcoat like Uncle . . . like Hraben's . . . thrown over her shoulders. Even so, she's still fat, with a face like a lump of dough into which the baker's pushed two currants for eyes; he's tweaked her out a long, sharp nose and slashed a wide line for her mouth but forgotten to add any lips. Her hair is long and bright yellow, except next to her head, where it's almost black. I'm trying to work out where I've seen her before as she looks from me to Daniel and back again.

"I thought I heard something. Decided it must be mice, but no. How did you two escape?" When I don't answer, she comes closer and stares very hard at Daniel. "By God, you need fattening up."

"You're not eating me," he snarls.

"That's one sort of meat I never tried." The witch laughs. It's not a nice sound. "I believe some did."

"*Wynocha z nią! Uciec!*" Daniel hauls himself to his feet. The effort makes him cry out. "Go on. Get out of here. Clear off."

The witch frowns. "Polish?" She stares at him, her forehead creased as if thinking hard. "Now there's an idea. If they thought—"

"Leave us alone." I brandish my weapon, thrusting the metal blade so close to the witch's face that she jumps back. "Go away."

"I'm not going to hurt you." She pretends to smile. "I'm the same as you now. We're all on the run. I think we can help each other."

"How?" I lower the handle but keep a firm grip, just in case. "What could you do for us?"

"For a start, that must be painful." She points at Daniel's shoulder. "Looks as if it's dislocated. I can put that right easily enough. . . ." She pauses. "Very quickly, too, if you'll promise to tell them I was kind to you and made you better."

Daniel and I glance at each other.

"And," she continues, "I'll feed you. You tell them that, too." Another pause. "More importantly, I can take you to safety. In return, the boy must teach me some Polish . . . simple things, enough to get by. We haven't got time for anything complicated." Her eyes grow distant. We watch as she paces the floor, muttering as if to herself. "After all, why should I be punished for obeying orders? We all knew what happened to anyone who objected. Everything I've done, I was forced to do. No good telling *them* it had scientific purpose." She comes closer, looking straight at Daniel. "I'll need you to describe a town in Poland I can make my own. Do you understand?"

Now I see what the witch is doing. She's hoping he'll talk to her like Hanna did to me. She's after Daniel's memories so she can invent a wicked story of her own. Before I can warn him, he's made up his mind.

"Verpiss dich!"

Daniel's blunt rebuttal doesn't have much impact on the witch. She perches on the workbench, untangling her hair. "Please yourself. Stay a cripple for the rest of your life. Starve. But don't forget I can guide you out of here. The Swedes have come to rescue the women and children before the Allies get here. Yanks, British, Russians, they're a murderous, uncivilized lot and they'll be hunting down Germans, innocent or not." She glances meaningfully at me. "You know what happens if they find us."

Greet's voice starts whispering close by. *"In come the evil men, betrunken wie Herren, dragging after them a young girl."* I swallow hard and clamp my hands over my ears, even though I know she's inside my head. The witch's mouth continues to move, and Daniel, who's been staring at the floor, suddenly looks up, silencing her with a shout so loud I hear it even with my ears covered up.

"All right!" He glances at me, and I take my hands away. "All right, I'll tell you."

"Good," she says. "Very sensible. Where shall we start?"

"First make his arm better," I demand, in the same moment that Daniel asks for her name.

"It'll be painful." The witch smiles as she says this. "Soon over, though. Me? I'm called . . . Agnieska." It's a lie. I can tell by that long pause. "What about you?"

I smile right back. Two can play at that game. "My name's Lilie. He's called Benjamin. Now fix his arm."

"I know a few Polish words, Benjamin," she says, talking to Daniel and ignoring me. "*Chleb, woda, kiełbasa*. How's my pronunciation?"

He nods. "Bread, water, sausage."

"*Piwo, wino* . . ."

"Beer. Wine."

"*Ser? Proszę?*"

"Cheese," he says, looking puzzled. "And *proszę* means 'please.'"

"*Zatrzymaj mnie rani.*" Now she's watching him more closely. "*Dlaczego to robisz? Bóg mi pomoże.*"

Daniel's mouth works. "The first means 'Stop hurting me.' The second, 'Why are you doing this?' And the last is 'God help me,'" he says in a small, flat voice.

"That's what I thought. You'd be amazed how many times I was forced to listen to that sort of stuff. One remembers after awhile." Agnieska slides from the workbench. "So far, so good . . . Now I'll see to your shoulder. Take off your jacket. Lie on here."

I go to help him, dragging the hoe after me. Daniel flinches from her touch. His body is purple-black except for the bite marks and raw places oozing blood and clear liquid, or the puffy bits that have turned a foul brownish yellow. He's frightened and trying hard not to show it. I squeeze his good hand to let him know I'm watching her every move.

"Turn on your stomach," orders Agnieska. "Move nearer. Come on. Come on. Your arm has to hang over the edge."

"Don't hurt him," I growl.

"Stop being ridiculous," she says briskly, and grasps his arm very firmly above the elbow. Her other hand seizes his wrist and pulls. Daniel screams, a terrible sound, his mouth momentarily so wide it's like a great dark cave. I'm just about to swing the hoe when I hear his groan of relief. Whatever the witch has done, his arm looks normal again.

"*Dziękuję,*" he whispers. His eyes close. "Thank you."

The witch repeats the word several times—it doesn't seem to be one she knows—before taking off her apron and folding it to make a sling. "Let him rest. You, come with me."

"No. Why?" I want to stay with Daniel. His face is running with sweat and he's doing the terrible silent panting again. I write a bit more story in my head: *By midafternoon the boy's condition had worsened. Clearly his internal injuries were even more serious than suspected: Benjamin was feverish, raging, speaking in tongues.*

The witch interrupts me. "Stop daydreaming, girl, if you want to eat. And don't forget he'll need water."

I follow Agnieska unwillingly along paths littered with fallen bean flowers that look like crushed butterflies; already some of the parent plants are bending under the weight of swelling bean pods. When she unlocks the door to the tower, I catch my breath, covering my nose against the acrid stink of bird shit. The birds panic, taking flight in a blizzard of cast feathers: Mother Holle is shaking her quilt. As the air settles, I see the curved walls are lined, floor to ceiling, with nesting cubicles set into the thickness of the bricks. At the center, a tall wooden pillar rises from heaped droppings. It has two stout movable arms at right angles to which ladders are attached, and the doves fly up again as the witch begins to climb the nearest.

"Madhouse," she says, but it's not the one I'd hoped for, and my story is slipping away from me. The characters are becoming hazy: Gudrun has been overlaid by Greet and when I try picturing Benjamin I see only Daniel. Even Josef is fading back into history, where he belongs. Perhaps I am a ghost to him . . . *And Lilie was walking along the corridor away from him, already made small by distance. Josef began to run, his footfalls heavy against the polished wood, but every step widened the gap until she was little more than a pale shadow, a phantom, an illusion, a creature spun of moonlight.*

"Wake up, girl," bawls the witch, passing me down a clutch of small white eggs. The ladder moves on, nest to nest, and I follow behind, holding the harvest in my cupped hands.

After she's collected enough, Agnieska climbs down and leads me out into the sunshine, pushing though overgrown shrubs until we're standing in a courtyard behind the ruined house. Water drips from an old-fashioned pump. Feathers blow backwards, forwards, over the mossy cobbles, and flies gather around the bloody remains of previous massacres, partly covered by roof tiles. Nobody else lives here. A heap of bones at the end of a long chain show where the watchdog was left tethered to the wall. I take its empty drinking bowl to carry water for Daniel.

This side of the house is in worse shape than the front. Walls have fallen in; beams and tumbled masonry block every door. The witch jerks her head towards a window opening. "In you go." When I hang back, she gives me a little push. "Get on with it. Pull yourself up on the frame. It's easy enough. I'll be right behind you." She must think I'm *einfältig*, not right in the head: everyone knows what happens next in the story.

"I can't. I don't know how. I'm scared of falling." Just to prove the point I pretend to blub.

"*Dummkopf. Jammerer.* Watch carefully where I put my feet so next time you can do it without sniveling." Once inside, she turns to give me a hand up, but I'm right behind her. This used to be the kitchen, now open to the sky but still with pots on shelves, pans hanging from hooks, and just as I thought, there's a huge cooking range with an oven big enough to roast an elephant. I sidle round the witch, keeping my back to the wall, only to discover it's safe for now: she's forgotten to light it. Instead she's breaking up bits of half-burnt wood, making a fire inside a metal drum to boil the doves' eggs. When they're cooked, she shares them equally, but I still don't trust her.

ALL AFTERNOON, Agnieska badgers Daniel to teach her more Polish. At first, he deals it out reluctantly, one word at a time.

"*Medycyna*—medicine."

"*Medycyna. Medycyna.*"

"*Penicylina*—penicillin."

"*Penicylina. Penicylina.* This is easy enough," she crows. "Nothing to it."

Daniel frowns. "My father told me Polish is one of the most difficult languages to learn."

"And where's your father now?" the witch asks nastily. He doesn't answer. "Teach me some numbers," she says. "I should at least know how to count up to twenty."

"*Jeden, dwa, trzy, cztery* . . ." Daniel begins. After eating, he'd seemed better for a while. Now his eyes look strangely bright and he's panting again. If Agnieska really was a nurse, she can't have been a very good one.

"What's wrong with him?"

"An infection," she says with a shrug, and goes on repeating the numbers, turning the list into a sort of silly chant, until I feel like screaming.

Outside, I carefully nip off a bean pod and open one of the tiny beans to see if there's any sign of a soul. I'm trying to think myself back into my story and make Josef real enough to make that trip to Linz. I still haven't decided how I'll kill the little boy Adolf, but it won't be difficult—I've seen it done in lots of different ways. Hanna said she'd heard he was a lonely child, so it ought to be easy enough to befriend him.

WHEN I RETURN to the shed, the witch is demanding to know about Polish towns. She wants a quiet place where it would be easy to find work and somewhere to live. Daniel's slumped against the wall. His eyes are closed and he doesn't answer for a long moment.

"Jedwabne," he says, sitting up, suddenly more alert. "You could say you're from Jedwabne. It's in the northeast, near Białystok."

"Jedwabne?" The witch frowns over the name. "I'm sure I've heard of the place. Is it famous? Did something happen there? Have you been to the town? More to the point, would it be a good place to live?"

Daniel nods, but I notice he's clenching his fists. "Jedwabne was once a weaving town. My grandparents lived there. It's surrounded by beautiful forests and has long, warm summers. So many people have . . . *left* . . . in recent years that there are plenty of houses and shops standing empty." His mouth tightens. "I think you'd fit in there. All you have to learn is *Pochodzę z Jedwabne*—I come from Jedwabne."

"Now we will eat," declares Agnieska, apparently pleased with this prospect. "We'll have a feast. The boy will sing Polish songs for us. And afterwards you"—she looks at me—"can help cut off my hair. Then I'll tell you about my new idea."

But before the feast there must be bloody murder. Back we go to the tower.

Evening's drawing in and the doves are coming home to roost.

Thump, thump, thump, go the witch's feet as she mounts the ladder—*Fee-fi-fo-fum*—and the big wooden ratchet that allows the arms to turn round the central pillar creaks and groans. Some of the doves fly outside, many more flap and jostle beneath the roof, a few even try mobbing Agnieska's buttercup-yellow head . . . but the mothers only crouch lower, spreading their wings in a vain attempt to protect their babies. Nothing makes any difference: the witch will kill every last one if she has to, she'll wipe the entire dove population from the face of the earth. Her big hands lunge, dashing the mothers against the wall, snatching up the squabs. *Snap!* and their necks are broken. *Thud!* The small bodies land in my outstretched skirt. I try doing what I've always done—escape into that secret part of me where by magic or heroism I make things turn out differently, leaving behind an automaton, a machine with no feelings whatsoever—but today I can't. A door has closed. The ideas have gone. The words aren't there. Perhaps this is what happens when you invent stories inside stories that are themselves inside a fairy tale: they become horribly real.

In the yard, the witch gleefully lays the young doves out for the count. She hacks off their wings with her nurse's scissors, twists and pulls until their heads come free, plucks the sparse feathers from their breasts—which she then tears from the carcass, throwing the rest away. We climb into the kitchen where she makes *Jungtaube* stew, flavored with garden herbs, in a battered cauldron. When it's bubbling and spitting over the oil drum, Agnieska leaves me for a few minutes.

"Stay there and make sure it doesn't burn," she yells over her shoulder. From the noises that follow, she's climbing over rubble in the rooms beyond, but although I'd like to see what she's up to, I'm more interested in a certain pan the witch surreptitiously pushed out of sight when we came in. On lifting the lid, I realize things aren't happening in the right order, because Gretel didn't find the precious stones until after the witch was dead. There again, Gretel wasn't as curious as me, or as clever. Also, these are gold watches, rings and brooches, pearl neck-laces, and gold teeth rather than fairy-tale gems.

I want and don't want to eat the baby-dove stew. It's very different to the soup we'd grown used to. In the end, I manage a few mouthfuls and Daniel gobbles the rest. There is no singing or dancing afterwards, and no haircutting, either: Agnieska is too eager to present us with her re-vised plan.

"No." Daniel is shaking his head while she's still talking. "No. I can't. I won't. I'd rather die."

"You probably will, in that case," the witch says pleasantly. "We're running out of time. I'll give you tonight to think it over."

"What does she mean?" I whisper as we curl up on the sacks. "How can we run out of time? What does she know that we don't?"

Daniel is silent for so long I think he's asleep. "Perhaps there's going to be fighting," he says at last. "I don't care. Like I said, I'd rather stay here and die than pretend she's my mother."

"If she can show us where to go, what does it matter what you're forced to say?" I demand. "What does one more lie matter?" He doesn't answer. "Say she's your wicked *step*mother, then. Could you do that?"

He sniffs. "Maybe . . ."

"You must. We're not staying here, and we're not dying."

"But my mother—" There's a catch in his voice.

"Don't." We promised to stay silent about these things until it was over. "Look, you never had a stepmother so it doesn't matter if you pre-tend. Anyway, Agnieska, or whatever her real name is, won't fool any-body for long. With that great big bottom of hers who will believe she's ever gone hungry?"

"Ugly fat cow. *Dziewka. Suka. Kurwa.*" He recites his entire stock of bad words, his voice slowing and fading as he runs out of steam.

"And you'll say she's your—" But now Daniel really is asleep, his stomach gurgling with surprise at finding itself full. When I can't stay awake any longer, I dream I'm back in Ravensbrück, inside the infirmary, running down endless white corridors calling for Papa. And here's Agnieska. The witch emerges from doors to the right and to the left, her hands bloody, clutching pieces of raw flesh or whole legs that are sometimes feathered, sometimes still with shoes attached.

THIS MORNING I hardly recognize the witch. Instead of her nurse's uniform, she's wearing a striped dress like mine, but better fitting and a lot cleaner, though there's still blood under her nails from yesterday's massacre. Half her hair has gone and she's frantically chopping off the rest even as she yells at us to get up.

"He's fixed the bloody thing. Even now he's putting it back together. This is our last chance. They'll be going soon."

"Who has?" I ask, still fighting free of my nightmare. "Who's mended what?" Daniel jumps up without a word and lurches towards the door. He's holding his stomach with one hand and covering his mouth with the other. "What's the matter?" Agnieska stops me from following him. "Let go!" I shriek. "I need to find out what's wrong—"

"It's only gut ache. Everything out, both ends, I dare say. That's what happens when you guzzle food after being kept on a simple diet."

"Why didn't you stop him?"

"That's what they're like, these *Kreaturen*—worse than animals. No self-restraint." The witch shrugs and goes on cutting her hair. "*Judenscheisse*. Who would have thought I'd be relying on one to save my bacon?" She laughs, as if at some private joke, then grows sober. "Still, in a tight spot, needs must." I bite my tongue and watch the locks slide down her back like evil yellow snakes. "We'll be off in a minute," she says. "This won't take long."

"But where are we going?" I force a smile. Never trust a witch, but if you want to get the better of them, it's best to pretend you're their friend.

"To the bus, of course." Agnieska puts away the scissors, shakes her head, and runs her fingers through the uneven tufts of black. "That feels wonderful: quite liberating. I really don't know what all the fuss was about. Vanity, I suppose. Now, where's that boy?"

"What bus?" I demand, following her out of the shed. "I don't understand. And where is it?"

"By the lake—it's not far. Come along, Benjamin." She jerks her head at Daniel, who's crouching by the rhubarb. "We follow the drive down to the road and head for the village. The bus is well hidden—set back, among the trees, plenty of cover—that's how I was able to keep watch on them. I'll show you."

I stop dead. "How can you be sure it isn't one of the other sorts of buses? The ones that took sick, old people to the—"

"Because," she says with exaggerated patience, "it's got a bright red cross painted on each side. You know what the Red Cross is, surely? Anyway, Lilie, it's not one of ours. It's Swedish. There were several—all the rest have loaded up and gone home—this last one had some sort of engine trouble. It's held them up for three days."

I hang back, waiting for Daniel, who's looking worse than ever. In addition to everything else, he's now what Greet called "green around the gills." His teeth are chattering but his skin feels as if it's on fire. "Did you throw up?" He nods miserably and falls in beside me, dragging his feet, walking so slowly that in the end I put my arm through his. "Just don't puke on me, right?"

The witch is stamping her feet with impatience at the end of the garden. She's got a lumpy cloth bag tucked under one arm and I don't need to ask what it contains. Maybe my own story can't end properly and everything will stay the same, but at least in this one I won't do any worse than Gretel.

"Let me." The witch takes Daniel's weight. "Straighten up, boy." She's smiling but her tone's sharp. "Make an effort now." After a few moments of trying to make him move more quickly, she stops walking altogether and a peculiar expression crosses her pudding face. "Benjamin, in case we get separated, tell me again how to say 'My name is Agnieska.'"

"*Nazywam się Agnieska,*" says Daniel, and groans. He sways as the witch loosens her hold and steps away. I'm so afraid he'll fall that I put both my arms around him as she walks to and fro, memorizing the phrase.

"One last thing," she says softly. "What about 'I am a nurse'?" I feel Daniel tense. When I look at him, his expression is almost as strange as hers. "Such a useful skill might make all the difference," she adds.

Daniel nods. "*Jestem zabójcą dziecko,*" he says, very clearly. Something's not right: his hand searches for mine, holding it so tightly I'm getting pins and needles in my fingers, and he's never taken so much trouble making sure her pronunciation is correct. "*Jestem zabójcą dziecko.*" He says it a dozen times.

"Good." The witch pushes me aside and takes Daniel's arm again. "Best foot forward, Benjamin. Not long now." She smiles, but her eyes look hard and mean. "Lilie, my dear, why don't you run ahead and make sure they wait for us."

Icy fingers pluck at my spine. The witch is planning something bad. Daniel feels it, too. His eyes plead with me and he shakes his head.

"But I don't know how to find them," I whine.

She clicks her tongue with annoyance. "I told you once already—"

"I'm too scared to go on my own."

We're approaching the tower. My heart begins to pound as I get myself ready. One more step and another—*now!* I snatch the bag from the witch's hand, run to the door, and fling it inside. The doves rise. The witch screeches. Letting Daniel fall, she rushes after her treasure, scrabbling among the ripe droppings for the scattered jewels and golden teeth. Quick as a flash, I turn the key in the lock. Already she's pounding on the door and roaring threats. She can't escape, but try as I might there's no getting Daniel up again, and now I'm afraid the rescuers will leave without us.

"Go," he breathes, closing his eyes. I drop to my knees, hating how peaceful he suddenly looks.

"I'll come back," I promise, putting my cheek against his. "I'll find these people, tell them to wait and come straight back for you."

Through the yard I race, along the side of an old stable block, dodging broken carts and rusty farm machinery, running until my bare feet stumble onto the weed-stippled gravel that once marked the sweep of a grand driveway. Before me loom massive iron gates, so overgrown they can't have been opened in years. It's only by luck that I spot the witch's secret trail through the undergrowth. Nettles unleash their stings, brambles seize my wrists and ankles, painting my legs with strings of scarlet beads, but my spells are stronger than those of the witch and her path leads me to a narrow stone stile at the edge of the road.

Although I can feel cold air rising from the lake, the water's invisible, completely hidden by trees and bushes. There's no sign of any bus, either. The witch said we should head for the village, but although I remember seeing its distant buildings as we descended the hill, I've no idea whether to follow the road to the left or the right. I run to the right for a count of two hundred, turn and run the other way. I'm up to one hundred and ninety-nine when I hear voices, plunge through the bushes, and almost crash into a white bus, so well is it concealed by broken branches and armfuls of ferns. It's almost definitely the one we jumped into that ditch to avoid. There's no sign of whoever was speaking. I inch forward, flattening myself against the vehicle's side, stop to look at the blood-red cross . . . and trip over someone's outstretched legs.

"*Hej!*" The man lying beneath the engine eases himself out and lumbers to his feet, brandishing a large spanner. He's a giant of a man with a dirty face and short blond hair exactly like Hraben's. Even so, I don't run far before remembering to be brave. "*Vänta, lilla!*" he bellows, but then lowers his voice and reaches out an oily black hand. "Wait, little one. Olaf not hurt you." He turns away, roaring even louder. "Lotten! Sigrid! *Var finns dessa kvinnor när du behöver dem?*"

Someone laughs. "*Du behöver inte svära*, Olaf. *Här är vi, tillbaka från vår simtur.*" The woman has come from behind the bus. And I can see others following behind her. She looks at my funny clothes with the blood-stains, the rips and tears, my bare feet. Her eyes flicker, but all she says is: "Hello. Never mind Olaf and his cursing. You must be from the camp at Ravensbrück. How did you manage to get away?"

"Daniel—" I want to say more, but the words stay stuck in my throat.

"Are you from Ravensbrück?"

I nod.

"All right, child. There's no need to be frightened. You're safe now." She calmly finishes tying her damp hair back with a length of blue ribbon. "None of us will hurt you. We've come a long way to help."

I *am* frightened, but there's no one else left to trust, so I examine her carefully. She's tall, wearing men's clothes. Her eyes are the same color as the ribbon, and where her hair's dried it's turned red-gold. There are freckles on her nose and along the tops of her cheeks. She reminds me of someone. When she puts her arm around me it feels nice.

"Daniel—" I say again, and point towards the house. The woman nods.

"Is Daniel hurt?"

I nod furiously. "He can't stand up."

"All right," she repeats, and reaches inside the bus for a doctor's bag almost exactly like the one Papa had. "You'd better show us where he is."

I start off immediately, glancing back to check they're following. When we get to the nettles, Olaf wipes his black hands on an even blacker rag before carrying me over them. He still leaves oily prints on my sleeves.

The doctor woman laughs when he apologizes. "We'll soon find her something better to wear." She lengthens her stride, easily keeping pace with me, even though I'm walking faster now, nearly running, because I'm afraid that Daniel might have . . .

"By the way," she says, "everyone calls me Lotten. It's short for Charlotte."

"I had a Charlotte. We buried her in the aviary."

"That's very sad."

"She took all my stories with her."

"I see." Lotten walks in silence for a moment. "There will be more stories. There always are. Are you going to tell me your name?"

"I'm Krysta." We've reached the tower and Daniel's lying where I left him. He smells really bad but he's still breathing. His eyelids flicker as I sit on the ground next to him, holding his hand. Lotten kneels, too, and gently opens his jacket. Her face changes; I see her swallow hard.

"All right," she says, reaching in her bag for a stethoscope. "All right."

"*Hallå,*" says another voice. "*Här är vi.*"

"Yes, here we are. Sorry we took so long."

Two other women, one dark, the other as fair as Lotten but with a wide, calm face, have caught up with us, and it's now I see Olaf has tears streaming down his face. I didn't think giants could cry. He must have hurt himself quite badly. When I ask Lotten about this, she shouts at him. Olaf scrubs his eyes and shambles off, lighting a cigarette. There's still a lot of noise coming from inside the tower and he's unlocked the door before I can stop him.

"Witch," I whisper.

Lotten is too busy flicking at a big syringe. "This is for the pain, Daniel."

Agnieska bursts from the tower, hands covered in shit, jaws stretched open to spit toads and vipers at me. On seeing the others, she tries looking small and pitiful. One of the other women, Sigrid, I think, starts talking to her, but the witch opens her eyes wide and stares straight in front of her, pretending to be like one of those poor people on the march who no longer knew where they were or what was happening. *"Nazywam się Agnieska,"* she mutters. *"Nazywam się Agnieska."*

"Witch," I say loudly enough for everyone to hear. But the women are too busy comforting her and Daniel chooses this moment to squawk a protest at the prick of the needle. The witch's eye alights on him.

"Mój syn!" she shrieks. "Benjamin."

"His name's Daniel," I remind Lotten.

Lotten sighs. "The poor woman."

Daniel opens his eyes a crack. "And she's only pretending I'm her son."

"She's confused," Lotten says, examining his broken skin. "Sigrid speaks some Polish. She'll get to the bottom of it. Are these dog bites?"

"You don't understand," I insist. "That's one of the bad nurses. They cut people up. I saw her. She's only pretending to be one of us."

"Uh-huh." Lotten is hardly listening.

"Einer der Engel des Todes," breathes Daniel. "She's one of the angels of death."

Lotten stands up. "You need proper care, young man. Don't try to talk." She beckons Olaf, who stubs out his cigarette and lopes over to unroll the stretcher. He's stopped weeping but his eyes are still very red. Together they lift Daniel, and I help slide the canvas underneath him. The witch swoops down on us, both hands clutching her bag of teeth.

"*Jestem Polskiej,*" she shrieks. "*Pochodzę z Jedwabne.*"

"No, she doesn't," says Daniel sleepily. He yawns. "And she isn't Polish."

The witch's eyes flash as she draws herself up. "*Jestem zabójcą dziecko.*" She speaks the words she's memorized. The phrase is her trump card and I can see by her face that she doesn't understand why Sigrid has recoiled. "*Jestem zabójcą dziecko.*"

"She says . . ." Sigrid frowns. She hesitates and her lips move as though she's going over the words in her head, making sure she has understood correctly. "She says she's a child killer."

"My little sister . . ." mutters Daniel.

I touch his cheek. "Don't." It's still not the right time to speak of these things.

"*Schmutzig doppel-Kreuzung Jude!*" The witch's face turns white and she shows her teeth like an angry dog. "Filthy double-crossing Jew— should have put you down while I had the chance." She screws up her bag as if it's a wet dishcloth and a scatter of gold teeth falls onto the cobbles. Without another word she turns and runs towards the forest, into the clutches of the red bear, the bulldogs, or the Yanks. I try not to laugh. Now that the witch is dealt with there's only one thing missing from this particular tale, but when we're finally on the bus, I realize we've found something better than Gretel's white duck to carry us over the water to safety.

All the stories, good and bad, are mixed up now. I went back for Daniel, just like the girl in "The Pied Piper," but in this one, too, I'm doing better than she did, because Lotten has promised me that we're being taken from this place where they cried "Rats!" to a beautiful land on the other side of the mountains. It's only my story that didn't finish properly. I suppose Cecily was right when she said that some things just can't be changed, however hard you imagine them . . . but only a *little* bit right because I know for sure that some things can. This morning I overheard Lotten telling Sigrid it was a miracle Daniel was still with us. They don't understand it was my storytelling that kept him alive. And that's why I'm staying at his bedside—even though they say he probably can't hear me—whispering a new story into his ear about Lilie and Benjamin leaving Vienna to grow cherries and apricots in their little cottage garden.

AND I WAS RIGHT—I usually am—for the scientists finally caught up with me and declared hearing to be the last sense that leaves us.

So here we are, two generations later, and once again I'm sitting at a bedside, holding Daniel's hand, retelling the story of Lilie and Benjamin, the happy-ever-after fairy tale we made our own, willing my words to keep him anchored to the earth, to the life we have built together . . . *to me*. There have been many such times since we fled Ravensbrück, many night watches, many retellings: the results of the hardships we suffered did not lessen when the world grew weary of our pain, our grief and fears, our strangeness; and the worse the memory, the stronger its stranglehold on the present. We survived. We went on. It seemed enough. But this time I suspect my storytelling will not be enough to keep Daniel beside me. He feels too old, worn out by his search for answers.

"For the first time in days," I whisper, "Josef managed to rouse himself from his apathy and plodded outside. He stood breathing in the frost-tinged autumn air. Gudrun's comments were justified: the garden was unkempt. Docks and nettles were winning the eternal battle between Man and Nature in Mathilde's herb patch. Even the bushes on which the weekly washerwoman spread laundry to dry had become leggy and looked dead at the crown. He nipped off a single remaining flower spray and breathed in its fragrance. 'There's rosemary,' he muttered, 'that's for remembrance.' The smell awoke in Josef a troubling sense of something too soon forgotten, but whatever it was continued to elude him. He wandered farther along the path—"

I stop as the door is gently pushed ajar, knowing it will be Sara, our young granddaughter, bringing me coffee. She's a beautiful child, delicate, almost elfin. Daniel opens his eyes as she comes into the room. The evening sunlight catches her hair, turning it gold.

"Krysta?" His voice sounds faintly alarmed. Still cradled in our story of times past, he's confused. It's understandable: although Sara is named for the little sister who perished in the camp, Daniel swears she looks exactly as I did at her age.

I squeeze his hand. "I'm still here."

"Don't leave me," he begs.

"Why would I start now?"

He manages a weak smile. "It's very dark in here." His eyelids droop. "Go on with the story. Tell me the bit about Lilie and Benjamin finding their cottage. The big apple tree . . . our vegetable garden, your books, my music, those long sunny evenings by the river . . ."

"Still telling Grandpapa stories?" Sara hooks her long hair behind her ears and places my steaming coffee within reach.

"Not stories," I correct her, "*the* story."

"But it's always the same one, over and over—don't you both get bored? It's been so long—you must have told it a thousand times. Doesn't it ever change?"

I gently release Daniel's hand and pick up the cup. In silence, I sip the bitter brew, feeling it rushing through my veins, giving me new strength. When I look at Sara, her face has grown anxious. She's biting her bottom lip and her eyes are suspiciously bright. It's only the good looks she inherited from me: the child gets her tender heart from Daniel.

"I didn't mean . . ." she mumbles. "I'm sorry, Grandmamma. I know it was terrible running away from the camp and the killings. I never meant . . ."

"Come here." I rise, a trifle unsteadily, and hold her close for a moment. "I know. I know." She's taller than I ever was. I have to stretch up to pat her cheek. It's an additional torture that this generation, too, should suffer for our memories; almost impossible to find the point of balance between burdening them with the vile details and ensuring the truth is never forgotten. "As for your question, the story of what happened in the camp never changes. How could it? It's a memory written into our blood and bones."

I hesitate. Can that really be true? I decide to believe it is. Just as I also decide it's impossible to pass such memories on fully. When it comes to recalling my years in Ravensbrück, every sense is involved: ravening hunger; the sweet, sick smell of burning flesh on the wind; the cries of infants muffled by desperate mothers; the ringing of my ears after being dealt a blow in passing; the taste of blood in my mouth; the ache in my calves from standing hour after hour in the pouring rain, the snow, or the harsh August sunshine; the dull flinch deep inside at what the eyes cannot avoid seeing, the pain, the loss, the—

"Grandmamma?" Sara is bending over me and I realize I've fallen back into my chair. "Are you sick? Shall I call my papa?"

I shake my head. Daniel's hand is blindly searching for mine, a palely wrinkled starfish against the blue of our counterpane. I cling to it, unable to say in that moment which of us needs the other most. "I was about to add that the other story, that of Lilie and Benjamin, the one that saved our lives by leading us to our rescuers, is bound to change a little with each retelling. Not the essence of the story, just the details . . . and the *way* of telling it." I remember Greet telling me how proper stories change with the wind and the tide and the moon, and add: "It's like a fairy tale, shifting around a little as time passes."

"Like a fairy tale. I see." Sara nods, her face comically solemn.

"I was younger than you, Sara, when I first started making it up. Since then, I've learned so many new things, from life, from friends, from books . . ."

I pause, hearing a distant echo of Erika's voice fiercely insisting that I attend the secret camp school.

"Books," I repeat, for they've not only been a solace during the long years but also provided the keys to understanding other people's ideas and achievements, their hopes and fears, quirks and foibles, their dreams . . . their demons. Dear Josef, I've read so much about his life that sometimes I think I must know him better than he knew himself. Others, too, though the actions of a few are still inexplicable. . . . I give myself a little shake, turning from those grim memories and adding with a wry smile: "I've learned a little about myself, too! And so the story was bound to grow longer—and more complex, I suppose—as time passed. At the same time, parts of real life and my story became intertwined. Benjamin and Lilie went on to have a happy and peaceful life, a son—and a beautiful granddaughter. So of course it's changed."

"I've never heard it." Sara blushes. "Well, only bits and pieces."

I smile again, knowing she listens at doors. It's a family trait. "Sit down. I'm sure your grandfather won't mind if I start again from the beginning." I take a deep breath, conscious that this may be the very last time this tale is told. "The town of Gmunden, with its placid lake surrounded by high mountains, was a peaceful summer retreat until the morning Mathilde observed that a certain General Pappenheim had brutally suppressed a peasant rebellion there in 1626. The name stirred up a hornet's nest of resentments. Pappenheim was also the family name of that Bertha creature—the young patient Josef had been so pre-occupied with. . . ."

ACKNOWLEDGMENTS

My thanks to Richard Marggraf Turley of Aberystwyth University for his unstinting support and encouragement throughout the writing of this novel.